# A VAMPIRE'S SIN

## THE ORDER OF THE BLACK OAK - VAMPIRES

## MARIE-CLAUDE BOURQUE

SEA STORM PUBLISHING

This is a work of fiction. Names, characters, businesses, places, events, locales, and incidents are either the products of the author's imagination or used in a fictitious manner. Any resemblance to actual persons, living or dead, or actual events is purely coincidental.

Edited by Jennifer Bray Weber
Cover Design by Frauke Spanuth
Paperback ISBN: 978-1-956115-05-5

*"Bourque develops a world of mages and sorceresses unlike any other. "*

-- **Night Owl Reviews**

**www.marieclaudebourque.com**

*To Logan and Finlay, nothing is stronger than a mother's love.*

# CHAPTER 1

Old-Montreal,
Early March, Present Time

*N*yssa Vlahos marched into the *Serpent Maudit* nightclub. She blinked as her eyes adjusted to the darkness, a sharp contrast from the bright day outside. With a deep breath and straight spine, she slipped off her leather gloves but kept her winter coat primly belted at the waist.

This meeting wouldn't take long.

She'd come to the club to talk to him countless times in the last three months, but today was different. Today, her quest was personal.

The one she was coming to see was the most infuriating man of her acquaintances—as if nothing serious ever touched him. Keeping her persona at the highest level of professionalism was the best way to approach him.

And there he was.

She watched him work at his usual corner booth beside the bar.

Magnovald St-Amand. Owner of this trendy Montreal nightspot, his actual wealth a secret, even to her. No doubt its origin tethering between both sides of the law, some legitimate and some probably criminal.

And this time—even though it killed her to have to do this—it was the latter she had come for.

Mag, as they called him, was pouring over a pile of ledgers spread across the table and punching numbers on a printing calculator, his demeanor unusually focused on the menial task.

A nudge of respect rose with a flutter in her stomach to see him work on his own accounts.

Such a contradiction. Nothing in his laid-back facade indicated a thriving business owner. As always, his dark hair brushed his neck, the curls a little too long above the plain black t-shirt emphasizing the defined broadness of his shoulders and arms. His skin—a tad too pale to be healthy—contrasted gently with the sculpted cheekbones and dark determined brows.

And as she watched him check his calculations, she knew she had mere seconds before needing to brace herself from his immense charm.

Once his dark gaze hit her, when his lips curled into that constant amused expression he had every time they met, she would have to fight hard her attraction for the man who was nothing like her.

His life was far from the world she came from. His was late evenings and sensual pleasures. Dubious connections all over the city and the lording over its luxurious nightlife.

Hers was pondered and orderly. Charity balls and business bureaus. A continuous quest to keep her tight hold on the Montreal's real estate power.

As she looked at him now with a slight weight lodged in her chest, in those few seconds before he would become aware of her presence, she couldn't help but wonder if there was perhaps a possible place where they might be alike.

But that small hopeful moment was soon over.

He knew she was here.

Magnovald St-Amand slowly lifted his head. With a profound inhale, she took hold of herself as the dark undercurrent of his gaze seized her and threatened her very soul.

"*Tiens, tiens*. Nyssa Vlahos." His lips curled into the familiar wolfish grin. "My favorite Greek tycoon."

She tightened her grip on her gloves and took another deep settling inhale while the back of her neck stiffened with minor irritation at his comment.

She should never have told him about her family background—her dad an immigrant from the old country and who had started their large family business by managing apartment buildings in town. Magnovald brought it up at every encounter. She was never sure if he was teasing her, or truly considered her an outsider, his own family having been in the country since the foundation of the city centuries ago.

Her stomach still quivering, she strode toward the devastatingly handsome club owner with all the confidence she could muster, her chin high, her chest opened and her gaze aloof.

The grin was still on his lips as he reclined and stretched his arms along the wooden railing behind him to consider her. His gaze trailed down her body from the tip of her classic leather boots all the way up to the flushed skin of her bare throat. The attention nearly changed her mind about the purpose of her visit.

Thank goodness for her coat, the heavy wool garment providing a little protection from his appraisal. She would *not* let him see how he affected her. Their relationship had been purely business since the beginning and would remain that way.

She swallowed, pursing her lips as she realized that today was an exception. Her request was very private.

"Mr. St-Amand," she drove right to the point with a curt nod, "I need your help."

He raised an inquisitive brow then the cocky smile returned. "Mag."

She frowned and leaned back on her heels with her arms crossed at her chest.

"I've told you before, *poupée*." An impossibly dark twinkle appeared in his eyes. "Call me Mag."

"Fine." She shook her head and took a decisive step forward. "Mag, I need your help."

"Now that's interesting," He lazily stretched his long leg under the table as he watched her with a slight tilt of his head. "No new offer for my club today?"

She nodded at the finance paperwork scattered on the table in front of him, momentarily distracted from her current purpose. "You're not up to code, Mag. It's just a matter of time before the city board forces you to comply."

She surveyed the area and the exposed wires alongside the mirrored wall behind the bar. The steps leading to the stage by the dance floor were crooked and old pipes were exposed just over the DJ area. The place was an opulent den at night under the colored strobe lights, but the day exposed its potentially harmful flaws.

4

"I can offer you more money than you can spend in a lifetime," she added.

"A lifetime, really?" he snorted. "You'd be surprised about that."

"Look, I'm not here for your club." Her current quest was so much more important than making him another generous offer for the premises. She just had to go for it. Ask him for his help. Now.

"Then you came for me." His features lightened, a crinkle appeared at the corner of his eye. "About time. Want to go upstairs right away? Or you want romance first, maybe dinner?"

"No." She brushed his banter aside with a wave of her hand. There were no chances in hell she'd ever go out with him.

Perhaps it was her own assumptions, but everything seemed a joke to him, from the casual banter he constantly used on her to the laid-back way he ran his business. Life was no laughing matter. Hers had been a challenge which she had met head on at every turn.

But all that was not important right now. She eyed him hard. "I need you to give me access to Moreno."

"Ennio?" He chuckled and slid his tall body back farther. "What happened? Are you late with your protection payment? I thought you'd be the type to go straight to the police."

"Mr. St-Amand." She huffed, correcting herself. "Mag." She grabbed a chair to sit across him. Her back stiff, she leaned in towards him. She had no time to beat around the bush. "It's about my little sister. Stepsister, actually. She's missing."

He shook his head and his expression changed. His

forehead creased with gravity for the first time since she'd walked in. "Missing?"

"She ran away with her boyfriend. He's much older than she is. Some rapper named Oliver LaChance. My sources say he's connected. She's only thirteen." Nyssa swallowed, her mouth parched. "Mr. Moreno might know where to find her."

"A kid. *Sacrament.*" Mag leisurely ran a hand through his hair and bent forward, unease warring upon his features. "Not sure I can help you, though."

With her heart racing, she pushed her shoulders back. Her gaze was unwavering. "I'm willing to trade for your help."

"Trade?"

"I promise not to bother you about the club for at least one year if you only give me an introduction."

"What about that petition you sent to the board about my so-called code violations?" He shot her a harsh squint.

"Dropped. Called it off this morning." That was the least she could do. She had hoped rescinding the appeal would be her olive branch. That the gesture would convince him to at least make a call to the mob boss on her behalf.

"Really?" He remained unnaturally still, a brow slightly raised.

"Yes."

"Wow, you've been a pain in my ass for months. You'd really drop it? No more visit to the club before opening hours?" The easy grin returned, and she shifted on her seat.

"It's withdrawn," she stated with a slow nod.

"No more letters. No more calls?" The change in his

6

voice almost sounded as if he'd miss her contacts. That he would miss *her*. No. That was a wild thought.

With her jaw tight, she lay her gloves flat on the table. She let the fact that she was a purely goal-oriented woman sustain her. It had helped her escape her troubled home life, had helped her build her empire. And now her drive would help her save her sister. She would never let something like lust for a bad boy club owner distract her from her mission.

"One year." She held his gaze in hers steadily.

"Even for one year, I'm shocked to see you back off so easily." Despite his laid-back manners, she detected a hint of interest in his tone.

She scowled, her teeth clenched with impatience. "I will, I promise."

"Just for an introduction?" He showed genuine attention now.

"It's my sister." The pain she had so far managed to keep in check bubbled to the surface to lodge itself at the back of her throat. How could she explain to him that her half-sister had no one but her in life? No one who cared.

Her breath was seized by visions of what may have happened to Cat—her body lying in a frozen ditch somewhere along the highway, or hunkered in a sleazy basement room with that rapper, forced into things she was not ready for.

Nyssa closed her eyes and rubbed the bridge of her nose while taking a deep inhale. Panic would not be useful here.

"I wish I could help you." Mag's tone was apologetic, his brows drawn together.

"Why won't you?" Her shoulders drooped. If he didn't

help her, how on earth would she be able to approach the known mob boss without a recommendation?

Her mind raced through the possibilities but nothing sensible came to mind. She had been adamant in running her business as clean as possible—following safety protocols and builder unions demands to the letter. There were definitely people who did not like her methods. Ennio Moreno being one of them.

She sighed. "I'm willing to add another year."

She would have to say goodbye to her plan for a series of condominiums with quaint street-level shops in the area. She had desperately wanted to renovate this neglected part of old-Montreal—months of historical research, costly handshakes and late-night deals—but right now it did not matter. She had her sister to think about.

A sudden numbness hit her limbs. She would sell her soul to the devil to get her sister back. "Anything you want," she pleaded.

"Damn, I'm sorry, Nyssa. Another year won't make a difference." With a slow exhale, he cast her a pained look, his voice tainted with a trace of emotion. "Didn't you know? Moreno's dead."

*Her sister. Damn.* Nyssa Vlahos had a little sister that she cared about.

For the first time in the few months he'd known her, Mag looked upon his favorite ice queen with something like empathy instead of his usual amused attraction.

In the moments she digested the news of Moreno's passing—like every damned time she came to his club—his blood tingled with the need to touch her.

He wanted to let his fingers skim along the vulnerable line in the sway of her neck. Wanted to taste that tender part of her skin.

He felt a tiny prick of fangs brush his tongue and tightened his fist. There was nothing he could do to quench that deep desire that had not let go of him since they met.

He had thought of compelling her, as his kind would do. Oh, it would have been so easy. But something strange and powerful in the recesses of his mind had always stopped him.

"Dead?" She wrung her hands together with anguish over the leather gloves she had set on his table.

"Heart attack. Just fell over his dinner at Enzo's Palace. Sometime last weekend." He offered her a small nod. "Funeral's tomorrow."

She slumped back in her chair, her body seemingly curled upon itself.

An unusual heaviness settled across his chest at witnessing her distress. He had never seen Nyssa Vlahos defeated. Since they met, she had been nothing but an elegant blonde radiating a frost that was colder than any Montreal winter day.

She carefully patted her straightened hair, smoothed the flyaway strands escaping the well-coifed head. The tiny vertical scar that broke the perfect curve of her lip was an imperceptible gap in the glossy red lipstick. He always wondered how she'd hurt herself. One day he'd have to ask her.

But now she needed him. And despite decades of not caring about mortals and their problems, this time was different.

"Okay." He threaded his fingers together upon the table. "Tell me."

She straightened her spine and stared at him with a blank look.

"Tell me about your sister," he urged.

"Catalina." She licked her bottom lip and took a deep exhale. "My dad remarried, when I was a kid and he and my stepmother had a child together. The kid's a mess. She's turned rebellious all of a sudden and lashes out at everyone."

"I see." Mag wanted to know it all. But the haunted look in her eyes hinted that it could take a while. "Want a drink?"

She shrugged with a huff. "It's two in the afternoon."

"Is there a rule that you can't drink at two?" His lips curled into a smile he meant to be lighthearted. He raised his hand in the air to call out Sandrine, his head waitress, who was stacking drinks in the cooler behind the bar. "*A couple of beers, fille*. Please?"

Nyssa frowned but didn't protest.

"So Catalina ran away," he repeated.

"Yes. Our dad is sickly and disconnected. Her mom doesn't care." She pursed her lips while slowly rolling her gloves into a tight ball. "Lucinda's such a bitch, she won't even search for Cat. Once she gave birth, that was it. Got her hooks into Dad with a child and left the poor kid with nannies. Now she has my father convinced that Cat is fine, that she is old enough to make her own decisions. Ever since his stroke, he's a shadow of himself and believes everything Lucinda says."

"When did Cat disappear?"

"About a week, or so Lucinda said. She can be such a liar. I wasn't there, I don't live at the estate anymore. Haven't for years." Her movement unusually slow, she reached for her crisp leather satchel and unzipped the top. "Didn't take long for me to leave that dysfunctional family."

"Oh yes, I remember now." He raised a brow at her with a slight chuckle. "You got your own place at the top of Vlahos Tower. There was a feature about the building in the papers. You built that eyesore in less than a year.

"You read about me?" She dropped the gloves into her bag and swiftly zipped it shut.

"Gotta know my enemies." He smirked. She was anxious over a sister, but he just wanted to see her combative spirit return.

Yet her features were still slack. "I'm not your enemy."

"You want to eradicate the heritage of this street." He considered her, reflecting on their many heated interactions. "That makes you my enemy."

"The buildings are old. Not safe." The zeal had returned to her eyes as she tapped her pointed finger on the table to prove her point. "I'm just looking out for the people living here."

"If you have your way, those people won't be able to afford to live here anymore," he huffed. That, there, was the part that infuriated him. He worried about his neighbors—old Bourgeois on his pension next door, the Chakirs with their small family bakery across the street, the weird kid with the comic book shop farther down—they would all have to move.

"Can we not do this?" She shot him a feverish gaze, which stung him straight at the center of his heart.

"Right." He grimaced at the unfamiliar twinge of guilt rising inside him. This was not the time to bring up their feud. "Your sister. She's gone."

Nyssa nodded grimly. "I really hoped I could talk to someone who knows LaChance. He's in his mid-twenties. What would he want with a thirteen-year-old? I heard he's connected, got his start-up money in shady deals. What if he's grooming Cat for the sex trade or something like that?" She shuddered upon her last words.

"Sex trade?" He let out a slow and measured sigh. "Is the man that twisted?"

"I believe so. Cat's best friend Livy is really concerned. The two texted for a bit. Cat was all excited about the new clothes LaChance bought her for her first job."

"A job? What kind of job is there for a thirteen year old?" Mag shifted in his chair, suddenly invested in Nyssa's plea. "Can you not track Cat through her friend?"

"No. That's the problem. Livy said LaChance was insisting Cat switch to the new phone he got her. So now we can't find her. She went totally dark last week. I tried to locate him too. All his known contacts lead nowhere. Email, phone, social media, all dead." She threw her hands up in the air, her voice choked with emotions. "The staff at the club where he played wouldn't talk to me."

"Why did you think Moreno would help?"

"Doesn't he run most of the prostitution in the city?" Her gaze was alert now, her expression entirely focused. "Or at least he's connected with the gang that runs thing."

"You're well informed," Mag noted, "but underage prostitution, that's not like Ennio."

"Why not? I know he had friends in high places, but he's basically a crime boss," she exclaimed before leaning forward over the table. "Regardless, I came across a police officer who brought up your name. She said she could help."

"Captain Akande," he asserted. Another human he considered a friend. Amelia Akande was a captain of the *Sureté du Québec* provincial police and knew a lot more about the supernatural than most. If she had sent him Nyssa, she meant for him to help the real estate tycoon.

"She seems like a sensible woman. If she trusts you, I figure it was worth a try." Nyssa seized her handbag from the table while her expression fell. "Now I guess I'll need a new lead."

She shrugged and pushed herself to her feet.

Prompted by a slew of strange feelings rushing inside him, he grabbed her wrist. "Stay."

She looked down at him, her brows knitted together. "You can't help me if he's dead."

He gently pulled on her arms, his senses drumming to

13

feel the strength of her determination under his fingers. "You can meet the widow, Señora Moreno," he suggested. "She's taking over the business."

"His wife?" Nyssa was taken aback. "Is she involved?"

"Oh, doll, she's aware of all of it." He let go of her and shot her a knowing smile. "Some say she was running operations behind the scenes for the last few years."

"I was willing to pay the old man a good amount of cash for the information. Would his wife be swayed by money?" Nyssa didn't look convinced but was listening.

"Probably." He shrugged and nodded at her to sit down. "And she has granddaughters—she may be empathetic to your situation."

"From what I hear that fact doesn't stop the Morenos from running the town's prostitution trade." Nyssa grumbled but returned to her seat.

Mag's heart beat a little faster. He *could* actually help her. He had no idea why, but he wanted to be part of this search for her little sister.

Wanted to keep this banter between them going. And that poor kid, if she was in danger, he ought to get her out of there.

Unable to help himself from countering Nyssa's reasoning however, he raised a brow at her with a half-smile. "One may argue that facilitating a business of consenting adult sex workers is a bit far from dealing in children."

"Still illegal." Her bottom lip remained stiff.

"And you would never cross the law?"

"No. I wouldn't." Her posture was ramrod straight.

"Yet you were willing to run to Moreno for answers," he counteracted. "Not willing to wait for the police to find your half-sister."

She let out a heavy sigh. "The city's police are swamped. They have tons of cases like Cat. Not a priority."

"Your dad surely has influence over the mayor?" He narrowed his eyes at her, his mind racing for ways she could influence the Montreal police to look for her sister.

"He won't try. He's been detached from Cat's upbringing since he had a mild stroke a decade ago. Lucinda was pushing him to work harder and harder, and it nearly killed him. The woman is one greedy snake." Nyssa's tone had turned bitter. "He thinks Cat will be all right. Like I told you, Lucinda convinced him to let Cat lead her life."

"At thirteen?" He frowned with surprise. "Your stepmother truly doesn't care."

"Not one bit." Her hands flew out with exasperation. "She always looks at me like I'm something dirty under the bottom of her shoe. Barely acknowledged me when I was a kid and when she did, it was *not* kind. She has a foul temper and likes to take it on vulnerable people. And now, even with her daughter gone, she's planning her next cruise. Honestly, all Cat has is me."

"Wow, no wonder you left." Mag blinked at the nasty stepmom and the absent father. He suddenly wondered what Nyssa's childhood had been like.

"Yes. I left young." Her expression turned numb. "But Cat is not street smart. Her head is in books and fairytales. She's convinced this guy is her soul mate. She snuck out to his concert one night and that's when trouble started."

"Shouldn't be too hard to find her. If this rapper is connected to organized crime in the city, Señora Moreno should be able to point us in the right direction." Mag cleared his throat. "I'm warning you, though. The lady is not that fond of me."

"Why?"

He nodded at his empty club. "Moreno liked to come here and play."

"You were his pimp?"

"No, not like that." He dismissed the accusation with a careless shake of his head. "But she's very old-fashioned. Church every Sunday. Kids in Catholic school, devotion, that kind of thing."

"And you're far from the church-going type."

"Yet, one of my best friends is a priest," he chuckled.

"Hard to believe."

"It is, isn't it?" Father Grégoire had always been in his life. Ever since the holy man had come to the St-Amand Immortals as a young novice of the Notresdame Disciple.

He was old now and at the head of the monks who assisted the undying siblings with their yearly ritual blood feeding. He was closest to Mag's brother Val, having aided him in rehabilitating young, cursed vampires at the *Sanctuaire des Truants*. But now that Val had moved to Berwick Hollow with his true love Maisie, Mag has sort of taken over and helped when he could. Things had been quiet in the last three months, so Father Grégoire was the one who checked on Mag now and again, to make sure he didn't miss his brother too much.

Nyssa had proven to be an interesting distraction from the pain of having to say goodbye to his brother. But now the diversion was turning into a serious infatuation and a mission to rescue a kid who could be in real jeopardy.

"So, this funeral?" Nyssa disrupted his thoughts.

Mag didn't have a chance to answer before the hair on the back of his neck prickled with an ominous feeling.

16

His entire club suddenly darkened, the room clad in a heaviness that crushed his shoulders and sank into his very soul.

A clattering of broken glass echoed from the bar area behind them.

*What in the hells…*

Stunned, he witnessed Nyssa slump forward on the table between them. Her frame turned completely inert, her cheek plopped sideways on the pile of his business files.

He bolted from his chair, his whole body corded in alert as he reached out for the crook of her neck to search for her pulse.

Nyssa's heartbeat was slow but thankfully steady, as if she were merely asleep.

His fangs elongated as he surveyed the deep shadows while shielding Nyssa with his bulk. His vampire sight finally kicked in and he made out the bar area through the unnatural darkness.

*Fuck.* Sandrine had also fallen, her bar tray to her side, the drinks she'd prepared for them spilled on the flagstone floor.

Mag clenched his fist, ready for an attack.

A wide glow rose from the dance floor in front of him, just under the podium where his dancers usually worked. The mist lifted and thickened, obscuring the sight of a human-like form.

The being was a whole head shorter than he was. Mag couldn't make out the face but recognized at once the nature of the low mumbling escaping from its lips.

*A spell.*

*Sacrament.* A magic-user had appeared out of nowhere and had put some spell on the humans.

And this was a strong sorcerer if he could pass the magical wards set up around the club against supernatural attacks.

With Nyssa unconscious right behind him, Mag faced the trespasser.

His fangs were sharp and ready for battle. The predator in him viciously resenting the intrusion into his territory.

Damn, his own legacy magic was rusty. He'd given it up in some brash retaliation when his mom had abandoned him the day his father died.

"*Igirah!*" he intoned, calling powers from the enchanted bracelet at his wrist for a protective barrier. He had his mom's magic somewhere deep inside him, all right. But his grudge against her was stronger than his need for the Ice Witch's power.

The magical cuff he'd bargained from the old indigenous witch across the neighborhood was powerful enough. The teeth and claws of his vampire side, along with his compelling powers, had always been plenty against his enemies.

"*Igirah Gayrdyeth.*" He splayed his palm forward as he cast the shielding spell with confidence.

"*Stryos!*" the magic user spat.

Mag flinched at the clear and fierce female voice that reverberated against the stonewalls of the club. The assailant's spell hit his shield with a flash of indigo light.

The edge of his invisible bubble wavered in a fit of hissing sparkles but it held tight.

Hells, this was a goddamn witch. And one with a hell of magic.

*Fucking bitch!* His whole body tensed as he held up the barrier protecting the humans. His nostrils flared with anger. If it had been only him, he would have jumped

18

straight for her throat. But he had Nyssa just behind him. And Sandrine a little farther.

"Whoever you are, get the hell out of my club." He had no idea what that witch wanted but it couldn't be good. Fury pounded loud in his ears. He would not let the bitch sorceress hurt his two favorite humans who were currently under his roof and protection.

She would pay for her intrusion.

"*Anyenthex!* " the female voice shouted again in the dark.

At the booming word, a lightning bolt shot straight out in Nyssa's direction.

Mag's shield quavered under the spell. Fear for the woman shook him to his core.

"*Koir idash.*" Without thought, he called upon the magical mark just under his wrist—the sigil of his mother, *la Sorcière des Glaces*.

He had not wanted to use the magical bloodline inside him since she'd left the city three hundred years ago. As a kid, the act had felt as natural as the fangs and sharp claws that came with his legacy vampirism. But right now, the ancient familiar magic seemed wrong somehow. The mark not glowing blue as it always had but shining a pure red hue.

"*Pour l'amour de dieu*, Magnovald. Get out of the way."

The voice sent a chill to his spine. *No, it couldn't be!*

The figure of the sorceress detached itself from the dark fog and his throat closed with shock at her sight. He nearly dropped the mystical shield.

In awe, he stared into the delicate ageless features. He took in the thick chestnut hair falling over delicate shoulders and down the long black lace and velvet dress. A rush of confusion tumbled in his chest and he brought a shaky hand to his forehead.

Charlotte Callan St-Amand, the Ice Witch, stood before him. His long-lost mother.

Glowing energy currents were humming and dancing around her palms, now lowered to her sides. Wrath tightened her expression as she eyed the unconscious Nyssa.

"*Maman*." His voice came out hoarse, the tone glacial.

"*Oh mon pitou*. I heard the *chienne* wants to take over your club." His mother crossed the distance between them to pat his cheek. Her hand heavy with magic rings felt cool upon his skin. "When Valerian told me about her, I did what any mother would do. I came to help my son."

Paralyzed from the multitude of thoughts racing in his mind, his witch mark still prickling at the inside of his wrist, Mag remained speechless. She had been gone for *centuries*!

His mother cast another wrathful look at Nyssa who still hadn't moved a muscle. "Now give me some space, *mon fils*, and let me kill her."

# CHAPTER 3

"*A*re you out of your fucking mind?"

"Magnovald, your language." His mom leveled her chin at him and took a step back, ready to strike again.

Mag was furious. "I have not seen you in over three hundred years. What the hell are you doing here?"

"Three hundred and thirty-two."

"Oh you counted, did you?"

"Of course I counted. You're my son."

His lips twisted grimly. "Drop the spell, *Maman*."

"She's your enemy." Her small shoulders were stiff, her body tensed with power.

"No, she's not my enemy." Mag huffed with frustration as he glanced back at Nyssa, still slumped unconscious over her arms. "Bring her back!"

His mom shrugged and dropped her hand. "Why would I do that?"

"Well, first, she's human. We don't attack humans."

"In your world maybe," she sneered. "Not mine."

"She's no threat." He'd forgotten how stubborn she could be. "Lift the spell."

"It's just a sleeping spell." She tilted her head to the side to take in the real estate magnate. "She's in no danger. What's her name?"

"Nyssa," he said without thought. "Nyssa Vlahos. But it's none of your business."

Her features softened and she looked at him. "If she's in your life, it *is* my business."

"She's not in my life." He dug his nails in his palms to contain his irritation. "Come on, *Maman*. Just bring her back."

"You obviously care about what happens to her." She watched him with shrewd eyes.

"Of course I care. This is my place," he stated, incensed by the fact that she didn't care for consequences in the human world and that, even after centuries, she still had a good read on his personal feelings. "No one should be attacked under my roof. Bring back my waitress, too."

"Fine." She rearranged the strap of the leather satchel resting against her hip. "Under one condition."

"Condition?" He protested. What was it with these women and their bartering system?

"Dinner at Justinien's. Tomorrow night."

"What?" he asked with genuine confusion. When on earth had she been in contact with his brother?

*Damn Justin.* He'd never mentioned it. Hells, Mag had stopped discussing their mother with his brothers a good century ago, when it was obvious she no longer care about them.

And if Justin knew, why had he not bothered telling Mag she was in town?

"I'm hosting dinner. I want you to be there."

"Dinner?"

"Yes, you, Justinien, and Renaud."

He shook his head, still perplexed. "You abandoned us three hundred years ago without an explanation, and when you come back you want to have dinner?"

"It's a special dinner."

"I'd say," he smirked, thinking of the conversation ahead around the table.

"Don't be like that, *mon fils*. It doesn't suit you."

"Like what?"

"Snarky."

"I'm not snarky." He just couldn't believe the woman. She acted like a mother, but had she actually been one?

"Yes, you are. A little." A tremor of emotion tainted her words.

"Mother, you put a spell on my…"

"You're what?" She smirked and took another closer look at Nyssa. "Your enemy?"

"No. *Sacrament*, Mom. Again, this has nothing to do with you. Lift the damn spell."

"Dinner?" Her contemptuous expression vanished to be replaced by what looked like hope.

His frustration lessened. Three hundred years. And now dinner. What had caused her change of heart in deciding to come see them after so long?

Whatever the reason for her sudden appearance, he wanted to know. "Yeah, I'll be there."

"Oh wonderful." Her eyes brightened and she pressed her hands together at her chest. "I'll make something you all like."

"The spell," he grumbled.

"Deal is a deal." She snapped her fingers and Nyssa

23

shuddered from her slumber. Sandrine let out a low moan from the back.

With a finger to her lip, his mother shot him a warning look not to give her presence away. *Tonight*, she mouthed.

She slowly dematerialized to leave nothing behind but a faint purplish haze.

"The funeral." Nyssa blinked at him. "What time?"

*Damning hells.* Shaken, furious at his mom, and more than a little overwhelmed, Mag sat back into his booth.

Nyssa had noticed nothing. She seemed to be completely unharmed.

At the back of the club, Sandrine was cursing at the spilled drinks and picking herself up from the floor. She too seemed fine.

"Sorry?" he said.

"Moreno's funeral, what time should I be there?"

"Oh right." He shook himself, returning to her quest. "It's tomorrow at two in the afternoon. Meet at the cemetery at three?"

"Which one?" Her gaze was alert, her poise cool.

"Mount-Royal," he answered. "By the gate."

"You'll introduce me?"

As he shifted forward, he noticed the distress in her expression. The businesswoman was hurting.

His mother could have very well killed her, right there before his eyes.

Pissed at her audacity, he vowed to let his mother know exactly how he felt at that bloody dinner of hers. The witch had no right to interfere with what was his. Not his favorite ice queen. Not any human he even remotely tolerated. It wasn't his mom's place to meddle in his life.

"Don't worry, Nyssa," he told her, feeling back in charge once again. "I will introduce you to the señora."

"Thank you." Her expression was so grateful that his heart thawed a little more, distracting him from his bitterness at the mother who'd abandoned him so long ago.

"Tell you what." Satisfied with his rash decision, he grinned. "I'll do more than just introduce you. I'll help you bring your sister back home."

# CHAPTER 4

*C*at had been offline for six days now. Dread seeped into Nyssa's bones as again she imagined the worst for her little sister. The child could be hidden somewhere in a filthy rundown trailer outside of town. Forced to be high on drugs, unable to leave. Or worse, she could be dead. Her body discarded in a garbage dump at a sleazy back-alley downtown.

Nyssa repressed the bile mounting in her throat at the possibility of her sister's death. Seated at the back of her limo, she absentmindedly watched Mag—as he insisted she called him—take powerful strides towards her car parked beside the tall stone gates of the Mount-Royal cemetery.

His strong legs were planted firmly on the packed snow as he stopped to wait for her under the ancient arch with an air of complete ease. His wide chest was barely covered by a motorcycle leather jacket, his hair tossed by the icy wind. How could the man not be cold?

With gritted teeth, she repressed the feverish desire growing uncomfortably for the enigmatic man and refocused on the sole reason she had asked for his help. Find her sister.

The temperature had been relentlessly below freezing for the last three weeks and she wondered if Cat would be warm enough wherever she was. According to her young au-pair, her sister had left all her parkas and warm coats at home and had last been seen wearing a thin silk bomber jacket.

Nyssa shook her head as Mag rested his gaze on her chauffeured Mercedes. She guessed that this was her clue. He had come down from the Moreno family's mausoleum to greet her. The funeral was ending.

In preparation to brace herself against the harsh winter, she slid on her leather gloves.

"You want me to come with you?" Mr. Julien, her chauffeur, glanced over his shoulder at her.

She appreciated his concern but shook her head to decline the offer.

"I have to do this alone." Mag had insisted she keep things discrete. The Morenos preferred their affairs private.

Protected from the elements by a dark full-length over-coat and a Greek fisherman's cap, the loyal middle-aged man slipped out of the car and walked around it to open her door.

She placed a steady footstep onto the slippery snow-covered pavement and stretched into the bright and frigid day.

She'd been feeling queasy since she'd left the club the day before. With an eerie feeling that she'd missed a few minutes of time just as Mag had agreed to help her.

She rubbed the back of her neck. It was probably just stress. She'd been working much too hard lately, with barely four hours of sleep each night. There were meetings she couldn't reschedule. The deal for a new development in Brussels was turning into a reality. Vlahos' first foothold into Europe. Mom and Dad's dream of expansion into the old country finally realized. Too bad her mother would never see it. She'd been gone for more than a decade, but Nyssa had to carry on, if just for her memory.

She concentrated on the condensation of her breath creating frozen clouds in the air to compose herself.

She'd sleep after she found Cat.

Her sister's behavior was infuriating but Nyssa's fear for her fate meant that she just couldn't be mad at her.

With a sigh, she touched her lip—just where her scar was—in a much too familiar habit. The poor kid had it worse than Nyssa ever did. Lucinda was the queen of narcissism, parading her child like an accessory when Cat was a baby and now only using her as a target to her volatile temper. At least Nyssa had known what a loving mother was like. She'd experienced real love for a part of her childhood.

Cat had none of that. And while Nyssa could never be as nurturing as her own mother was, she could be there for her sibling. The kid was just looking for love in the wrong places.

And just then it hit her, and Nyssa made a decision. As soon as she'd found her, Nyssa would not return Cat to her bitch mother. Her sister would come live with her. At Vlahos Tower. Nyssa would put pressure on their dad if needed. He desperately wanted her Brussels deal to go through. It should be leverage enough for a quirky kid that he was too sick to enjoy.

With a purposeful stride, her plan solid in her mind, she closed the distance between the devilishly handsome club owner casually leaning against the huge, weathered pillar and herself.

She raised her chin and, genuinely grateful, laid a very light hand on his arm over the sleeve of his leather jacket. "Thank you for arranging this."

He stared at her touch with a slow curl of his lips before nodding toward the crowd coming out of the crypt in the centuries-old cemetery. "They're done. Here's our chance."

Nyssa watched as, one by one, the family and closest friends of the deceased mob boss exited the extravagant stone building, with its gilded carvings and trio of alabaster chubby cherubs covered in ice glittering in the frigid sunshine.

"Is this the archbishop?"

She turned to Mag, shocked at the sight of the man of the cloth in full regalia who was nodding with a solemn smile at a middle-aged lady.

The woman's bare hands were joined together over what looked like a dark beaded rosary. Her jet-black hair streaked with a red tint remained stiff under the black fur hat despite the winter breeze.

A trace of amusement appeared at the corner of Mag's eye. "The Moreno family is not all bad. Definitely friends in the highest places."

Anxious at having to associate with mobsters, Nyssa tugged at the collar of her coat, worried about how to approach the widow.

The archbishop and his entourage of somber priests took their leave of the small mourning party and retreated on the path of the cemetery in a swish of white robes upon the snow.

"Come." Mag took her elbow and his strong presence

enhanced her courage. She looked up at him and, for the first time in forever, felt she had someone she could trust to take the lead. If only for a moment, and in this environment she knew nothing about.

"Señora Moreno." He approached the lady with a bow.

From up close, Nyssa could see that the widow was much older than she had originally thought. Despite the youthful henna-dyed glossy waves of her hair and the expert heavy make-up, the señora's features lined with age put her at least over sixty-five.

Buried within the folds of the señora's long raccoon coat was a little girl of about four dressed in a tiny black peacoat and matching hat over red-colored wool tights and shiny black boots. The child was looking up at them all through wide black irises and with silent respect.

"Mag." A tall and broad man in a dark overcoat blocked their path to put his body right in front of the lady and child. With his jaw set, his gaze belligerent, he narrowed his eyes at Nyssa.

This was Montreal's mafia and despite the priests and child, the threatening thug before her underscored how out of her depth she was.

"Vince. Sorry for your loss, man." The words were oddly respectful but the deadly undercurrent in Mag's tone was unmistakable. His presence seemed to widen and cast a shadow over the whole funeral party.

"You shouldn't be here." The man named Vince crossed his arms at his chest and settled back on his heels, his expression unreadable.

"You're out of a job now, I believe." Mag's hand was now at Nyssa's back and she felt grateful for the contact.

"We're never out." Vince shot a quick glance behind his shoulder. "I work for the lady now."

"As you should." Mag nodded to himself.

"This is family business, bud." Vince rested his gaze on Nyssa. "You shouldn't bring strangers."

She leaned a little closer to Mag, not sure what to say.

"She's my guest." Mag's tone was like ice. His hand slid around her waist, his stance solid as if he were warning Vince against touching even a strand of her hair.

Once again, Nyssa was grateful to Mag for going beyond a simple introduction to the mob family.

The widow suddenly spoke. Her words a fast string of Italian behind the rigid bodyguard.

Vince nodded quietly and stepped aside. "She said it's okay. But don't overstep your welcome."

"It's nice to see you too, Vince." Mag's tone lightened but turned sympathetic as he bent down to the tiny woman. "*Le mie condoglianze, Señora*. Ennio was a good man."

The lady nodded silently, then spoke animatedly in Italian again, her gaze hard on Mag.

"Not always good," Vince translated with a half-smile. "He liked to stray sometimes. But he was an excellent provider and father to their children."

"I know you run things now." Mag was straight with the elder as he tilted his head at her. His words measured, he started to explain what they needed from her.

The tips of Nyssa's fingers dug into her palms. There was no way this short little lady could be at the head of the biggest crime empire of Montreal. Bookmaking, loan sharking, racketeering, arms trafficking, it always seemed to come back to this family.

Yet Señora Moreno looked like a grandmother ready to light a candle to her departed before kneeling in church with her rosary for hours. Not some mob boss one expected to see at the smoky back room of an illegal gambling club.

As Mag continued to clarify who Nyssa was and why they were here, the Italian woman settled her gaze on Nyssa.

Her spine stiffened as she detected a harsh and keen glint in the old woman's watery eyes. She hoped Mag would find the right words to convince Señora Moreno to give them the information they wanted.

"Your sister," she finally said in broken English, looking straight at Nyssa.

"Yes." Nyssa raked her throat. "Catalina. She's thirteen."

"*Ah si…*" The woman concurred with a knowing smile. "How do you say? Teenagers."

"I'm very sorry for your loss," Nyssa offered her condolences, realizing the lady did understand English.

"It was time." Her jaw stiffened and, still clutching the little girl at her side with one hand, she made the sign of the cross with the other, her rosary wrapped around her gnarly fingers.

"I just need to know how to find Oliver LaChance, the rapper," Nyssa pleaded. "Catalina is with him."

"LaChance?" Señora Moreno turned a puzzled eye at Vince who replied something back in Italian.

"You know where we can find him?" Mag furrowed his brow.

"And why should we help you?" Vince's sharp chin was thrust forward.

"You know why." Mag chest expanded. His body was coiled, ready for action.

"Easy, Vincenzo," the lady barked. "I like this one."

"Told you the lady liked me," Mag told Vince and eased back, his usual slow smile returned.

"I like *her*." Señora Moreno pointed a decisive finger at Nyssa. "Señorita Vlahos."

"She's heard of you." Vince's gaze on Nyssa softened.

"Those big towers," Señora Moreno said, her smile wide while her eyes took a dreamy shade.

"Yes. That's me." She was uncomfortable with the knowledge the mob knew of her.

"Very, *como le dice*, nice." A light flush rose at the lady's cheeks.

Nyssa caught Mag's amused arched eyebrow at her before she returned her gaze to the widow, hope rising in her chest. "Thank you."

Señora Moreno cast a fond gaze to the child by her side before taking a step closer to Nyssa.

She grabbed both her hands in hers. The gloveless parched fingers appeared brittle against Nyssa's black leather gloves. "You help your sister," she told Nyssa, her eyes bright. "Bring her home."

"You will help me?"

"Vincenzo?" Señora Moreno dropped Nyssa's hands, wielding surprising authority in her call.

"Yes, Señora."

She waved her ornate jeweled rosary into the air. "Tell her."

Vince nodded back at his boss while she took the hand of the child and spun away from them to amble forward in the snowy path of the cemetery. Their meeting was over.

"So," the big man began, loosening his stiff posture, "what do you wanna know?"

# CHAPTER 5

"*S*o you're actually going to help her. Why on earth, *mon fils?*"

"Mom." Mag's voice was low, the word pregnant with everything he felt and didn't want to express.

His family sat around the sturdy dinner table in Justin's brownstone townhouse in the Plateau Mont-Royal.

Renaud was there, elbows on the table and, as usual, dressed like a lumberjack in his plaid shirt over a white tee. With his expression aloof as always, he watched Justin, still in the formal tweed he wore at the university, pour a rare bottle of Bordeaux into an old crystal decanter.

Then there was their mother, the Ice Witch of the Callan Clan, lording over her three sons—as if she hadn't been gone for three hundred years. Ageless in her beauty, she occupied the head of the table like a queen of the occult.

Missing were his brothers Cassiodore and Griffon. Cass was still touring with his band and Griff was somewhere in Asia looking for their elusive birth father.

Mag huffed as he leaned back in his chair, wishing his closest brother Val were here. He always had Mag's back.

But Mag knew Val had his hands full with the Black Oak warlocks in New England and that his heart and soul now belonged to Maisie Thibodeau, the High Priestess of the White Holly. His brother was happy in Berwick Hollow.

After Valerian had turned a lover into a vampire in the 1600s and she'd transformed herself into a blood-addict monster, Val had spent centuries ridden with guilt. He'd spent his life atoning for his mistake by rescuing the cursed teen vampires turned by his ex, Emmeline.

The immortal female vampire had mellowed a little and was now best friends with Maisie. Something had happened between the two when Maisie had to endure a ritual that had made her immortal. Mag didn't know what, but the friendship seemed tight.

*Sacrament*, he should have told Justin to invite Emme to their family dinner. She was always fun. Mom despised her for what had happened with Val when they were all barely eighteen. She always blamed the shopkeeper's daughter for the forbidden ceremony that had turned her. Watching Mom being annoyed at Emme's presence would have made this affair a little less gloomy.

He cringed to see her now presiding at the end of the table—with a beaming smile for Justin who was filling his brothers' drinks— and he endeavored to ignore her familiar scent of heathery perfume, which tossed his soul in a shadow of melancholy.

As if she tried to recreate their old lost life, Mom had commandeered Justin's small kitchen and actually cooked dinner for her three sons—something from the old days, she'd promised.

Ren cut a large slice from one of the traditional thick golden meat pies their mother had placed at the center of the dinner table. Mag leaned back on his chair with his wine glass in hand, not really hungry. It would take more than a hearty meal for Mag's soul to soften when it came to his mom. Why the hell had she just decided to show up like that?

"Wasn't Ms. Vlahos the one who kept trying to buy off your club?" Justin tore a piece of bread from the crusty loaf their mother had bought from the bakery down the street, his expression grave as he laid a heavy gaze upon his brother.

"She spearheaded an injunction with the city board to have me closed." Mag shifted in his seat and sat the glass in front of him with a slow exhale. "She wants the land for another of her ugly towers."

"I wish one of you would have told me earlier," his mom said. Despite her small frame, she radiated confidence, her shoulders spread wide under the velvet dress adorned with silver filament. "I would have nipped this in the bud. Just a simple spell and she's gone, *mon enfant*."

"Nyssa wanting to buy me out can't be the only reason you came back after all these years." Mag squinted at her, searching his brain for his mom's real motive in coming to Montreal.

"Valerian called." She clasped her hands together in front of her empty plate and cast Mag a concerned look. "He was worried about you. Said this Vlahos woman could truly have the power to close you down. After the witch Maisie Thibodeau called upon my powers to help your brother, I realized I'd been away from my boys for too long."

*Valerian, dammit.* Mag slowly shook his head, not sure how to feel. "You *have* been gone too long, *Maman*."

Her admittance was an understatement.

She had left in 1690. They were just twenty years old. Her departure, merely hours after their beloved adopted father had died, had been like a punch in the gut.

Papa Antoine had been Mag's anchor. His strong silent composure leading him in what it meant to be a man. And to see him brought down by a rabid animal had shattered Mag's sense of certainty. He still remembered his mom by Papa's side, wetting his feverish brow with a weaved cloth. The strong man mumbling in his delirium.

And all Mag could think was, *Maman, why aren't you using your magic? Why aren't you easing his pain with your gift?*

But she hadn't. And had stopped Mag and his brothers from trying to use their own magical abilities.

Papa hadn't lasted the night.

Why be different and have all these powers when you wouldn't help the ones you love?

And he needed an explanation as to why a night had barely passed after their father's death, and she'd disappeared from their lives. Leaving her sons with the task of burying their father.

Val had still been suffering the consequence of having unleashed a monster rampaging the city while Justin had just decided to pass as mortal and study at the *séminaire*. Mag had no direction, no idea what to do with his immortality. The others were equally lost.

They'd finally received her letter a month later from Salem in Massachusetts in which she told them she had needed to leave Montreal to process her grief. That they were men now and would know how to carry on. That the Nostredame disciples were there to support their vampirism.

They later got news that she had moved south after the Salem's witch trials and, when Griffon had looked into the history of the Black Oak Order warlocks, he suggested that their mom was likely the witch who had brought them their power.

Mag snorted inwardly. How ironic that the warlocks' leader Diesel Stanford resented Mag's hold of magical artifacts. Without his mother, the Order would be nothing.

In the end, their mom had sought out her own kind. When the Acadians had eventually made their way to Louisiana, after their expulsion from their lands during the Great Upheaval, Charlotte Callan was already there to help them settle in their new home. She'd found kinship in the witches of her own ancient traditions she had discovered amongst the new Cajuns settlers.

Mag harbored a great deal of resentment. The only reason he knew all this history was not because his mother had kept in touch, no. His brother Griffon had kept him informed. Griff had turned his grief from Papa's death into a single-minded quest—find their birth father. And in the process had kept abreast of their mom's fate through various sources.

"Isn't your club the most important thing in your life?" Mom interrupted his grim deliberations, her brows knitted together. "Why would you have me leave this Vlahos person alone?"

The club *had* been his life. First being the brewery he'd opened on his own in the seventeenth century to avoid spending too much time brooding over his father's early passing and his mom's betrayal. Founding a place for the local lads to enjoy a drink late at night had been the solution.

Then, as Valerian started rehabilitating the cursed teen vamps created by Emmeline and her legacy, he had slowly hired some of them for odd jobs in his establishment.

Words got out and soon the Domaine-Lassalle wolves dropped by occasionally, witches and warlocks from the area also making a point to stop at the *Serpent Maudit*, knowing that most mystical beings would be welcome, so long as they blended in. Because humans, too, enjoyed the premises, Mag always had the best-looking serving wenches and drinks for every taste.

The brewery had changed over the long years, from tavern to jazz club to the modern nightspot that it was now. Mag had been thankful that his province had never gone for that prohibition nonsense. But while the club's style changed, the heart of it remained. It was a place to let go of the daily life's toll, forget your problems. And all the while, at its center was the same cool owner, as Mag pretended to age and made himself inherit the establishment over and over.

The place had endured the red coats and the rebellions, the industrial changes and quiet revolution, and had fended greedy thugs who had wanted to push Mag out, the last being old Moreno in the 70s.

Taking hold of the city's crime as a young rising gangster, Ennio Moreno had set his eyes on Mag's place. But after a few violent skirmishes where the emerging mob boss lost too many of his men to Mag's bite, the man eventually keenly aware of Mag's vampirism, the two had found some sort of truce. Mag even let the family run a small betting book from the *Serpent*'s premises.

"The club is the *only* thing in my life," he finally acknowledged to his family. How would he have survived his immortality without it? "But I made a deal to help Nyssa. I plan to keep it."

"Why would you get involved?" Ren stopped chewing his dinner to chime in. His usually taciturn brother tilted his head at him with a frown. "This is mortal business."

"It's a kid, Ren." Mag narrowed his eyes at him with a harsh glare. "A thirteen-year-old kid."

"And?" Ren scowled.

"Renaud has a point. Why this particular kid, Magno-vald?" Justin was polishing his glasses. "Is it because of Akande? She told Miss Vlahos you're connected, right?"

"Akande?" Ren added. "That police officer?"

Mag nodded. Aware of his true nature, Captain Amelia Akande knowingly kept a blind eye to his small illegal enterprises as long as he left the law-abiding citizens alone. She had never truly called for his help to fight crime. But if she had sent Nyssa to him, he had to honor her request. "If Amelia wants me to help—"

"What, you do the police's bidding now?" His mom stared down at him with a snort.

"You have no say in what I do, Mom." He shot her a direct stare, his jaw stiff. "You've been gone for three hundred years."

"Magnovald…" She settled back in her chair to take in the city lights twinkling as they hit the iced windowpanes. Her tone was wistful. "One thing hasn't changed here, this snow. It's all so white."

Anger rose in him that she still wouldn't talk about why she left them.

Ren said nothing. Twirling his glass between his fingers, he stared at the wine swirling inside.

"You like Louisiana, Mother?" Justin tried to dispel the tension in the room.

Mag was surprised that Justin didn't seem to be angry at her desertion. But maybe he'd thought it for the best. If you intentionally live like a mortal, it didn't serve to have the most powerful witch of the continent as a mother.

Mom turned to Justin with a small smile. "I *do* miss the snow."

"Can't call yourself the Ice Witch now, if you're not here, can you, *Maman*?" Ren sneered, for the first time showing a hint of his feelings.

"Oh Renaud, *mon pitou*." She straightened her spine to reach to him across the table.

He looked down at her hand as if offended, a shadow crossing his aloof expression.

"What?" Mag took in her mark tattooed on the inside of his wrist, the same sigil on all of the St-Amand siblings. "Is that right? Your magic is tied to the city? I wouldn't have guessed."

"No, it's not." She shook her head. "It's tied to my people. Plenty of French descendants where I live now. The *Sorcière des Glaces* is just a name the people here called me. In fact, I think Antoine came up with it." Her expression turned pensive.

"We all miss him, Mother," Justin said, once again trying to ease the tension.

She looked at all of her sons, one after the other. "And he would be so proud of you all. So strong. Leveled. A professor at the University. A well-respected business man."

"Respected," Ren snorted.

"Hey man, watch out," Mag spat back at his brother in a similar bantering tone.

She smiled at him. "And you Ren, a landowner."

"They don't call us that anymore, Mom. And I don't really own Domaine-Lassalle."

"Honestly, Mom, the only one of us who's worthy of praise is Valerian." Mag crossed his arms at his chest, his teeth still clenched. "He's been selfless his whole life. Helping people. The rest of us, we're as egotistic as it comes."

"Mag is not wrong." Justin pressed his lips together.

"Immortality is not an easy cross to bear, *mes enfants*."

"And you bear it more easily where it's nice and warm," Ren scoffed.

"I bear it more easily amongst my people." She breathed out, cool and calm, as if supported by centuries of wisdom.

"Witches," Mag sneered.

"Yes," she admitted. "Can you even do magic, Magnovald? All that I have taught you when you were child?"

He remained silent. Unable to express that every time he'd been tempted to cast a spell from her essence after her departure, he'd been reminded of her betrayal.

Since he couldn't depend on her, why would he rely on the magic she gave them? He could very well fight his fights without her interference.

And he had.

The vampire in him was plenty. And he had his magical artifacts for more.

Calling upon her mark when she had attacked Nyssa earlier had come from pure instinct, brought upon by his deep fear that the real estate magnate could be hurt.

"You couldn't even fend me off yesterday." She clasped the Celtic pentacle at her neck and rested a pained stare upon him. "I could have killed your precious Nyssa in an instant."

"Stop," he suddenly snarled under his breath, his fangs elongating at the repressed fury that came bubbling to the surface at the mention of Nyssa.

"That cuff you wear, it's to bring the magic, isn't it?" Her mouth was pinched, her tone tart, while sadness lined her forehead. "You can't even call it from your own legacy."

"Mom, no." He balled his fists tight as a low growl resonated deep within his chest with his mounting anger.

But she wasn't finished. "Val told me about the magical artifacts you stockpile. Why? It's all in you. My blood. The ancient Callan legacy. Do you even know how strong it is? You're the only one of your brothers to forsake it all."

"You!" he abruptly bellowed, unable to contain his rage. Bolting straight up from his chair, he towered over her with an accusatory finger towards her chest.

"Mag, let it go." Justin was by his side, a palm at his shoulder.

"You, *Maman*, have forsaken us!" Mag fumed, his blood pounding in his ears, wrath blinding him. Centuries of pent-up anger right out and furiously in the open. Finally shouting his pain at her departure.

He realized he was holding her upper arm in his grip and dropped it with a huff.

"I had to." She stared at her hands—the slim digits covered in heavy pewter rings—her chest suddenly caved in, her posture stooped. "I couldn't stay with so many memories. With him *dead*."

"Mag." Justin's measured touch was doing nothing to calm the tempest within him.

Here was his mother, the one he had loved and trusted as any child would, and who, as they'd lost their mortal father and were haunted with grief, had just vanished. The one person who was supposed to be there for them had abandoned them all.

For centuries. As if she'd never birthed them.

How were they supposed to learn how to deal with the misery of an immortal life without her support?

Mag's tight fists relented and he sat back in his chair. He grabbed his wine, gulped it all in one slug before leveling with her. "You were not the only one grieving for Papa. We all did."

"I know," she sighed.

"You didn't even come see us when you returned to help the *Fils de la Liberté* hide." Mag's lips were razor thin at recalling the plea of French-Canadian fighting for their rights. "The city was in chaos and you disappeared into the countryside with them."

"You could all have come with me."

"And abandon the ones who didn't flee to their fate? All our friends? The St-Amand cousins, all of Dad's family who fought in St. Eustache."

Mag, Renaud, and Griff had been right there with their St-Amand extended family for the last face-off of the rebels against the government during the Lower-Canada rebellion. Even with three vampires in their midst, most had perished under the gunfire of their more organized assailants.

"They all died, Magnovald," his mom huffed. "All of them."

"Not all," Renaud said.

"Antoine's family?" She turned to him in disbelief. "You know his descendants?"

"A few."

"Mother, no." Justin's brows closed together with a grave expression. "You have to let them be."

"Justin is right," Mag sneered. "There is no extended family for us. Just us, here, pathetic beings who can barely deal with their immortality. And don't get me started with Griff still searching for our birth father."

"Don't. Ever. Mention this beast!" His mother's cheeks were flushed red with ire.

"I do just fine, brother," Justin interrupted, his lips curled into a slow smile. His chin rose as he stared at Mag, an amused current crossing his dark pupils. "Wouldn't call myself pathetic."

"You might be the only sensible one here," Mag agreed. His anger receded as fast as it had risen to be replaced by his usual lack of care about his existence. Why bother looking for answers after so many decades. "Living like a human sounds like bliss sometimes. How many wives have you had now?"

He instantly regretted his last comment as Justin's eyes turned dark, his expression unreadable.

"Just the one," his brother replied, "I don't recommend it."

"Don't you go fall for this Nyssa, bro," Ren snorted.

"Oh hells, why would I do that?" he protested a little too loudly. "Didn't you see my club? The women in there?"

"She hasn't fallen for you, has she?"

Mag couldn't deny that as soon as Nyssa had stepped into his club that first time just before Christmas, with that ice queen demeanor in her sleek pencil skirt and elegant coat, her clear gray eyes cool and sharp as she'd surveyed him, everyone he ever knew had paled in comparison. And he hadn't touched a single woman since.

Initially thinking he was meeting the spokesperson for a new wine cooler, he'd been shocked when the supremely composed blonde in the silky business attire had slid him a check for an insane amount of money. She wanted his club.

She'd been equally stunned when he had laughed in her face, righteously insulted. Did the woman really think someone like him would let go of his life's work just like that?

And so their little dance had started, her cajoling with money one time, followed by threats the next. She'd found loopholes in the deed, which didn't surprise Mag since the *Serpent*'s foundations dated all the way back to 1692 when he'd first opened the place. Now she was onto code violations. As if such things mattered at the turn of the twentieth century when he'd had the electricity installed.

He had started to enjoy these little jousts, preferring the times when she came in person, in the dead of the afternoon, where her chic persona contrasted with the stark atmosphere of his nightclub during daytime.

"I did try," he grumbled. "I asked her out a few times."

"Wait," Ren said. "She resisted your compelling powers?"

"I didn't compel her," Mag sighed. "It just felt wrong somehow."

"It's always wrong," Justin asserted.

"Yeah, okay, Justin." Mag rolled his eyes at his straight-laced brother. "Thanks for reminding us why we actually don't want to be human. Too many rules."

Mag had no intention to let any mortal, with such little life expectancy, dictate what he should do. He knew who and what he was and had no desire to change it.

He was an immortal bastard, with a taste for human

blood, super strength, and the power to compel whoever he wanted to satisfy his lust.

And frankly, he'd found plenty who had let him drink from them without even being encouraged. His flat above the club had seen a heap of willing partners, finding the thrill of being drunk from an intense aphrodisiac. So why not make them and himself happy?

Hadn't killed a single one yet.

But Nyssa, dammit, she was different.

"What does Father Grégoire say of your feeding on the patrons?" Ren asked lazily as he leaned back into his chair, casually holding his wine glass at his side.

"Nothing." And Mag appreciated that the elder knew better then to speak on it. "I help him at the *Sanctuaire* as I promised Val I would. He's a good guy. Doesn't judge like some here."

Justin sighed. "We're just trying to give you sound advice, brother."

"I'm fine," Mag barked. He glanced at their mother who was studying them back and forth, cautiously holding her tongue. His anger at her was now carefully tucked behind the recesses of his subconscious, his cool nonchalant persona firmly back in place.

"Except that you just promised the biggest business-woman in town that you would retrieve her kid sister for her," Ren pointed out.

"It's nothing," he shrugged. "Small time thug."

"Oliver LaChance," Justin mused. "Cass know him?"

"Cass knowing a two-bit rapper? I doubt it." Ren sat his glass back on the table with a chortle. "He's too busy anyway. He's playing Detroit right now. Chicago next."

"What are you, Cass's time keeper?" Mag turned to

Ren, not quite surprised—the two had always been a bit closer to each other.

"We're tight, okay. He always hides in Domaine-Lassalle when he's in town. Away from the crazy fans. Sorry we don't feel the need to inform you each time."

"I bet those wolf friends of yours keep the undesirables away," Mag chuckled.

Ren cast him a dark dismissive look. "Something like that."

"Well, Mom," Mag finally said, examining the witch carefully. "Where are you staying? Here?"

"I've been staying with my friend Lakota above her *Sortilège* shop."

"Ah." Mag smirked and folded his arms at his chest. Not even with one of her sons.

"Why have you never visited me in Lafourche, Magnovald?" she said, her voice steady. "It goes both ways."

He looked at her stunned. "You expected me to come see you?"

"Why not? Valerian calls me. Cassiodore and Griffon have stayed with me twice. And I met with Justinien when he was on layover in NOLA last year. Why not you?"

"Ren?" He turned to his brother looking for backup.

"He sends cards at Christmas," she informed him.

"You do?" Mag's mouth turned slack.

Ren shrugged lazily. "I didn't think you'd care, man. Honest."

Mag looked once more around the table trying hard to contain the warring feelings in his chest.

Mom had always been a moot point with them. He seethed on how she'd abandoned them to the task of breaking the news of Papa's passing to his friends and family, of settling his affairs, and having to decide what to do with his forge and land up north. And later, on how they learned to live an unending life without a compass to rely on. The Nostredame disciples were their assistants, but each one died eventually. None could replace the powerful, immortal figure that was a parent.

And here he discovered that every single one of his brothers had reached out to her, except for him. Was he supposed to cut her some slack?

He wondered how different things would have been if he had contacted her.

"You've lived such a good life since you built that club, Mag," Justin said. "You got your parties, friends, women, and your dealings. Honestly, I thought you'd actually forgotten about mom. It's been two hundred years since you last mentioned her."

Mag turned a questioning look to Ren. "You, too?"

"Sometimes it's better not to ask."

Of course, Ren, as usual, was no help. Mag suddenly wished Val were here. But then why hadn't his brother told him he called their mother. Dammit.

He grunted and grabbed the wine decanter to fill his glass. To be fair, Justin had a point. Mag never mentioned Mom once in the last few hundred years.

Of course, he hadn't forgotten her.

In fact, the memory he retained of her while Papa Antoine still lived was of a high-spirited mother full of joy and love for them.

The St-Amand household was a lively one, dotted with warm family gatherings in the winter and summer trips to the mountains at their cabin by the lake. Mom had six boisterous sons and time for each of them. Tucking them into bed a night and chasing them out of her kitchen with a wooden spoon and a laugh when they got rowdy during the day.

Mag had pushed those memories back in the deep corners of his mind. Her struggles with their father's death had exposed a weakness in their lives that he had never wanted to explore.

Had he started to seek magical artifacts as a replacement for her void in his life?

*Hells no!* He took a swig of Justin's century-old Bordeaux. That was some heavy psychological shit right there.

"I do live a good life." He smirked to himself and shook his head hopelessly at his mother, relenting a little. "Fine, *Maman*. You're welcome here."

"Just stay away from Nyssa, you hear me?" he added with a scowl, remembering his panic at seeing the businesswoman slumped limp over her arms at his mom's spell.

He was glad to be helping Nyssa with her quest to find her sister. Warmth rose inside him at the anticipation of seeing her again soon and he slid his thumb slowly across the crystal glass, wishing he could be gliding his fingers along her delicate throat instead.

"Of course, *chéri*," his mom promised. "She won't know I exist."

"Good." He quelled the emotions tugging at him to think of the challenges the real-estate magnate was facing. And of course, with her being human and him an immortal, there could be no future between them. "I just have to find this kid and Nyssa will be out of my hair."

"Shouldn't be too hard to do." Ren snickered. "Just another mortal woman to add to Mag's collection."

"Not a problem." Mag choked on his words and poured himself some more wine to mask the conflicted feelings about Nyssa that warred in his chest. He raised his glass to his family with a forced smirk. "Then I'll stick with what I do best, right? Enjoying my favorite cardinal sins."

# CHAPTER 6

"*Y*ou didn't have to come. I could have handled it." Nyssa had agreed to ride with Mag when he'd call the day after the funeral to tell her Vince had a lead.

The rapper had first contacted the Morenos wanting to provide them with fresh recruits for their sex trade business in exchange for a finder's fee. When the mob family had found out that the bastard meant underage teenagers, they had sent him packing.

But they kept an eye on him. Vince had been told through his network that LaChance had an important meeting for his music career tonight in the East Side area.

And that was how Nyssa found herself staring at Mag's strong grip on the leather steering wheel of his sports car as he parked in front of the *Chez Tonton* diner in the middle of the night.

Jumpy, she rubbed her hands on her thighs and looked out to the grim restaurant's glass storefront and its badly shoveled sidewalk. The red neon sign above the door flickered under a dim streetlight, right above faded Valentine's

Day decorations still plastered in the window a month too late.

"You, Nyssa Vlahos, alone at night in the East Side?" He turned off the ignition as she opened the door to the elements with a firm grip.

The night was calm, with the air just below freezing. The frigid temperatures of late finally relenting to give them a slight taste of the spring to come. The night sky hung in smoggy orange hues above the city lights, the moon obscured by clouds which rendered the atmosphere thick and humid.

Mag came around his car to her side. The sleek black paint of the Ferrari gleaming under the streetlight was a sharp deviation from her companion's rough exterior in his black jeans and rugged leather jacket.

She frowned at him with puzzlement. "I'd be fine."

She'd had her share of dealing with shady characters in derelict buildings. Though, usually during the daylight hours.

He tipped his head at the overflowing garbage cans and black trash bags upon the snow in the alley beside the diner. "Doesn't seems like your kind of place."

"You're right, it's not."

"You grew up rich. Fancy house in Westmount," he said, referring to her childhood neighborhood, home to many well-to-do English-speaking families. "Private school abroad."

"Switzerland. Yep." Her voice was chilled as she mentioned where she had spent most of her teenaged years. As if the money could erase the pain of being cast away by your family.

She had been only eleven years old when everything had changed. *Nyssa, pumpkin, Lucinda will be living with us now. She's your new mommy. And guess what, you'll soon have a new sibling.*

Oh, Nyssa hadn't been upset at the sibling, no. Actually, she'd been really excited at first by her stepmom. Lucinda was tall and graceful, looked so sweet. She had brought Nyssa this amazing historical porcelain figurine and a box of fancy chocolates.

Who thought that such an evil witch hid under that beauty? At first, Nyssa had tried to shield Cat from Lucinda's worst treatment of her daughter—things like ripping the poor kid's artwork and calling it amateur or dumping Cat's favorite plastic dolls in the trash because they didn't fit in with her décor.

And herself, after years of seeing her favorite things being thrown away for no good reasons and being yelled at for just being alive, combined with physical blows on the worst of days, Nyssa had given up on finding any hint of a caregiver in her stepmother. She had resorted to protecting herself behind a shield of quiet frosty judgement that the bitch had never been able to shatter.

In the end, the *Institut Bossart* school in Switzerland had been a blessing.

The wicked stepmother of fairytales, Nyssa smirked to herself.

Lucinda had left her daughter with the nanny pretty much since the day of the child's birth. But now there was no one to look after Cat. Her faithful old caretaker had been replaced two years ago by college-aged au pairs who never stayed for more than a few months, unable to tolerate Lucinda's stiff rules and harsh treatment.

Cat was now in trouble and since no one at home would take care of it, Nyssa would.

Embolden by her unhappy memories, she straightened her spine despite the dingy surroundings.

"It doesn't matter where I come from," she proclaimed. "I can easily just walk into this diner and retrieve my sister if she's here. You did not need to come."

"I'm the one Vince called." Mag gently took hold of her elbow, his rich manly scent folding over her. "Señora Moreno seems to like you, but Vince and I go a long way. I saved his skin out of some tight spots a couple of times."

"Mob henchman." Nyssa shook her head. "It was written all over him."

"And you disapprove?"

She shrugged and looked up at him. "If you don't follow the law, how do you know what to do? What's left to believe in?"

"Oh, I don't know. Ourselves. A moral code."

"You have a moral code?" As she teased and took in the strong jaw and sculpted cheekbones, she knew deep inside that whatever rules Mag followed, they were guided by a steady ethical compass. Starting by his presence here helping her. He had paid his part of the bargain, introduced her to the Moreno family. And now he was here with her. "That bodyguard of Señora Moreno, Vince, he's just like you, isn't he?"

He shot her a wicked grin. "Oh, and how is that?"

"Contained, confident." She paused for a moment to survey his features further, noting the strong-minded brow.

She had never expressed to herself exactly how she viewed Mag beyond the enticing but stubborn club owner. She'd always been annoyed at his casual attitude around legalities, where he'd laugh at her for inquiring about things like the noise bylaws and urban planning regulations for his neighborhood. But things were different since she'd asked for his help. He'd turned out to be a surprising ally.

She searched for the right word to describe him and his friend. "Loyal?"

"Vince *is* loyal to the Moreno family. He's been there since the motorcycle gang war."

"A biker?"

"Yes. When it all came down early on during the *Guerre des Motards*, he was swept up in one of the raids. Veteran, just back from Iraq. Never truly belonged with the bikers. Moreno intervened in his favor."

"Paid a bribe."

"Something like that. Vince has been faithful to the whole family since then. That little girl you saw is Ennio's granddaughter. Vince would die for that little girl.

"And what does he do for them now? A leg breaker?" She smirked as she pushed open the glass door to the filthy diner. The scent of cold fried meat and cigarettes cloyed her nostrils.

"More or less." Mag pushed the door wider for her and held it out.

She swallowed, his words and the scene around her a reminder that she truly was out of her element.

Maybe it was for the best that he had chosen to come.

The crowded place made her nose wrinkle in distaste. A mismatched group of people sat around Formica tables at the front and booths at the back, waited upon by an older woman in a ghastly pink nylon uniform. Night-shift workers with tired appearances composed most of the clientele, along with two streetwalkers taking a break from solicitations with coffee and cigarettes, and a group of youths in washed-out parkas sharing a plate of French fries by the window.

Everything seemed dirty and coated with despair. Nyssa could have sworn she saw a fat cockroach crawl away behind the counter propped with an unattended old-fashioned till.

"This place should be closed down and demolished." She glanced back at Mag.

He took her elbow again as if to protect her from the unsanitary environment.

"And replace it with what?" he whispered in her ear, sending unexpected shivers along the crook of her neck. "You want to build another one of your complexes?"

"Maybe." She turned a dark look at him. "Clean and safe apartments for the neighborhood, that's for sure."

She shuddered at the sight of plates filled with left-overs and dirty napkins piled haphazardly at the end of the counter.

"Is that her?" He tapped her shoulder, and she followed his gaze to the back of the diner.

Her heart sank to her gut.

There, at the very back booth, next to a skinny guy in a too large canvas coat, was Cat. A very different Cat. The young girl she usually saw in basic jeans and sweatshirt, with a mop of puffy hair and cute hairclips, had been replaced by someone she barely recognized.

Her sister's eyes were heavily lined with black, her naturally dark curly hair had been straightened to harsh poker-straight strands. Her mouth was tainted a vivid pink.

She looked to be about twenty, the garish makeup erasing all traces of the innocent teen.

She was slouched against her companion—likely the

rapper LaChance—the metal chains of his coat digging into her nubile bare shoulder, her flesh barely covered by the thin strap of a lacy red top. Her eyes were fixed as if hypnotized on a man sitting across them. All Nyssa could see from the third party was his neatly barbered hair and the collar of a well-fitting dark suit.

Raw anger rose inside her at the two adult males with her sister. Cat was just a kid. She should be at home, reading one of those fantasy novels she liked. A glass of milk and pile of cookies by her bed at Doukas House, where the Vlahos had lived since her dad had bought the mansion from a rich Greek boat builder just before Nyssa's birth.

"Let me do the talking," she spat. She strode to the back of the restaurant.

"Wait," Mag called in vain after her.

"Cat," she barked, purposefully ignoring the two men sitting with her sister. "Time to go home."

"Nyssie?" Cat frowned at her. Her voice was hazy as she blinked with confusion. "What are you doing here?"

"What am *I* doing here?" Nyssa's fury redirected to her sister. The little twit had her worried for days. "What are *you* doing here?"

"Just hanging out with my boyfriend." She shrugged and then nestled her small body closer to the rapper who was ogling Nyssa with a leer on his razor-sharp features.

"Who's this, boo?" His pierced lip slid into a cold smile.

"Just my sister," Cat breathed.

"Beat it, Sis." LaChance shot a quick glance at Mag before thrusting his sharp chin at Nyssa with defiance.

With her fists balled at her side, she took a step forward

to tower over him. "You got some nerve taking a thirteen-year-old kid from her family."

She felt Mag just behind her. He was quiet, his hand very light at her upper arm.

"I ain't taking anything." LaChance snorted, his palms out by his sides. "Am I, baby doll?" He trailed a proprietary look over Cat's leg, bare under a vinyl skirt that hardly covered her crotch.

Nyssa finally looked at the man across from them. Business suit. Lone crystal earring. Yeah, she knew him. Disgust rose in her. Jacob Martin.

"Vlahos?" Martin's hands were joined together over the paper placemat on the diner's table. "How interesting to cross paths with you."

She looked at him then at the rapper. "What is this?"

"He's a record producer," Cat chimed, her voice bright. "Isn't it exciting?"

"I know he's a producer, and a sleezeball at that." Known for the many lawsuits against him—sexual harassment, abuse, and also fraud and tax evasion—the media mogul was the last person she'd want to be associated with.

Martin cast her a nonchalant look, as if he found her outrage nothing more than inconsequential amusement.

"Man's signing me on." LaChance narrowed a flat look at her, his hand splayed wide on Cat's thigh, making her cringe.

"Yes, and I get to go with Mr. Martin to his big weekend party tomorrow." Cat's eyes sparkled, bright with excitement.

"A party?"

"Yes." She shot her sister a wide grin. "With all these businessmen, just like you do, Nyssie!"

"Nice little favor." LaChance leaned back lazily into the booth. He squeezed Cat's thigh a little too hard and gave it a slap while Martin smirked with a slow lascivious appraisal of Nyssa's sister. "Right, boo?"

"You're not going to any weekend party, Catalina." Nyssa's tone was steady, her pitch low. "I'm taking you home."

The kid's eyes widened. "No."

"Come on." Nyssa reached across LaChance to grab her sister's wrist. "Let's go, Cricket."

"No, you can't make me do anything." Cat shrieked and pulled back her arm.

"Hey! Leave her alone, bitch." The rapper shoved Nyssa hard across the chest.

The punch blasted painfully through her torso. Shock seized her breath.

She would have fallen if Mag had not been right behind her.

LaChance had now bolted from his seat, mad as hell, everything from his lazy rapper persona gone. A knife appeared in his hand. He waved it nastily toward her. "Now, get out of here, *lady*."

Her heart hammered hard in her chest, her ribcage aching where he'd hit her.

Cat was fixed on the bench, her mouth open in shock.

"*Sacrament!*" Mag's snarl was unmistakable. "You shouldn't have done that, boy."

The rest of the events happened in a flash. One second, Mag was behind Nyssa, the next he was shielding her body with his. The knife fell on the linoleum floor. Mag had the rapper pinned by the throat on the wall, his back coiled with power under the leather coat.

"You shouldn't have hurt Ms. Vlahos." Mag's voice

61

was a purr so deadly the entire place fell silent from the chill in the air.

Stunned, Nyssa watched the rapper's feet beat the void as he twitched under Mag's grip, his face a mask of fear. She couldn't see Mag's expression but whatever it was, it left LaChance terrified.

She shook herself out of her trance to grasp what looked like Cat's things, a tiny pink fur coat and a small plastic purse on a chain. "Come on, kid," she said. "There's nothing good for you here."

Cat cast an uneasy glance at LaChance and reluctantly slid across the booth to Nyssa's side.

"She's just a kid," Nyssa spat at Martin who had remained quiet and unconcerned through the whole encounter. "You should be ashamed of yourself."

She had no desire to go into the details of how exactly she felt about the slimy businessman—she just wanted Cat away from the two scumbags.

The teen teetered in heels much too high as she attempted to put on the cropped furry coat.

Nyssa stared at her sister's get-up with a shake of her head. Her heart sank again to see the exposed navel, her sister looking no different than the two streetwalkers at the front of the diner.

"Here." Nyssa grabbed the tiny fur from her sister's hands before sliding off her own long wool coat and wrapping the girl in it. "Let's go home."

Cat shuddered in the too-big garment and Nyssa noticed the tears in her sister's eyes. "You can't make me, Nyssie."

"Oh, I can, and I will. Dad's sick with worry."

"I really doubt that." She suddenly sounded much more mature than usual.

"Well, *I've* been sick with worry." And that was the absolute truth.

She stared back at Mag who was shoving LaChance into the booth, his brutal grip reminding her how he actually associated with mobsters. She had been worried enough to accept the help of a connected and perhaps shady man against her very own instinct.

After having been threatened with a knife, she couldn't deny that she was glad Mag was here with her.

She gritted her teeth with anger, mad at herself for her weakness. She had years of martial art training behind her but when LaChance had shoved her, she'd frozen on the spot. She'd been scared. Not confident enough to retaliate. *Damn.*

And Mag had swooped in like a hero of noir movies, saving the dame in distress. Conflicted emotions rose inside her. She'd been so used to taking care of herself and now, when she hadn't, he'd been right there.

"Let's go." She pushed her sister to the door, annoyance at herself still lingering in her chest. Well, this was over now, and she could get on with her merger, take care of her sister properly, since no one else was.

They exited the diner, the cold air making her shiver in her thin blouse.

"Here," she nodded at Mag's Ferrari. "Get in."

"I'm not going." Cat's small feet in her spiky heels were planted in the dirty ice.

Mag came out behind them. "So this is her, huh?"

"Who are you?" Cat's shot Mag a quizzing look, her expression closed in, brows drawn together.

"A friend of your sister." He opened the car door and pulled down the front seat to make way to the back. How he'd said "friend" made Nyssa pause. Were they now friends?

Nyssa was not ready to ponder the nature of their connection. "Get in the car, Cat."

But Cat had her own ideas. "What did you do to my boyfriend?"

"Boyfriend?" Mag's lips curled with amusement. "Kiddo, you should be in bed."

"Catalina, in the car."

"Why?"

"Because I said so, that's why," Nyssa snapped.

"You're not my mom."

"Thank goodness," Nyssa smirked. Lucinda was the last role model on earth.

Mag looked at them both with a slight grin that made her tense with uneasiness. She could not let him see her lack of authority.

"Cat, you have no choice." She endeavored to sound calm and possessed while taking her phone out of her purse. "I'm calling the police right now if you don't get in."

Cat glowered fierce eyes on her, her feet solid in a wide stance. "I love him, and he loves me." Her vigor was like some tragic heroine of her favorite teen show. "And there's nothing you can do about it."

# CHAPTER 7

*T*he kid had finally agreed to get into Mag's car after Nyssa had shown her the missing person alert on her phone and threatened to call the authorities. Both were seated in the backseat. It was as if Nyssa felt the need to keep the kid as close as physically possible.

Mag was impressed by the businesswoman's cool demeanor after she'd been obviously furious at her sister. Especially after she'd been struck by the "boyfriend."

He let out a forced breath as he turned a close corner under the green traffic light. As he left the East Side area toward the high rises of downtown, the icy streets were almost free of traffic, deserted by their usual commuters until the next business day.

He stretched his tight neck as he recalled his actions in the diner.

Neither of the Vlahos sisters had seen his fangs. Or the way his face thinned when he let the predator out. His vampire's features were not hugely different from his everyday traits but enough to look inhuman. Enough to scare a worthless punk trying to be tough.

LaChance would not lay a hand on that kid again. No. Not after what Mag had promised him if he did.

Rage at seeing Nyssa hurt had provoked him. He hadn't planned to scare anyone. In fact, he hadn't planned anything. Had just been drawn to be there with her in a place where she obviously did not belong.

Why did he even care?

He glanced at the little sister through the rearview mirror. The kid's eyes were smudged with black, her harsh makeup ruined from her tears. He detected the child in her in the still chubby cheeks.

His lips thinned. How did a young girl like that—with all that money could buy—end up being sold for a weekend to a sleazy music producer?

His gaze shifted to Nyssa. Her face was her usual chilly mask, her spine straight. She had done what she had set out to do. Recover her sister. Even if it meant she had given up on buying his club. He couldn't help himself the hint of a smile.

She got the job done. No doubts about that. She had her sister now.

"Where do you want me to drop you?" he asked.

"My place." Nyssa shot another pained glanced at her sister. "Downtown. "

"Oh, I know where you live."

"Right. Saw it in the papers." She cocked an eyebrow at him through the mirror and her genuine smile carried all the way to her gaze. "Thank you for this." Her words were short but spoken with true gratefulness.

Just as he was about to ask her about the blow she'd received from LaChance, Cat spoke.

"I'm not going to your place." The kid's voice was strident, her arms crossed solidly at her chest.

"Well, I'm certainly not taking you home." Nyssa faced off with her sister. "Ever since Nanny Brown left, you've been a mess. I should have done this sooner. No one is looking after you."

"Mom's back from Dubai." The kid slumped back in the leather seat, her chest caved in.

"Your mom can't seem to take care of you," Nyssa's virulence was palpable. "And she's going on a cruise to the Maldives next month."

"She doesn't hit me, you know. Not like—"

"Still not great," Nyssa interrupted sourly.

Mag frowned, listening in to the sisters. They bickered as if they were alone in their own bubble, just the two of them against the world. Despite their current spat, he sensed the deep sisterly bond between them.

"She may never have been physical with you, but the verbal abuse is real." Nyssa had become sympathetic. "I've heard how she talks to you."

"Physical?" Mag's curiosity prickled at the word.

"Mom used to hit Nyssa." Cat railed, wincing as she caught his gaze in the mirror.

"Hit you?" Stunned, Mag peered over his shoulder at Nyssa. "Your stepmother hit you."

"She's a real bitch." Nyssa held herself rigidly contained on the back seat, avoiding his gaze in the mirror.

"But that's not right."

"It's none of your business, really." Her tone was frigid as she unconsciously touched the top of her lip and her gaze darted out the window.

"That scar." His grip clamped tight on the wheel.

"It's not important." Her steady voice now had a piercing to it.

"Your stepmother hit you." Mag repeated, his teeth grinding with fury. "Cat, it's true?"

"I was just a toddler." Cat wrinkled her nose in a small grimace. "I don't remember much but Mom sure doesn't like to be crossed. She yells a lot."

He repressed a growl at the fate of the Vlahos sisters. The two girls sat turned away from each other sulking. Aside from their very different styling, they were so similar. Each sported a brave and defiant look that said they were ready to take on the world. And despite being angry with each other, their attachment was unmistakable. Forged under duress of an abusive caregiver. Who, from the likes of what he heard, didn't care at all.

He experienced a great deal of animosity for the unknown woman.

"I didn't stay long after she gave birth to Cat," Nyssa explained in her usual reasonable voice. "I was sent to Switzerland when she was about three. It fitted with her ideas of high society to have a stepdaughter at a fancy European school."

"You didn't answer my question," Mag nudged again. "Did your stepmother beat you?"

"She slapped me around a few of times." Nyssa took in a sharp breath and shot him a flat smile, downplaying the events. "Stopped when I came back from boarding school. I wouldn't let her."

"She gave you that scar?"

"Yes." The word was spoken so coolly it chilled his spine.

His throat tightened with empathy. Dammit, to be reminded of the abuse every time she looked in the mirror.

"I don't care what you want right now, Cat." Nyssa

dropped the subject, her confident tone chiding her sister. "You'll be living with me from now on."

"No way. Your place is no better than Doukas," the kid protested. "You don't get it. I want to go back to Oli'Vrai."

"Oli'Vrai?" Mag raised a brow with a small curl of his lip.

"It's his true name," Cat stated with extreme conviction. "His rapper name. *Vrai*, as in real. He's speaking his truth. He's the only one who loves me."

"By selling you out?" Nyssa interjected sharply.

"He's not selling me out. He just needs connections, okay?" Her voice trailed on the last syllable with annoyance. "To break out. That guy was giving him a deal."

"Child prostitution, that's what I saw," Nyssa huffed.

"No." Cat recoiled, offended at the idea." He just wants me to stay with his friend for a couple of days."

"His friend?" The kid had no idea what risks she was taking.

"Yes. Mr. Martin is a big producer. It's just a party."

"Look at you, Cricket." Nyssa took a gentler approach. "Look at how you're dressed. What do you think you'd be doing at that party?"

"Be a hostess, you know. Dance, talk to people. Make them happy. Serve them drinks."

"Are you high?"

"No—"

"You know what making them happy means, kiddo, right?" Mag interjected, disgusted that those adult males were taking advantage of children like Cat.

"Oli'Vrai wouldn't do that to me." She petulantly lifted her chin. "He loves me."

"God, you're so dumb sometimes, Cat." Nyssa snorted. "And his name is Oliver."

"You know nothing, Nyssa." Catalina's tears shone under a passing streetlight illuminating the cabin. "He has the courage to be his true self. Not like all the other fake people out there."

Mag looked at the kid, a little girl, really, aside from the makeup and all that. Nyssa was right. It wouldn't have taken long for the child to be drugged and used. He was now mad as hell. He wanted to go back and beat this Oli'Whatever to a pulp.

But that wouldn't help.

Maybe he'd text Vince instead. The Morenos were crooks but would not get involved in sex trafficking. Vince would happily see to it that the punk no longer targeted underage girls. Mag smiled, remembering how Vince and his team had helped him remove the dealers hanging in the back alley of his club the previous year. He didn't care what his patrons did, but he wouldn't have drug deals outside in his street. Not with the small merchant's families and their children living there.

He always sent his bouncer Evan after closing time to check that his patrons hadn't left anything for the kids to find. Condoms, drugs, needles. He wanted none of that. And the streets were always clean when the little ones came to play in the morning. One call to Vince and his crew was all that had been needed. They'd seen the gang packing.

"I'll run away again," Cat blurted out.

Nyssa sighed. "Cat..."

"I'm serious. You can't cage me in your glass tower. Plus you're so busy, you won't even notice me."

Mag frowned, listening to them. He took in the dark night. "It's late. Maybe you two could spend the rest of the night at my place until you figure this out."

His own words stunned him. Where the hell did that come from?

"Uh?" Nyssa shot him a puzzling look through the mirror.

"Yes." He nodded, now convinced it would solve their imminent problem.

Something in him was prompting his desire to jump in and help. He was no hero. But the sisters' lives were no picnic, despite their gilded environment. And he hated to risk Cat going back to that bastard. A bitter taste rose in his mouth at remembering the two men in the seedy diner who had looked at the child as if she was just chattel.

"At your club?" Nyssa wasn't convinced. "That's no place for a kid."

"I'm not a kid," Cat protested.

"Well, you're much younger than my usual patrons." He smiled back at her.

"Exactly," Nyssa chimed bristly. "No place for Catalina."

"There's a priest I know." *Yeah*, he thought to himself. Calling on Father Grégoire was a good idea. "He works with teens. She could maybe have a chat with him."

"She needs a therapist, not a priest," Nyssa grumbled.

"You have a night club?" Cat was suddenly interested. Her eyes in the mirror brightened.

"I do. Yes. And you are both welcome to stay in my apartments above.

"She'll be fine at Vlahos Tower."

"No," Cat griped. "You'll just abandon me tomorrow morning."

"Tomorrow morning, I'll take you to school." Nyssa's tone was unwavering. "Principal Baker has been asking about you."

Cat's mouth was a thin line, her brows knitted together. Then she gave a small shrug. "I'll just run away again."

"Look, I don't know much about kids and it's not really my place, but maybe a neutral territory for now?" Mag said. "It's one in the morning."

Nyssa seemed to mull over his proposition. As she took in her sister, a deep shadow darkened her expression. And for the first time since he'd known her, she seemed like she did not know what to do.

He'd been annoyed at her persistence to buy his club, but her self-confidence was what had always made his blood hot for her. Now, she looked lost. She needed help.

And he desperately wanted to be the one to relieve her of her troubles.

Their gaze connected through the rearview mirror and something passed between them. A connection he didn't understand, born of the confrontation in the diner, of their concerns for the child in sleazy clothing in his back seat. A tie that made him madly hope that she would take his imperfect offer of sanctuary for the night.

She broke their eye contact to look uneasily at her hands and eventually said, "Fine. We'll stay at the *Serpent*."

Cat let out a cheerful whoop and a little string of happiness rose inside him.

He had no idea why, but it was right there, next to his heart.

He said nothing else for fear she'd change her mind. He peered at the tall modern towers around them in Downtown Montreal. Then with glee, he took a swift turn and set his car towards the old part of town.

To his place.

# CHAPTER 8

"Wow, I love this." Cat twirled before finding a seat on a rose-tinted Art Deco settee with plush velvet curves. "It's like being in a movie from the thirties with all those gangsters and lounge singers."

"Well, it's... fine." Nyssa eyed the suite cautiously, taking in the sectioned mirrors edged with gold, the heavy dark wood furniture and geometric-styled Tiffany lamps dotting the space. It was indeed as if she'd stepped back in time by a hundred years and expected to find bootlegged liquor in the ornate credenza. "You take the bedroom. I'll take the couch."

"What are you talking about? These antiques are priceless," Cat said before disappearing into the next room.

"That, they are," Nyssa agreed. She felt drained, somehow.

She rubbed the tender area just under her ribcage where LaChance had punched her. She lifted her shirt and took in the large bruise, which was getting darker by the minute.

*Dammit*, she should have reacted. She had a few years

of martial arts training, graduating from basic self-defense to actual weekly karate lessons when she was in college. She was a few months from earning her black belt.

She could have taken him. Retaliate. But no, she'd frozen.

The hit had brought an onslaught of memories and her body had just seized. Forgetting all she had learned. As if she was still fourteen years old. On the receiving end of that bejeweled cruel hand.

Lucinda knew exactly how to slap so that no one knew.

Except for that one time when the blow had been hard enough to send Nyssa flying into the corner of her desk and lose consciousness for a few minutes.

The woman had been furious when Nyssa had accused her of being a gold digger after the woman had boasted of the new extravagant diamond bracelet, she'd convinced Nyssa's father to buy.

Her upper lip had required stitches. The incident had been explained as a simple misstep. Nyssa never dared criticize the woman again after that. And Lucinda had switched to words instead of blows. Then exiled her step-daughter to Europe for good.

Nyssa hadn't protested. She would have given anything to make the cruel confrontations stop. And the educators at the *Institut Bossart* were strict but fair.

She had missed her baby sister terribly but at fifteen years old, she felt powerless. Terrorized by the woman who was supposed to take care of her.

And there was not much she could say about it to her dad, weakened by his fragile health. The stroke had made Nyssa fear she would lose him as well. Lucinda made sure to warn Nyssa constantly that her dad would surely get another one if Nyssa mentioned their little "scuffles".

So, she'd kept quiet.

The private school staff was not family, but they'd made her feel safe.

And the years of therapy in adulthood had helped her cope.

"Wow, you should see the bathroom, so cute. So many different shampoos in there. And scented candles." Cat walked in as Nyssa swiftly dropped her shirt over the bruise. No need for her sister to witness the results from LaChance's violence.

"You can use the shower first." Nyssa forced a smile. Cat's face was a mess, her little crop top askew. "Mag said there should be some nightwear in here."

"Right,." Cat shrugged and disappeared again.

Nyssa slumped into a wingback chair, removed her tall leather winter boots and glared at the small glitzy purse Cat had left on the coffee table. How had her kid sister gotten so misled?

The jittery feeling in her belly wouldn't leave as anger at the wannabe rapper rose inside her again. Maybe she *should* show Cat her bruise. Show her how nasty he truly was.

She breathed out and strangely the *thump-thumping* of the club below had a calming effect on her hammering pulse. She stared at the luxurious carpet under her feet. Everything in the room was designed for pleasure but still warm and cozy. And she—who preferred clean and unaltered lines—was suddenly comforted by the rich colors and sensual fabrics. A faint scent of sandalwood permeated the atmosphere and further lent her comfort.

Who would have thought that Magnovald St-Amand would have been the one there for her in her time of need?

Oh sure, she lusted plenty after him when he shot her

his bemused smile and that sinful look. The one that made her cheeks grow feverish each time it caught her in its pull. But she hadn't thought he would come to her defense so swiftly, jumping at LaChance's throat as soon as the jerk had touched her.

And now, offering his place like this. For them?

Because of the whim of a teenager?

Nyssa was still shocked at the suggestion. Nyssa and Cat were nothing to him. Heck, she was the one who had wanted to relieve him of his club. Going against him to have it condemned.

She had been wrong in assuming Mag's home was a depraved den. The place, at least this suite, was charming. A haven where one could hide from the world. Away from nefarious predators, cutthroat businessmen, and evil step-mothers.

Her gaze landed upon the lovely antique table in the corner with its ivory inlay depicting patterns of roses and exotic birds. A deep desire to sit there with her laptop and phone and conduct her business in peace overcame her.

Away from it all.

And with that bedroom right there on the other side of the suite.

Heat rose inside her as she pictured the man she *could* meet between those bed sheets. Those powerful thighs between hers, those wide shoulders above her, those sensual lips…

*Oh god*. She pressed a hand to her chest and swallowed. *Don't go there, Nyss*.

What was she thinking? She could not mistake a phys-ical infatuation and gesture of kindness for the real thing. No.

He was not the one for her.

She had always wanted to take her business abroad. Meet someone equally wealthy and driven, a minor royalty perhaps, needing a little extra cash to restore a stately country home. Someone at ease with charity auctions and state dinners.

Not a local club owner.

No, that was *not* in the plan.

She stood and padded to the bedroom to find some pajamas for herself and Cat. She purposefully ignored the four-poster antique bed with its thick dark green coverlet to push away her lustful thoughts as deep as possible.

She opened the wardrobe and rummaged the drawers to stumble upon a silk bra and panty set—expensive, with the price tags still on.

She shook her head, pondering if the fine lingerie belonged to a girlfriend.

A tug of disappointment hit her. Girlfriend? She suddenly wondered if he had one. He was awfully fond of the waitress named Sandrine. The woman—who Nyssa usually saw wearing a short leather skirt and fitted white top exposing her pierced bellybutton— was extremely sensual and attractive. She had an ease around Mag that wasn't present in the other staff.

So, what. Mag might have a girlfriend. What was it to her?

She closed her eyes as her stomach hardened. No, she wasn't jealous. That would be crazy.

Her jaw stiff, she marched to another chest of drawers. Forget Mag, she had to figure out how to handle her sister.

Digging through the bottom drawer, she found a pile of club t-shirts in various sizes tucked under a spare blanket. They would have to do to sleep in tonight.

*And what about tomorrow?* That little planning voice

crept in. The last thing she wanted was to think about tomorrow.

But she had to. She had left a message for her dad that Cat was with her safe and sound. But what next? She needed to convince Cat to come live with her.

She could not leave her little sister here at the club, even if Mag offered. Who would watch her during the day? And Cat needed to be at school.

*Right*, a vague plan formed in her mind, *maybe that would work*. Get Cat to school, where the staff would be watching her like a hawk, and then pick her up right there at the end of the day.

Nyssa was mulling over the schedule when Cat stepped out in an oversize fuzzy white bath towel. Without her makeup, she looked like a small child, her wet hair curling naturally like a halo around her.

Nyssa smiled at her kid sister. She was just a misguided child. Once back with her school friends, she would forget all about how two sleezeballs had tried to take advantage of her innocence.

"Your turn," Cat said, chirpily. "Try the ocean salt wash. Smells really good."

"Here." Nyssa handed her sibling one of the oversized tees. "To sleep in."

"Mag said I could stay here as long as I want." Cat held the shirt out to admire it. "I love this place. He's so cool, don't you think?"

"If you like degenerates." Nyssa blurted out the stereotype without thinking, maybe to dismiss her attraction for the rugged club owner.

"You're such a snob, Nyssie. Just like Dad and Lucinda. Why do you think I left?"

Anger at Cat's words came rushing in out of nowhere.

She bit her lips tight as pressure built in the back of her throat. Her fist tightened as she let out a controlled breath and narrowed her eyes at her sister.

"I am nothing like Lucinda," she seethed.

Cat shrugged and flopped on the bed. "Mag is nice. He talks to me like I'm a real person, you know. Not like some burden to pass back and forth."

Nyssa's sudden irritation receded. "You're not a burden, Cat."

"Then why didn't you come see me more often."

"You know why." She wished Cat could understand that building a successful career carried a heavy load of responsibilities. And she wouldn't be caught dead under Lucinda's roof.

"Well, Mom is not there all the time. And you could pick me up more often."

"I have to work, Cricket," she countered again. "I'm there every Saturday."

"One day a week. Like a duty. And you never really listen to me, you know."

Nyssa sat next to her on the bed, wondering if Cat was right. She'd been so focused on her own career; she hadn't been listening deeply enough to Cat's teen problems. "You should have told me about LaChance."

"Why? You never care."

Nyssa paused, assaulted with guilt before saying, "I love you—you're my little sister. You should have told me these things."

"Maybe. But all you ever care about is my schoolwork. Did I pass this class, am I set to graduate?"

"I *am* very focused on achievements. On the ability for you to be independent." A sad smile etched upon Nyssa's lips. "In the end, that's all you got."

"There's more to life than work, Sis."

"Maybe." Nyssa slid her hand on the silky fabric of the bed. Her sister wasn't wrong. Work had always been her way to escape reality.

"You don't even have a boyfriend."

"Boys are not a career plan, Cricket."

"But they're nice to have." Her tone turned wistful.

"Maybe. But not your rapper."

"He loves me." Cat's cheeks flushed with embarrassment.

"Are you sure?" Nyssa tried to keep her tone steady.

"Yes, I am." Cat's lips were thin with resolve. But doubts started to show behind the pinched expression.

"Let's talk about it tomorrow, okay?" Nyssa stood, her body aching, her neck stiff. She hadn't really slept since Cat left. "I'm exhausted. We need sleep, Sweetie. It's late."

"Yeah. Okay." Cat nodded and her features eased.

Nyssa was stepping towards the bathroom for a much-needed bath when her sister called her back.

"Nyssie?"

She turned towards her wearily. "Yeah?"

"You shouldn't discount Mag so quickly. I think he really likes you."

# CHAPTER 9

"You ou called me all the way over here for high school math?" Justin had stopped flipping through a thick textbook to raise a brow at Mag with disbelief.

Cat was scribbling furiously next to him in a spiral notebook.

The three of them were sitting at Mag's usual booth in the *Serpent* at midday. Closed, chairs were overturned on low tables and the bar counter gleamed with polish. The place was dead quiet aside from Sandrine stocking the fridge.

"Cat has missed a lot of school." Mag shrugged. "Aren't you a teacher?"

"Sort of." Justin looked uneasily at the teenaged girl sitting next to him. She chewed on her pencil as she stared at her notebook with a deep frown.

Still wearing her leather skirt and heels but covered by a giant hoodie with the *Serpent Maudit* logo, she looked totally different than she had the previous night, her face fresh and with two small buns at each side of the top of her head.

"Principal Baker said I have to do all these worksheets before going back to class." She turned to Justin eagerly. "Do you know anything about systems of equations, Professor St-Amand?"

Justin glanced over her paper and offered her a kind and patient smile.

"Nyssa had to swing by work for a couple of hours. I said I'd help." Mag shrugged helplessly at his brother.

When he'd suggested that the Vlahos sisters stay the night with him, he hadn't expected Nyssa to jump into her efficient self so early in the day. She'd called her driver first thing and by mid-morning she had Cat's schooling all under control. By the time the teen woke just after noon, a pile of work was waiting for her.

After much protest, Nyssa had agreed they could stay at Mag's place longer if the kid got right to her work. Her personal assistant hadn't stopped texting her through it all and, torn, she had finally left for her office after Mag assured her that Cat would be perfectly safe with him for a few hours.

Honored by the trust she'd put in him, he now found himself having to supervise math homework on the main floor of his club.

"In here?" Justin took his gaze off Cat's scribbles to stare around the area, his gaze settling on Sandrine in her skintight leather pants and satin push-up top.

"Where else?"

"At the sister's house, maybe?"

"Cat prefers to stay here."

"Hey, you two. Don't talk like I'm not here," Cat

complained. Immediately, her shoulders drooped in defeat. "I'm sorry, it's just…this math is so hard."

"Sorry kiddo," Mag replied. "My brother can be a bit rude sometimes. Goes with the job."

The teen tilted her head to the side as she considered Mag's brother with narrow eyes. "Are you really a professor at the university?"

"Yep. Astronomy." With a benevolent smile, Justin reached for her pencil and examined the series of equations scrawled over the page.

"I tried, Justin, really. But this is gibberish to me."

"Right, school has never been your thing."

"Hells no." The small one-room school crowded with children of all ages and led by the harried schoolmistress was no fun. He'd learned all he needed from Papa Antoine.

"Shouldn't be swearing in front of a kid, Magnovald." Justin shook his head absentmindedly, as he carefully wrote in Cat's notebook in a neat print.

"It's okay, Professor. I'm not eight. My boyfriend swears all the time."

"Boyfriend?" Justin paused to frown at her.

Mag widened his eyes in a silent warning behind Cat's back. The whole boyfriend thing was not his territory. It was Nyssa's. Talking about that subject with a girl in the midst of puberty was certain to be riddled with landmines.

Yet, seeing this child with her skimpy clothes in the dirty diner's booth, with that scrawny bastard squeezing her thigh as if he owned her, had brought a rush of rage inside him.

And he was glad he had helped Nyssa getting her sibling back.

Once he'd seen the jerk shove Nyssa, Mag had lost it.

He would have left the rapper for dead if not for the two sisters there, no matter the consequences.

But beating LaChance to a pulp might prompt Cat to run right back to him.

As he watched his brother pour over the teen's homework with her, he wondered how he'd ended up in this situation. One day minding his own business and now with two human sisters under his roof, a kid doing homework in the middle of his club and himself worried that she would not finish in time. Because he wanted to impress the sister and prove he could be trusted to watch after Cat.

Her school supplies looked completely out of place next to the vintage brass dome-shaped lamp at the center of the table. Mag pondered how to make this all fit. He grunted inwardly. Himself with mortals, where would it go?

Justin seemed to take it in stride, the calm professor helping a pupil, even if Cat was somewhat younger than his own university students.

Mag tamped down unwanted envy of his studious brother. What the hell was he trying to do, helping a child with school.

A kid, dammit. Under his very roof.

He would never have a kid of his own—he was unable to procreate.

A slight lump lodged in his throat. He knew this because he had tried. Many, many times without success.

The first was just after his mother had left them. He was a young adult of twenty, then, but her departure, merely hours after their adoptive father had died, had been like a punch in the gut.

Antoine St-Amand was the only father he ever knew

and seeing him like that, gasping his last breath when Mag himself was immortal, had been too hard to bear. His death had devastated him. He could never understand why his mother, the freakin' Ice Witch, had not attempted to turn their father immortal and save him from his human fate.

As he grieved for the father he was so close to and having been abandoned by his mother, he deeply felt his loneliness and his need for a legacy.

His own biological father had managed to impregnate his mother in the sixteenth century and bring forth Mag and his five brothers, so why not him? Mag could have immortal children, too. None of the countless women he had bedded over the centuries had ever managed to become pregnant.

Lost in his longing for a moment, he aimlessly fiddled with Cat's school papers, letting out a slow sigh.

As his friends died and his brothers pursued their own obsessions, Mag kept on trying to have a child. He'd turned to supernatural partners, hoping their non-human side would help. There had been Hannah, the wolf-shifter from the pack in Domaine-Lassalle and Rachel, the banshee in Rhode Island. And there was Kari, the shaman from the Ioshta clan. and Megan, a selkie up north in the Maritimes. None of them had conceived.

Even Csilla Mihaly, the powerful Hungarian witch who'd agree to carry his child in exchange for his prized collection of magical artifacts, had not been able to become pregnant, no matter how many spells she tried.

Mag had attempted one last time with Sylvie, the woodland nymph, in the 80s—reproductive medicine so advanced by then. But nothing had worked. So he'd put his desire for an offspring deep down in the depths of his soul and moved on to enjoy the nightlife.

But children still remained his weak spot. Their innocence so far removed from his own life, they brought back memories of happier times, when his dad would bring him hunting for deer in the snowy woods or teach him the tools of his trade at the town's forge.

Mag was now happy to let children play hockey and build snowmen in his corner of the back alley during winter. The kids would spend hours in the sweltering summer drawing cute pictures all over the pavement with chalk.

But if Mag ever wanted to be a father, he was failing at it now. He couldn't even do math. His desire of fathering a child had always been about legacy. The actual responsibilities of parenthood had never entered his mind.

He had wanted some part of him walking and talking in this world. Maybe something like Papa and himself had, some gruff bond based on what needed to be done that day to keep the family going, working hard to learn the trade of a blacksmith, take a week away from home to hunt furred mammals for pelts. A few drinks at the local establishment at night.

Yes, that was what he had been looking for. Someone who'd be just like him, take over the club. Sure he was invincible. Immortal actually. But the events of last fall when his brother Val had been taken down with drugs had disturbed something in him. He could be killed. The thought had brought back his deepest desire for posterity. Now he wanted more than ever to leave someone behind.

He fingered the bracelet at his wrist with a shiver, quickly repressed. He'd been given the artifact from that old crone Madame Ioshta who had a heap of magical paraphernalia in that shop of hers a few blocks away from the *Serpent*. He was not invulnerable, his mother had been right earlier. He had not used his own magic in centuries. He was weak.

And now Nyssa and Cat were unwittingly showing him that maybe he actually shouldn't *be* a father. Aside for the fact that, so far, he couldn't even produce a child, he knew nothing of raising one. Homework, unsuitable boyfriends, meeting teachers? And what about illnesses and doctor's appointments? It was obvious that he hadn't given this any real thought beyond bringing to life an extension of himself.

And yet as he recalled the three of them in the car last night, something had stirred within him. He'd instantly felt a kinship with the kid. Felt relieved that she was safe. Deeply satisfied that he had helped rescue her from a terrible fate.

The tiff between the two sisters had brought an extra dimension to his life. Despite their quarrel, their bond was absolutely timeless. Unyielding.

What on earth was going on here? When had he ever felt something more than amused lust for a human? But there it was, now wanting to do something nice for Nyssa, making sure Cat was okay, protect them both.

They had such a crummy childhood. Who could ever hit a child? Fury rose again inside him. For her sake, he hoped he'd never cross paths with Nyssa's stepmother. To be sent away like that after losing her mother, hells that was the horrid stuff of fairytales.

His own mother wasn't perfect, but she wasn't truly evil. And Mag had his brothers. They were tight.

He couldn't help but feel impressed at how efficiently Nyssa was dealing with the situation. The woman was tireless. Getting her sister back to normal as quickly as possible. Well, as much as doing math homework in an empty nightclub with a pair of vampires could be called normal.

*Right.* He raked a hand through his hair, conflicted. He suddenly wanted to be part of their lives. But how would he explain his true nature to them? The eternal life, the extra strength. The magic and the vampirism and, dammit, the yearly ritual blood feeding!

Revealing it all was foolish thinking.

"Here, you just have to solve for 'y' first." Justin pointed to the equation, his tone benevolent.

"It turns out this is super easy, Mag." Cat turned a pleased expression towards him. "Why couldn't you do this?"

"I told you, kiddo." His muscles relaxed at seeing the girl happy. "Math is not my thing."

"What *is* your thing, then," she inquired with glee.

"Yes, Mag. What *is* your thing?"

The clear female voice echoing Cat's words produced a startling tide of lust in him.

*Nyssa.*

He hadn't noticed her come in. He was losing his edge, distracted by this weird new world he had brought into his place.

He took her all in. The tips of her blonde hair brushed the turned-up collar of her sleek wool coat, the opalescent of her small drop pearl earrings emphasizing the complexion of her clear and fresh skin. Her mouth, perfectly drawn in a deep red, was curled into a half smile.

He wanted to draw his finger gently over the flaw at her upper lip, as if he could make the memory of her abuse disappear.

"Nyssa, meet my brother Justin."

"Justin. Nice to meet family." She extended a strong handshake. Her steady eye contact with Justin made Mag wince a little. Was he jealous of his more respectable brother? She looked down at the table with an amused look. "Are you helping my sister with school work?"

"Apparently this was very important to Mag." He rolled his eyes at his brother then shot her an easy grin.

"Was it, now?" Her playful gaze shifted. The affectionate look she gave Mag rattled him to the core. Somehow, he felt it deep. He had playfully danced around with the ice queen, but this...this was entirely different. The sudden connection between them elicited a hope for something more.

"He's a professor, Nyssie. He's so good at this." Cat broke their bond and Nyssa reluctantly turned her sight back to her sister and Justin.

"You came down here just to help her?" Nyssa's eyes slightly widened in surprise.

"Mag insisted." Justin shrugged with a half-smile.

"Wow, I don't know what to say." She nodded gratefully.

Mag was the one being speechless now. With him and his brother there helping Cat and with Nyssa coming back from work, bringing in the fresh outside air, it felt oddly domestic.

That transient moment was so close to the one thing he had truly wanted when he longed for a child. To be a family man.

"Anyone would have done the same." Justin shook his head pleasantly. "Don't worry about it."

"Well, we should be out of your hair now." She turned to Cat. "It's time to go home now, Cricket."

"You mean your penthouse." Her mood turned sour.

"Our home," Nyssa insisted. Frostier now, her lips thinned as she stared intently at the teen to assert her authority.

"Why can't I stay here?"

"Here? At a nightclub?" Nyssa wrinkled her nose ever so lightly and Mag's heart sunk. Of course this was no place for a child.

Still he interrupted. "You can both stay here as long as you want."

Justin raised his brow but Mag shrugged. He didn't care for his brother's disapproval. It was none of his family's business. He could invite whomever he wanted.

"I'm sorry." Nyssa sighed, loosening up before taking a seat at their table. "I don't mean to dismiss your club, but this is really no place for a child. She has to settle in my home eventually."

She was right, of course. Why did Mag ever think he could have a family of his own? He had chosen a different lifestyle and had endeavored to thrive in it. Maybe deep down to ensure he'd never acquire anything like a family. His way of closing the door to his stupid dream for good.

He looked at the kid. "Your sister's got a point, Cat. You're welcome here but it's a noisy place, not for someone who has school in the morning, and all that."

The girl looked crestfallen and his heart broke. How many times could a child be rejected before they cracked?

"Sorry, kiddo," he said. "You can come see me, though. Anytime." He peered at Nyssa to catch her reaction. "Well, before the club opens."

Cat's happy demeanor disappeared. "I need to go home first."

"What do you mean?" Nyssa frowned.

"Doukas. I need my stuff."

"I can send my assistant, surely Lucinda can get it packed up for you. I'm sure Daddy will understand."

The kid's lips pursed. "I need Mr. Baba. She won't know where to find it. It's somewhere safe."

"Your teddy bear?"

"Nanny Brown gave it to me before Mom sent her away. As a way to keep me strong. I didn't bring it with me to Oli'Vrai's, though." She bunched her features and bit her bottom lip. "I was afraid he'd think I'm too childish."

"I see." Nyssa said.

Mag watched the interaction between the sisters. The teary-eyed kid carried an undefeated stance in the way she pushed her chin forward while Nyssa studied her silently as if trying to make her comply. He could feel the pain they both experienced impregnate the air.

A silence had fallen over them all, broken only by the sound of Justin's pen scrawling lines of mathematical equations on Cat's sheet. His brother always had the uncanny quality of hiding from unpleasantness behind academic work.

"Would you like me to come with you?" Mag made up his mind. Whatever pain was lingering in the two sisters' lives, he vowed to do anything he could to alleviate it.

"Would you?" Cat's tone shifted and she turned a bright face to him. Whatever this child was going through, she had decided that Mag was somehow her hero.

He shot her a good-natured smile. "Of course, I would love to see your house."

"Doukas," Nyssa spat. Her tone was still bitter but her expression was softer as she took in her sister.

"You don't like the place."

"I used to." Her eyes turned melancholic. "It's changed a lot since my days."

"Mom keeps redecorating." Cat said absentmindedly dragging her math sheet towards her on the table.

"Yes, she does." Nyssa seemed to wilt, her expression wistful. It had to be painful to see her old home be taken over by someone else.

He wondered if this was not why she worked tirelessly to reconstruct buildings all over town. Taking one neighborhood after another to make into her vision. A way to make up for her own lost home.

"Well, Cricket, we better go, then." She straightened her posture decisively, her hand stiff on the crisp leather tote at her shoulder. "Get all your work together."

Cat gathered her schoolwork in a neat pile before glancing back at him with a look full of hope. "Mag? You're coming with us, right?"

Justin reclined back on the bench and silently considered him, an amused look plastered on his face. His gaze went from Cat to Nyssa, then back to Mag.

Mag gave his brother the slightest helpless shrug and turned to Nyssa.

With his look heavy on the elegant blonde, he answered Cat. "Yep, kiddo. I'm all yours."

# CHAPTER 10

"*O*h shit." Nyssa cringed at the colossal stone façade of Doukas House as she stepped out of Mag's car.

"Nyssa?" Mag stood from helping Cat out of the back seat and caught her gaze over the Ferrari's roof with a concerned expression.

"They're having a cocktail party." She clutched her hands together over the handle of her tote, a bout of dizziness making her blink.

The bright porch lights illuminated the slew of luxury cars parked along the curved driveway and dotting the snowbank that had started to thaw in March's uncertain weather. Silhouettes could be seen through the wide glass windows of the conservatory. Nothing but Lucinda's fake friends, Nyssa thought, as she recognized a few cars.

"So, what's the problem?" Cat asked her sister as she circled the car and grabbed her by the arm, her breath leaving condensation particles in the cold air. "I want to see Dad. He always looks so nice at parties."

"Right." Nyssa nodded, her lips pressed together as she held her breath.

"I'll wait here." Mag's deep voice sounded strangely reassuring.

Nyssa turned to watch him as he leaned back on the hood, his wide form clad in his usual motorcycle jacket, his long, powerful legs in the black jeans stretched in front of him. His expression was so at ease, it was as if nothing would ever bother him.

"Oh no, Mag," Cat protested. "You need to see my house." She grabbed his arm.

He shot Nyssa a sorry look and together, with her sister in the center, they climbed the stately steps up to the front porch of the mansion.

The weather was still below freezing, making their footing treacherous. Small piles of snow still remained in the corner of the wraparound porch. Nyssa recalled how her mom would always come and sweep the snow off it every morning, a welcome to their home, she'd say. Keep it safer for the postman.

Nyssa couldn't imagine Lucinda risking her pricey boots by shoveling her own porch.

*Okay, let's do this.* She mentally prepared herself for a potential battle. She would usually stay in the car on Saturdays. Waiting for Cat to come out for their weekly time together.

But this time, Nyssa was entering the actual house. On Lucinda's territory.

Where the woman was surrounded by *her* friends.

The door opened as soon as they reached the top.

"Mademoiselle Catalina." The old butler was delighted to see the teen, a crinkle at the corner of his eyes. "I'm so happy you're back. Mademoiselle Nyssa." His lined features softened further, genuine pleasure in his expression. "It's been so long."

"Well, yes, Denis." They ambled into the foyer and she took off her gloves before shaking his hand in a warm handshake. "I've been busy. How are you carrying on?"

"Oh, holding the fort, you know." He gave the smallest shrug under his black suit jacket. "Your father…"

"I know." An understanding passed between them.

Denis had been with her father ever since their days in the Air Force, even before Nyssa's mom. The only staff member Lucinda had not been able to fire. Dad had slowly let go of most of their original employees and turned a blind eye when it came to Cat's upbringing, but Denis was still untouchable.

"Sir?" Denis turned to the club owner standing silently beside Cat who had Mag's arm in a tight grip.

"Oh, Denis. This is Magnovald St-Amand, a…." Nyssa struggled to define him. A friend seemed too close and yet he was more than an acquaintance. "Business associate," she eventually stated, watching the slow and amused grin curl upon Mag's lips at her uneasiness.

"Oh." Denis' eyebrow rose as he took in the leather jacket and tousled hair.

"Monsieur Denis." Mag extended a firm yet deferent hand. "*Vous êtes de Montréal?*"

"*Non, Monsieur.*" Denis' stern expression thawed at the question about his origins. "*J'viens de Gaspé.*"

"Gaspé, really? Beautiful mountains." Mag nodded with enthusiasm. "Great fishing there also, isn't it?"

"*Un vrai beau pays,*" Denis said, melancholic about his birth region, before turning to Cat and Nyssa. "I used to go fishing every weekend with your dad when we were on leave. Right out at the Lake of Two Mountains."

"You never told me that," Cat marveled.

"Oh, it's so long ago. But your dad and I did for a while, you know. Before his company took off."

"How is Dad tonight?" Her father was never too keen to don an uncomfortable suit to play host to Lucinda's friends.

"Happier I think now that our Catalina has been found."

"We're only here for a few minutes, Denis," she clarified, "to get Cat's things."

"Are you not coming back with us, Mademoiselle Catalina?" he kindly asked.

"I will be living with Nyssa now."

Nyssa's heart lifted to hear that her sister had finally made up her mind and accepted to stay with her.

"Oh well, very sensible," the old man huffed, while a knowing look passed between him and Nyssa.

Denis noticed so much more than he let on. She'd often wondered if he hadn't been the one to suggest she went away to boarding school. Although she doubted he expected her to be shipped out all the way to Europe.

"Yes, it's for the best," Nyssa agreed. Again the quiet understanding passed between them.

She sensed a shift in Mag's posture and caught his serious gaze on her.

The look was dark and heavy. He seemed to inherently catch the fact that while her stepmother wasn't at the entrance to greet them, her influence had started as soon as Denis had opened the door. Nyssa recalled how he'd questioned her about Lucinda hitting her. The hint of anger had been obvious in his tone.

Her own bitterness was mostly gone. Hatred was not helpful. But some of her resentment still ran under the surface, always ready to burst every time she heard the woman's shrill voice. Which is why she'd avoided this place and preferred to see her dad in his old office down by the docks in the Port of Montreal.

She'd dropped by every Friday, bringing coffee and the Greek pastries he liked. She'd fill him in with a weekly report on Vlahos Enterprise, make him feel like he still had a say in things. Truth was that when she'd taken over three years ago, things were going downhill with the business. He'd kept the company going, but his heart had not been in it since his stroke. Building her tower has saved the business and put them back in the black.

She shook off her melancholy to take in the foyer behind the butler. She hadn't been inside in two years and it was all very different now, her mom's Old-World touch obliterated. Everything was stark with gilded trim, from the curved staircase leading upstairs to the bleak modern artwork on the walls. The polished marble floor made her shiver with cold despite the heated air.

She gave Denis a bright and brave smile, then turned to Cat. "Come on, Cricket, let's go to your room."

"Can't wait to see it," Mag added, keeping his tone eager.

"Oh, I have the best fairy figurines collection," she exclaimed. "And you should see my comic books, too. Some are very old."

"Sounds great." Mag nodded with exaggerated interest while shooting Nyssa a lighthearted look as they all stepped into the hall. He obviously had no idea what Cat was talking about.

Nyssa gave him a shrug, both palms up as they

reached the bottom of the curved double stairs leading to the upstairs rooms. Cat was still a child in so many ways.

"Oh! Isn't it our Nyssa!" The high-pitch, earsplitting voice stopped her dead in her tracks. A chill snaked down her spine and she gulped.

She slowly turned toward her worst enemy.

Lucinda advanced in a low-cut gold lamé dress that emphasized the brittleness of her collarbone. "Look Kostas," she called out loudly to the crowded room behind her, "your daughters decided to show up!"

"Mom!" Cat glanced at her and back at Nyssa, her voice shaky as if they'd be caught doing something they shouldn't.

"Run along upstairs, Catty." She waved a hand in the air, her wrist jingling with the multitude of gold charms at her bracelet. "We're having a party right now."

"But Mom…"

"It's a party—you're too young."

"I want to see Dad," she demanded.

"He's talking with the mayor," Lucinda huffed heavily. "You know how he might run for a council seat. Now go on up. I'll get your au pair, what's her name again? I can't keep up."

"I'm just here to pick up my things," Cat declared. "I'm going to Nyssa's place."

"Nonsense. Your sister doesn't want you there." Lucinda narrowed her heavily made-up eyes at her daughter. "And what have you been eating, girlie. You're so pudgy again."

Nyssa's fists balled with anger at seeing her little sister crumble under the insult.

Mag turned very still as if his aura attempted to shadow Cat from harm.

"Go get your things, Cat," Nyssa said to her quietly. "I'll deal with this."

"And who is this beefcake?" Lucinda's gaze settled onto Mag. She sashayed to him, her bony hips tensing the fabric of her glittery dress.

Mag didn't bother giving in to politeness and offer an introduction. Instead, he watched Cat disappear upstairs.

Nyssa edged closer to Mag as if to shield him from her horrible stepmother.

"How's Dad?" she asked Lucinda between her teeth.

"Fine, fine as usual." She rolled her eyes before leaning back on her spiky heels to settle an appraising gaze on Mag. "Really, Nyssa, please introduce me to this gorgeous man."

Mag raised an amused brow at Nyssa and the corner of his lip curled into a dangerous half-smile.

"Mag," Nyssa said with a huff. "Magnovald St-Amand. This is Lucinda."

"Oooh. The owner of the *Serpent Maudit* nightclub. Oh, Mag, I *have* heard of you." Without warning, she grabbed his arm and dragged him towards the conservatory, which echoed with bright laughter above the low-key music from a hired pianist.

Mag cast Nyssa a wide-eyed look over his shoulder and she mouthed "sorry." She had forgotten to warn him that Lucinda liked men, any man. She was forever flirting with the gardener and pool staff, or whatever male contractor she had hired for a remodel.

Wearily, Nyssa followed after them. The small and brittle middle-aged woman with her bleached blonde hair held tight onto the brooding man, his heavy black motorcycle boots hitting the newly installed glossy flooring.

Nyssa would need to figure out how she'd save Mag

from Lucinda's clutches. She had no time to say hi to her father, either. The sooner they were gone, the better.

As she took in the party room, a lump rose in her throat. It had been a true conservatory once, full of tall plants and her mom's prized orchids. Nyssa's mother had spent much time making sure they grew beautiful and healthy, showcasing them every year at the city's flower shows.

Every afternoon after school, Nyssa would join her for tea in the pretty room. The chintz table was packed with different kinds of pastries, her dolls all lined up in the extra chairs. Denis would attend them, asking each little figure what they wanted, remembering the fancy names Nyssa had chosen for them—Lady Esmeralda, Princess Tam, *Mademoiselle* Francine. How on earth did she still remember that?

And now the plants were gone, and the area had been expanded into another stark room with metal sculptures, dark drapes, and odd-looking furniture.

The bar was fully loaded at the corner, serviced by a tall and willowy brunette, while catering staff in white uniforms and silver trays darted between guests. Nyssa recognized a well-known news anchor and her boyfriend talking animatedly with two middle-aged friends of Lucinda, both laden with heavy jewelry. An over-the-hill lounge singer leaned upon the white baby grand piano, as if waiting for his turn to take over for the young man currently at the keys.

And Dad was indeed talking to the mayor. Her father looked tired and uncomfortable in his navy double-breasted suit, far from his usual faded chinos and roomy button-down shirt.

Dad had started from nothing, first as custodian then owner of a small set of apartment buildings in the East Side, before expanding to managing new constructions. Always hands-on, he had never quite fitted into formal affairs like this.

But this was all Lucinda lived for.

Nyssa glanced back at Mag. With his leather jacket and black jeans, he was in complete contrast with the elaborately dressed guests, but he radiated a worldly charm that was hard to miss. It was as if he could turn it on and off, violently taking down a shady jerk one minute and charming an elderly lady the next. His movements were slow and deliberate as he gently shook the hand of old Mrs. Harris from next-door. Did the man ever feel out of place?

Nyssa smiled wistfully. She would have liked him by her side and introduce him to Dad. But Lucinda's laughter suddenly echoed throughout the whole room as the woman possessively took hold of the back of Mag's neck, the gesture filling Nyssa with dread.

She had to get him out of there. This was not fair to him. He'd come for Cat, not to be trapped in Lucinda's web.

She tightened her fists and straightened her spine, cast one more look at Dad who was nodding meekly at something the mayor had said. She'd talk to him tomorrow, at his office. Discuss her plans for Cat. Make sure his health was okay.

For now she had only one thing to do before getting out of here. Make it clear to her bitch stepmother that Cat was coming with her to Vlahos Tower.

Taking in a sharp breath, she settled her hammering

heart in anticipation of an ugly confrontation with the cow. She marched through the small group where her enemy was holding court.

"Lucinda," she called out, her voice as frosty as the icicles dripping from the eaves of the mansion outside.

The woman's animated features dropped and she shot Nyssa an annoyed scowl. "What!"

The sight of her nemesis's hand on Mag's skin made Nyssa gag. Her loathing of Lucinda grew tenfold.

"I'm taking Cat with me tonight." Nyssa took a decisive step towards the woman, her chest now a mere foot away from Lucinda's shoulder. "She won't be coming back."

Lucinda lazily let go of Mag to turn towards Nyssa. The small group had stopped talking and a hushed silence fell over them.

"Why are you always so dramatic, Nyssie?" She snickered before peering sideways at her friends. "This one will be the death of my dear Kosta, I swear."

Hearing Lucinda use the nickname reserved only for Cat pumped her anger up a notch.

But she remained cool, controlled. Even as Mag studied her.

"No drama here, Lucinda." Nyssa pronounced her name slowly, scorn palatable in each of its syllables. "I'm just *telling* you."

Lucinda's mocking expression shifted to wrath. She leaned into Nyssa, ignoring her guests who were now whispering to each other with curiosity. "You are *not* taking my daughter with you."

"She's not really your daughter, is she?" Nyssa scoffed, her tone accusatory. "She was gone for ten days and would still be missing if I hadn't found her."

"She was safe with her boyfriend," Lucinda sneered before letting out a mocking laugh. "You have no say in what I allow her to do."

"Safe? Being sold to the highest bidder, you mean?" A bout of dizziness shook her. Cat could have been servicing lecherous businessmen at this very minute if Nyssa hadn't intervened. Her anger at Lucinda's apathy knew no bounds. "I'm taking her and that's that. I should have done it sooner."

"No." With surprised force, Lucinda grabbed Nyssa's wrist. "She's *my* daughter. I decide what she does. She stays."

"Nothing here is yours, bitch," Nyssa hissed, not willing to start a scene for her father's sake. She dismissed Mag's alarmed look at her retort. She could take care of this on her own. "This house, my dad," Nyssa snarled. "These so-called friends. None of it is yours. You're just a cheap whore."

With her mouth taking a vicious twist, Lucinda dug her talon-like nails deep into Nyssa's wrist.

The pain caught her off guard and Nyssa let out a tiny yelp.

Mag had suddenly materialized right at her side and laid a hand on her back. But Lucinda held her close. The too familiar cloying scent of patchouli and gardenia over-powered Nyssa's nostrils and in a fraction of a second, she was fifteen years old again. Her throat thickened and an unhealthy tingling shook her body, scattering up along her neck and to her cheeks.

Under her breath, Lucinda warned, "Get out of my house." Her nails dug even deeper, her grip a solid vice ready to crush Nyssa's bones.

And then she let go.

The tide of post-trauma disappeared as Nyssa breathed and focused on her senses. Three things, she recalled from her therapist. Focus on three things—the touch of her fingers on her stinging wrist, the fat snowflakes falling slowly outside, and Mag's warmth against her body.

Within a few seconds, she was herself again and facing her foe with disdain.

"Gladly." Her tone scathing, her chin high, she was back in control. She should never have let the witch get under her skin like this. She glanced at her dad, then narrowed her eyes back at her adversary. "Cat and I are leaving."

"The kid stays here." The corner of Lucinda's eye twitched with disdain.

"You're a pathetic excuse of a woman." Nyssa stared down at her, contempt bristling from every parts of her body. "You'll never fill my mother's shoes."

Mag's steady palm at her back and his calm presence enhanced her confidence.

Lucinda held Nyssa's gaze for a moment then dropped it, defeated.

"Come on, Mag, you haven't met all my friends yet." The woman's voice came out whiny, like a spoiled little girl, as she grabbed the club owner by the top of his arm.

The hint of a primeval snarl suddenly came from deep inside him. He shot Nyssa's stepmother a look so deadly that she nipped her hand back from him as if she'd been burned. And suddenly, he was taking all the space around them. A deep shadow cast over the entire ballroom, silencing Lucinda to a stop.

People watched as if they couldn't take their eyes off him.

Lucinda bit her lip as he took one step towards her. She

folded onto herself as if to escape him. He bent his imposing form over her and whispered something into her ear.

A look of pure horror fell over Lucinda and she swallowed rapidly. She looked at Nyssa, hesitantly, like a terrified child.

"You take Cat," she finally choked, her voice trembling. "You're right. She'll be happier with you."

Nyssa blinked in shock at the woman's turn of heart. Mag straightened and his touch returned to the middle of her back as if it were the most natural thing in the world.

Lucinda flicked the tip of her tongue on her lip as she cast a nervous glance at Mag who still held her in his gaze. "I'll tell Kosta, Nyssa. It's for the best."

Mag's lips curled into a slow smile and he nodded in amusement. "Sounds like it's all settled then."

Nyssa, while still stunned, was relieved. How on earth had he done that? Her skank of a stepmother was stubborn as hell.

As Lucinda retreated with a forced laugh to her group of friends, he put his hand on her wrist. His thumb trailed lightly over the bruised skin, attempting to erase the red marks from Lucinda's claws. "Does it hurt?"

"It'll be fine."

"Didn't Cat want me to see her room?" He was obviously eager to get Nyssa out of there.

"That, she did." The extreme tension she'd held in since she'd stepped into the house released like an open pressure valve. "Let's go help her pack."

As they stepped away from the ballroom, she cast one more glance at her vile stepmother. She couldn't help the small thrill that fluttered against her ribcage to see the evil woman standing in the middle of her friends still with a look of pure shock on her face.

Nyssa's chest expanded with gratefulness at Mag's intervention. Her biggest foe had, finally and for the very first time in her life, been completely silenced.

# CHAPTER 11

"So you just compelled the stepmom." Justin leaned on the doorframe of Mag's office, casually polishing his glasses.

"Yep." Mag reclined farther back in his swivel chair, his feet on the desk, feeling smug as he looked at the three vampires across from him.

Justin in his usual tweed jacket embracing wholeheartedly his professor persona, Renaud, his jeans and flannel shirt underscoring how he was much more at ease in the forest of Domaine-Lassalle. And Emmeline, the unstable beauty, sitting next to Ren on the couch, and clad in a fitted dress, thigh-high boots and her favorite long suede coat. The blonde was not quite an Immortal like the St-Amands but she was also not one of the young vampires cursed to die sometime in their late twenties.

Mag hadn't planned to compel anyone last night. But when he'd seen the harpy dig her pointy nails into Nyssa's perfect skin, his blood had boiled over and he had to defend her. Not willing to cause a scene, he had simply compelled the nasty stepmom to agree that Cat was better off with Nyssa. He'd described in great detail what would happen if she didn't comply, making sure she'd remember the consequences once released from his persuasion power. If he recalled, turning entrails inside out might have been mentioned.

"Mag." There was a hint of criticism in Justin's tone as he shook his head, his glasses now back on the bridge of his nose.

"*Sacrament*, brother." Mag crossed his arms at his chest, his mouth pinched. "Nothing wrong with that. I'm a vampire, after all."

"He's right," Ren intervened, lazily stretching his legs. "Why not use his vampire powers?"

"Well, technically you're an Immortal," Justin corrected. "Not quite the same, is it?"

"It's the bloody same, Justin. Super strength, speed, what else?" Mag sneered. "We can change into freakin' bats if we want it bad enough."

"And you like the taste of human blood." Emme's lips curled into a slow leer, a twinkle of appreciation in her pupils.

"Exactly." Mag shot her a broad smile as he uncrossed his arms and linked his fingers at the back of his head. He always liked Emme's no-nonsense approach about their place in the world.

"Only once a year." Justin's forehead remained lined with reproach.

"Maybe for you," Mag's voice was terse. "But not me. Emme? Ren?"

"Well, Emme drinks synth." Justin turned to the blonde with a look heavy with concern. "Tell me you haven't broken your promise to Valerian?"

"No, I haven't." She rolled her eyes. "Last I had human blood was this gorgeous hunk in Seattle. And I remember it so well. A scientist from out of town, having a beer at a pub downtown. Actually, looked a little bit like you, Justin."

"Did you kill him?" Ren's voice was flat, devoid of judgment.

"No! And I haven't turned anyone since Evan," she said mentioning Mag's bodyguard. She had made vampires of the runaway kid and his friends before helping them escape to the Pacific Northwest the year prior. "I do like humans. I don't want them dead."

"Then why did you kill so many in the 1800s?" Justin reminded her, referring to the carnage that had destroyed for good any love Val may have had for her.

"Not killed, turned." She cast him a defiant look, her chin lifted with self-assurance. "I saved them from a life of drudgery."

"And what good did your little mission do to us?" Justin accused. "You created a bunch of bloodthirsty kids who rampaged the city."

"Not anymore," she shrugged. "Val reformed most of them."

"Compound effect, Emmeline. You make one, he makes ten, they each make ten and then you get thousands. It never stops." Justin's usual calm composure was crumbling, his tone wrought with righteousness. "They left our city. They are all over North America."

"Oh, shut up, Justin. You're so pompous sometimes. I'm not dumb."

"Sometimes I wonder," he huffed, annoyed.

"Good thing you're sexy, otherwise no one would ever listen to you," A twinkle of amusement appeared at the corners of her eyes, her expression easing as she bit her bottom lip seductively.

"Sexy?" Justin's assurance was suddenly shaken, his pale skin taking on an unusual flush.

"Yeah, that stern professor's look you got." Her brows rose with appreciation. "The jacket, those glasses. Makes one want to be just a little bit bad, you know."

Justin cleared his throat uncomfortably. "Emme."

"See, that tone, that's sexy." She purred now, her body shifting ever so slightly to reveal more of her curves under Justin's gaze.

Fed-up with Emme's game, Mag frowned back and forth between her and Justin. "Why are you even here, Emme? Getting bored at the sanctuary?"

"It's awfully quiet, yes. Father Grégoire is gone to see Val and Maisie in New England. He missed Sasha," she said, mentioning Val's trusty dog. To think of it, Mag missed the fluffy lovable animal, too.

"He put me in charge, but I was getting bored and had to step out for a bit," she added. "Ariane is looking after things right now. Came to ask you about Momma." She shot him a big smile. Emme truly loved drama.

Mag's chest tightened at the mention of his mother. "Oh you heard."

"Charlotte in town, oh my," she snorted.

"Don't tell me you kept in contact with her, too?" Mag frowned.

"What, why?" She looked at Ren and Justin with confusion.

Ren shrugged while Justin clarified. "Mag's a bit upset Mom kept in contact with us but not him."

"Oh." She sat straighter on the couch, her expression impassive.

"Yeah," Mag croaked.

"She hasn't talked to me, that's for sure." She shrugged. "That woman has hated me since Val set eyes on me. Why is she here?"

"Apparently she heard about Nyssa wanting to buy my club and wanted to help me fight her off."

"Really." She tilted her head to the side.

"Mom's always been a bit fragile." Oddly, Ren was trying to justify their mother's unforgivable actions. "She genuinely wanted to help."

"Fragile? The bitch's the freaking Ice Witch. She's more powerful than Maisie and that's saying a lot." Emme's arms moved with animation as she underscored Mag's mother's power, having been witness to it when Maisie had been turned immortal by the ancient Callan magic running in the witch's veins.

"Ever since Papa died, she's been lost," Justin interjected. His agreement with Ren made Mag feel like an outsider.

"For three hundred bloody years?" Mag's nostrils flared as his anger mounted again.

"True love." Justin sounded wistful.

"And that's why you can't fall in love with a human." Emme's posture shifted, her tone taking an unusual serious strain. "It was Val's love that turned me into this."

An uncomfortable silence fell in the office as a look of pain passed on Justin's features. He cast a long look upon her. "Sorry."

"Not your fault, Justin." Her fun-loving persona utterly vanished.

"You lost your soul," Justin stated, and something deep passed between them.

"And for that I am grateful. Although it was more fun

when I was still rampaging bordellos." She tossed her head back with an easy smile, her flippant self returned. Yet Mag couldn't help but sense her regret.

"Glad you're not doing that anymore." Justin had settled back into the admonishing professor's role. "Can't hide any more bodies."

"What are you, Justin?" she smirked. "The vampire police?"

"Well, Val was the one to keep you in check. And Maisie was there for a brief second. " Justin winced. "I guess the responsibility now falls to me."

"I'm almost freaking four hundred years old, Justin. I'm not a child."

"No, you're not." Ren's voice cut through it all, his pitch deep. "But it does us no good to bring our existence to light. So you better stay under the radar."

She looked at him with defiance before shrugging him off. "Fine."

As they bickered, Mag became detached. It was always the same. Emme wanted to feed on a human and one of his brothers—usually Justin or Val— convinced her it was wrong.

Emmeline Dubois was different than they were. She needed blood to survive like humans needed food and water. The brothers didn't. They could go for months without anything and not wither.

But Mag liked human blood. Female human blood, mostly. He loved how each of them tasted slightly different on his tongue. Enjoyed how they swoon when his teeth pierced their skin and his saliva mixed in with their wounds. That little sound they made at the first bite, it was so endearing—it stoked a fierce and lustful drive to possess them entirely.

Visions of Nyssa's graceful neck crossed his mind. *Oh hells*. To hear that little yelp from her… He breathed in his cravings and dug his fingers into his skull to quiet the deep desire churning inside him.

Seeing that bitch's bright pink nails pierce Nyssa's wrist last night had given him nothing but rage. Fury and horror. Because, while Nyssa could obviously deal with her stepmother's cruelty, she had once been a young victim to that evil bitch.

He hadn't been able to help himself from taking her wrist, trying to erase the red marks Lucinda had created.

"You can't go on compelling people, Mag." His brother interrupted his thoughts with another one of his stern warnings.

"That woman is evil, Justin. You don't understand."

"She's human. I agree Nyssa is lovely. But you're too involved. And having the little sister here at your club, that's too much."

"You were happy to help the kid."

"I was. But not in a bar." He offered Mag a small smile.

"Wait, what?" Emme brows shot up with confusion.

"Keep up, Emme." Ren sneered. "Mag brought the woman and her kid sister here and called Justin over to give the kid math lessons."

"Uh?" She shot Mag an incredulous look.

Justin leaned back on his heels with a cross of his arms. "I think Mag is falling in love with a human."

"Oh hells," Emme warned. "That's a real bad idea."

"What, were you in love with me, doll?" Mag jested, shifting in his chair.

"Mag, stop joking. Look at me!" Her playfulness had entirely disappeared. The only time he had seen her that serious was when her friend Maisie had been victim of a terrible curse.

"It's all good, Emme." He tried to lighten the mood and took his feet off his desk.

"No," she insisted, her blue eyes like slits. "*Look* at me."

"Fine," he grumbled. "What's wrong."

"What do you see?" She squinted further at him.

"A hot blonde who can be a pain in the ass." Mag snickered before turning to Justin for reinforcement.

He was struck by his brother's crushed expression, Justin's lips a thin line, his jaw tensed.

"Wrong answer." She unfolded herself from the couch and towered over them all, her shoulders back, her chin high. "What you should see is a human who lost her soul. A young human woman who had the course of her life changed forever because of you people."

"Emme." Justin's voice was hoarse, the empathy obvious in his gaze.

Mag didn't know what to say. He rearranged the files on his desk with uneasiness, unwilling to really look at her.

"It's true," she admonished. "You, St-Amand, turned me. You changed me into a vampire, and why?"

None of them said anything. There was nothing to say. Something heavy hung in the air. The weight of their commonly shared guilt.

"I'll tell you all why. Because of love. That's why. The love between an immortal and a human will always result in this... thing." She drew her hand down across her body and took a breath, nostrils flaring. "This monster. Me."

"You're not a monster, Emme." Justin pushed himself from the doorframe to close the distance between himself and the blonde. He laid a careful hand on her shoulder, his gaze on her unreadable.

"We're all monsters," Ren interjected.

Emme shot Justin a grateful look then turned to address Mag with a huff. "Is that what you want for this, Nyssa? You love her, right?"

"No. Maybe. Oh… I don't know."

"He loves her," Justin said.

"Justin," Mag protested.

"Brother, I usually go along with your crazy plans." Justin's lecturing tone returned. "I supported you against the Black Oak warlocks when they found you stockpiling magical artifacts. I don't say much when you feed on your staff and the occasional patron. But this, this is too much."

"She's a well-respected Montreal real estate tycoon, Mag," Ren said. "You can't just feed off her and hope people won't notice."

"Take my word, Mag, if you love her, truly love her, stay away." Emme was adamant.

"She's right, brother." Justin crossed the room to stand right in front of Mag's desk. "Nothing good can come from this. And there's a kid involved for crissakes."

"You can't turn them both, bro," Ren attested, his brows drawn together. "I have to agree with Justin and Emme. Even if you could make the sisters immortal. They'll lose their soul."

"What if I could do it? Turn them but with their souls intact."

"How on earth?" Emme asked. "The disciples have tried for centuries to bring back my soul."

"Mom." Mag clasped his hands together over his desk, the possibility becoming more real in his mind. His mother owed him. This was one way to repay him.

115

"Your mother?" Emme's jaw turned slack.

"We don't know the full extent of her powers," he reasoned. "I bet she could do it."

"Mag, stop." Justin shook his head in reprobation. "You can't seriously be thinking about bringing a human into our world like that."

"Captain Akande knows all about us." Mag shrugged rationally. "She's as human as they come."

"She does," Justin conceded. "I wasn't keen about her at first, but I admit it helps to have her in the know."

"So why not Nyssa and her little sister Cat?"

"Akande remains human," Ren added. "And let's say you do bring them in? Then what? She'll tell her parents. Her business associates. What will happen when she doesn't age? When the kid doesn't age?"

"Can you truly condemn that kid to immortal life—at the risk of losing her soul— just because you're infatuated with the big sister?" Justin questioned.

"I think I *do* love her." The words came out without thought.

*Oh shit*, he did love her. It had been obvious the minute he witnessed her bitch stepmother grab her wrist. But it was the way Nyssa had stayed cool and collected, her head high and dignified during the assault that had won his heart.

Oh, of course it hadn't come out of nowhere. He'd been shaken since the day she strolled through his door. He'd admired her persistence, had been impressed by her attention to detail, the research she'd done about the history of his neighborhood. She knew about zoning laws, tax breaks, and building codes. Hells, he bet she could rewire his club if she put her mind to it. The way she sleeked her blonde bob every time she stepped into his place made his heart expand with warmth.

And there was her steadfast love and patience for Cat. Her loyalty to her sister was admirable and he wished some of it would be directed towards him. He wanted to be there for them. *For her.*

"Then stay away, Mag. Just stop," Ren cautioned, his tone unusually stern. "Don't call her. Step away from her life."

"Compel her to forget you," Justin advised.

"What?" A rush of disgust at the thought overtook him. To take such a determined woman's willpower would be all kinds of wrong. He still seethed at his mother for having done just that with her sleeping spell.

"Brother." Justin paced the floor again. Then he stopped right in front of him, and grabbed each side of the desk to lean in and emphasize his logic. "One of the hardest things I ever did was to say goodbye to Marie-Louise."

"Sorry, man." Mag's body stilled as he looked up at his brother. Marie-Louise was a distant past. A spouse he had taken when all humans of their generation were alive before dying one by one from age. She had passed peacefully as an old woman in her eighties. Mag knew this was a sore point in Justin's life.

"Like you, I didn't listen," Justin continued. "I tried. I took a human wife. I wish I hadn't. For her sake. For mine."

"You have to give up Nyssa, bro." Ren said.

Mag's fists tensed and he let out a heavy breath. He just couldn't. He knew it was selfish, maybe wrong, but he just couldn't let go of his obsession with the business-woman. He'd been searching for something all of his life.

117

Something to fill the deep void at his soul, and here she was. He had found what made him feel complete.

"I can't stop seeing her," he told them. "No, brothers. This is the first time something like this has ever happened to me. And I bet Val would approve."

Justin's gaze turned dark while Ren let out a heavy frustrated huff.

"And I told Cat I'd take them skating tomorrow." He looked at the vamps with defiance, a slow smile appearing on his lips. "I just can't break that promise."

# CHAPTER 12

"*O*f course, you can skate perfectly." A genuine smile of appreciation brightened his rugged looks. "Isn't there anything you can't do?"

She shrugged, unable to ignore the pounding of her heart with him so near as they glided on the outdoor skating rink installed in the city's Old Port area for the winter.

He radiated strength and sexiness in his perennial leather jacket over his black t-shirt. He again appeared unbothered by the crisp late evening air, while Nyssa was bundled into a hip-length ski coat over her casual jeans to fend off the freezing temperatures.

They were skating in circles side by side under the rink's spotlights among a cheerful crowd in vivid colored parkas, ski hats, and woolly mittens. People were indulging in the last few weeks of winter sports before spring weather would close the venue. Cat was doing a graceful layback spin in the middle. She loved skating, having taken lessons since she was a toddler, participating in local competitions attended faithfully by Nanny Brown.

Nyssa reflected on the drama of the last few days. *He likes you,* Cat had said.

She bit her bottom lip as she glanced at him, noticing how the planes of his sculpted features gave him an air of danger that had her shuddering with lust.

"Do you ever get cold?"

"Cold?" A twinkle appeared at the corner of his dark eyes.

"It's subzero and I've never seen you wear more than this jacket."

"I like this jacket." He shrugged lazily and gave another solid push of his skate.

"It suits you." A craving for him descended down to her navel. She wished she could just grab the lapel of that coat and snuggle safely against the powerful chest, surrounded by the intoxicated leather scent.

He chuckled. "Does it now?"

"Very much so." Her heart skipped in crazy palpitations.

"I'd thought you preferred the suit and tie types."

"Not always." She gave her skates a few more gentle thrusts and wondered why she was so attracted to this bad-boy entrepreneur. In truth, this was a first. She had indeed played it safe and dated the suit and tie types. Up until today that is.

And if this was actually a date, she was enjoying it immensely.

She shot him a bright smile. "So you don't get cold?"

"Nah, I'm a tough guy," he teased. What could have been an obnoxious statement on anyone else was nothing but the truth. He *was* a tough guy.

He cocked a brow and returned her smile. A deep current of unspoken emotions seemed to pass between them. She couldn't pinpoint why exactly but she was more and more drawn to him.

Oh sure, on the first day she met Mag, she had been so attracted to him. It had taken everything to quench the lust at her core to focus on her offer to buy his club. His banter was actually quite clever. He was considerate of his staff, asking civilly instead of barking orders like some bosses she knew. And the way he treated Cat—taking her seriously while also realizing she was just a child—had melted Nyssa's heart. Seeing him pore over math worksheets with her sister had been an amusing sight that had quickly turned into sincere gratefulness.

And how he had changed Lucinda's mind at the cocktail party, swooping in to help her just like a hero from the movies—as he had done when retaliating against LaChance—created goose bumps all over her skin.

"You skate really well, too," she admitted. "When did you learn?"

"Oh, I can't remember. Feels like I was born on skates. I played hockey with my brothers."

"Your brother Justin?" She wanted to know more about his family.

"Justin? Yeah, a little. But he preferred to stay home and blow things up with his experiments. Mom hated that." Mag chortled with a shake of his head. "Val and Cass were the ones I hung out more with in those days."

"Cass St-Amand? The rock singer. Of course, I forgot. When I asked around about the *Serpent Maudit*, someone did mention that you two are brothers."

"That he is."

"Does he ever come back here? I read he's mostly on tour or in the studio in the US. We almost forget he's from Montreal."

"Don't tell anyone, but he *is* here a lot. He goes to Domaine-Lassalle when he's in town. We own a few getaway places in the area. My brother Ren has a huge log cabin at the top of the mountain, just up Briac Falls. Cass likes it there. Away from everyone."

"That's sensible." They maneuvered past an older couple bundled in long wool coats and fur hats. They were holding hands.

"Very." He shot her a small smile. "Don't you get tired of all these charity balls you attend? I see your picture in the papers all the time."

"You *do* read about me." She recalled their earlier conversation and she was giddy at the thought that he'd been interested in her life.

"I have." His appreciative expression was so intimate that she quivered under his penetrating gaze.

She shrugged dismissively to calm her inner turmoil. "It's all work."

"Ah, yes. Stealing people's homes," he quipped with an amused rise of his brow.

She sighed. "Hey, I'm no longer trying to buy your club. The city council has dropped the case."

"Actually, you *were* right about one thing. I just hired someone to fix the old wiring."

"You have?" She was sincerely surprised.

"Yes. You were right. I've been a bit too attached to the old system. But I do want my patrons to be safe."

"So you see how I'm not wrong?"

"Well for some things." His lips were still curled in amusement. "But destroying our city's heritage is not right either."

Frowning, she pondered his comment. "I've never been one to hold on to the past."

Her own past hadn't been the greatest, so she was inclined to always looked forward to the future.

"I can tell," he noted. "The structures you build, they're all so modern."

"I have a great architect firm working with me. I want to move ahead. Our city is full of talented people." She lightened with excitement for her work. "I want to show what we can do, always pushing into the future. Have you ever seen Singapore?"

"I have. And no thank you." He chuckled. "Not my style."

"You're happier in places like Paris then?"

"I'm happier here." His traits became serious. "In my city. I don't want Montreal turned into Singapore."

She surveyed the devastatingly handsome club owner as she mulled over his strong opinion. "You know I was born here but it's not truly my city. I left when I was fifteen. And returned after college in the US."

"Your stepmother didn't give you much choice."

"Lucinda." Her eyes rolled with scorn as she crossed her foot over the other to maneuver the curve of the ice rink. "NYU was my choice, though. Anything to get away from her."

"Then why did you ever come back?" He edged closer and her heart raced with his nearness. "Why try to modernize the city?"

"Oh I don't know. My mother's memory maybe." She craned her neck to catch his gaze, which had deepened with interest at her answer. "I guess it was my parents' dream to make this construction business expand into a successful real estate powerhouse. Dad still has his old office just up the hill where Mom worked the books in her days. She liked to tell me how ecstatic they were when they could afford the house in Westmount."

"Doukas?"

"Yes. It's so different now with Lucinda's changes." She was bitter, no doubt about it. "Dad brought in Denis from his time in the force and hired a cook. All I remember from our live was happiness. Mom inherited all these old-word pieces of furniture and artwork from a great-aunt in Greece and the house was packed with them. I don't even know where they are now. Dumped at some charity store, probably."

Pain lodged itself at the back of her throat, as she remembered too well her lack of resources to prevent Lucinda from giving away Mom's precious secretary and dressing table. And along went the beloved antiques still touched with the patina of her mother's memory, out of the house, with no means to ever recover them. Maybe it was why she'd blocked her heart from ever becoming sentimental about historical objects. They would all be discarded one day anyway.

Mag's look on her was empathetic. "And your father doesn't say anything?"

"Dad is distant, not always there, to be honest. Even before his stroke, he just let Lucinda runs things." She sighed. "He was a lost shell of a man when he met her."

The social climber had seen his weakness, Nyssa was sure of it. The bitch had played him in his loneliness and trapped him. Maybe he thought his void would be filled by her and a new child. Maybe, through it all, his grief from losing Nyssa's mom had been too much, and he'd disappeared within himself.

"I'm afraid he failed Catalina." Nyssa watched her

half-sister do a fancy skating move, a beaming smile upon her face. "She really is a good kid, you know."

The kid in question glided towards them. "Nyssa, Mag, did you see that? A backward three turns!"

"That's great, Cricket."

"You're an amazing skater, kid." Mag seemed honestly astonished by Cat's figure skating talent.

"Been taking lessons since I was five." She hooked an arm through Mag's and pushed him forward. "Come on, go around with me."

"Sure."

Mag and Cat moved to the inside of the circle of skaters who drifted casually around the rink under the starry sky. Soon the pair was sailing across the ice at incredible speed. Mag's muscular thighs powered through, his entire body radiating strength. Nyssa glimpsed him as a youth playing hockey with his brothers in his current drive to keep up with her sister. They were both masters of the ice, people turning to watch them with admiration.

Nyssa sighed with longing. Could this be possible? Mag with her, as a couple?

He was so wrong for her. Or was he? Nyssa wrestled with a jumble of sensible thoughts and brittle feelings.

Dammit, she was falling for him. And Cat loved him.

Nyssa was incredibly worried that her sister would go back to LaChance and the school counselor had insisted she keep things normal and busy for Cat. Was hanging out with Mag normal?

He was a businessman like she was. She had thought him stubborn but now she saw that he was just hanging on to something he was passionate about. A tingle of satisfaction rose in her that he had called in an electrician. He had actually listened to her and followed through.

She had misjudged him.

"Nyssa, watch out!"

She heard the call too late and Cat slammed into her from the side.

Nyssa would have fallen if not from Mag catching her. At once, she was embraced by warmth and solidity—his clean spicy scent filling her senses with delicious stirs—as his arms captured her.

"Let me try that move again," Cat called out before zipping back to the center of the rink.

As Nyssa recovered her balance, Mag slid beside her but kept his arm around her waist. She placed a tentative hand at her back, her mouth dry from jitters. They slowly skated together without a word, Nyssa much too aware of his body alongside hers, her cheeks flushed, the sensual tension unbearable.

"I can't believe you're not married yet." He finally broke the silence.

"Oh, I almost did." She was nervous to see his dark gaze so close.

"Really." Both brows rose with surprised interest.

"Yes, Karl." She nodded with a small dip of her chin, acknowledging her last boyfriend. "An honest-to-god Austrian baron, titled and all."

"No shit." His jaw dropped and he missed a step. "What happened?"

"Not quite right," she explained. "Very charming, but he was a bit cold to Cat on a few of our Saturday outings. I just couldn't see the relationship working out long term."

In fact, while they got along so well in Europe during her three months' stay the year past—attending small soirées and a few glamorous balls, interspersed with romantic holidays to the Alps and the Riviera—Karl just

126

didn't have it in him to deal with her hectic schedule and supporting her sister once they came back together to Montreal. Even then, Nyssa knew she would need to be more involved in Cat's life as her sister was growing into a needy teen.

And over time, his aloofness reminded her more and more of the snobs Lucinda liked to entertain.

"I see." Mag nodded to himself.

"She likes you a lot." Nyssa's throat tightened. Had she just implied out loud that Mag could succeed where Karl had not?

"She's a cute kid." Mag's tone was measured. "We just have to keep her away from LaChance and others like him."

"We?" She swallowed. There was no denying he intended to remain in her life.

"Yeah, why not." His smile took the most tempting turn and her heart suddenly pounded against her ribcage with unmeasured desire. Her knees weakened.

She licked her bottom lip and looked at him through her eyelashes. "She's not the only one who likes you," she admitted. "I misjudged you."

"You did?" He tilted his head to the side and his grip on her waist tightened.

"I think I like you, too," she breathed, dizzy from her forwardness. There was no turning back now.

Mag slowed their pace and skated in front of her, his gaze smoldering. He leaned towards her ear and her blood rushed to her head. When he brushed her temple with his lips, her entire body warmed with an inner glow.

"I like you a lot, Nyssa Vlahos." His hand slid lower to the small of her back and he pressed her against his rock-hard body.

Losing her balance again, she teetered against him. He led her to the side bank, and they stopped skating as she beamed at him, her hands on his chest, his at her waist.

Unbelievably happy, she peered into his gaze, riveted by the strong connection passing between them. "Then I supposed we'll have to see where this leads us."

"Exactly." His forehead was tipped towards her, his face so close, she was dying for him to kiss her. She had sampled the thrill of his enticing lips upon her temple and now wanted them on her own, desperately desired to have him mingle his warm breath with hers.

And she was sure he would have kissed her had Cat not come zooming by to interrupt them.

"Oh, come on, you two." The child was happy, her face flushed with exercise, her breath condensing in the air. "Let's go get some hot chocolate. I can't feel my toes."

"Right." Nyssa checked her watch reluctantly. "It's past dinnertime. We should go."

They ambled together to exit the rink—Mag holding the gate open for them both—before sitting on the wooden bench to untie their skates.

A few minutes later, they had returned them to the small booth by the ice rink and were taking a shortcut to the coffeeshop through an old alleyway.

"You want to come to dinner?" Nyssa asked as they walked side by side, her heart hammering wildly. Was she being too eager?

"Oh yes. Please, Mag. Nyssa promised to make these spinach things." She gazed up at him filled with cheerful hope. "Her mom's favorite. It's so good."

"You cook?" He turned an amused expression in Nyssa's direction.

A bout of nostalgia rose in her. She had endeavored to

try different Greek recipes for Cat to connect with their father's roots. "Yes, I—"

Mag had suddenly stopped dead in his tracks. A deep growl emerged from his throat.

"Nyssa, Cat. Run," he ordered abruptly under his breath.

She frowned at him, blinking rapidly.

"Mag?" Cat whispered with unease.

"Run!" With his jaw clenched, he seized Nyssa by the shoulders and gave her a sturdy push. "Now! Take your sister."

"I don't—" Nyssa squawked, following his gaze.

There at the end of the alley stood two men surrounded by a dark, ominous fog.

An uncontrollable fear rose from the pit of her stomach up to the back of her throat. She unconsciously grabbed Mag's arm as she stared at the menacing forms advancing slowly towards them, blocking their exit.

While dressed in everyday clothes, khakis and nondescript parkas, it was their evil essence that made Nyssa swallow with dread. Everything about them seemed lifeless and brutal.

"Nyssa?" Cat's voice again came out small and charged with terror.

"Magnovald St-Amand. Mount-Royal Immortal." The tallest one called out, his cavernous pitch a spine-chilling threat that bounced against the bricks of the towering buildings enclosing the alley. "I come from Prince Norwell of the Daeva Realm. You have insulted him deeply. Prepare to die."

# CHAPTER 13

*hat the hell.* Incredulous, Mag faced the soul-sucking monsters.

Because that was what was in front of him. Daevas.

Those beings from the beyond that survived in their world by drawing out the life force of humans. They hadn't been seen in Montreal in decades. Where did these come from?

Dread scattered in his chest in a myriad of glacial tingles at the risk to Nyssa's and Cat's safety.

"Nyss, take Cat and go back inside to the rental store," he said under his breath, trying to keep calm, while cursing inside that they hadn't taken off running yet.

He had to get them both out of here before he could pounce on the supernaturals to destroy them.

"Let's go, Cat," Nyssa finally snapped.

With the sisters retreating, Mag sized up the two daevas. He'd get to the bottom of this. Find out just what was going on and then swiftly, fatally dispatch these creatures.

Cat screamed in a razor-thin pitch. "Mag!"

"Oh god," Nyssa echoed.

Keeping the two monsters in his range of view, his body in a loose defensive pose, he did a quarter turn to see what terrified Cat and Nyssa.

*Sacrament!* Another dark cloud hovered over the ice-covered cobblestones, coalescing into a third humanoid form. *Not another, dammit.*

"You thought we'd come alone?" One of the daevas sneered.

The newcomer was different. He was clad in a long dark red robe hemmed with gray fur and painted over with a multitude of black runes.

"Mag. What is this?" Nyssa's feet were planted on the snow, her grip firm on her sister as she gazed back and forth between Mag and the three daevas. "You know these people?"

"Let them go." Mag growled at the monsters, glancing at the parka-clad ones before settling on the cloak-covered foe. "It's me you want."

"True." The daeva shrugged in a rustling a velvety fabric. "But they'll be much juicier than you could be."

"Mag." Nyssa had retreated closer to him. She pulled on Cat's arm and dug through her purse.

"It will be okay, Nyss. Just stay close." Mag was trying his damnedest to sound reassuring, but he didn't like this one bit. His fists were balled at the ready as he addressed the daeva. "Who sent you?"

A slow and malevolent smile stretched the monster's lips as Mag racked his brain.

He had probably insulted many people, but he did not remember any daeva on that list. In fact, the last one he'd seen a hundred years ago was a pathetic rotten soul he'd found in the back of an abandoned bakery where Mag had sought refuge with his latest human conquest—a sexy little nursing student full of curiosity—during a particularly vicious blizzard one night. The supernatural thing had tried to attack his lover, but a few well-placed fang bites had seen the being dissolved back into its gray cloud and into the floorboard of the bakeshop in minutes, destroyed for good.

"Prince Norwell," the daeva finally spat, repeating what the other two had said.

"Of the Daeva Realm." Mag frowned, trying to remember where he had heard the name. "He's here?"

"Mag, who are they?" Nyssa fished her cellphone from her purse, her arm shaking.

He took a side step to position himself closer, wanting to shield her and the kid from it all. He wasn't sure how to explain the three otherworldly foes to the sisters.

"She doesn't know who you are?" The daeva in the robe cackled while the other two exchanged an amused look.

"Mag, I'm scared," Cat murmured. "Can we go now?"

"Not yet, girlie." The tall daeva in a parka took a few steps closer and Cat whimpered, huddled against her sister. "I'm gonna taste me some vampire before I get to you."

*Ah, yes.* It suddenly came to Mag. *Norwell.* A wretched prince with something to prove. Damn. He'll have to fight. Right there in front of Nyssa and Cat. All the way around, this was going to suck.

"Does Princess Merritt know her little brother is here?" Mag commented, trying to buy time.

"Prince Norwell doesn't answer to his sister."

"Oh really?" Mag was muddy on the whole Daeva Realm order of things, but fuck, he didn't care. His fangs elongated, scraping his tongue. Anger mounted in him that anyone had dared threatened the Vlahos sisters. "He does answer to the Daemon King. The Necromancer. He won't be pleased to hear minions descended upon Montreal under the prince's bidding."

The Necromancer was his brother's friend. Malcolm Dunsmuir had taken over for his father and now oversaw the whole Daemon world—which lay at the border of the human world and hell— and to which the Daeva Realm now belonged, having been annexed when their ruler, young Princess Merritt, had pledged allegiance to Malcolm's kingdom.

But the Necromancer couldn't help Mag now. How could he battle the three daevas without revealing his true nature to Cat and Nyssa?

*Sacrament*, he had no choice. It was their safety above all.

He looked at Nyssa with sadness. "I'm so sorry."

"Mag?" She tilted her head to the side in puzzlement, her hand frozen over the screen of her smart phone.

He tore his gaze from her lovely face and centered all his intentions to the warlock band at his wrist.

"*Igirah!*" he boomed.

A giant protection sphere appeared at his call. The translucent silver shimmery globe glowed under the flickering spotlight at the end of the alley as it settled around himself and the sisters.

He sensed them gasp at the sight.

"Whoa! What is this, you can do magic—real magic." Cat was no longer afraid. Her small body shook with wonder.

"Yeah." A tiny flutter of pride made him cast her a small smile over his shoulder, but he couldn't help the knot of anxiety as he glanced at Nyssa, worried at how she would react.

And she was not okay. Her eyes were wide with bewilderment, her hand clutching her phone frozen in the air at her side.

He had to focus, get them out of here.

"We don't have much time. These are not regular thugs. They're monsters. I don't know why they're after me. But they'll suck you dry."

"Like zombies." Cat appeared surprisingly fine with the whole supernatural thing.

"Sort of." His palm was out holding the shield up as he glanced down at her. He forced his other fist back, ready to punch anyone who came too close.

Nyssa suddenly shook herself out of her trance. Grit lined her forehead. "I'm calling the police."

"Yeah, why not," he huffed as she brought her phone to her ear.

All he cared about was getting rid of these three freaks before any of them touched Cat or Nyssa. Police sirens might be enough to disperse them. Prince Norwell might not want to let humans know about his existence and the daevas would run before being uncovered by the human authorities.

The cloak-covered one mumbled under his breath.

*Oh shit.* A fucking magic-user. The shield Mag had raised wouldn't hold very long. He considered his mother's tattoo on the inside of his wrist with distaste. The last thing he wanted was to call on her powers. He had vowed he would rather die than ever use it again.

Damn. He clenched his jaw. There was more than his life to consider now.

Nyssa was talking on the phone to the dispatcher. She

had recovered quickly. It was as if she had the ability to block her fear entirely to focus on action. Her resilience was astonishing.

"Cat." He looked down at the kid, who was gawking wide-eyed back and forth from one monster to the next as their assailants closed in on them. The alley was completely deserted, the path icy with crackling snow and dotted with discarded crates and garbage cans behind the different local shops. "As soon as I drop my arm, I'll hit the one with the robe. You have to grab your sister and run back to the main street with her, you get me?"

"You're a wizard." Cat turned a gaping look at him, her gaze filled with both shock and wonder.

"Sort of," he grumbled.

"Will they hurt us?" She was taking it in stride. Her small features pinched in concentration.

"Not if you run, kiddo. They only want me. If you run now, Nyssa will follow you, okay? You'll both be safe. Find the police." And with chance on his side, the monsters would be long gone by the time they arrived.

"But you?" Her features bunched together with concern.

"I can get rid of them. But not if you're both here."

Her lips thinned and she nodded with gravity.

"Got it?" His muscles holding his shield were strained, but ready to attack to cover the sisters' escape.

"Nyssie, we gotta go." She tugged on her sister's purse.

"Mag?" Confusion warred with rationality as she continued to describe the scene urgently to the dispatcher on the other line.

"To the main street, Nyssa," Cat insisted, pulling harder.

"No." A glimpse of fear, quickly repressed, shadowed her gaze. "The police are on the way."

But Mag had no time for that.

"Go. Now!" he roared.

He dropped the shield and swiveled to the mage blocking the sisters' way.

"*Colebex yth!*" He blasted him with a lightning bolt that catapulted the daeva high up in the air.

The evil spell-caster hit the brick wall and his body thumped down in the snow, his red robe pooled around his inanimate body.

"Holy mother of god!" Nyssa's mouth gaped open, her eyes widened in shock. She stood frozen, slowly lowering her phone from her ear.

"Nyssa." Cat took off down the empty alley.

"Cat, wait!" The real estate mogul shook herself with a blink and took off after her sister.

"Let's get him!" The tall daeva shouted to his sidekick as he bolted towards Mag.

*Sacrament*. He took a leap back and landed on a pile of wooden crates a few feet above ground. "Run, Cat, run! Get out of here."

Cat pounded the ice in her flat furry boots. Nyssa was running as fast as she could behind her but was slipping in her booted heels. If they could just get to traffic, they would be safe.

And Mag had no magic left, his warlock's bracelet depleted from holding the shield too long.

The tall one was on him first, knife drawn from beneath his parka, wildly swinging around his blade. The other one postured widely behind his pal.

Care be damned, Mag dove down into him and

grabbed the monster at arm's-length by the throat. He would not let this nasty beast near him.

Daeva would suck a human's essence in a minute flat. Immortals were resilient but Mag didn't want to test it.

The tall daeva gasped under his grip and swung back at him, his claw-like hands digging into Mag's forearm. A swipe of the knife cut deep at Mag's flesh.

Damning the pain, Mag lifted the foe's entire weight by the neck, crushing his windpipe in his grip. He flung the lifeless beast across the alley where it lay, his body broken at an odd angle on the ice.

*So much for that.* Bastard had it coming.

Mag shrugged in his leather coat and glanced in Nyssa and Cat's direction.

*Fuck.* The mage had awakened and was now after them. They were still running but the evil freak had almost caught up with Nyssa.

But he couldn't help. He faced the daeva built like a barrel now charging him. Mag waited for him by the crates, feet planted solid on the snow. These were not men, they almost matched him in speed.

"Come on, asshole!" He was eager to finish it and quick, fear for Nyssa fueling his ire. He had to stop that goddamn magic-user before it was too late.

The thick creature rammed into Mag like a Mack truck. Mag let his momentum carry him down. At the last moment, he twisted the daeva's body under him. They smacked onto the ground. Mag wrestled with the monster until he had the wretch's neck in the crook of his arms. Mag flexed until he heard a gurgle.

*Oh what the hell.* He grabbed the head in both hands and snapped his neck. The beast slumped forward. Dead.

If what he remembered was correct, both deceased

creatures would soon dematerialize, and their essence would vanish into the concrete under the packed snow at their feet.

"Cat, keep running!" Nyssa's warning echoed breathless into the night.

The evil mage had grabbed her purse. She dropped it before scramming forward.

His pulse racing, he knew Nyssa would not make it far. He had no choice.

Mag bolted at vampire speed. And with two vaulting steps on the brick wall, he landed right in front of them all, blocking the way to the main street.

"Leave her alone." His voice was a deadly chill as he pinned the evil spell-caster under a lethal gaze.

The daeva mage froze.

"You know I'll kill you," Mag snarled, retracting his upper lips with wrath.

Cat scurried into the main street past him. But Nyssa stopped to stare.

"Magnovald." Nyssa's hesitant voice came out as if from far away.

His teeth were bare, incisors fully out in a rictus he knew was horrifying.

His heart fell at the reality that she was no longer looking at the club owner she said she liked. His hope for any relationship with her deflated.

But her life was at stake.

"Run to the street, Nyssa," he said quietly with a nod. He swallowed his pain at having this happen this way. "Go with Cat."

But it was too late.

The mage flicked his palm open and a dusty cloud temporarily blinded Mag.

When the smoke cleared, the evil daeva had Nyssa by the hair, a look of pure hunger upon his face. This was more than a minion carrying out his duty for his prince. This one wanted food.

She screamed and the creature pulled her towards his chest.

"Don't move or she's dead." He placed her in a head-lock, her back to the monster. His open red velvet cape revealed a bare emaciated arm, its flesh gray against Nyssa's dewy cheek. Mag wanted to gag.

Instead, horror and fury swallowed him whole to see the monster lay a palm upon her forehead.

She howled a bone-chilling scream that cut right through Mag's soul. She fell limp against the horrific arm, her eyes glassy.

A look of pure pleasure passed upon the freak's face. He was feeding on Nyssa's life force. In moments she would be dead.

"You bastard, let her go." Mag took a slow step forward, searching for a weakness.

The color was returning to the mage the more he fed. But Nyssa's skin turned paler by the second.

"My master told me I could feed today. And that's what I'm going to do."

"Let her go," Mag snarled. He took another step and narrowed his gaze at him, trying to force the daeva to look at him.

"Don't even bother, vamp." The daeva tipped his head back with a malevolent chuckle. "With her essence in me, you can't compel me."

Mag took another slow step, his fangs ready, his body buzzing with ferocity.

What happened next took him completely by surprise.

With astonishing force, Nyssa slammed her high heel in the daeva's foot. She rammed her elbow into his gut, and he grunted with pain.

*Sacrament!* That was enough to loosen the monster's grip and she slid down along his body to the ground.

In an instant, Mag had the fiend by the throat, pinned to the brick wall.

She was watching—he should have been hiding his true nature. But adrenaline pumped in his veins and he no longer cared.

His growl knew no bounds. The bastard had dared touch her, feed from her. He would end him right there.

The sound of sirens erupted in the night and reason somehow prevailed.

With his teeth bare, he sneered. "Don't ever lay a finger on my friends. Go back to your prince and tell him. If he stays one minute longer in my city, we will end him."

Mag slammed the freak hard against the wall, the spell-caster's head cracking against the bricks.

The sirens were now upon them and soon flashing red lights pulsed along the alley's walls.

"Police!" Flashlights illuminated the scene as a gruff voice called, "Stop. *Arrêtez-vous!*"

"Nyssie, Mag?" Cat called out from behind the blinding lights, her voice shadowed with worries.

Mag let go of the daeva's neck. The mage dropped to the frozen snow, scrambled to his feet, and scurried away in the alley.

Two officers in fur caps and thick black blouson coats approached, shining flashlights at Mag and Nyssa.

"No problem here, *Monsieur l'Agent*. Just small-time thieves. They ran away." Mag impressed upon them with a deep compelling look as he strode forward, his hand extended for a shake. "I'm Magnovald St-Amand."

"Sir." The young female officer shot him a stern nod. "Are you okay?"

"Yes, of course." He cast a worried glance at Nyssa behind him. She was retrieving her purse from the ground.

"And you, miss?"

Nyssa stood straight and advanced towards them, her chin high. She brushed her coat and stopped in front of the two officers, her expression unreadable under the red lights of the police car.

"Cat." She had eyes only for her sister who ran into her arms with a squeal of relief.

"Miss Vlahos. She's with me." Mag suddenly realized that she never would be.

With his breath shortened by intense torment, he contemplated the two sisters embracing each other.

Whatever Nyssa saw and experienced tonight, that would be the last time she'd ever let him near her or her little sister.

# CHAPTER 14

"Well, that's it for us. We'll be in touch if we need anything else." The police officer closed his notepad while his female partner strode back to the patrol car. He shot a quick nod at Nyssa and Mag. "Miss Vlahos. Mr. St-Amand. Good they did not take off with your belongings."

"Thank you, officer." Nyssa's cool and collected tone seemed to come from outside of herself. Inside, she was a storm of turmoil, her heart battling her ribcage, the back of her head in a vise grip of tension.

"Catalina." The officer turned to Nyssa's sister with a softened expression. "You're a brave kid running for us like that."

Cat was still out of breath, her eyes bright with excitement as she loudly declared, "They were really scary."

Suddenly feeling wobbly, Nyssa gulped, realizing what her sister had been through.

"Will you be okay, miss?" The officer narrowed a concerned gaze at her.

"Her driver will come pick them up in a minute." Mag

sounded as he always did. Strong, commanding. In charge of the situation. Like the normal club owner he was.

But he was not normal.

And Nyssa still refused to look at him.

The police left the scene, the snow glittering in the patrol car's headlights as it drove away.

Her heart was tumbling with too many emotions— terror, anguish, shock, and disbelief.

She finally settled with anger.

Nostrils flaring, pulse speeding, she pivoted to Mag and shoved him hard in the chest.

"What was that?" she exploded. Her hands were on her hips, her body flushed with a rush of wrathful heat. "What the hell *are* you?"

He took a step back, distress and pain both mixed in his expression.

Nyssa closed her fists tighter, her muscles quivering. Whatever this was, he had no rights to expose them to it.

"What are you, Magnovald?" She threw her hand out to the now empty alley. "Who, no, what, attacked us tonight?"

"Oh, Nyssie, didn't you hear the monsters? He's some kind of vampire." Cat chimed in and turned eagerly towards him. "You're immortal, like on TV."

"Cat?" Nyssa's stomach hardened along with her mounting disbelief. "How on earth can you be cool with any of this?"

And how was this even real? Her entire grip on truth shifted under her very feet.

Mag let out a slow and measured breath. His posture eased as he avoided her gaze, his arms loose at his side.

"The people that attacked us are called daevas." His

tone was so unnervingly calm that her fury rose up to another notch.

"What do they want, Mag?" Cat asked, like an attentive student and apparently taking it all in stride.

Nyssa frowned and said the word "daevas" slowly under her breath as if to keep hold on her reality.

"They are not of this world," he said simply, finally catching her eyes.

She was stunned by the unrest raging in his dark irises.

"What, like demons? From hell?" Because what she'd experienced under the monster's grip had been something worse than a horror movie.

She forcedly refused to let her mind return to that gruesome moment. Damn, she was off in the deep end now. Her heart raced madly, her skin clammy, and she unconsciously reached out for Cat to shield her from the stranger facing them. She didn't know whether to run away from him or urge for a full explanation.

Her knees weakened. But she tightened her fists again and continued to glare at him.

"Hell?" He kept his head down, his expression indecipherable. "Yes, sort of. More at the border between our world and true hell."

"And where are *you* from? Hell?" Her voice was frosty now. It was the only way she could cope.

He snorted and his jaw clenched, showing emotions for the first time. "Not hell, no. I'm as much from this world as you are."

"He called you Immortal." Cat was all perked-up and full of curiosity.

Nyssa put her hand around the teen's shoulder to protect her from the person—no, the thing— she no longer understood. She shuddered. "You have fangs."

"Really?" Cat exclaimed. "You saw them? How cool."

"Yes, I have fangs. And so what." His posture changed and he took a step forward, his chest wide, his expression defiant as he retorted, "I was born this way. Fangs and all. I can even turn into a bat if I put my mind to it, believe it or not."

She just couldn't imagine this. Mad at his defensiveness, she tightened her grip around Cat's body.

"Immortal." She narrowed her eyes at him, her mind racing. Her tone like ice. "Then how old exactly are you? And don't lie to us, Magnovald."

"I have never lied to you." The crooked smile returned and he was back to his carefree swagger as he casually leaned back on his heels. "Just over three hundred and fifty years old. Born in 1670."

"And the club?" Her jaw slackened at the unbelievable confession.

"Yep." He crossed his arms at his chest. "Mine, all those years."

"Wow. That is so cool," Cat gushed.

"It can be." His tone warmed as he cast Nyssa's sister a genuine smile.

"Oh, hell no." Nyssa took a step back, Cat in her arms. She was shaken at the attraction still churning inside her, despite the incredible revelation. Her mind hurried to grasp her next course of action and she narrowed onto one single thought. "You put us in danger. You put *Cat* in danger."

"I'm really sorry." His swagger disappeared and he shoved his hands into the pockets of his leather coat, his expression aggrieved. "Are you sure you're okay? You handled that last one pretty good."

She shook suddenly as the repressed memory came crashing back.

Horrific slimy appendages had slid across her skin. So cold, so hungry, like slithering squid-like sucking cups pulling at her bare flesh, pumping out her essence all the way from her soul, drawing excruciating pain as the invisible limbs found every intimate corner of her private self. They twirled and dug deep until her entire being had been exposed, with nothing left untouched. The worst being her inability to scream her agony.

She'd been violated in the worse possible manner. But there was no way she would share any of this with him.

"Martial arts training," she said absentmindedly. "It just kicked in."

"You fought the thing off?" Cat was clearly impressed.

Nyssa straightened her spine. "Did it really suck my life force?" she asked Mag in a cool and collected voice. Falling into her habit of rationally collecting and cataloging information when overwhelmed.

"Yes. You'll feel drained for a couple of days." He reached out to her with familiarity, his hand useless in the air as he reconsidered before dropping it at his side.

And suddenly she let herself feel it, the draining, her weakness at coping with it, and she wanted to fall into his arms. Let him give her some of his extra strength.

He had defeated three monsters, just like that. And he had magic in him. Something like it, anyway. Lightheaded from the trauma, she held a hesitant gaze on him, no longer knowing what to feel or think.

"Do you feed on people's blood?" Cat asked.

"Cat," Nyssa warned her sister.

"Actually, I do," he responded slowly.

Horror felt over her like sudden nightfall, numbing her heart further.

"You do *what*?" She wasn't sure she had heard him right. Or did want to.

"So you *are* a vampire?" Cat said as if it was the most normal thing in the world, while Nyssa continued to stare at him in disbelief.

"Not quite," he explained. "I'm what is called an Immortal. All my brothers are. We need to feed on human blood once a year."

"So you just find someone and bite their necks. Like in the movies?" Cat couldn't hide her excitement, her eyes wide with eagerness.

"No. Not exactly." He casually shrugged, his features steady as he tried to find the right words. "There is an order of monks dedicated to keep us alive. They draw their own blood in a cup and offer it to us. Just once a year."

"So you never drink from humans, like sucking the blood directly." Cat wouldn't let it go.

"Well… I have." He winced, his hands again dug into his pockets. "I do."

Nyssa tightened her grip on her sister and slightly turned sideways. "Mag, this is way too weird for us."

Her mind full on denial, she had retreated behind her aloof persona. It didn't matter what he was. Or that he was still hot as hell. She had to cut ties with him this very second.

"Look, I never drink from innocent people." He folded into himself further, his usual pale features—the shade no doubt due to his condition—slightly flushed. "I don't kill people. It's just… fun."

"Fun?" Her brows shot up in astonishment. How on

earth can any of this be anything like fun? Her resentment mounted again, her heart pumped heavily at the center of her chest.

"Yes." He was defiant again, his firm chin thrust sharply at her as he pinned her under his solid gaze.

"Fun?" she repeated. Her anger grew fully, her vision tunneling and seeing only *him*, the brazen leather-clad rebel who had brought this upon them. "There was nothing fun about tonight. Three monsters claiming to come from some prince of hell that you somehow insulted."

"Nyssa, calm down. He saved us." Cat interjected with a measured tone, swiveling away from her embrace.

"No, Cat. I will *not* calm down," Nyssa shrieked. Her hands flailed in front of her, her body boiling with rage as her fear, astonishment, and exhaustion took over any reasonable thoughts. "I got you from the grips of a sexual predator and now this. A fuckin' vampire!"

"Immortal." Cat corrected, again her tone oddly rational.

"Whatever. He drinks blood, Cat. Human blood!"

She stared again at Mag, wanting him to apologize. Telling her that this was not real, just an illusion.

But he remained silent, watching them carefully and no longer posturing. The casual smile was gone, the wide shoulders withered.

He stood under the glow of the streetlight, an aura of darkness enveloping him. His dusky gaze was shadowed with secrets. Snow had started to fall around them, and he didn't even brush the damp flakes falling upon his bare neck, his leather jacket wide open to the elements over the basic black t-shirt. Now she understood why he was never cold.

Her fury disappeared as soon as it had risen, replaced by incredible sadness.

She looked at her little sister—the thick pink woolen scarf wrapped three times around her neck, the furry earmuffs at each side of her head. She exhaled long and slow as each of her tensed muscles relented.

Cat was just a kid. Forced to grow up too fast before her eyes. Lucinda, then LaChance grooming her into some kind of child prostitute, and now this. Her sister had become attached to some creature, a vampire—or immortal if this was what he called himself. No matter how natural Mag may be, this was a whole other level of messed-up.

Nyssa didn't care to know more. She just couldn't.

"Mag..." She turned to him and his crestfallen expression shot her with a surge of unexpected emotion. She blinked painfully, soreness mounting at the back of her throat for what *could* have been. "We can't."

"I know." He pressed his lips and nodded as if to himself, his gaze on her dark and somewhat tragic.

Sounds of wheels on the snow interrupted them. Nyssa's chauffeured Mercedes had pulled up to the curb.

"Your car." His chin dipped slightly as a sad, wistful smile emerged from his features.

"Yep." She braced herself and pushed Cat towards the vehicle where Mr. Julien was standing with the back door open. "Get in, Cricket."

"But he's coming for dinner." Her face had slackened, her eyes full of hope and pleading.

"Let's go home, sweetie." She gently pushed her sister into the car, her heart in turmoil at having to do the hard thing.

"Then when?" Cat poked her head out of the door to

call after Mag. "You'll come see us, right, Mag? Maybe tomorrow?"

Nyssa's heart broke to see her little sister essentially bidding farewell to her newly found friend.

"We'll see, kiddo," Mag said. But it was clear in his gaze that he knew this was over.

Nyssa sat next to her sister and with one foot still out of the car, she took a long look at him, unable to put her emotions into words.

"Goodbye, Magnovald." Her tone was just a little chillier than she'd wished.

"Goodbye, Nyssa Vlahos." His meager smile dug straight through her heart.

She nodded at Mr. Julien who closed the car door for her. And the last vision of Mag she retained was that of his sturdy and broad-shouldered silhouette cutting against the snow gently falling down upon the deserted street.

An immortal man, utterly alone under the cold Montreal night sky.

## CHAPTER 15

*M*ag was sitting at the back of the bar in his personal booth.

His place was packed as usual. Hues of pink and purple lights twirled with each other in the dancing area crammed with sweaty patrons bopping the cold away.

Hands on naked skin, slinky fabrics, wild hair, it was hard to distinguish who was who in the entanglement of overheated bodies springing below his crew of professional dancers on the platforms. His performing team undulated expertly in their signature outfits of skimpy leather shorts and matching top, the star twirling with her pet live royal python curled around her shoulders and waist.

His DJ was in tonight, bouncing to the heavy beat behind his podium, one hand on his heavy headset, the other on the console, his features in furious concentration to give the crowd the very best experience.

The *Serpent Maudit* was rocking. So why was Mag so tormented?

It had been three nights since he'd watch Nyssa's luxury car disappear into the snowy night, leaving his heart empty and cold. He was unable to appreciate any of his usual pleasures. He watched the crowd, trying to enjoy the sight of the women's bouncing curves, the expensive scents permeating the air, or the thumping beat so heavy it resonated through his leather bench. But none of it reached his dulled senses.

"Here's your drink, boss." Sandrine put another plain Scotch in front of him and he looked up at her.

She wore skin-tight cropped jeans under her waitress apron tonight, with a tiny polka-dot top making her look like a movie star from the sixties. Her blonde hair tumbled in waves over her shoulders and down her generous breasts.

"Thanks, *fille*." He gave her a curt nod.

She put her bar tray on his table and sat beside him. "You don't look so good."

"I'm not." After three hundred years, he should be able to handle disappointment better. And that was all what losing Nyssa was, a simple letdown.

He tapped his fingertips on the glass of his drink with gloom. So he would not get to ride in the sunset with the ice queen. Hells, until a few days ago, he didn't even know he had true feelings for her. Getting closer to the woman had been a mistake. He could even hear Val's fatalistic voice in his mind. *And what did you expect would happen, brother?*

They couldn't make Nyssa immortal.

And Mag couldn't live with her and see her die, either.

Sandrine leaned in to brush a lock off his forehead. With a worried expression, she lifted her hair off her shoulder, baring her throat. "You need to… you know?"

"Don't you have a boyfriend, now?" Mag countered.

They'd had an understanding, she and he. She had loved the thrill of the bite. But he had stopped months ago when she'd told him about Donatien—the boyfriend.

"You just seem so sad." She dropped down the mane of her hair with a fretful huff.

"It'll pass." He shrugged and leaned back farther in his seat, attempting to ease the heaviness at his chest.

"You have girl trouble." She raised a knowing brow at him.

"Not anymore," he stated with a shake of his head.

It was over and he knew it. Better spend his time figuring out why the hell Prince Norwell was in his city with some sort of vendetta against him. Maybe he should put out some feelers with his shadier contact to find out where in Montreal the daeva prince was hiding. He'd pay him a surprised visit. That would do it.

His jaw clenched with determination as he steadied his gaze on Sandrine. "I'll be fine, *poupée*. Don't worry about me."

"I better go then." She nodded at the crowd, grabbed her tray, and stood straight, her posture fierce for such a petite woman. "The place is hopping, and they want their drinks."

"Thanks, Sandrine." His gaze softened with gratitude.

"For what?"

"For checking up on me. You always have my back."

"We all do, Mag. This is a good place to work, you know. You're a good boss." She tilted her head to the side with warmth. "And you're my friend. I want you to be happy."

"I am." He stretched his arms wide over the wooden railing behind him and admired a small group of girls dancing right in front of the mixing stage, exaggerating their hip thrusts to catch the attention of DJ Al-Walid above them.

Their sexy poses should have brought him lust, but nothing stirred. They were not who he'd wanted grinding against his own body.

"I *am* happy," he reassured his waitress again despite his acute dejection. "This is the life. What more do I need?"

She pursed her lips unconvinced and departed to serve his customers.

He remained there for the next few hours, doing what he always did. Holding court. He first discussed the bar supplies with his barman, then planned the next big summer bash, and followed that up to conference with the bookie working out of his club. The quiet little man settled every night at the back of the bar, the blue light of his laptop glowing upon his pale weedy face while he managed the betting deals that was one of Mag's many sources of income.

Mag facilitated all this, while also attended to the constant interruption from his bouncers and the many small brawls that always arose throughout the night.

He was basically taking care of business to make sure his club was still what it promised to be. Enough thrills, drinks, and entertainment, with some side businesses that remained just at the edge of the law.

And now up to safety code. Thanks to Nyssa's suggestions.

The hollowness in his chest deepened. No. He wouldn't go there.

He reached for his phone to text Val about the where-abouts of Malcolm Dunsmuir, Necromancer and King of the Daemon Realm, for more information about the royal family of the daeva world.

Daevas were under Mal's dominion. The beings and Princess Merritt, their ruler, answered to him. The Scotsman wouldn't be pleased to hear that an underling of Merritt's little brother had attacked a human in the streets of Montreal.

"Boss, someone's outside to see you." His bodyguard Evan interrupted Mag texting mid-sentence.

"What for?" Mag cocked his head at him with annoyance before resuming his typing, his mind sorting through the underworld royalty system.

"Not sure, sir. But you should definitely let her in."

"Her?" A trickle of hope pierced his heart. *Nyssa.* No, it would not be. And his people knew the real estate mogul. They would just let her in as a matter of principle.

Could it be his mother? She'd been pretty much out of sight since the family dinner at Justin's. He curled his upper lip, just above his teeth, as his resentment mounted. Nah, this couldn't be his mother. She would likely appear in the middle of the dance floor in a poof of smoke just to make a grand entrance.

"Yeah, boss." Evan nodded, his deep respect for Mag, as always, infusing his tone. He was still a kid and a true vampire—like in the movies, as Cat would say.

The mean-looking vampire bodyguard was more for show than necessity. Because who would dare attack Mag? Aside from Prince Norwell, apparently.

With a huff, Mag sent his text to Val. Then scrolled through his screen once more, just in case, his heart racing a little but soon thumping with disappointment.

Still nothing from Nyssa.

With irritation, he glanced back at Evan who was hovering over him waiting for an answer. "Just send this woman away," he said. "I'm busy."

"Well, boss, it's awkward. She's a kid."

Mag dropped his phone on the table. His gut tightened with foreboding. "A kid?"

"She's all dolled up, like," Evan continued. "Without the makeup, I'd say she's fourteen. Sixteen at most."

*Sacrament!* Mag bolted from his seat. "Where is she?"

"At the door, sir."

Pushing patrons out of the way, Mag raced across the club to the entrance, while typing a quick text to Nyssa. It was past one in the morning. Did she even know her little sis had snuck out? And why would that wretched kid come to him in the middle of the night.

He found her waiting at the entrance under the awning, next to his doorman Raphael guarding the entry-way. There was still a huge line of patrons waiting to be let in.

Thank the heavens Raph had not sent the child away.

"Raphael." He shot his doorman a discrete thumbs-up. "Good catch."

"Sure, Mag."

"You know her, boss?" Evan was right behind him.

"Sure I do." With a grim twist of his mouth, he stared at her, the teen completely out of place and mismatched with her fishnet stockings and cropped top, a girly canvas pink backpack at her back.

"Cat, what the hell are you doing here?"

"I came to say goodbye." Her face was pinched and small as she took in the massive form of Raphael with his muscular arms bulging out of his black tank top, before trailing her gaze to Evan in his dark-on-dark suit and tie outfit.

"In the middle of the night?" Filled with concern, Mag raked his hair back and kneaded the tension mounting at his neck. "Surely Nyssa doesn't agree with this."

"She doesn't know. I'm leaving her place. She's got way too many rules." Her mouth turned into a small pout as a gleam of defiance appeared in her eyes. "I'm going to live with Oli'Vrai in Laval."

"Oh." He pressed his lips together while taking a slow and deep inhale at the frustration rising inside him. He was so damn close to yelling at her for her recklessness. But that would be a goddamned bad idea. He didn't want her to bail. With a huff, he laid a hand on her backpack. "Let's go to my office."

"I wanted to talk about what happened," she said as they walked into the vestibule. "You know, at the ice rink. But Nyssa would have none of it. Oli'Vrai says she's stubborn and he's right. I can't stop fighting with her! He said we should get out of the city for a bit, take a break from her. So this is the last time I'll see you for a while."

"I see. Let's talk." He nodded at Evan that everything was fine and led Cat towards his office.

"Oh, wow!" Her excited gaze darted back and forth around the club. "This is such an awesome place at night."

He shot her a small smile. "And you will be welcome when you turn eighteen."

Her eyes were wide as they passed by the full-length bar illuminated for the night with its flashing light combination making it look as if a sleek snake undulated above the stretched mirror. With the pulsing music and thick crowd, the place was far from the quiet space that Cat had experienced earlier in the week.

A couple of guys leered at her, taking in the bare skin of her nubile waist. Mag shot them a stare so deadly that they quickly scurried away. He breathed noisily as anger shook him to the core. Cat was just a child. He cursed the bastard LaChance to hell. He shouldn't have let the pig off so easily.

"Sit," he told Cat before closing his office door behind him, shutting away the raucous nighttime noises.

"You're really a vampire?" She found a spot on the couch and laid her bag tidily at her feet.

"Immortal. Raphael is a vampire." Another of Val's rescued pupils. The cursed youth of Asian descent had been turned by Emme about five years ago. She claimed he was so sexy she hadn't been able to stop feeding from him.

"Raphael?" Cat's curious mind was in high gear.

"The doorman who stopped you tonight." Mag leaned against the edge of his desk, his palms at each side of him on the solid wood antique.

"Oh. What's the difference?" Her eyes were like saucers, as she demanded to know everything.

"Well first, he needs to feed on blood daily to survive. I only need an offering of blood once a year in a special ceremony."

"They need real blood?"

"All the vampires here feed on synthetic blood," he explained. "Justin created the alternative about a century ago. We used pig blood to calm them before that."

"Wait, Professor St-Amand." She blinked with surprise. "He's a vampire, too?"

"Immortal," Mag corrected her with a smile. "Yes, didn't I tell you? All my brothers are immortals."

"Okay fine," her brows furrowed deeper together, "but

how are you any different than vampires. Nyssa said you had fangs—she saw them."

"Right. She did." With a shallow breath, he stared grimly at the kid. "Where do I begin?"

She continued to survey him with wide eyes, ready to take it all in with zeal.

"Well," he started, "first, vampires, the ones in town anyway, were made. They were bitten by other vampires."

"Like in all the legends."

"Exactly," he agreed. "They were humans before. My brother and I were never humans like you are. We were born this way."

"With fangs?"

"Yes."

"Your parents must have freaked out." Her gaze sparkled with wonder at the thought.

Mag chuckled at her fascination, his heart lightening a little. "Well, my mom is a French witch. She met my father, my birth one, before crossing over to New France."

"New France," she thought for a second then added, "you mean like in the 17th century?"

Oh hell, there was so much to the story, Mag just didn't know where to start. "In 1669," he finally said, hoping he remembered correctly, "with the other women called the King's Daughters."

"And she was a witch."

"*Is*. She's still alive. In fact, she is here in town right now," he huffed with an eye roll.

"Can I meet her," she pleaded.

"Probably not a good idea." After what his mom had done to Nyssa, there was no way in hell he'd have her anywhere near any of the Vlahos sisters.

"And your father?"

"Well, the man I consider my true father, Antoine St-Amand, died when I was twenty. My mom was already pregnant with us when they met. But he raised us as his sons." His heart was hit with a twinge of melancholy. "Best father I could ever have."

Cat thought about Mag's explanations for a moment. "Your mom must have been really sad when he died."

"She was."

"And it must have been weird for him to have you all stay young and him getting old like that."

"Actually, we all aged normally until it kind of slowed around twenty-five. He was no longer alive then. But mom, yeah, she always looked the same."

"So that's why you and Nyssa can't be together." She raised a brow at him, surprisingly perceptive beyond her age.

"Why do you say that?" He suddenly perked up, hope flooding him. "Did Nyssa talk to you?"

"Not really." She gave him a small sad shake of her head. "We talked a bit about that night, but she told me to forget it all. Cold as ice, you know what she's like."

"Yep." A silent but connected moment passed as they both shared in that common experience.

"She told me you were not safe for us," Cat started again, "and she kind of left it at that. But she was upset. I could tell."

"How can you tell?" He just couldn't let the matter alone. He wanted Nyssa to be thinking about him. Missing him, just as he pined for her.

"She gets really straight-faced when she's truly upset. She looks like she has no emotions whatsoever. Like an android, you know, like in those sci-fi shows."

"Right," he agreed. It was obvious that this was how Nyssa dealt with unwanted emotions.

Conflicted, he studied Cat, not knowing what to do. He couldn't let her leave. Not into the clutches of LaChance. He had been responsible for the child the moment he'd agreed to help Nyssa and he would not fail in his duty. He hoped Nyssa got his text.

He should really be calling her now, but that would cause Cat to bolt. Mag needed to stall a little longer.

"Since you're so curious about our world, want to see magical artifacts?"

"Artifacts?"

"Yep, I have quite the collection." He pushed himself off the desk and ambled across the office to the brass door of his private vault. He punched in his code and soon dragged out the hefty purple velvet bag full of his precious loot. "Here you go."

He dumped the whole shiny lot straight onto the couch beside Cat.

"Oh my god!" Her hands went straight to her face. "That is amazing."

"It is." With pride, he rummaged through the clanky pile to fish out a pendant. "Here, this medallion is supposed to make you smarter."

"Do you think I need that," she questioned.

He chortled. "No, not one bit. And I'd be careful before using any of them. I just like having them around."

"Can I...?" She slowly reached for the pile.

"Yeah, sure. Haven't hurt anyone yet." He winced, suddenly recalling that a piece of his treasure had once caused chaos when Emme had managed to steal one and taken off with it to the Pacific Northwest. "Just don't tell anyone, okay?"

"Sure, Mag." She beamed at him and pushed aside a gold and ruby tiara to pick up a tarnished goblet encrusted with jewels. "What does this do?"

"Not sure," he shrugged. "Maybe call a demon? Can't remember."

"Yikes!" She dropped the cup as if it burned.

"Here." He took a small gold ring out of the pile. "This is supposed to help you find your true soulmate."

"I already have my true soulmate." She wore a dreamy look that broke his heart. His mirth vanished.

"You're a smart girl, Cat," he cautioned. "You could do better than hanging with a loser like LaChance in a crappy diner in the East Side."

How could he reason with a youth so in love? He briefly mulled over compelling the teen to forget her sleazy boyfriend. He didn't like the idea since she was so young. If not LaChance, she might find someone else just as bad.

He'd have to give her some real talk. There was no way around it. Explain the facts to her. Just like he saw them.

Cat was wrinkling her nose at him. "Rappers are not losers. He was getting a music deal when you and Nyssa came to get me."

"From what I saw," Mag swallowed, careful of his words, "he was trading you for sex."

Cat grimaced. "Is that a bad thing?"

Mag winced at her reply. Did she know what LaChance truly had in mind for her? He bit back the scolding outburst on the tip of his tongue. He had to control himself and this conversation. "What do *you* think?"

She looked at the pile of artifacts and fingered a silver circlet engraved with twirling waves and seashell inlays—

a mermaid enchanted crown if he recalled correctly. "I can help his career."

"Is he that good of an artist?"

"Oh, he is. That first time I heard him, I was hooked." Her dreamy tone had returned. "His lyrics, they just get you, you know."

"No matter how good he is, why would you sacrifice yourself for him."

"I'd do anything for him. Anything to help with his music." Her lips parted slightly, a glow rising to her cheeks. "I love him."

Mag couldn't humor her anymore. He looked down at her inadequate clothes before catching her eyes with intent.

"If he truly loved you, he wouldn't change you. Would not ask for anything." His nostrils flared with a burst of anger. "If he loved you, he'd protect you."

"Is this what you do?" Her voice was very small, her determination shaken.

"That's what a real man does." And there was one lesson imparted by his father that had always stayed with him. *Protect your family, son. Protect those you love.*

Had he ever loved anyone? He sorted through the artifacts absentmindedly.

There were his brothers, of course. And Mom, well that was hella complicated. Sandrine, he did wish her well. As a friend. Then the myriad of women he had partied with. They all blended into one another. He had liked them. Never hurt one. But he couldn't really recall any one in particular.

No, his mind was haunted by clear gray eyes, sculpted cheekbones, and a small scar on the upper lip.

Damn, he had to let Nyssa go. This was about Cat's safety.

"Your sister," Mag's voice turned quieter, "she loves you very much, kiddo."

"It's not the same." Cat had lifted her chin. "Not romantic."

"And this guy," Mag continued, "how do you call him again?"

"Oli'Vrai." She bit her lips upon his name.

"He's romantic?"

"He texts me cute pictures all the time." Her expression lightened into a happy smile. "Bears with little hearts, kittens jumping all over. Sometimes he sends me some of his lyrics."

"What else?" Mag pressed. It would be helpful to know how they communicated.

"He wants me to leave Nyssa." Her expression took a somber hue.

"Is that love?" he inquired, keeping his disgust in check. "Cut you off from your family."

"I don't know." Her voice shook, her earlier resolve vanishing.

"Do you have to rush into this?"

"He wants me to." She bit deeper into her lips, her eyes downcast as she fingered the glittery chain attached to a gilded hand mirror, which was an old Latvian tool for divination.

"If he loves you, he'll wait."

"Like you and Nyssie?" She raised her gaze to him. And the gray shade, so like her sister's, sent palpitations to his heart.

"Maybe." The truth was that right now, despite not knowing whether his attraction was pure infatuation or

166

something more, he was willing to wait forever.

"You didn't call us," she admonished.

"Sometimes, it's best to respect other people's space."

She thought about that then said, "But you want to."

"Yes, I want to," he admitted, "but I respect your sister's wishes. And LaChance should not push you to run away from your life. You have your family, your school, your friends."

"Yes, I miss Livy," she chimed. Despite the makeup and skimpy clothes, Cat was indeed just a little lost kid. She shouldn't have to deal with the pressures of a predator. "I kinda like school, actually. We're planning our big spring field trip with my class. I want to go."

She chewed over this for a while and dropped the gilded chain. "Maybe I could date him in Montreal instead of going to Laval. Invite him home."

"That might work." Mag nodded, relief easing his tensed fists.

"I'll have to tell him. He'll be mad when I don't show to our rendezvous."

"If he loved you, he shouldn't be mad at you."

She looked at him with a downturned expression. "People get mad easily."

He'd met the mother and realized that this was what Cat had lived with all her life. Someone who was supposed to love her, her mother getting mad and diminishing her constantly in front of people.

"If they get mad for being who you are," he gently told her, "then they don't deserve you."

He wished he could take his own advice. He had come clean with Nyssa, told her who he was, and she had not accepted him. Yet, why could he not let go of her?

He would, he finally reasoned with himself. In fact, he had.

He hadn't contacted her since she told him goodbye and without Cat here tonight, there would be no connections between them.

Just let time make him forget her. She would eventually die while he carried on.

Still, Cat was here now. And naturally, he had to do something about it.

"Well, then," he told the little Vlahos, "should I drive you back home?"

"Please." She nodded, her hands on the handle of her backpack. "I hope Nyssie didn't wake up."

He was picking up his car keys from the desk when the door burst open.

"Catalina! Oh sweetie." Dressed in yoga pants tucked into furry boots and with her hair curling in disarray, Nyssa flung herself into Mag's office and ran straight to her little sister.

"Nyssa," he choked on his emotions. Seeing her like that, so unlike her usual poised self, was like a sucker punch to his gut.

All that sensible reasoning to give her space went right out of his brain. His longing for her came back full force and flooded him with the euphoria of having her right here again, in his home.

And as she embraced her runaway sibling, her love for her sister radiated with warmth.

Cat would be okay. She had a horrible mother but also someone in her life who truly loved her. Someone who would not think twice before rushing to a vampire's lair in the middle of the night to get her back.

Someone who truly loved the kid for who she was.

He caught a hint of Nyssa's fresh scent and a tingling of hope scattered within him. A floating sensation buoyed him upward at the possibility that all might not be lost for the two of them.

And as she cared unconditionally for her sister, there was one chance, one tiny chance that she could do the same for him.

# CHAPTER 16

*R*elief had flooded Nyssa as soon as she'd seen Cat standing in the middle of the office, her backpack dangling from her arm.

When she'd gone to check on her and found the bed empty, with Cat's jeweled pink smart phone gone from the night table, Nyssa's system had gone on overdrive. Cat didn't—or wouldn't—answer her calls and texts. Panicked, she had called everyone she knew, even the horrible Lucinda. The snickering of the evil bitch had deepened her distress and only one possibility had remained—LaChance.

In desperation, she'd been about to dial Mag's number just before his short text appeared on her screen.

He had her sister, everything would be okay.

And the tension had just melted away.

Mag had come through for her again.

And he now stood in front of her, looking as hot as ever, a plain black t-shirt with the club's snake logo on the chest emphasizing the muscular planes of his torso. His half-smile underscoring his sexy aura and making her inside melt.

"Oh god, Mag, thanks." She wanted to embrace his shoulders, grab both his hands in hers in deep-felt appreciation.

"It's okay." His gaze connected with hers sending her pulse racing. "She agreed to go back. Right, Cat?"

"Cricket, I was sick with worry." She looked down at her sister, a mix of emotions battling within her as she held Cat at arm's length.

"You were awake?" She stared up at Nyssa, guilt forcing her lips together.

Nyssa exhaled slowly, taking in the ridiculous outfit and choosing not to say anything.

"I've been calling everyone I know," she explained, calm settling over her. "Lucinda wasn't keen on getting woken up."

"But not me," Mag interjected, with what sounded like sadness in his voice, "you didn't check with me."

Standing in the middle of Mag's office with an arm around her sister, she surveyed his devilishly handsome features.

"Actually, you were next," she admitted. "I got your text first. Thanks for letting me know."

"Always," he murmured.

Something deep passed between them. Another impassioned connection that she couldn't deny.

*Always*. And in his world, always meant forever. An eternity.

She shook herself out of her trance. Unable to shed the emotions stirred inside her. Cat had run to him. That had to mean something.

She shifted her weight forward as her tense shoulders

relaxed further. She was overtaken by profound respect for Mag at the realization that Cat saw him as some sort of anchor.

"You can't run away like that, kid," she told her sister.

"I know. I was just really upset." Her brows furrowed with focus.

"We got attacked just three nights ago, and we're still in shock." Nyssa was keenly aware of Mag's stare, waiting on her to address the fact that she had shunned him since the event in the alley. "Jeez, Cat, we saw things we didn't even know existed."

"Didn't seem to bother you," Cat protested, drawing herself taller in an accusatory posture. "You wouldn't talk."

"Oh, sweetie," Nyssa huffed and leaned back to face her sister.

Mag remained silent but his presence permeated everything in his surroundings, the imposing antique work desk with the turn-of-the-century club chairs for visitors, the wet bar at the side with its many decanters of amber liquid, and above it, the tall oil painting of an aristocratic-looking man dressed in historical clothing. Oh hell, she suddenly realized with a tumble of her heartbeat, the man in the painting was *him*.

She swallowed. Trying to find the right words as the reality of the ancient immortal messed with her head. She leaned forward to take Cat's hand in hers and looked upon her ingenuous features.

"I was scared." She let out her breath slowly, her memory making her blink. "I was scared when they appeared, and I first thought they were thieves. And then one grabbed me and I believed I was going to die."

Mag came to her side, bringing with him a sense of safety that she had never ever experienced before.

Both Mag and Cat were quiet, and she felt the deep knot always inside her relent. The defenses she'd built to protect herself had been breached. Those barriers carefully erected for years gave way and she wanted to tell both of them how she truly felt.

"I was scared for you, Cat," she continued. "When you were running ahead of me. Then I saw things…"

She glanced back at Mag, knowing deep down that he would understand. That he would not lash out at her for being weak.

"I was scared, too, Nyssie." Cat's eyes welled, her voice tiny.

"I know, Cricket." Nyssa nodded slowly, her lips pressed together as she reached within to share her true experience. "Look, sweetie, when I get scared, I go some-where inside of me. I have this place there, where every-thing is safe. Where there are no emotions. No fear. Because I know that if I allow any of it to come out, I won't be able to control them. And I'll be lost."

"You grow cold, you mean."

She shot Mag another hesitant glance, saw in the soft-ening of his expression that, in this moment, he completely understood.

"I guess. It's been only me my whole life, Cat. Until recently, I thought you were fine. It took me to see you run away to LaChance to grasp that you need me in your life." Guilt was strumming her heart. "But I'm not used to thinking of someone else. I should have recognized that the attack would be a shock to you, too."

"I'm not scared of Mag," Cat proclaimed with a bright smile for him.

Nyssa let out another slow breath and turned her full gaze onto him.

He was so close that she could smell his woodsy cologne along with that smallest hint of something raw. Something wild and untamed. She recalled how he had skillfully fought the monsters in the alley. Fierce and true. Like a knight in shining armor coming to save her.

He was not quite human. How could she have fallen for someone like that?

Maybe because humanity had failed her?

"I'm not scared of him, either." She held his gaze within her own. She had been scared of her stepmom as a child, scared of the monster holding her in the alley, terrified by the visions, but never *of him*.

A faint hint of relief crossed his eyes and he reached out to her. His palm settled on her arm. A gentle touch that ran through her body, creating a warmth that reset everything racing in her overactive mind to a peaceful calm.

"I would never hurt you or Cat," he ascertained.

"You protected us." She knew it to be true to the depths of her heart.

"Always," he promised. "I will always be there to protect you."

She never had anyone protect her. But he had against Lachance and again in the alley. Like a hero he had swooped in and saved her life. And again she wondered what *always* would actually mean to someone immortal.

He would live forever.

She wouldn't.

Her heart paced as a small part of her brain considered the possibility of them. Mag and her, together. That was crazy thoughts. Impossible thoughts. But here he was, so real and well, just *there*. Her body called out for him.

Wanting so much more. And her heart. Well, her heart was filled with him.

She had always been resilient. Life had forced it upon her. She'd been on her own, longing for someone to lean on when she just no longer had the strength to carry on. She yearned to be weak, for just one second.

No, she was not scared of him. Not at all. In fact, she wanted all of him.

And shaky, she just continued to hold his gaze, not knowing what to say.

His lips finally curled into the familiar half smile she loved so much. "You didn't really need me, though. You fended off that daeva no problem."

"Pure instinct." She shrugged with a dismissive shake of her head.

"Cat," he turned to the teen. "Did you know your sister is quite the fighter?"

"Yeah," Cat chimed in. "Nyssa's been doing martial arts classes for, like, forever."

"You're strong." He nodded in appreciation.

She was still surprised that the move had come to her when she had barely enough strength left. She had frozen when LaChance had shoved her. Shocked. But the next time, pure adrenaline had done the trick.

"Was that him draining my life?" A chill trickled along her spine at the horrific memory. "The pain was unbearable. I had to stop it."

"If you hadn't, you would be dead within a few minutes."

"Oh my god, Nyssie," Cat cried. "I had no idea."

"Thank goodness you weren't there." She shot her sister an alert gaze, protective feelings rushing through her limbs.

"I'm so sorry." Cat wrapped her arms tight around her waist, her head buried in Nyssa's chest. "I didn't want to make you upset. You were so cold and you broke up with Mag. And I was so lonely. And Oli'Vrai called me."

Nyssa pondered the words about breaking up with Mag. Is that what it looked like to her sister?

"We were not breaking up, Cat." She pushed her sibling gently away, deeply aware of Mag's silent but heavy charisma beside them. "Well…were we even…" She stumbled on her words as she caught his amused gaze. Her breath remained wedged in her chest as she struggled to express what might lie at the depths of her heart.

"I don't know," she continued, intensely aware that he was waiting for what she would say. "I guess we need to figure this out."

"I really like your sister, Catalina." His expression was steadfast, his confession unwavering as he smiled fully at her.

Her knees weakened and she was rendered speechless.

"I knew it!" Cat shouted with glee. "And you like him too, right, Nyssie? You were pretty excited to go skating with him. You changed your outfit three times."

She *had* been excited for the date, yes. But that was before she knew Mag was different.

But now?

"Mag and I need to talk about this alone, Cricket." She lifted her chin with determination as she made her decision. There was no more skirting around the issue. "This whole vampire business. It's insane."

"He's an Immortal, Nyssie."

"Yes, fine. Whatever." She found herself suddenly exhausted, her initial drive failing. "We should go home,

Cat. It's late. And we need to discuss this whole LaChance thing. He's not good for you."

"It's okay, Nyssie. Mag and I talked about it."

"You did?" Surprised she looked at him.

"Yes. He made some good points. It's too early in our relationship for me to live with him, anyway. There's a lot I want to do. We can just see each other for now. With me at your house." Cat's features were bunched in concentration. "Plus, I need to finish the school year. I actually like it there. I'd miss Livy and Josie."

"Wow, that's good." Nyssa nodded a few times, shocked at her sister's sensible reasoning. There was no way she'd welcome LaChance into her home—that bastard exploiting children like this. But Cat had taken a huge step in the right direction. She'd figure out the next move later.

"We do need to set some ground rules for you if I'm to be your guardian," she added. "You can't be leaving at all hours of the night. You're still underage."

"Fine," she grumbled. "I'm sorry, sis."

Nyssa stared at Mag, still in disbelief he had succeeded where she had failed. "Thanks."

He shrugged, dismissive of his contribution to Cat's change of heart. "No problem."

But Nyssa was stunned. Mag had shielded them. Saved their lives, even. And now he had convinced Cat to slow it down with LaChance. This went against all notions she had of him at their first encounter. The devilishly handsome rule-breaker who didn't seem to care beyond his nightlife was at heart a fierce and loyal protector.

Someone knocked on the door, interrupting their reunion.

"Come in." A touch of annoyance lined Mag's forehead.

"Oh, boss, sorry." One of Mag's bodyguards—the young one in the dark suit—poked his head into the office. "Ms. Vlahos's driver is here. He's worried about the kid."

"Mr. J!" Cat shouted to see Mr. Julien standing in the doorway in his heavy overcoat, his cap in his hands.

"Miss Catalina." The heavy lines at the corners of his eyes lightened with pleasure. "You're okay! I was really worried."

"Mr. Julien, please come in. I'm so sorry. I didn't think we would take that long."

Nyssa had him wait for her while she fetched Cat, feeling guilty to have raised the man at such a late hour when she had checked with him on the odd chance Cat had told him where she was going. The older gentleman, filled with fears, had insisted on driving to the tower and help with Nyssa's search.

"Cat, would you mind going with Mr. Julien and wait in the car?" She glanced at Mag. "I'll be right there."

Mr. Julian lifted Cat's backpack from the teen's hand. "Come on, miss. I'll show you some more card tricks. We can pump the music real loud while we wait."

"Oh, I got a really good song I want you to hear," Cat replied, her eyes bright with excitement. She'd forgotten all about how she had just run away from home.

"I'll just be a minute," Nyssa called as Cat and Mr. Julien left the room behind Mag's employee. She turned to Mag, not knowing what to say.

"You won't be long?" His gaze on her was impenetrable and she couldn't help but suddenly focus on the bottom curve of his inviting lips. She remembered how close his breath had been on the bare flesh of her neck at the ice rink.

"No." She gulped, the silence around them underscoring their intimacy.

"He's a vampire, by the way." His lips curled into that familiar jesting smile and she found herself weak at the knees.

"Who?" She steadied her stance as she looked up at him.

"Evan. My bodyguard who just left with Cat and your driver. A vampire. And so is my other bodyguard, Louka. And the bouncer, Raphael."

She blinked a few times, being reminded that he was so much more than a sexy club owner. "Oh."

"Yeah." His expression turned serious as he acknowledged how complicated this all was.

"Thanks."

"For what?" He tilted his head at her in confusion.

"For telling me."

"You should know it all," he insisted. His brows furrowed with determination, his well-defined jaw tense. "Everything about my life."

She nodded again and leaned into the outside back of the couch. "How much more is there to know?"

"Not much, I guess. My mom is a witch."

"Oh." She shot him a tentative smile while letting the news sink in. "Like a real one with magic?"

"Yes." He showed her the tattoo at the inside of his wrist. "She's kind of a legend. The *Sorcière des Glaces*—the Ice Witch. This is her mark."

"Ice Witch." She nodded to herself. "I heard the tale somewhere I think."

"It's real. She's my mom. In fact, she put a spell on you when you came to ask me to help with Cat."

"Wait, what?" Her tone raised a notch.

"I'm sorry. I was furious with her." He frowned as he

rubbed the back of his neck. "Her spell caused Sandrine and you to fall asleep for a moment."

"Whoa. Why on earth would she do that?" She took hold of herself, suddenly feeling faint.

"She can be a bit dramatic," he huffed. "She just wanted to talk to me in private, without humans seeing her. She totally violated my respect. It won't happen again, I promise."

She blinked again, trying to take it all in. "Magic. You have some too, right?" She replayed the attack in her head, trying to focus on the details.

"I do. Though I haven't used my own in a while. That's why I wear this leather cuff here." He shook his wrist covered by a thick black leather band adorned with silver. "It's enchanted. I used its power to fend off the daevas."

"Wow." She was overwhelmed by this knowledge. Supernatural beings existed. Legendary witches, vampires, and the like found in books and made into movies were real. And why not? She'd seen it with her own eyes.

"And my brother is married to a witch," he continued, undeterred by her overwhelmed sagging posture. "She's the high priestess of her coven in New England. Maisie. She's about your age. You'd like her."

"So all you St-Amand brothers are immortals?" Might as well get the whole story now.

"Yes." He fixed a dark insistent gaze upon her. "Nyssa, we were born this way. We don't prey on people."

"But you mentioned blood feeding."

He shrugged. "I do sometimes—did—feed on people. I like human blood. It tastes good. And it makes the person I'm feeding from feel euphoric when I do."

She ran through the few horror films she'd seen. "Like vampires."

"Sort of. But unlike a vamp, I can control it so it wouldn't kill the person I feed from."

"And how many....uh...how many people have you fed from?"

"Oh, I don't know. Over a thousand, more. I've been alive a long time."

"Oh god." She brought her fist to her mouth.

"I stopped a few months ago though."

"Why?" Despite the dreadfulness of it, she saw the man desperately trying to have her understand him.

"You."

"What?" She firmly gripped the back of the couch, each hand secure at her sides, and leaned forward toward him. Had she heard him right?

"I have not consumed the blood of anyone since I met you."

"You're serious." How could that be? She was in utter disbelief.

"Yes. It's a thrill. Something I did for fun, usually with the waitresses or one of my patrons. But I met you and somehow, I don't know..." He paced the floor as he spoke before standing right in front of her, a tortured expression on his features. "It felt like a cheap kick compared to how much I enjoyed bantering with you each time you came to convince me to sell the club."

She was speechless and could do nothing more than gawk at him, dazed by his confession.

He gently took hold of both her shoulders. "Nyss. Look, I have to come clean with you. I'm not a saint. I have hundreds of years of age on you. I have slept with many women. I have drunk their blood. And no, I don't have any diseases or anything like that. I seem to be immune to sickness. "

"I—" She started to say something, but he stopped her with a light finger in the air in front of her.

"I like you, Nyssa. A lot. And it's true, since you came to buy my club that week just before Christmas, I have not been able to get you out of my head. You're like no one I've met. I have not slept with, touched, or drank from a woman since I met you."

"Truly?" She shook her head, still unable to believe what he was saying.

"Yes. Everyone is so...bland. I don't know." A genuine smile brightened his gaze, lightening the shade usually so dark and deadly. "You're so accomplished. All these things you build."

"You hate my buildings."

"It's not my taste. But I admire the drive behind it. And how you care for your sister. You're so levelheaded through it all. And so kind." His touch was warm on the bare skin above her casual shirt. "I never thought I could fall for a human. A witch maybe. A fairy. Hells, even a female werewolf."

"Fairy, werewolf. Wait." She shook her head breezily with sudden acceptance of this whole new world. "They all exist, too?"

"Yes," he chuckled. "It's all real. Humans know this at the unconscious level. And in some cultures, non-humans are very much present. The modern world just seems to have forgotten."

"I had no idea." She let those notions sink in, blinking in that maybe, yes, it had been there all along, for those willing to see.

"Does it matter, though?" His voice was a deep purr as he stepped in closer, his hands now cupping her neck, his handsome face inches from hers. "Don't you feel it? This thing. Between you and me?"

She stood off the couch, falling into the intensity of his stormy irises, drawn under his incredible attractiveness. His masculine scent made her lightheaded and ready for more of his sexy aura.

She leaned closer and croaked, "I do."

His smiled turned wolfish and possessive. "Good because there is something I've been wanting to do for a long time."

And without warning, he slid his hand to the back of her head and crushed her lips with his own.

*Oh god.* Her knees buckled and she would have tumbled if not for his strong arm across her waist. She reached up for his neck and dug her fingertips into the mane of his hair. Her entire world disappeared as she succumbed to his hold and returned his kiss with equally matched hunger.

The relentless *thump-thumping* of the music from the club receded and she heard nothing but the small groan in his throat.

As their breaths mingled together, the rough stubble of his chin scratched against her skin. Such a contrast to the silky softness of his hair under the pads of her fingers.

She was shaky with sensation, with passion. His corded muscles pressed against her body, his arm steady at her waist. A lump of emotion blocked her throat as if she wanted to cry from the release of her powerful and still unnamed feelings, while her entire body was flooded with pent-up yearning.

She had wanted him for so long and here he was. In her embrace. Even more magnificent than she ever could imagine.

Heat pooled straight to her core as his lips left hers for a moment to settle at the little curve of her throat, right below her earlobe.

"*Mon amour*," he whispered against her skin, his palm sliding deliciously from her waist up to the middle of her shoulder blades.

Somehow, in the tangle of their passion, his desk was behind her and he stood, tough and steady before her, holding her tight. All she wanted in this moment was to have him take her right here and there in his office.

"Oh hell." He brushed her hair back to dig his fingers into her strands, his expression pure and raw longing.

"Mag." She couldn't help herself but be apprehensive of the lust taking over her. "Is this sensible?"

He drew back and shot her that smile that always drove her senseless. "I'll stop if you want to stop."

The deep frequency of his voice sent scorching heat straight through the center of her chest and she struggled to think.

What the heck. There were so many reasons why she shouldn't be doing this. So many *rational* reasons. She was drained, her sister waiting for her outside. And him, good grief, an immortal man she barely knew.

But that man, in her arms, was also the one reason why this was what she wanted most of all in this very moment.

"No," she replied in a heated moan. "I don't want to stop."

She pulled down his head towards her and pressed her mouth against his again. His lips were soft and welcoming, his breath enticingly warm. A warmth she had been searching for her entire life. It was like finally coming home.

He let out a powerful groan as he swept his arms under her to sit her fully on his desk.

Her knees parted to welcome his powerful thighs between hers. As he reached up to cup the back of her neck in a sturdy grip, she let her head fall into his hand.

Her touch had lowered down to his waist and she held him tight, her palm tracing the planes of his sinewy lower back under the t-shirt.

She wanted everything he had to offer her. Now. Tonight.

Dazed with pleasure, she wondered if he would want to pierce her throat with his fangs. She should be terrified, but she wasn't. She knew with absolute certainty that he would never do anything that she didn't want herself.

He was now fiddling with the buttons of her shirt. He had undone most of them when the door crashed wide open in a loud thump.

"Boss! The kid!" Evan stormed inside, supporting her driver slumped under his arm.

Her body temperature dropped to ice in horror at the sight of Mr. Julien's beaten body.

He looked barely alive. His face was swollen black and blue, one of his eyes completely shut. His suit was torn to shreds, his fists covered in blood.

She let go of Mag and toppled to her feet to race to the poor man.

"Cat?" The bottom of her world was slipping away as she looked back and forth from Mr. Julien to Evan.

"What happened?" Mag demanded.

"They took her," Mr. Julien managed to rasp before spitting out blood and sagging farther in Evan's grip. "They took Cat."

# CHAPTER 17

"*D*amn this!" Mag wrapped his arm around Nyssa's shoulders. Her whole body shook with panic. And he was in a right fury, adrenaline pumping through his veins.

The driver's face ballooned with swelling, his eyes glassy.

"Sit him down," he ordered Evan as he gathered his artifacts off the couch and onto another chair. "Get the first-aid kit behind the bar and bring back Sandrine."

Evan laid the driver onto the couch before rushing out for the waitress.

"He needs a doctor." Nyssa rushed to her employee. She knelt beside him and brushed the hair caked with blood from his face. "I'll need a cloth, something to clean his wounds. Can you talk, Mr. Julien?"

"Who took Cat?" Mag urged, the kid's fate the only thing on his mind. "Do you remember?"

The driver carefully raised his arm to press the bottom of his palm to his head. He squinted in pain but was able to nod.

"There were four of them." He stopped for a moment to catch his breath, a deep frown on his swollen brows. "One was someone Cat knew. She bolted out of the limo to meet him as soon as he tapped the window."

Nyssa flashed Mag a look so haunting it broke his heart.

He placed a comforting hand on her shoulder. "We'll find her." He tried his damnedest to sound calm while a brazier of wrath burned inside him.

Evan returned with Sandrine. The waitress gasped at the beaten man and kneeled beside Nyssa before opening the safety kit.

"I'm sorry, miss." Mr. Julien blanched as Sandrine cleaned his wounds with alcohol pads. "I got out of the car right after her. She called him Oliver, something like that."

"Shit!" Nyssa bolted straight up before Mag could react. "That fucking little bastard."

"The boyfriend is back." Mag planned to make good on the threat he'd given the son of a bitch at the diner. "But why attack Julien?"

"Well." Mr. Julien flinched with pain as he tried to prop himself up. "It seemed okay at first. I waited outside as Miss Catalina told him she would call him later. That she was coming back to your place at Vlahos Tower."

"He didn't like that." Mag surmised. His upper lip retracted at the thought of tearing the fucker's throat with his teeth.

"Worse. There was this strange man with him…" The driver took another shallow breath while Sandrine carefully placed a bandage just under his eye. "Unusually tall, weird hair, dressed in all leather. He was hanging in the background with his two cronies at first. But then he stepped forward and told Miss Catalina that it wouldn't do. That she had to come with them."

"A man?" Nyssa pressed.

"Yes. This Oliver called him a prince or something."

"Prince." Mag's throat closed in as his mind raced. "No, that couldn't be…"

"What?" Nyssa's trepidation was tangible. But Mag couldn't explain what he was thinking. Not yet. He needed to know more.

Mr. Julien rubbed his forehead again, his face now cleaned but still tumefied. He tried to push himself to his feet but was too weak, and he fell back on the couch with a gasp. "I swear I was on them, Miss Vlahos. I just couldn't let them take the kid."

"We should really take him to a hospital," Sandrine admonished, clipping the first-aid kit shut.

Mag agreed. The man had taken a pretty bad beating. He could have a concussion.

"It's not your fault, Mr. Julien." Nyssa was back down at his side, patting his back.

"They jumped me," he griped.

"Can you try to remember anything else," Mag asked. "Do you recall the name of this prince?"

"Let me think." Mr. Julien frowned as he accepted a glass of water from Sandrine. A deep line dug in his battered forehead. "Yes, I remember now. Prince Norwell."

"*Sacrament!*" Mag balled his fists tight in pent-up frustration at being so helpless in the moment.

"That's the one they mentioned in the alley." Nyssa's brows slowly drew together, her voice ethereally calm. "What would they want with Cat?"

"The young man mentioned some house he lives at," the driver continued as his memory returned. "That she had promised to go there with him. That's when Cat said no. The odd one, this prince, grabbed her and hoisted her over his shoulder. He's freakishly tall, miss. She fought like a tiger cub."

"Oh god." Nyssa closed her eyes for a second.

"I fought him too, Miss Vlahos, I swear. I didn't care how big that bastard was." Mr. Julien's distress was obvious. "But the others just pounced on me. I was down in a minute. Lucky the patrons came out to see what was happening. I was barely conscious when they ran away. I couldn't see the car they took her in. My vision was blurred."

"You're lucky to be alive. Really lucky." If these were daevas, they could have sucked him dry in minutes. "You must be pretty strong, sir."

"Did some wrestling back in the day." He shot Mag a sad smile. "Didn't help Miss Catalina any, though."

Mag patted his shoulder and turned to his employees. "Sandrine will get you to a hospital. Get him there safely, will you?"

"I'm so sorry, miss," he said to Nyssa. "We have to find her. I can help."

"You already did help." Nyssa stated quietly, her inner thoughts unreadable. "Just work at getting better, Mr. Julien. I'll call your family."

A mix of emotions could finally be seen through her features as she watched the man struggle to make his way out of the office with Sandrine and Evan's help.

She straightened her spine and her expression hardened.

"I'll find her," she said after Mag's employees closed the door behind them. With her shoulder set back and her lips thin, she took her cell phone out of her purse. "I'm calling the police."

"Not yet." He stopped her, a hand on her arm.

"Why not? The police will get them first. Arrest them." She shot him a hard look. "I think I know where they took her. She told me. LaChance was talking about this house in Laval. That's why we had a big fight today."

"But why would a daeva prince be involved with Cat and LaChance?"

"The attack in the alley." She lowered her phone. Tears began welling in her eyes as realization sank in. "Mag, these things, this monster that grabbed me, this prince is the same?"

"Worse." He hated having Nyssa and Cat mixed in with this supernatural vendetta, whatever it was.

She had come to him for help, but by accepting, he had pulled them both in his own dangerous world. The enemy saw his weakness—the sisters—and were using them against him. His desire to be closer to her was what had brought the horrific consequence. Dammit, it was all *his* fault. There *was* no world in which they could be together and where she and her sister could be safe.

"Oh god." She drew her hand to her mouth with a sob.

*Sacrament*, he had never seen her at such a loss.

"She's not dead. They wanted her over there." He took her wrists as he forced himself to repress his growing fury. "They won't hurt her."

She nodded as she caught his gaze.

"You're right. But oh god, when that thing attacked me, Mag. The pain was excruciating. I can't imagine. Cat with these monsters." She shook his grip off with urgency to scroll through the screen of her smart phone. "We *have* to call the police."

"No." He pressed his lips. "If this is supernatural, we can't."

"Why not." Her face was deep in concentration as she squinted at her device. "This is my sister's life."

He rummaged through the pile of artifacts still in a jumble in the club chair. He grabbed the Latvian mirror and discarded it right away before seizing some tarnished metal disks.

"What's all this?" She groaned in frustration. "Trinkets won't help."

"Maybe. I don't know. Look, calling the police won't help, either. Mr. Julien didn't even see the car they took Cat in."

"They could search Laval." Her lips were razor thin as she narrowed her eyes at him.

"So can we. I think..." he picked up a small milky marble, "this orb could help with a locator spell. We can't have the police involved in this. This is a supernatural matter."

"This is my sister." Her voice was deadly cold. "She's human."

"Nyssa," he tried to reason with her. "Daevas took your sister. How would the police be able to fend off the creatures? With guns and procedures? There wouldn't be much they could do up against these beings."

"What about the Moreno family?" She tilted her head to the side, her gaze alert but not quite looking at him. "They have the resources. And don't they know about supernaturals?"

He paused, his hand on the useless demon summoning goblet. Shit, he had zero option. He might have to ask his mom for help.

"Could you not call your friend Vincenzo? I know they're thugs but..." Nyssa wouldn't let it go.

He stopped sorting through the artifacts to really look at her. He took in her gritty tenacious face and his shoulders dropped. It *was* all his fault.

"*I* will find her."

"Mag, the police," she pleaded. "We have to."

"Fine." He relented and reached for his own phone. "I'll call Captain Akande directly. She knows what I am. And she's provincial police. Maybe she can ask the Laval precinct, see if there is anything unusual going on. Pinpoint a location."

"Yes." Some ease lightened her high-strung voice. "That would work. Then we can go look ourselves. Maybe with all those vampires you have here."

"I need to call on mom." A heaviness settled at the center of his chest to realize that he had no choice but ask for help.

"Your mother?"

"Yep," he grumbled. "Like I told you, she's a witch."

"She could find Cat?" Hope laced her question.

"Yes. She might be able to," he acknowledged reluctantly. "I just have to convince her to help. She's not big on assisting humans."

"Boss." The door opened wide to Evan, his vampiric face unusually pallid. "There's someone here to see you. Calls himself Prince Norwell of the Daeva Realm."

*No.* Mag hadn't heard that right. Halfway through dialing Amelia Akande, he stopped and slowly pocketed his phone.

"Prince Norwell." He raked his hair back to stare at Evan with disbelief. "Here?"

"Sounds like it. Scary-looking dude." Evan looked to Mag for guidance. "Not good for business."

"Well, fuck me." Mag glanced at Nyssa, and clenching his fists, he slowly leaned back against his desk.

He let his wrath flood his entire being. His lips curled back over his fangs to bring the predator that always sat at the shadow of his consciousness.

So Norwell wanted to meet with him on his turf, his home, surrounded by his people. This ought to be good.

Now he'd find out just what the hell had this prince riled. What Mag had done to offend him. And where Cat was taken.

He smirked at Evan. "Bring him in, then!"

# CHAPTER 18

*P*rince Norwell strode into Mag's office with his head high, his poise supremely confident.

Nyssa shivered as his eyes—of a pale vivid green that bordered on yellow—surveyed the room. There was no warmth to them, no hint of compassion, no humanity.

He was tall, barely fitting into the doorframe, his build slimmer than Mag's. His sleek straight hair was shoulder length and silver. Not gray but a shimmering metallic hue that didn't exist naturally nor could have possibly been done at an upscale salon. He wore black leather motor-cycle pants and a jacket over a black shirt of a silky mate-rial she couldn't identify. His entire aura was something so dark, it seemed to absorb the light around him, like a black hole leaving nothing but destruction in its path.

The stranger barely glanced at her as he strutted into the middle of the room in front of Mag. She always consid-ered Mag to be huge, but the prince towered over him.

"St-Amand."

"Where's your crown, Norwell?" Mag smirked, his

shoulders loose, his stance steady. "Not looking very princely, if you ask me."

Prince Norwell stared at him for a second, then a wide cold smile stretched his lips. "I leave the royal trappings to my sister."

"Merritt."

"Princess Merritt to you, worm." He inflated his chest out wider, his brows rose lazily.

"You're not in your kingdom, Norwell. We don't bow to your kind here." Mag shot Nyssa a reassuring glance before sneering again at the daeva prince.

"No. You don't. So egalitarian," Prince Norwell huffed, followed with an ugly twist of his mouth. "Maybe why I like it here. These humans, so much hope. It's amusing."

"Leave humans alone." Mag stepped closer, a low growl now emanating from deep inside him.

The manner in which the prince stared down at Mag drew unidentified repulsion from deep inside Nyssa. Despite his absolute beauty, the frostiness he emanated made her skin crawl. His nauseating scent of cologne was too heavy, his voice edged with a shrill that rattled in her ear. There was something parasitic about his whole being.

As if he needed everyone to revolve solely around him.

Nyssa shunned her revulsion for Cat's sake and positioned herself right under the prince's nose.

"Where's my sister," she barked.

"Ah. Your little woman," he said of Nyssa with an unpleasant drawl.

The way he mentioned her, as if she were no more than a nuisance, raised her blood to a boil. She would not be dismissed. "What did you do with her? We're calling the police."

"Oh, so much drama for such a little thing. My friend

LaChance knows how to find the juicy ones, doesn't he?" The prince seemed to enjoy her distress and suddenly burst into laughter. "You'd do very well, too. A little old for my patrons' taste but I, personally, appreciate a little… experience."

Unable to control her fury, she took one more step right into his face, her nostrils flaring.

"Nyssa." Mag raised his hand out to stop her.

Mad as hell, she knew the daeva was dangerous, but couldn't help herself.

"Return my sister," she growled.

Prince Norwell cut short his hilarity. "Oh, be quiet, human." Before she could respond, he tapped a finger at her forehead.

She screamed. Searing pain seized her from the inside out. Clenching agony radiated from her skull and down to every nerve ending.

"*Sacrament!*" Mag grabbed her from behind to pull her back from the prince.

The piercing torture receded to leave her with a dull pain that charred her bones.

She moaned in torment as the prince grinned, his greenish eyes sparkling with conceited joy.

Barely able to stand on her two feet, she leaned back against Mag.

"You son of a bitch!" Mag roared.

"Now, now, St-Amand. Not that vampire look. You should know better," the prince snorted, his nose now wrinkling with distaste. "Have you never encountered a peer of the Daemon Realm? You can't compel royalty."

Still shaky, Nyssa looked up at the monster who didn't even glance in her direction as he paraded around the office.

"By *Ell'zoth*, this is a bit shabby but will do quite well." He circled around Mag's desk with a swagger and rocked the office chair. He shoved Mag's papers aside to clear the desk as if he were moving in.

"What did you do to my girlfriend?" Mag's arms quaked with fury as he nestled her farther into his embrace.

Any other time, his words would have warmed Nyssa's heart, but she was lost in the torment of it all. This beast who held her sister captive had reduced her to a pawn with a mere touch. And she thought Lucinda was bad. She had not been prepared for such horror.

"Oh, it's nothing serious." The prince waved his hand facetiously. "One of my sister's tricks. That's how we tame them all. "

"Them who?" Mag growled.

"The girls, the boys."

"What do you actually want from us, Norwell." Mag was seething. "Why did you take Cat? And what the hell are you doing here?"

"Well, the kid is just one of many." Prince Norwell made himself comfortable in Mag's office chair and swiveled it back and forth, a small frown on his pale brows. He turned to adjust the setting. "This office is pretty grungy. Will have to change that. It's not swanky enough to make Merritt jealous."

"Get out of my fucking chair!" His words enraged Mag further.

"Why? This will all be mine soon." Prince Norwell spread his arms wide, a satisfied smile on his lifeless features. "Nice place. The *Serpent*? You own it, right?"

He opened a drawer at his side, closed it before bending forward over Mag's desk. With his elbows upon the blotter, he threaded his fingers together and rested his chin on his knuckles.

"Must I explain *everything*?" he grumbled with a roll of his eyes.

The blood had returned to Nyssa's limbs and she found her footing again. "Where is Cat?" she demanded through clamped teeth.

"Didn't have enough, human?" His brows rose in amusement and he turned to Mag with a chuckle. "She's quite tough, that one. I may have caught the wrong female."

"We want Catalina back." Mag's tone was icy cold, the lethal undercurrent unmistakable.

"Well, see here," Prince Norwell shot them a smug look, the playfulness gone from his eyes, "that is exactly why I'm here."

Nyssa glanced behind her and jolted to see Mag's features drawn back with pure hatred, his fangs out, his irises bottomless pits of darkness.

"Oh fine, Immortal." Prince Norwell bristled under Mag's gaze. "I suppose it will make more sense if I let you in on my plan. I am quite the business entrepreneur, you see."

"Go on," Mag spat, his hands eerily steady on Nyssa's shoulders.

"I'm like you, St-Amand. But I deal in, what do you call it… forbidden pleasures. That's why I need the young people. Children like this Cat girl that LaChance was grooming for me. You know, I actually do love that part. Takes a while to break them, sometimes I even watch." His lewd expression bore into Nyssa, while she silently raged at his implications. "The rapper is just one of my many suppliers."

"You deal in sex trafficking." Bile mounted in the back of Nyssa's throat. "You're just a pimp."

"Humans should do better than talk," he warned her.

His boastful look switched to one so evil—the irises taking on a full yellow hue—that she quaked. She reached back for Mag's hands in a panic. Her little Cat was in the clutches of this arrogant monster. She trembled at the thought of what he had planned for the teen.

"I have this compound in Laval just on the outskirts of the city," Prince Norwell continued. "Nice and quiet. Serves a large variety of very—shall we say—demanding clientele, humans and daevas alike." He slid his palms at the edge of the desk in an unhurried propriety motion. His expression took a distracted turn. "You know, there is beauty in seeing these young people's spirit slowly leave them with each encounter. Human dreams squashed, willpower gone as they gradually shut down, turned into mere things to be used. Anyway, the rapper was preparing me your random kid, and that's when you got involved, St-Amand. You threatened my employee."

"The diner in the East Side," Nyssa gasped.

Mag was still silent.

"You made one mistake, Immortal," the prince snapped, narrowing enraged eyes at Mag. "You showed LaChance your true nature. He saw your fangs. I had no idea immortals lived here, but now I know. You insulted me, Magnovald St-Amand. Interfered with my business. This will be my city. My lair. My patrons. And you will pay for daring coming between me and what's mine."

"Your daevas were easily defeated." Mag's voice was so low, it resonated ominously against Nyssa's ribcage.

"So was she." Prince Norwell pointed at her and she shuddered inwardly.

"You can't kill me," he continued to brag. "You know that. And if you don't give me what I want, I will come after the humans in your life. Her, your staff. I'll take out your patrons, one by one."

Mag gave Nyssa's hand a squeeze and let go. He strode forward to stand at his desk across from the prince and planted his palms flat upon each side of the antique, his imposing frame towering over the daeva.

"You won't," he stated under a growl. "There is more than just me you have to worry about in this city."

"Your brother Renaud, I know. I've done my research." The prince dismissed the threat with a wave of his hand. "But what, two Immortals? I've little concern. My compound is well guarded. More and more daevas have been hiding in the city, crossing over to this world. They prefer my more easygoing ways over my sister's iron fist."

Nyssa's mind raced, uncertain about what any of this meant to the humans of Montreal. As if reading her thoughts, he expounded further.

"I don't want to hurt people of this city. No, not at all. I am not a dictator. I love it here. And the people will love me. I have so many delights to offer them." The prince shot Nyssa an almost pleasant smile that made her gag. "But I'm growing tired of the Laval compound. It's quite bland. And I deserve so much better."

"So you see, St-Amand," he continued, as Mag remained simmering in silence, the immortal containing his hatred behind a stony facade. "Your interference was in fact a blessing. I have something you want, and you have something I want. A simple deal. Makes good business."

"What is it that you want?" Nyssa was fed up with all the posturing. She needed to pinpoint how on earth she would save her sister from this sadistic monster.

"See, she gets it. She wants her sister, she's ready to deal." He chuckled with contempt, not even bothering to look at her. "Don't you, little human?"

She didn't reply. Her worry for Cat pressed upon her, various horrific possibilities making her nauseous and restless. What if LaChance was abusing her sister right this minute? With monsters like Norwell watching!

She bit the inside of her mouth hard. Her fists tightened with the urgent need for action.

"It's very simple, St-Amand. *This* is what I want." Prince Norwell leaned back in Mag's chair and stretched out his limbs. His gaze swept across the office. "This club."

Nyssa shot Mag a look of panic. With her knees weak, she fell back into an armchair while she gaped at the daeva prince. Mag would never give up the home he built and nurtured throughout the centuries.

"It's really that easy. I bring you your little girl. And you give me this." The prince clasped his hands behind his neck and sized Mag up with a complacent grin. "The *Serpent Maudit.*"

CHAPTER 19

*N*o. *Fuck, no!* Mag reeled with torment at the choice before him. Then rage washed it all away.

"Fucking bastard," he bellowed at Norwell. This pretentious twat would not steal what had taken sweat and grit to build. "Get the hell out!"

"You have until tomorrow." A smirk stretched the prince's features. He wetted his lips with a leer at Nyssa as he strode out of the room as if he already owned it. "I'll leave the girl untouched until then."

"*Sacrament!*" Mag smashed his fist through the wall. The plaster caved in and his old portrait fell to the ground upon the rebound. "Fuck!"

His body shaking, he caught Nyssa's blank expression. She sat completely still in the armchair. Her knuckles white, her lips thin.

His heart shattered at her pain. With a slow breath, he leaned back against his desk. "I'm sorry, Nyss."

And he wasn't sure if he was apologizing for his

outburst or for seeing her trapped in this impossible dilemma.

"Oh what the hell." Without thought, he slammed his hand on the inside of his wrist, right over his mother's mark. "*Koir idash!*"

"What are you doing?" Nyssa's voice came out small, but her face had now taken a determination that wasn't there a second ago. She stood and rubbed her palms on her yoga pants. As she paced the office, her initial stillness had been replaced by a fretful stride.

"*Koir idash, Sorcière des Glaces,*" he intoned again. A pool of mist coalesced at their feet. "I'm calling my mother."

"Oh." Nyssa stopped marching and swiveled to face him.

"She's been wanting to help me," he rushed through his teeth. "This is it."

"How can she beat this thing when he overtook me with just a touch?" Nyssa was all business, her brows tense with focus. "Is a witch strong enough against something like that? I think we should still go to the authorities, Mag. We can find the compound and attempt a rescue of Cat and the other kids."

"Mom will find it," he spat. "Hells, she can probably obliterate this two-bit prince with one word."

He wasn't certain that his mom had that kind of power but goddamn, she could find the fucker and Mag would deal with him.

"Cat's probably in there, we can't just blast the whole place." Nyssa's features were pinched tight. "She could get hurt."

His mad tension eased as he looked at her. He crossed the distance between them to hold her by the shoulders.

"We will get Cat back, I promise. I will give up my club if I have to."

"You would?" Stunned, she went completely motionless. Her eyes took a dull sheen.

"Of course, sweetheart. No question there." His tone firm, he shot her a look meant to reassure her. "Nothing is worth more than Cat's life right now. Which is why I'm calling on my mother. I'm not letting anything to chance. You saw how twisted Norwell is, he'll likely not give Cat back."

She nodded and again his emotions for her soared. He hated having to call on his mom, but he would, for Nyssa. And the child.

"*Koir idash.*" He let go of her and intoned the words once more with a flick of his hand.

The small pool of twirling mist at his feet slowly solidified in a mass of dark indigo fog. As the form of his mother slowly rose from the floor, her black velvet dress took shape before her mass of dark curls appeared. Soon soulful brown eyes, so much like his own, were fixated upon him with quiet questioning.

He heard Nyssa's gasp being quickly repressed as her eyes widened in surprise at the apparition. He stepped to her side and slid an arm around her waist.

"It will be fine. Mom will help," he reassured her. Or at least he hoped his mother would. He never knew with Mom, but she did owe him for what she did to Nyssa.

"Magnovald, *mon pitou*." Mom stepped towards him with her arms wide before stopping herself. Her hands dropped to her sides. "Oh, it's her."

"Mom, this is Nyssa Vlahos." He kept his tone as steady as he could manage. "Nyssa, this is my mother, Charlotte Callan."

Nyssa blinked a hint of annoyance before her cool persona returned.

"The one who put a spell on me," she said, her voice measured.

Mag's mother leveled with Nyssa. "You are trying to take over my son's life's work."

"Not anymore." Nyssa said carefully.

"Mom. Nyssa. Please, we need her magic," he told them, realizing that both women were strong-willed. He hoped having them together was not going to be a mistake.

The businesswoman straightened but she didn't add any more.

"You need my help. Finally. Please do tell, *mon p'tit,*" his mother fussed with excitement. "Your mom is always here for you."

"You haven't been, but never mind," he grumbled. A conflicted set of emotions ran through him. He had to ask her. This wasn't about him but about Cat.

The gullible girl's image ran through him and his stomach churned at the thought of her naivety in the clutches of the pompous prince.

"What do you know about Prince Norwell of the Daeva Realm?"

"Norwell? Morgious' little brother?"

"Morgious?" Mag frowned with confusion.

"The former king of the Daeva Realm," his mother explained. She strolled to his wet bar and served herself a drink. "They don't have a king anymore since the warlocks killed him. Their king now is Malcolm Dunsmuir. He rules over Hell's Gate. Daemons and daevas and all the other nasties. Princess Merritt oversees the daevas. Malcolm let her keep her title."

"And she's Norwell's sister."

"*Oui*. Older sister. He's the runt."

"A narcistic runt clearly jealous of his sibling," Mag sneered. "So, what do you know of him?"

"Little Norwell? Oh I've only encountered his dad when I was younger, visiting Malcolm's mom—Flora is ancient, and of my tradition, you know. The prince is just a kid. Spoiled little brat. Why do you ask?"

"Because the prince is here, in Montreal. Definitely grown up. And he wants my club."

"What?" His mom blinked with surprise.

"What would he be doing in our world, *Maman?*"

She shrugged and took seat at the edge of the couch, her expression filled with concern. "Oh, I don't know. Merritt can be difficult, I heard. Maybe he finds life here a little easier. I truly have no idea, *mon fils*. That's daemon business."

"Right, you're more at ease with hell's business I suppose." He sneered his frustration. "Haven't you turned to voodoo magic now? Isn't that why you left? To seek new powers?"

Despite the dire threat surrounding him, he just couldn't let go of her abandonment. The hurt still lingered deep within him.

"What are you talking about?" she declared. "I'm still very much steeped in my Callan tradition. But I respect all my New Orleans' sisters. Voodoo yes, and Acadian magic, like Maisie Thibodeau's coven. They have nothing to do with hell."

"Whatever." He didn't know why he had brought up the subject. He was still trying to accept her reasons for leaving her sons. "I need your help in kicking this prince out of Montreal."

"I see." She frowned and his heart fell.

What had he expected? *Sure, Magnovald, let's go slam that bastard's ass.*

"He has Nyssa's sister," Mag added, hoping to jolt her sympathy.

"*Her* sister." Mom shot Nyssa a flippant look.

He heard Nyssa take a deep breath, but she remained motionless, standing straight beside him.

"She's only thirteen," Mag continued to plead. "Norwell wants to sell her to service a bunch of creepy twisted bastards. *Sexually* service them. Some are daevas, Mom. Others, devious humans who prey on children. A mere kid. Sold to depraved clients."

"I see." His mother nodded to herself. "This little sister, she's human? Like *her*?"

"Nyssa, mom. Her name is Nyssa." His anger was rising fast. But he had to contain it to save Cat. He didn't want to take on the daeva compound alone. Even with Justin and Ren and maybe Emme and a few disciples with their ceremonial magic, he wasn't sure they could overpower a nest of daevas.

No. Mom was the better solution. He had witnessed his brother's wife—the High Priestess of the powerful White Holly Coven—obliterate a pack of wraiths and mothbeasts the year before. He was very much aware of what a witch could do. And Mom was the most powerful of all witches, apparently.

"Catalina is human," he said. "Just like Nyssa."

"No powers at all? Banshee?" his mom pressed. "Psychic perhaps, an empath even?"

"No." His fingers curled with contempt. It was obvious that his mom would prefer to help someone with even a smidge of supernatural blood over a powerful human. But he was done playing nice. "I'm asking for your help, Mom. Don't you owe me?"

She tilted her head to the side, with a quizzing look on her face. "Owe you?"

"For leaving me behind," he fumed. "Just like that."

"Like I told you at dinner the other night, Magnovald, you never made an attempt to contact me." She crossed her arms, somewhat miffed. "And now, you actually need me, so you call upon me. Summon me even, like a creature at your beck and call."

"It was faster," he muttered, shoving down newfound guilt at his complicity for their estrangement. "Mom, I'm worried about the child."

Nyssa bristled imperceptibly under his arm at the mention of Cat.

"Oh, son," his mother replied, the corner of her eyes mollifying. "You've always been a softie when it comes to protecting children. I see so much of Antoine in you."

Her voice was kind as she added with a slow shake of her head, "He was not your natural father, but he raised you to be just like him."

"Mom, this is not the time to bring up *Papa*." Nor was it time to rehash his grief over his father's death. He missed the man, sure... "He's been gone for three hundred years."

"And yet," she placed a hand over her heart, "he's with me every day I walk this earth."

"*Maman*," Mag urged. "Will you help me or not?"

She let out a measured breath. "I can't."

"What do you mean, you can't?" Distress seized the back of his neck.

His mother unfolded herself from the couch and suddenly it was as if she took the whole room, her presence so large that Nyssa unconsciously pressed herself against Mag.

He knew his mother was much more than the small dark-haired woman who had given birth to him. He rarely saw the other side of her but at the moment—taking in her limbs crackling with power under the shimmering black dress, the pentacle at her throat humming with unnatural energy, and the smoldering look she was casting upon him—he was facing the Ice Witch.

And the Ice Witch stared at Mag with the entire weight of her ageless power shadowing his office.

"I have been in this form for a long time," she stated. "But you know my true soul is much older. From the original witches of the Celtic Island, of the Callan Clan. We are forbidden to interfere with human business unless they are magically bound to us. Had the kid been a witch, like Valerian's wife, or even simply an empath, perhaps I could have helped. But to go against a prince of the Daeva Realm, of the Gates of Hells, for a human—*that* I cannot do. My deities would punish me dearly for trying."

"Can you not find some ways?" His voice was strained as he pleaded with her. "Help me. Something that could circumvent your laws."

She let out a restrained breath and her expression on him eased. "As soon as this prince shows up with his minions to storm your club, I will be right here. I'll obliterate them and send him home. But not until he does."

"They attacked me already, Mom."

"And you killed them easily. Didn't you, son?"

"Yes, but—"

"No buts." She shook her head. "You don't need me."

"You don't care about us, do you?" Nyssa suddenly spoke, her tone frigid.

"About you and your sister?" Mag's mother sounded detached as she answered. "No. Not really."

"Well, I personally don't give a damn that you're a witch older than dirt," Nyssa countered through her teeth. "You're just one cold bitch."

"Magnovald, *mon fils*." His mom turned a shocked look at him. "You're going to let her talk to me like this?"

"Actually, Mom, she's right." He held tight onto Nyssa, half glad to see her tell his mom off and half worried of what the witch could do to her.

"Listen, *ma p'tite*." Mom stepped toward Nyssa and Mag realized that his mother was a good foot shorter than the real estate tycoon. "You're just a puny human. And you'll die soon, like all of them."

"So what if I die." Nyssa's eyes were sparkling with anger. "At least I will have died knowing I did the right thing by my sister, my family. If I get this correctly, you refused to see your son for centuries. You, a mother! And when he needs help, you turn him down. That's the most selfish thing I know."

"You know nothing, *fille*." Mom was right in Nyssa's face and he felt the air hiss with electricity. "You think it's all good fun, you and Mag. In love with an immortal. What will happen when you get old. When your pretty face turns gnarly and he no longer looks at you like the fresh young thing you once were?"

"Mom. Stop." Mag put his body right between them with wariness.

"No, Magnovald, listen to me. It *will* happen." His mom wouldn't let it go. She was pointing her finger up and down with vigor to emphasize each of her words. "Nyssa will be an old woman, and you, you will still be you. With pretty women wanting to bed you while you turn them down to go home to a dying crone."

"I've seen it with Justin. How unfair it was to Marie-Louise. It was heartbreaking for him to see her wither away with age until her death." She stepped back and eyed them both, one after the other. "Your relationship is doomed, and I am not about to help you get there faster by interfering."

"This has nothing to do with you!" Fuming, Nyssa looked at his mother then at him. "It's not about either of you. Fuck, it's not even about me!"

Filled with anger, her eyes welled for the first time since his mother had materialized in the room. Nyssa's ice queen poise was long gone.

"This is about *my* little sister," she raged. "This is about a kid who has never known a mother's love and whose life is now in the hands of the most horrible thing I have ever seen." Her face was red, the pain dug deep into her features.

"Nyssa," Mag coaxed, sliding his hands along her arm in an attempt to comfort her.

"And you both..." Ignoring him, she shook her fist in front of her with fury. "You're bickering about things that has nothing to do with my sister. If you can't help, fine!"

"Nyssa," he said again softly, trying to calm her.

But she no longer heard him. She stood there, her eyes like slits, her nostrils flaring.

"The hell with you all!" She broke his embrace and raced to the door before he had a chance to catch her. "I'm going to save Cat myself."

# CHAPTER 20

*W*ith her fury subdued back into place, Nyssa closed her fists tight before releasing them with control. There was only one person she could think of who could help her now.

She had first told the cab driver to go to the police station. But as she reviewed what she had to tell them, she realized that they would never believe her. She could report the kidnapping but after Cat's earlier running away, it likely wouldn't be a priority for the authorities.

Which is why she found herself pent-up with adrenaline and, despite the late hour, walking up to the guarded gates of the Moreno family estate. A quick text to her ever-efficient assistant had produced the address. Nyssa made a mental note to send a bonus to the associate that was on the ready for her, night and day.

"I'd like to talk to Señora Moreno," she told the guard on the other side of the iron gate.

The man in the winter black blouson stretching over his paunch belly flashed his big flashlight at her.

"At this hour?" He frowned as he looked her up and

down. In her exercise pants and slim snow parka, her hair in disarray, she knew she didn't inspire confidence. "She knows you're here?"

"No. But she knows me." Nyssa cleared her throat hoping she could bluff the middle-aged guard. The matriarch *had* recognized Nyssa's name at the cemetery.

He smirked with an unconvinced expression under his black ball cap. "The old lady won't be seeing anyone in the middle of the night."

"Can you ask, please?" Nyssa shifted her weight back and forth in her furry boots. "It's important. It's about my little sister. She's in danger."

His expression softened a little. "Name?"

"Vlahos. Nyssa Vlahos."

He clicked his two-way radio. "Hey, Sandro, can you check in with Vince? There's a woman here who wants to see the boss. Says it's urgent. Nyssa Vlahos."

A crackle of static and muffled voice replied.

"Just go see if Vince is up," the guard answered.

They both waited a few minutes, the old guard staring at her while she tried to calm her hammering heart by rubbing her hands on her thighs to stay warm.

The radio came back to life. "He's coming to you."

"Your lucky night." The guard raised an incredulous brow and shrugged. "Looks like Vincenzo will see you."

"He knows me."

"He does, uh?" The guard placid expression returned, and he opened the heavy gate to let her in. "Well, he's coming down to get you."

She wrapped her arms around herself as she waited for the veteran bodyguard to come down to the stone steps. She prayed that Vince wouldn't kick her out. Now that her nervous energy had waned, the reasonable side of her took over. Maybe she *should* have gone to the police.

But she knew Vince was aware of Mag's immortality and the vampires at the club. It wouldn't be a stretch for him to believe in the daeva prince.

She wondered if he knew about Mag's mother—the French bitch.

Nyssa hadn't felt that powerless around a woman since she'd stood in her bedroom at Doukas House, lovingly decorated by her mother in shades of pinks and creams, while Lucinda had announced that she was being sent off to boarding school in Switzerland. She had lost her family and her home, all at once.

When Dad had married the brittle social climber, Nyssa had trusted that Lucinda would take care of her. She hadn't been prepared for the cruelty. But the tramp was not of her own flesh and blood.

This Charlotte Callan was Mag's *birth mother*. How harsh to refuse to help. Just as Lucinda had failed Cat, Mag's mom didn't care.

Well, Nyssa would never be that heartless person for her sister. She would not fail Cat. Not as long as she lived.

She bit her lip. Maybe she should have contacted Mag after storming out. It wasn't his fault his mom was a cow. But what would he do now? Offer his club? No, she *couldn't* do that to him.

With their muscle and manpower, the Morenos were the solution. She didn't have the time to wait for Mag while he bickered with his mother. The elder Moreno was fond of kids, and against trading them for sex. Nyssa had seen the empathy when the woman had told her to find her sister. She understood the family bond.

And Nyssa had one big bargaining chip. Money.

They were mob. And she would hire them.

She'd always prided herself in walking a straight line in her affairs. But this was different. Her spine uncurled, a plan forming in her mind.

"Miss Vlahos." Vince had reached the gates and, wrapped in his heavy navy overcoat, he stared down at her.

"You know her, chief?" the security guard asked.

"Friend of St-Amand."

"Oh," the guard's tone eased. "You should have said, miss."

She shrugged under her thin parka. "I didn't think you would know the name."

"He's been around a few times." Vince's smile was broad as he motioned to her up the narrow path. "Why on earth would you want to see the old lady at this ungodly hour?"

"It's my sister," she explained.

"Again? I thought you'd found her." He punched a security code by the regal entrance double doors. "Mag said it was all sorted. Cute kid, he told me."

She stepped into the huge foyer as he held the door for her. As if to indicate that the Señora was in deep mourning, candles were lit everywhere, their glow flickering on the gilded touches found all over the estate, from the plaster ceiling to the curved banister leading above and the many statues of various saints and angels.

Nyssa let out a pained breath. "Cat's been kidnapped."

"How?" Vince shock was genuine.

"This LaChance works for someone a lot worse than simple Montreal thugs." She pressed her lips together at the severity of her situation.

"Does he, now?" Vince showed her into what looked

like his office. "That fucking little weasel. He's been recruiting teens all over town."

He invited her to sit down before taking seat across her behind the serviceable desk. She looked around the simply furnished room. A few snapshots of military men in arms and official looking pictures dotted the bookshelf behind him but nothing betraying his biker past.

"How much do you actually know about Mag's..." she cleared her throat, "condition."

"Oh that." A twinkle lit the corner of his eye.

"Yes."

"He finally told you."

"You know about his family? The vampires in the club?"

"I do." He offered her a sympathetic nod. "And lot more than just the club. His brothers. His witch sister-in-law in New England. And that hot little vampire friend of his, Emmeline."

"Emmeline?" The name caught her by surprise. Mag had never mentioned he had a female vampire in his life. A strange ache caught her throat. Was she jealous? She shook herself inwardly. This was not the time. She had to rescue Cat.

"There's this compound in Laval," she said. "Some kind of whorehouse. LaChance is tasked to recruit young people and bring them there. If I'm correct, he lures them by grooming them first. You know, pretend to be their boyfriend, then pushing for more."

"Yeah." Vince winced. "I know the pattern."

"LaChance met Cat at a club he played. She'd snuck out of the house. He flirted with her, bought her trinkets, pretended she was special. He took the phone my dad bought her so we couldn't trace her. She ran away to him on her own volition. No one was really watching her, so she was an easy target."

"I'm sorry." His brows drew together, his tone grim. "But that's how a lot of the youth sex trafficking here operate. Usually they sell the girls out to Toronto or in the US. Families never find them. Some don't care to."

"Looks like Oliver LaChance is one of many recruiters for a kingpin named Prince Norwell," Nyssa informed him.

"Prince?"

"Yes, and not some exiled East European royalty. No. A creature from another world." She was trembling with repressed anger at remembering how easily he had hurt her. "Had Mag ever mentioned anything like that to you?"

"He *did* allude to other mystical creatures." Vince clasped his hands together over his desk. "Shifter types in Domaine-Lassalle where his brother Ren lives. Things out of fairytales, you know. The legendary *loup-garous*, as we call them here. Also real live witches."

"Like his mother."

"Oh yeah, he may have mentioned her. They don't get along."

"Well, whatever. The thing is, Cat has been kidnapped and is trapped at the compound." Nyssa leaned in forward over his desk and shot him an imposing look. "This prince has an army of soul-sucking creatures guarding the place and I want to hire you to help me get her out."

"Me?"

"Well, you and whatever men you can recruit." Her jaw was set with purpose.

He sat back with a careful expression. "I see."

"What, you never do this sort of thing for others outside the family?" She tilted her head with a frown.

218

He didn't answer right away and studied her, an inscrutable expression set on his rugged features.

"Señora Moreno is very fond of you," he finally mused with a somber twist of the mouth. "So that goes in your favor."

"Doesn't she hate child trafficking?"

"That she does." He nodded with a slight rise of his brow. "But what about Mag? Why isn't he here with you?"

"Family problems. His mom is in town."

"Oh."

"Yes," she said carefully. "And she doesn't want to help humans."

"Doesn't she, now?" The half-smile returned as if her words had brought some amusing thought about Mag and his mother.

"Look, I have to come clear." Nyssa lifted a bold chin at him. "This prince gave Mag an ultimatum. He will return Cat if Mag gives him the club."

"The *Serpent*."

"Yes."

"Shit. So you *do* want to go behind his back."

"We can't tell Mag. He's too caught up in this," she warned. With his club and all, she just couldn't risk his mom convincing him that Cat didn't matter. That she, Nyssa a human, also didn't matter.

And the witch was right. Humans died, grew old if they were lucky. She'd be no different. She would only be temporary in his world. She couldn't blame him if he chose his constant—the *Serpent*—over her. But she sure as hell didn't want to make him choose. The inevitable heartbreak would destroy her.

She eyed Vince hard. "I would pay you handsomely."

"I don't doubt it." He held her gaze and she felt the

strength behind the man. He must have been a formidable soldier. And as the late Moreno's right man, he would be able to lead a rescue mission to get Cat. Once they had her, she would hide the teen at the family cottage outside of town. This Norwell would have to find himself another bargaining chip.

"You have to help," she insisted.

"I suppose we could. It's been a bit quiet here lately. The guys need some action." His capable hands formed a steeple as he twirled his thumbs together while chewing over the idea. "And Laval is under our jurisdiction, so to speak. They scooped in and opened their whorehouse while Ennio was on his deathbed. Fuckin' snakes! Can't let them get away with it. It makes the old lady look weak."

"They're stealing kids," Nyssa pressed.

"Right." He groaned and placed his palms flat on his desk while staring at her. "Okay, fine. I guess things got slack since the old man became sick. God bless his soul."

"You're going to help me?" A trickle of hope grew at her chest.

"Yep."

"You won't tell Mag."

"For now," he said, his large body absolutely still.

"Thank you."

"It's not like me to hide things from him. I consider him a friend." His expression eased. "If he brought you to us in the first place, he cares about you."

"But I'm human, he's not."

"He's flesh and blood, just like you and I," he insisted, showing his loyalty to the immortal she cared so much for. "Shouldn't matter."

"No. It shouldn't." Her stomach tensed with the guilt at going behind his back.

"I can have my men ready in about an hour." He stood and glanced out the window, where the night still shaded the city with a cover of darkness. "Get this done before dawn makes us visible to the neighbors. We'll need you to come with us to identify your sister. Can you do that?"

"Yes." She shot him a curt nod, relieved at Vince's plans and ready for anything.

"You can wait in the señora's small parlor while I get us ready. Maybe catch some rest." His gaze weighed heavily on her and she sensed his respect. "We can protect you. But this will be risky."

"I know."

"Monsters you said…" A corner of his mouth curled upward.

"Yes."

He shot her a full smile. "That should be fun."

# CHAPTER 21

"What's up?" Emme walked into Mag's office as he was searching through the jumbled pile of the artifacts dumped on the club chair. "I just saw your mom storm out. She looks mad as hell."

He grunted back at the vampire and continued to dig through the stone and metal objects. If he could just find something, anything, powerful enough to go after that asshole Norwell...

"The bitch. She can *go* to hell for all I care." He picked the summoning goblet before laying a shrewd eye over his collection. His gaze settled on the Latvian mirror Cat had selected earlier and he choked up. Dammit. He had to find *something*.

"What did your mom do again?" Emme sassed with an exaggerated roll of her blue eyes.

"Being obstinate." He dug out a pair of leather vambraces strengthened with copper plates—parts of a Holy Shield, which he was told was the armors worn by a secret legion of demon-slayer knights somewhere in

Europe. "The whole 'I'm above humans and I want nothing to do with them' thing."

"Wasn't your dad human?" Emme took seat beside his artifacts and crossed her long legs revealing creamy bare thighs under the skintight miniskirt.

"Adopted dad. Yeah, probably why she's like that." He shrugged his history away and started to undo the laces of the mystical arm bracers. "But this is about me. She should help me. I'm her son."

"What do you need help with?"

He frowned with concentration as he traced the holy cross pattern embossed in the russet leather and felt the hum of power in the armor. Annoyed at the distraction from his task, he turned to Emme. "Oh, I gather you don't know?"

"I just walked in. Spent the night helping Ariane at the *Sanctuaire* with a new batch of baby vamps."

Mag didn't really care about the cursed teen vampires that had been his brother's mission. He was focused on the Holy Bracers right now. They would have to do.

He slid them both on his forearms, one after the other and extended his arms at Emme so she could help with the lacing.

"What time is it?" he winced at her. "I've been arguing with Mom forever."

"It's almost dawn." She pulled on the strings at his left arm, securing the magical armor tight above his wrist and all the way to his elbow. "The bar's been closed for a couple of hours. Sandrine is finishing your inventory. I just needed one last drink. You know how the disciples don't keep anything strong enough for me at the nunnery."

"You're welcome to live here if you want." He held still

under her strong pull as she tied the second arm bracer. "I have a couple of empty guest rooms."

"Last year I would have said yes. But Father Grégoire needs the help." She eased back onto the couch and stretched her arms wide over the backrest before narrowing heavily lined eyes at him. "We *did* promise Val to look after things. I had to step in—you haven't been there much."

"Sorry, been distracted." He had no time to feel guilty. Yes, his brother had to give up his mission to look after cursed vamps in order to save his wife, and Mag had indeed promised to take care of them. But that was before Nyssa had walked into his life and tugged at his heart.

"So what's all this for?" She waved at the leather armor on his forearms.

"Some prince of the Daeva Realm kidnapped someone I care about and wants to take over my club." He shifted his stance with a brief clench of his fists.

"What?" She flinched at his words.

"Yeah," he croaked, not willing to think about Cat at Norwell's mercy. He had to focus on getting her out and fast.

"The Daeva Realm?" she pondered. "As in where those soul-sucking creatures come from?"

"The one, yep. They're in town." He snapped his magical Ioshta Band over the bracer on his left wrist. "Well, out in Laval at the moment."

"And you tell me all this now?" she criticized.

"I just found out."

"Have you called Dunsmuir?"

"Why?" He picked up his car keys from his desk and slid them into his pocket as he turned back to Emme.

"Isn't he king of that world?" She was leaning forward, a deep frown at her brow.

"I thought you hated him," he smirked. There was a time when Emme had taken a little jaunt over in Seattle where Malcolm lived and had caused havoc within the Black Oak Warlocks. Val had been forced to bring her back.

"More like, don't want to mess up with him." She stared at Mag with a somber look. "But he does have dominion over all daemon-like creatures."

"Well, we kind of agree to stay out of each other's way." Mag shrugged. "He's Val's friend, not mine."

"What about Maisie?" Emme was genuinely trying to find a solution.

"Maisie, why?"

"The otherworldly seems to be her expertise." She was adamant that he needed to bring someone in to help.

"I have, Mom." He flicked his gaze upward with annoyance. "I don't need another witch."

"Charlotte didn't look like she wanted to help."

Mag leaned on his desk, his arms crossed at his chest. "She won't. I tried to convince her, but she says it's human business."

"Wait, why not? Why is this human business?"

"Because it involves Nyssa."

"Oh."

"Yeah." His shoulders dropped. "Prince Norwell kidnapped Nyssa's little sister Cat. He's willing to give her back if I give him the club."

"Seems like an unbalanced trade to me."

"You don't say. "

"The club is everything to you." Emme shook her head in disbelief. "Why would he think you'd part with it?"

"Not you, too." Anger again mounted inside him.

"What? You want to give him your club?" Shock at the prospect froze her features in place for a second.

"I'm considering it," he grumbled.

"For a human kid?" Her eyes squinted with doubt.

"Sure." He'd come to realize that, just like his father, he had found profound feelings for someone of a different world. Except that he was the one on the other side of the supernatural.

As fleeting as it may be in the end, he had been given the gift of knowing and caring for these human females. And that was worth so much more than his club.

His time was a constant, unending, and he would spend his eternity in regrets if he didn't do everything in his power to help. Even if saving the life of a human child meant trading the one thing that had brought him happiness.

He gave Emme a small shrug despite the turmoil at his chest. "Problem is, I don't think the prince will give the kid back."

As Emme continued to watch him with astonishment, he couldn't suppress his fear for Cat's fate in Norwell's grasp. He *would* give anything to save the kid's life.

And here he thought he'd make a bad caregiver because he couldn't do math.

His gut tightened as he surveyed his comforting establishment, the original stone still there at the back wall.

But the memory of proudly counting the take on opening night centuries ago receded and was replaced by the recent image of a child happily exhausted from a race with him around an ice rink. A child looking at him with fondness and trust.

"That's why you fought with your mom?" Emme interrupted his thoughts. "Because she won't get involved?"

"Hell yeah." Mag pursed his lips, fury returning to his chest. "It would not be that hard for her. A couple of spells and the whole thing would be down."

"And she'd have the whole Daeva Realm after her."

"Maybe." He leaned farther back as he paused to consider the idea.

"Not maybe. For sure," Emme insisted. "This is royalty. To mess with the prince for a human. That would totally destabilize the daemon world."

"When have you turned so clever?"

"I've always been," she sneered. "You weren't paying attention."

He shook his head and held his stance firm. "I better head down there and get the kid back."

"You're going by yourself?"

"I have to. Nyssa was here." He suddenly worried about what she might be feeling. Dammit, he *had* wasted too much time with his mom. "She probably went to the police."

"Did you call Akande?"

"I might. After I get the kid back." He strode to the door as Emme slowly unfolded herself from the couch, the heels of her thigh-high boots digging into the flagstone floor.

"So Nyssa doesn't know you're doing this alone?"

"Mom was a bitch to her. And she stormed out. She was angry."

"You should call her." She tilted her head to the side, an atypical look of empathy on her brows.

"After I get Cat." The only way to fix this with Nyssa was to come to her with the teen.

"Oh, Mag." She smiled. "I've been around humans

long enough now to know that you should let her into your plan."

He slowly let a breath out. His heart had crushed to see Nyssa storm out like that. She'd turned so cold again. Rage at his mom churned once more in his gut.

"I'm just going to sneak in, find Cat, and go." He brandished his leather-covered arm at her. "This should do."

"If it's so easy, why did you ask your mom in the first place?"

"I panicked, okay. And she returned to Montreal for me. To help me."

"You guys are so messed up. I think Justin is the only sane one in the family." She let out a breath. "Need help?"

"Yeah, maybe." He was about to step out when his phone pinged in his pocket.

He fished it out. A part of him hoped it was Nyssa. Maybe Emme was right. He hated not talking to her right now. He should let her know everything was going to be all right.

But not now, he reasoned. It was best to get this over with and show up at her place in a few hours with Cat.

As he swiped to get to his cellphone's texts, he smiled imagining how grateful she would be.

The harsh words his mom had said about their relationship had made him cringe. Yes, there was this complication thing between them, her mortal and him not. But they would make it work. All he could remember of his mother and Papa Antoine was happiness. That kind of bond was worth any pain that came afterwards.

And they had her lifetime to find a way to extend her life. He *would* go grovel to Malcolm Dunsmuir to find a way.

*Vince.* Mag looked at his text and frowned. What would Vince want with him?

He started reading and ice flushed straight to his heart.

"Uh-oh. I don't like that look," Emme said. "Something's wrong."

"No shit." His mouth turned dry with denial.

"What?"

"Nyssa went and hired the Moreno's men to get Cat." He reread the message grimly, hoping like hell it wasn't true. "They're about to storm the compound in Laval. Vince felt bad going behind my back."

"Oh, wow," Emme cried out. "I got to give it to her, your woman knows how to get things done."

"Emme, you don't get it." He slowly lifted his gaze, horror clouding his vision. "They're all humans. Vince and his crew. I don't care how many there are. They can't go up against daevas."

The blonde vampire shrugged with an amused smile upon her lips. "We better hurry then."

# CHAPTER 22

*N*yssa tiptoed up the wide staircases in the compound as her hired mercenaries lit up the way with their night gear. The place was an expansive old hotel from the seventies, some developer's idea of luxury that hadn't quite panned out with its garish wallpaper and the old smell of cigarette smoke and musky perfume still seeping from the faded furniture.

Her flat furry boots were dead quiet on the thick carpeted steps. Vince was at her left, his large form even more massive under the tactical equipment. His man Sandro, his small build nimble in black fatigues and t-shirt under the heavy protective vest, led the way with his firearm at the ready, while another one called Leone, was charting the perimeter with his scope, a black watch cap secure under night vision goggles.

Nothing moved in the compound aside from an occasional oomph as one of the Moreno militants silently took down lone sentinels.

While Vince's men carried everything from state-of-the-art rifles to military grade side arm pistols, no gunshot had been released. She had no idea where all these troops were from, but they were steadfast at hand-to-hand combat. There was a dozen or so lethal men and women with deadly expressions and what looked like real respect for Vince's authority.

And most likely, she acknowledged, her money.

After rallying in a nearby parking lot at the edge of dawn, they had nodded briefly at her and, with some short exchange in both French and English, Sandro and Leone had been assigned to stay close to her.

The plan was to quietly overtake the guards, then go straight to where the young people were kept. Her heart had broken as Vince speculated that if Cat were here, they would likely use her right away. Break her in.

She had no trust in the prince's promise that they wouldn't touch Cat yet. The thought of her sister being assaulted in the worst way tightened her gut with revulsion. An angry storm burned within her and she bit the inside of her mouth to retain her cool.

Vince's team had forcefully extracted the information from one of the security guards at the entrance that the party room was upstairs.

So far, the prince's security details were all humans. In fact, the guard they'd held at gunpoint for information didn't seem to know anything about supernatural beings.

That knowledge had bolstered her step. The prince had sent three daevas after Mag in the alley behind the skating rink. He'd kill two so there was still one around.

It could be that he was the only supernatural there.

She heard a faint commotion above her and looked up to see Sandro touch his helmet and motioned them up the last few steps.

She should have told Mag. The thought shot through

her mind as she reached the second floor. She really should have. He might not like to hear that she'd gone behind his back to hire his friend.

And there was more. He had made her feel safe. She trusted the professionals around her, but it was not the same. They were loyal to her money, not to her.

Well, it was too late now, she noted as she stepped past two other guards knocked unconscious.

Vince silently pointed to the two huge carved doors at their left. She mentally mapped the compound in her head. This had to be the hotel's ballroom.

With her heart pulsing, she tightened her fists. She had to rescue Cat. She'd deal with Mag later.

There were about eight soldiers from the Moreno squad around her. The two scouts who'd cleared the hall, Vince, Sandro, and Leone and three more who'd followed her, including Gia, a tough-looking female with black pistols and vicious blades strapped around each of her thighs. She kept chewing on her gum with a cocky smile plastered on her lips.

This looked much too easy. The prince had to descend on them any moment now.

Gia and another of Vince's men took a spot at each side of the doors while Vince signaled to the rest of them to line along the opposite hallway.

Nyssa's palms were damp with sweat as she watched him extend a hand to push open the door a few inches.

A small rustle echoed from the room, then nothing. Vince slid inside with surprising ability despite his huge size. He kept the door ajar and flicked his hand as a gesture for them to come in.

She tiptoed in the dark right after Sandro and gulped at

the scene she could make out from the mercenary's nightlights.

Beds and couches haphazardly littered the old parquet floor. Naked bodies, male and female and of varying ages, lay everywhere.

Everyone was passed out or sleeping, low sounds of snoring and moaning disrupted the otherwise quiet atmosphere. The smell of booze, weed, and cold sweat was prevalent.

Sickened beyond belief, Nyssa repressed a gag. *Could Cat be in that mess?*

The horror of the very thought propelled her forward. Her eyes started to adjust to the dark as she stepped amongst the mattresses, Vince inching beside her and sweeping the area with his heavy flashlight.

The ballroom was arranged with couches pushed to the walls, leaving the wide beds take the center with little room to walk between them. Nyssa winced at the various scenes of the orgy lit by Vince as they proceeded through.

A middle-aged obese white man slept with his flaccid gut flopping to the side and over a young girl's skinny legs, her nubile body barely formed.

With her jaw clenched with sadness, Nyssa resisted the urge to pull the child out and instead pressed on forward. But tears welled in her eyes at witnessing a mattress where a rickety, hairy old man was intertwined with two naked boys—their bare flesh crisscrossed with vicious lashes—who couldn't be much older than her sister.

Once she found Cat and got her out of this horror, she would wrestle heavens and hells to force the authorities to close this place and rescue those poor youths.

She glanced at Vince and, seeing similar disgust in his

face, she realized that she wouldn't have to. The Morenos would likely take care of it.

Her heart pounded madly in her ears with urgency. They had to find Cat. Now!

Another sweep of Vince's light made her gasp.

*Oh god.* She found her.

There at the very back wall, next to two underage girls passed out on an old ornate couch. Wearing nothing but a tiny satiny black slip, she was sitting upright, her eyes wide and looking at nothing. Perfectly awake but in complete shock, not moving a single muscle of her chubby child's features.

*Cat.*

Nyssa lunged down to her sister's side and seized her in her arms.

Cat shook violently. "Nyssie?"

Nyssa cupped her sister's face frenetically, looking for any signs of bruises or assault. She laid a finger on her sibling's trembling lips. "Shh. I'm taking you out of here."

Cat buried her face into her shoulder with a quiet cry and Nyssa's heart shattered on the spot.

Nyssa caught the shift in Vince's posture as he shot her a quick nod.

"Let's go," he said.

She pulled Cat up and the kid tumbled against her. Oh no, dammit. She seemed drugged.

Vince swiftly shifted his weapon to his back, secured his light at his waist, and whisked Nyssa's sister into his arms.

Cat yelped with a tiny sob.

Nyssa seized her sister's clammy bare shoulder and gave it a squeeze. "It's okay, Cricket," she whispered. "He's with me."

Vince stepped back amongst the bodies, careful not to wake anyone as Nyssa followed right behind him, her eyes glued to her sister who watched her over Vince's shoulder, her pupils glassy with fear.

In seconds, Sandro and Leone were at their side and no one stirred as they all reached the ballroom doors.

Relief swept over Nyssa as Leone carefully pushed the door open to let Vince through.

They were almost there. Just a few more minutes and Cat would be free.

They had rescued her, and Nyssa would never ever let that kid out of her sight.

She pondered hiring Sandro or maybe Gia to guard her sister day and night. The two mercenaries, wiry and pumped with adrenaline, seemed absolutely fearless.

"Oh shit." Vince stopped dead in his tracks, his wide body blocking her.

"What?" Her throat seized and she caught what he saw.

Gia and two other Moreno men were down on the floor, unconscious, their faces gaunt, eyes wide open fixated on the ceiling.

"Run," Vince rasped under his breath, shifting Cat over his shoulder, her sister's fingers white from gripping his soldier's vest with desperation.

Sandro and Leone bolted past her to their brother-in-arms sprawled on the carpet. Nyssa had no idea if any of them were alive.

"Down the stairs." Vince yelled at her.

"But Cat?" Nyssa's heart was pounding like crazy.

"We're right behind you. Go."

She tumbled down the stairs, Vince's heavy steps at her heels, as shouts and commotion erupted everywhere.

Everything seemed blurred as she darted for the exit, the only thing keeping her going was knowing that Vince, with Cat in his arm, was at the rear.

But as she reached the bottom of the staircase, she slammed into what felt like a brick wall. Two brawny arms seized her by the shoulders.

She screamed and, on pure instinct, rammed her knee up into solid flesh. But her kick did nothing to release her, and her blood curdled as a diabolic tone oozed in her ear.

"Now, now, there, woman. Decided to join us?"

*Oh god. The prince.* Nausea erupted inside her mouth and her entire body quaked at the revulsion.

"Vince! Get Cat out of here."

"Oh and look, you brought friends," Prince Norwell said above her head. "Handsome lot. I would love to sample them myself."

A slew of underlings materialized around him.

"Get them!" the prince snapped. "Get them all."

"Please, save her!" Nyssa roared frantically at Vince as the prince forced her to his chest, a scent of sickly-sweet aroma overpowering her. She managed to glance back at Vince.

He was hesitating, his eyes narrowing at the scene.

"Go," she mouthed at him.

He spun away to race up the steps with Cat firmly secured over his shoulder.

A group of Prince Norwell's minions whizzed past and she heard a series of footsteps above. Gunshots erupted, followed by shouts, and the crashing of glass.

The prince's slimy hands held her like a vice. In desperation, she smashed the toe of her boot on his shin with as much force as she could muster.

But he just chortled at her attempt. "What a delightful little thing you are. Like a tiny bird fighting to be free."

"Let me go, you creep." She struggled against him, trying to wiggle out of his tight grip.

"Oh my poor little hen. Have you never seen a cat toy with little birds?" His cheek was right next to her, his breath smelling like rosewater and clove. He let out a malevolent cackle. "The fowls never stand a chance."

He had her trapped against his body, her arms pinned to her sides. With her face pressed against him, she could barely breathe.

"They're gone, Your Royal Highness," someone said behind her.

"All of them?"

"Looks like it, sir. Certainly the big guy. He took off with the kid. They leapt out the window."

"Should we run after them?" another one asked.

"No. Sun's coming up. Wouldn't want to create a commotion in the street and have a neighbor make a fuss. By *Ell'zoth*, I'll be happy to leave this dingy area." He patted Nyssa's hair heavily, the false affection causing the back of her neck to crawl with dread. "Plus it turns out I have something much better than the kid. Right, sweetling?"

"You fucking rat." Nyssa tried to wedge herself out of his death grip. But it was useless.

"St-Amand will do anything to get this one back. Mark my words, friends. We *are* moving soon. We'll finally get out of this dump."

# CHAPTER 23

"What the hell?" Mag watched bewildered as Vince strode towards him in the parking lot across from the compound, his team behind him.

Vince's righthand gal, Gia, was limping supported by Sandro. Leone had an inert soldier over his shoulders. The rest followed equally defeated.

And wearing next to nothing, a shivering little Catalina was clinging to Vince's neck.

"Mag." His mouth pressed flat, Vince silently dropped the kid in Mag's arms.

Cat nestled against his chest without a word. She was shaking like a leaf.

Vince ripped his protective vest off, unzipped his thick hoody and passed it over to Mag.

"Cat," he carefully wrapped the layer around the half-naked child, "It's over, kiddo. You're safe."

"Is that the kidnapped kid?" Emme exited the warmth of his car to close the distance between them.

"Yeah." A heaviness settled in his limbs at the state of the teen huddled in his arms.

"Nice job." She shot Vince a rise of her brow.

"Where's Nyssa." Adrenaline suddenly rushed through Mag's system and he searched Vince's squad with panic.

Vince remained silent, his eyes somber as he slowly shook his head.

"What, she's not with you?" Emme said.

Vince opened his mouth to speak then closed it. He shook his head again. "He got her."

"What?" Mag choked on the word, stunned.

"I'm sorry, man. She told me to get the kid out."

Mag's entire body stilled as a ringing rose in his ears. *Norwell had Nyssa. No!*

The world suddenly narrowed to that one sickening fact and he disconnected from his entire being, as if in a dream.

"Here." He attempted to pass Cat back to Vince, but she hung on tight. He took an excruciatingly deep breath. "Cat, you need to stay with Vince for a bit."

Her face bunched up and she stared at him with a deep distress that tugged something inside him and shook him out from the shock he was under.

"He's got her. Nyssie. I saw him holding her—" She full-on sobbed. Big fat tears smeared with eyeliner rolled down her pallid cheeks.

His heart thawed further, and he addressed her gently. "Please stay with Vince and his crew, Cat. He's a friend. I need to go get your sister."

Her face was small and fearful. She bit her lips but nodded back.

"Keep her safe." He slid Cat back into Vince's arms.

"I'm sorry," Vince repeated, his voice shaky.

"It was the right choice." Mag steadily looked at his friend for a moment, then turned to stride towards the compound.

"Wait, what are you doing?" Emme was right behind him.

"Getting Nyssa back." His teeth clenched, he pulled on the leather bracers.

"You're taking the whole compound on your own?"

"Maybe." He actually hadn't thought that far ahead. All he knew was that Nyssa was in there and so he had to go in, too.

He'd let his mom distract him from what mattered. *Her.*

He had let her storm out of his office and now she was Norwell's prisoner. Scorching waves of anger pounded his chest. He *had* to get her out.

He would never, ever let her leave him again.

More even, he would reveal the depth of his feelings for her. And he would tell his brothers and his mother to shove it.

"I'm going to kill myself a few of these daeva bastards." Emme was stoked.

"You can kill whatever you want," he grumbled. "Just not the kids."

She drew her short sword out of her boot. "Right on."

"Just don't make this worse."

"I won't, I promise. I'm helping."

He looked at her, suddenly realizing she was actually going in with him. It was always hard to pinpoint where Emme's alliances stood but he was grateful for the backup.

"Don't let them touch you," he warned, unwilling to lose her, too.

They reached the entrance of the boarded-up hotel and with one blasting kick, he slammed the door open, taking it completely off its hinges.

His fangs were fully out, his blood boiling.

"Norwell, you fucker! Show yourself," he thundered.

A slew of daevas materialized from coalescing black smoke right in front of him. He counted a dozen or so.

"Now?" Emme was at his side, her sword poised.

"Not until I see her," he grunted.

His plan was to beat the bastard senseless with the enhanced strength his bracers would provide him while Emme tackled the minions.

Beyond that, they would have to wing it. Mag was all action, not the strategic type.

"Magnovald," the male voice purred sickly syrupy in the hallway as the prince, dressed in shiny leather pants and matching tank, stood in the middle of the staircase. Nyssa was under his arm, a furious expression lining her brows. "Welcome to my humble home."

Mag's heart picked up speed, overcome with wrath and worries at once. He forced his raging emotions down.

"Are you okay, love?" He peered at Nyssa with all the feelings he had for her, praying to hear her voice.

But all he was given was her strained and angry gaze. Of course, she was not okay. And it was all *his* fault. He should have bolted after her the minute she charged out of his office mad.

"And who's this," Norwell sneered. "You brought a friend."

"A very good friend at that," Emme declared. She had her sword straight out in front of her, pointed at the nearest daeva. "Go back to the hole you came from, ugly."

Norwell descended two steps down, dragging Nyssa

beside him. She was white as a sheet, so tiny and vulnerable next to the seemingly invincible daeva royal.

"Feisty," Norwell said, looking at Emme. "But I don't have time for all this nonsense. I want to be redecorating my brand-new club."

He waved his hand toward Mag and Emme and called out to his underlings. "Bring me the big one. You can have the female."

At his words, the daevas instantly swarmed Emme and Mag.

Mag leaped in the air before they could catch him, and he landed at the bottom of the stairs. But the daevas managed to surround Emme before she could move. She swung her sword in a wide arc, cleanly chopping off one head in a splash of black smoke. It looked like she'd found one way to dispatch them.

But Mag had no time to be impressed by Emme's victory. Her blonde hair disappeared under the bulk of monsters and she soon howled in pain.

One had his palms upon her head. Fucking hell, he was sucking the life force out of her. She was a vampire. How was that even possible?

"Shit!" Mag was torn between saving her and rescuing Nyssa.

Emme was kicking madly under the deadly grip, but Mag had to get Nyssa first.

And for that he needed to get to Norwell. The bastard stood on the staircase like a pompous king surveying the battle with amusement, his oversized arm clutching Nyssa against his chest.

Two minions, in drab fatigues and everyday shirts, stood guard behind him.

"Release her, you creep," Mag roared. The shields upon

his arms, called forth by the presence of a being from Hell's Gate, suddenly imbued him with a holy power that rushed up through his torso.

"Not until you give me the keys to your club, worm. Isn't that why you came?" Norwell sneered, his pretty-boy features suddenly distorted in a mean pout. "And you know what, I think I want more than that now. I want your club and the staff. Your bodyguards, those hot human waitresses, the dancers, all of them. Then I'll give you back both your women."

Mag took two more steps up. "Let her go," he seethed.

"Your keys." His heavy hand snaked to Nyssa's throat. He slid his fingers along her carotid artery and she whimpered. She would not be freeing herself as she'd done in the alley.

"Babe," Mag said, his voice hoarse. He wanted to tell her not to worry, that he would save her. But his brain was still trying to figure out how to get her away from the prince.

"Oh, for *Ell'zoth*'s sake," Prince Norwell suddenly raged. "Must I do everything myself?"

He shoved Nyssa to his daevas and leaped down right in front of Mag.

He was a good foot taller, even accounting for the staircase. But Mag had his artifact. Without the risk of hurting Nyssa, he could take the freak.

He crouched low in a fighting stance, one elbow protecting his side. Pumped with his bracer's hallowed energy, he jumped up a step and rammed his powered fist straight into Norwell's gut.

Pain scattered back into his elbow, searing his shoulder with hot agony. Had Norwell been human, the bastard should have been catapulted all the way to the top floor.

But this was like hitting a brick wall—Norwell barely moved.

The prince chuckled and grabbed Mag by the lapel of his leather jacket.

Mag tried to twist himself free under the colossal grip and shoved the heel of his palm square into Norwell's nose.

But the royal just shook his head with a laugh and lifted Mag into the air.

"*Annehyentx!*" Mag called on the power of the Ioshta Band, the artifact warming his wrist through the leather bracer.

"*Jalahran.*" Norwell spat lazily, neutralizing Mag's offensive spell. "Your magic is so feeble, Immortal. It's really no match for someone like me." He shook his head in a shimmer of silver hair before throwing Mag down the steps.

Mag hit the ground at an odd angle and heard the crack the instant his back seized with excruciating pain.

*Sacrament.* Breaking bones for the very first time in his life!

The agony slowly ebbed as his immortal body tried to heal. With the dull ache lingering in his spine, he finally scrambled to his feet, one hand holding his throbbing back. Dammit.

"Give it up, St-Amand." Norwell ambled down the steps to close the distance between them, Emme wailing in agony still behind him.

But Mag said nothing, his gaze focused on Norwell's neck. Right there. Above the collar. He could see the skin move over the vein. The royal being had blood. And if he had blood, he could be killed.

Fangs fully out, ignoring the torture in his back, Mag

dove upon his foe, this time sinking his fangs right into the flesh.

Norwell roared in pain and dug his fingers into Mag's shoulders, trying to wrestle him off.

But the man in Mag was gone and the predator prevailed. He would destroy the bastard. He would bleed him to death right here and now. Make him pay for hurting Nyssa and Cat.

Norwell faltered under Mag's bite. His knees buckled and he almost fell. But he managed to reach up and seized both sides of Mag's head.

And the scorching pain was like nothing Mag had ever felt. As if the white fire of a steel poker were applied directly to his skull.

Mag couldn't tell if he screamed. His consciousness just vanished. To a place where pain and torture no longer existed. A place filled with distressing feelings.

It was a bright sunny day. He saw Mom, Papa Antoine, they were walking on the beach along the St-Lawrence river.

And Mag was far, far from them. Buried deep under water. Trapped by sea kelp, the slimy strands binding each of his limbs, circling his chest. Pulling him down and taking him away from his parents' laughter. Away from joy.

Eerie sounds echoed around him, wails of despair, moans of agony. A sulfur smell of decay cloaked his airways as translucent moss-green tendrils slid across his vision.

Cold fear took hold as gyrating hungry suction cups appeared along each thick appendage keeping him captive. He wanted to scream but his voice was gone.

His head pounded in a defeating symphony of fear that swooshed through his temples. He fought like mad under the unseen grip but was left powerless. A viscous tentacle slid against his bare throat and he let out a voiceless wail as each suction sampled his skin. The searing burn dug into his insides, finding each of his crevices, leaving his mind lost to the unbearableness of it all, the torture breaking him as his guts clenched, gagging him.

The nightmare ended abruptly. Mag found himself slumped on his knees and violently sick, his skull burning with relentless throbbing.

Norwell towered above him, his features a look of pure malice as he gloated.

"Bring me the female vampire," he shouted with delight.

They dragged Emme forward and she tumbled at Mag's side. Her face was tear-stained, her natural defiance gone.

Mag's empty stomach clenched, rock solid with shock. In his entire life, he had never known defeat. Even his precious artifacts had not been enough against the prince. And now, when it mattered the most, when he had to fulfill his promise to protect the woman he cared for, he had failed.

His breath came out in rasps. Thought of despairs from his vision lingered in the deep recesses of his brain. He had never felt so powerless.

And for the first time in his life, he realized that there, here, was one fight he would never win. He looked at Nyssa held back by daeva underlings and her stunned expression broke his heart into a thousand pieces.

Her family had failed her. She only had him.

And he had to pay the price to save her. To get her out of this nightmare.

His body was broken but with all his might, he managed to raise himself to his feet. He picked up Emme who tottered at his side, her footing uneasy.

Norwell was looking at both of them, relishing their struggle to move. Waiting with a smirk for their surrender.

"Take it," Mag finally said as he slid the *Serpent's* key off his keyring and flung it at the monster. "Just fuckin' take the club."

He bared his fangs as his jaw gritted at the loss. The club had been his whole world. But now it meant nothing if Nyssa was not in it.

"Now, now, maggot." A satisfied smile stretched the prince's lips. "See how easy that was."

"Let Nyssa go," Mag narrowed a sharp look back at him.

Norwell tilted his head to the side. He patted his hand on his neck and looked at the blood on his fingers.

"Well…" he whined. "That was the bargain before you did this to me. It might leave a scar.

"Now, I'm willing to let you and the blonde go," he added, his expression turning nasty. "In good faith. It's a trade after all. And I wouldn't want the rest of the supernatural world think I'm unfair by double-crossing vampires. But her? Nah. She's human. No one will care."

Nyssa let out a choke of horror. Her bewildered expression hit Mag like a ton of bricks.

"Motherfucker!" Mag stood to his full height, suddenly full of righteous energy. "Fucking bastard. I'll kill you!"

"Now, now, we don't want to revisit this again, do we?" Norwell stretched his arm towards Nyssa, guarded by his minions in the middle of the staircase. "Come on, little one."

And just like that, buoyed by the sanctified energy in his bracers and the desperation that came from losing it all, Mag's palm found the inside of his left wrist.

The Ice Witch mark burnt red hot under the leather of his holy shield.

It was his last hope.

Words, power, he hadn't felt in centuries mounted like a tsunami inside him. It was all there. Still in him. And he fully embraced the familiarity of it.

"Fuck you!" he snapped.

In one move, he shot both hands straight out at Norwell, his palms out, full of the power of the Ice Witch. The icy blast hit the prince square into the chest.

Norwell flinched back, a stunned look on his face.

"S*tryos!*" Mag's arms shot to his side in a wide arc, his spell creating shards of frozen pellets that blitzed through every daevas surrounding him. They screeched and dissolved under the ice storm. Their bodies shifted and twisted before slowly turning to suspended dust near the ceiling.

"Oh god." Nyssa cried.

Her keepers had raced down to rally around Norwell.

"*Merde*, Mag!" Emme was ecstatic, her face lit with glee.

"*Strieahadhr!*" Mag shoved both palms out at Norwell and his guards in one last blast of primeval energy.

"You, maggot." A look of pure hatred shattered the prince's pretty face before it started to fragment under the frigid blow.

While the two minions turned to smoke, Norwell's

body lost its solidity, each of the molecules composing him disorganizing, one by one.

"Quick, Nyss." Mag motioned her down as she stared at the dissolving prince with shock. "We don't have much time."

She shook herself out of her daze and ran down the steps directly into his arms. "Mag."

He flinched as his back seized.

"You're hurt."

"It's nothing." He hugged her in a tight embrace and rested his chin on the top of her head. Her floral scent gently reached his nostril, making everything right again. "Emme?"

"I'm fine." She flipped her hair back over her shoulder before picking up her sword from the old, carpeted floor. She slid the blade back into the top of her leather boots. "These creatures are right nasty."

The hall was now completely deserted, aside from the dark cloud of immaterial daevas hovering at the ceiling.

"We better go," Mag said. "Norwell will reemerge again soon."

"You can walk?" Nyssa had her arms around his waist, her touch gentle.

"I'm healing already." He shot her a confident smile. He had won this one, after all. She was safe.

"Freakin' disgusting." Emme was wrinkling her nose as she stared at the smoke obscuring the painted ceiling.

"Let's get out of here. They won't stay like this for long." Mag reached to the floor to pick up his club key, which had dropped intact when the prince had dematerialized. "They'll be back. At least he will. He's too strong."

"He's insane. A real psychopath," Nyssa said. "The things he wants. I don't even know if he even believes half of it. But for sure he'll come for you, Mag. He's so jealous. He wants all you have."

"Don't worry, babe." Mag cast one last look at the ominous clouded ceiling before stepping out in the fresh air. "We'll be waiting for him."

# CHAPTER 24

"*Merde*, Mag. That was some awesome spell you used. Did that come from the bracers?" The blonde woman swiveled in the passenger seat of Mag's Ferrari with Vince at the wheel. She glanced to the back seat at Mag who sat beside Nyssa. Cat was nestled against her chest between them.

As soon as Nyssa, Mag, and his fierce female companion had exited the compound, they'd found Vince idling in Mag's car, waiting for them with Cat in the back seat.

Mag turned to Nyssa with a smile. "By the way, meet Emme. My crazy friend."

"Crazy?" The blonde in the long suede coat raised a flippant brow at him. "I saved your butt in there."

"Hardly." Mag shrugged with a bemused smile and Nyssa was struck by the close bond between them.

Pondering over their relationship, she hugged Cat closer as warmth filled her heart.

"How the hell did you blast a spell so strong?" Emme was saying. "It was as badass as what Maisie would do."

"Don't know. I just called on Mom's power. The holy shield was pretty much useless against Norwell."

"You came for me." Nyssa asserted herself in the conversation. Her brain was still a little numb as she tried to parse what exactly had happened after she told Vince to escape with Cat.

"I did." He held her gaze for a moment and all doubts she had about Emme vanished.

She swallowed carefully, her heart swollen with feelings. "You gave up your club for me."

"That was the only way."

"You would have lost everything." She was still shocked at having witnessed him toss his key at the prince.

The last time she'd seen him, he was debating with his mother whether a relationship with a mortal was worthwhile. And now, he'd given up all he had for her, a mortal.

"It's not even a good trade." He shot her that devastating half-smile of his.

"Thank you," was all she could say.

But her heart was in turmoil, full of emotion at remembering how hard he had fought for her life. And right there and then, she knew she was falling in love.

He smiled and his eyes softened as he looked down at her sister who was half asleep in her arms. "How is she?"

She rubbed the teen's back over the thick hoodie. "Cat?"

"They didn't touch me." Cat stirred as a little vigor returned to her body. "You came in time."

"Oh thank god." A flood of relief swept through Nyssa. "That room upstairs. That was something. Those kids there…"

She was still horrified at what she had witnessed.

"They gave me some alcohol to drink but when the party started, they basically ignored me. There were two others with me, Vicky and Jade." Her voice broke down. "They were new, too. We just watched before the two of them passed out from the drinks."

"I'm so sorry, kid," Mag told her.

"That's how they get them obedient. Groom them." Vince's chilled voice echoed in the luxury vehicle. "They make them watch first, then some groping before going full-on gang rape. The drugs and alcohol is to numb them."

An uncontrollable shake of horror passed through Nyssa's body and she tightened her embrace on her sister. "We need to do something about those poor kids. I'll call the police to come rescue them, bust the creeps who use them."

"I want to go home, Nyssa." Cat pleaded with her.

"To Dad's?"

"No. To your place. That's home now."

"Yes, home." Nyssa shot her sister a small smile as her heart lifted. Despite her rebellious tendency, Cat finally saw Nyssa as her source of comfort.

She closed her eyes for a second, letting the feelings of solace and safety wash all over her. They were finally speeding away from that nasty place.

She knew she had escaped a fate worse than death, she could still feel the monster's breath on her cheek. She'd been trapped by him for less than an hour but had felt the full expanse of his malice. She had seen his twisted pleasure as he tortured his enemy, had heard his mad rant of jealousy against Mag.

She'd been horrified to see Mag in the throes of torment and near defeat, wishing more than anything she could help him. Helped Emme who had disappeared under an assault of daevas.

She relaxed as Mag edged closer to wrap his arm around her. With her sister in her arms, it felt natural, sheltered. After she'd witnessed him destroy Prince Norwell, she knew he could do anything.

"Are you still hurt?" she asked Mag with concern. "Shouldn't we take you to a hospital?

"Yeah man, you got pretty banged up there for a minute," Emme chimed in. "I was almost worried."

"What are you talking about? I had him the whole time," he countered with a twinkle at his eye. He turned to Nyssa and leaned back against the leather seat of the Ferrari, with confidence. "It's already healing. One of the perks of being an immortal."

"So he could never have killed you." Intrigued, she stared at him, wondering at the extent of his abilities.

"Maybe. I don't know." He grinned, apparently unconcerned.

"Don't worry, *fille*. He can't be killed." Emme was smiling at Nyssa, looking more like an ally than competition for the club owner's affection.

"Thanks for getting me." Nyssa held Emme in a steady and grateful gaze. "That was some serious fighting with that sword of yours."

"Oh that? Just good fun." Emme jested and pulled at the top of her skintight shimmery silver dress. "Damaged my favorite outfit though."

"Emme's a vampire," Mag explained. "Well somewhere between a vampire, like Evan and Louka, and an immortal. She's as old as I am."

"Really." Nyssa stared at the gorgeous woman, trying to wrap her mind around that. "Do you drink human blood, like he does?"

"Nah, not anymore. I don't need to. Synthetic is fine." She shrugged and pointed at Cat and Nyssa. "You two girls are quite the survivors. Daevas are vile."

"They're not dead yet, though," Mag warned, his tone ominous.

"Your blast didn't kill them?" Nyssa asked.

"Hells no. With them hovering above like that, I barely dissolved them. They'll reanimate within a few hours."

"He'll be back for you," Nyssa cautioned, recalling the crazy desire the prince had shared with her. "He wants to use your club to propel his glory."

"It's jealousy," Cat chimed in with a tiny voice. "He wasn't paying much attention to me but when I told him Mag would come for me, he flew into this rage. He rambled that he was much cooler than Mag."

"For real?" Emme snorted.

"Uh-huh," Cat continued. "He claimed he could provide the city with all sorts of pleasures. He was going on and on during the party, talking up each of the guests. Like some flashy circus leader."

"Cat's right," Nyssa added. "Your club was all he talked about. Something about showing off to his sister."

"Merritt," Mag said with a thoughtful nod. "The ruler of the Daeva Realm."

"You think he'll come to the club, man?" Vince cast his gaze at Mag through the rear-view mirror.

"No doubt. He wants it all now." Mag frowned. "My staff, too."

"Your staff." Nyssa repeated with horror.

"Bastard," Emme said.

"No worries. We'll be ready when they come." Mag rested a steady hand on her thigh. "But first let us drop off Nyssa and Cat home. Then we'll call my brothers."

# CHAPTER 25

*M*ag tapped his fingers on the glass tumbler before taking a sip of his scotch as he gazed at the city below. The clank of ice cubes in his glass was the only familiar thing to him where everything in Nyssa's penthouse was luxurious hushed silence and snowy white-on-white comfort.

He'd taken off his motorcycle boots and stood alone in the open living area, uneasy with his toes digging into the plush cream carpet, while he waited for Nyssa to tuck her sister to bed.

He could have left them there to unwind but hadn't been able to leave them alone once Vince had driven to Vlahos Tower, and he'd let the man and Emme move on to the club without him for now.

He'd heard a bath being run in the upstairs level and now low female voices filtered in the quiet space.

Young Cat had taken to him, but this was a private moment between the sisters. He had no idea of the full extent of her trauma. But he knew Nyssa would be by her side to help the kid through it.

He smiled. No doubt the woman he cared so much about already had psychiatrist, therapist, and medical specialist appointments all lined up.

*Prince Norwell. The fucker.* His grip on the glass tightened as the fury again rose in large eddies from the bottom of his chest.

Yes, Mag was mad about his club. And he was livid that Norwell had used Nyssa to get it from him.

But worse were the kids. Cat had told them how the prince ran through underage teens as if they were mere cattle. Selling the fresh ones to whatever twisted fantasy was requested. And when beaten to submission and no longer useful, he'd ship them to the next city over or give them to his daevas for one last abuse before their lives just slipped away.

Children, dammit. Just a little over a decade of life.

Norwell had moved into the operation less than a year ago, bringing more and more daevas to his side. No doubt he'd managed to stay under the radar as Moreno had turned sicker and sicker.

And they, Mag's brothers and himself, had been none the wiser.

With a shake of his head, he turned to the wet bar in Nyssa's sprawling living room to pour himself another drink. He studied the urban environment she called home.

This was all Nyssa, from the soft pastel modern art on the walls, the clean lines of the cream leather suite broken only by his black leather jacket, and the sleek state-of-the art entertainment system that was offset by the unbelievable view of his entire city—the bright lights of skyscrapers dotted with soaring historical church steeples — making him love it even more. The efficiency married with the smooth lines around him were so like her that it thawed his entire heart.

Her safe place in the sky.

Could he blame her for being aloof, wanting to stay above them all? With what she had experienced in her life — seeing how easily adults could damage the most innocent child—he saw in this place the way that she was shielding herself.

But he was here now. He would protect her until the end.

He took another slug of scotch as Nyssa descended the steps to the living room.

"Cat's finally asleep." Clad in loose ivory silk pants and a matching top, she caught his breath away. A faint scent of soap clung to her skin and her hair was slightly damp, swirling at the nape of her neck.

"Oh good." His voice came out hoarse with his lust.

"You found the bar." Her lips curled in a genuinely warm smile. "Can you pour me one?"

"Of course." Seeing her like this, so sleek in her private environment made his heart soar. Everything fit so well together, matched in sumptuous elements that complemented all that she was.

She slid gracefully on the leather couch and crossed her long legs. "Whatever you're having."

He poured the drink, his breath short. Now that the imminent threat was gone and with just the two of them here, that something special between them hung in the air.

But Nyssa was as cool as usual, seemingly lost in her own thoughts.

"I called the authorities to tell them about the compound." She rolled her neck to relieve tension. "They're going to check on the place. I have to take Cat to the station so she can give a statement as soon as possible. I feel so bad for those poor kids."

He brought her drink and their fingers touched for a moment. Her essence permeated right through him.

"So do I." He sat next to her. Their bodies were not quite touching but her enticing body heat was so close he was aching to take her into his arms.

"You do, don't you? You care." Her head was tilted, her expression passionate. "Ever since I first told you about Cat in your club, you haven't stopped caring for her wellbeing."

"Nyssa, there is very little I cared about in those long centuries." A rush of warmth flooded through him as he considered her further. "My brothers, a few friends, my staff. The rest is… *was* entertainment."

She seemed to accept the last word without prejudice.

"Cat really looks up to you," she said.

"It's easy, I'm not the one telling her what to do and not do." He smiled as needs prickled his skin with hunger for her.

"Right." Her eyes lit up to see that he understood. "She doesn't like me bossing her around."

"But from what I've seen, you're the only one who cares enough to do it."

"Maybe."

"Watching you, I realize that taking care of a kid is a hell of a lot of hard work."

"Which is why her mother is not really doing it." Her tone shifted and it broke his heart.

He slid a hand to her cheek to tuck in a wayward strand of hair behind her ear. "Cat's lucky to have you."

She smiled and turned her head towards his palm. Her

gaze was feverish with intensity. "We're lucky to have *you*."

"I'm sorry about earlier. With my mom there, dismissing you like this."

"She's not very friendly, is she?"

"It's not that," he said, finally voicing what he had realized about his mother since she'd arrived in town. "I think our adoptive father's death really did her in. He was mortal and she wasn't."

"Just like us." She sighed.

"Yes."

"And I have Cat. She is also mortal."

"Too complicated for you?" He held his breath, waiting with apprehension for what she was about to say. He was dying for her to accept him in her life. To let him protect and cherish her.

"You're very complicated, Magnovald St-Amand." She raised her brows at him but didn't pull back.

He stared at her luscious lips and yearned to feel them under his. Taste them and feel them pliant under his claim, giving him a clue that she was willing to have him.

"Nyssa, I can't change this." He held her gaze steadily. "I will live for a long time. I don't even know the end of it."

"I wonder what it would be like." Her tone turned pensive.

"Being immortal?" he said with unnatural stillness, stunned to even think she could want to be like him. "You'd be devastated to see your sister die when you wouldn't."

"Wow." Shock registered in her stormy gray irises and she seized his hand cupping her cheek. "I hadn't thought of that."

"Yeah."

"I understand your mother."

"Tough," he nodded slowly at her. "When we were young, eighteen or so, my brother Valerian fell in love with the general store owner's daughter. She was mortal."

"So he saw her age and die?" She brought his hand to her lap and held it in both hers with gentleness. "Was he heartbroken?"

"Worse. He went to our disciples—those monks that take care of our yearly feeding, they can do some ritual magic." He paused, remembering Val's pain. "He turned her. His girlfriend."

"She died?"

"Worse. She turned into a true vampire, Emmeline Dubois."

"Emme?" Her brow rose at the revelation. "The blonde that came with you to the compound."

"The exact one." He reached for a strand of her hair again and felt her yield under his touch.

"So I gather they didn't walk into the sunset together." The corner of her eyes softened.

"No. She was never the same. In fact, she was quite horrible in her first century." He smirked at recalling the fallout of Emme's turning rampage as she created legions of young female vampires. "And Val kinda retreated inside himself. Never got over the guilt. He spent his life atoning for this by looking after the cursed vampires that came as her legacy."

"Legacy?"

"She bit and turned the first batch, literally like you see in the movies, buried them and all that." He twirled one of her strands around his finger. "Then they turned more and more. Only difference is that Emme's baby vamps all die in their late twenties, early thirties. Evan and Louka, my doorman Raphael, all are from Emme's line. Raphael has barely a few months left."

"Oh god, that's awful." She frowned with empathy. "Emme looks fierce and all, but I didn't realize she's got such a history."

"She hides it well."

"But your brother, he's married to someone else now, is he not?"

"Yes, head over heels in love."

"So it's possible."

"You mean human and immortal?" His heart sunk. "Maisie is an immortal witch. Making the transition nearly cost her sanity."

He recalled the events that had seen Val and Maisie daggered to the heart to save her and bind them forever. Val was a lucky bastard.

"I don't have any of those supernatural tendencies," she told him, her voice small.

"But you have so much more," he pressed. "I'm not sure why, Nyss. Maybe it's your bravery, your drive, or how much you care for your sister but, honestly, I have not stopped thinking about you since you walked in with all your big contracts to buy my club. There's something in you that makes me want to give up everything just to be with you."

"Honey, stop." She laid a finger on his lips. "Everything about you seems so wrong for me. Like seriously wrong. You run a nightclub, I know you have illegal deals in there, and your reputation... Dang it, you're not even mortal..."

He gazed at her, waiting for her to finish. Not sure if he liked where she was going, though it was all true.

"But mortals are not all that great." She shot him a small smile. "Lucinda, LaChance. And those men I saw abusing children. I know Prince Norwell is orchestrating it all, but he has clients. Human clients. And I saw them. Their disgusting paws all over those young teens."

She shuddered, a horrified expression shadowing her features.

"Oh, babe." He wrapped her in his arms, his heart breaking at her torment.

He held her tight for a moment, the two lost in silence as his heart beat in unison with hers.

She pulled back slightly. "I give to charity. But this time, I plan to open one in Cat's name, just to fight that sort of predator."

"Of course, you will." He gave her a benevolent smile.

"This thing between us, Mag, I don't know… I don't know where it leads. But I almost lost my life today. If it wasn't for you…"

"I will always be there for you."

"I know and that's what I'm saying. I want you to be. My life is short. I want you in it. See where it leads us."

He was speechless.

"Of course, you may not want to go that path." Worry etched her features. "Your mother…"

Nyssa dying in his arms was unthinkable. But the idea of not having her in his life was worse. Her neck was craned as she looked at him, her soft gray eyes shadowed with emotions and needs.

"Oh hells," he groaned. "I just want you, Nyss."

His lips seized hers and every misgiving warring in his mind disappeared.

She bent willingly in his embrace and wrapped her arms behind his neck, meeting his kiss with a passion equal to his. There were no doubts. With the deepest of yearning, he wanted Nyssa Vlahos, the woman who was so much more than the ice queen that had walked in his club three months ago.

He wanted all of her. Her skin, her breath, the desire that he sampled as their tongues met. His body was coming alive and his fangs elongated from pure cravings.

He pulled back and she made a small moan that dug straight through his inside and down to his groin. He was rock solid for her. Wanted to fill every inch of her, but not right away.

His gaze was instantly drawn to the curve of her neck. He watched the small artery pulse with the life that animated her.

He licked the tip of his incisive and slowed himself with a careful inhale. This was so new, so precious, he didn't want to pierce that perfect skin just yet. So, with great care he kissed that little hollow right under her ear and drew his lips along her throat and slowly down to the top of her shoulder. He slid the loose collar of her silky garment down and realized she wasn't wearing a bra.

Oh *sacrament*! He was hit again by a thumping of pleasure, his cock pressing hard against his jeans.

He dug his nails in his hand to slow down his cravings. Trying to remember that he was no longer at the *Serpent Maudit* and that this was *the one*. The one woman that he had lost himself over. The one he cared so much for, for whom he'd gladly give away his lengthy life's work.

"Hells, Nyssa, I want you. I'm not sure I can stop."

"Then don't." She was pushing curls of his hair from his forehead and the lightly warmth of her touch was like nothing he'd ever experienced. "I don't want you to stop."

"You sure you want this?" He had to make certain she

was one hundred percent on board and would never have any regrets about their intimacy.

"Oh god, yes." She took his lips with a loud moan of impatience.

He groaned with pent up craving at the wild passion in her usually measured tone. His ice empress was now fire in his arms.

"I want you, Mag," she whispered against his lips.

Her words called directly to the primeval part of him and he flipped her over the couch, his body poised above her.

"Then you will," he grunted before his lips curved into a wolfish smile. "Every bit of you, *mon amour*."

Her eyes were bright with desire as she cupped his butt within her palms.

He had no idea how long he would last before he could no longer hold back from forcing himself inside her. Hunger pulsed through every vein, his cock painfully scorched with need in his jeans. He unfastened the button of his waistband and zipped down his fly to ease the pressure, hoping it would buy him some time.

She trailed her fingers up his spine under his t-shirt. *Oh hells*. That was almost too much.

He edged his hip slightly to one side, leaving one hand free to explore her. His palm settled on her flat stomach under the loose silk of her top.

She called his name again and he quieted her with another kiss. He lifted the fabric of her top as he skimmed his palm gently atop of her breast, the skin soft under the pads of his fingers.

She shifted with a purr against his lips, the small moan mounting his cravings. He rolled her nipple between his thumb and forefingers and she jolted, releasing his lips with a small cry.

"Mag."

"You like that."

"Uh-huh..." She reached for his neck and drew him to her.

His breath mingled with hers again as he continued to fondle her nipple. She found the naked skin under his boxers and slid her palm down his bare butt cheeks and he nearly lost it. If she pulled the boxers down, that was it, done. He would be inside her in a second, unable to stop himself. And he didn't want that just yet.

"No. Wait." He wanted to savor this for what it was. Something real, something good. Something that happened once in a lifetime. Making love for the very first time.

Maybe Justin was right. Oh heavens, he did loved her. He truly did.

And he would love her body with as much passion as his soul yearned for her.

He broke their kiss so that his lips could find her breast. He nibbled at the tender bud and let his fang trail across it, delighted to see her arch her back with pleasure at the touch.

An overall feeling of weightlessness took over as happiness rose inside him. She didn't fear him, she took him as he was. All of him, the immortal vampire, the witch's son, and the man. And he badly wanted to feel her quiver under his lips, under *his* touch. All his.

He stopped playing with her nipple for a brief second and stayed poised right above her chest, looking at her striking face. Her usually perfect hair was a little messed up, her lips swollen, her soft gray eyes taking on a darker hue. "*Sacrament*, you're beautiful, Nyss."

"So are you." She had a hand at the back of his neck, her fingers digging in his hair, her touch drawing warmth and crazy sensations all along his spine. "I want you, honey. All of it."

With his entire body unbearably hungry, he slid on his knees on the lush carpet by the couch. His lips kissed her stomach, one hand held her shoulder down. He licked her sweet belly button as he tugged down on the elastic bands of her loose pants and panties. His mouth trailed along her hipbone and he slid her pants all the way to her ankles.

He pulled back to look at the length of her. Her top exposing flawlessly round breasts and dark pink nipples. Her limbs long and sleek, intimate blonde curls at her center. And he knew exactly where he wanted his lips.

"Perfect," he said, catching her feverish eyes.

"Your turn," she said, wrestling her underwear down farther with a wiggle of her body.

"Not yet."

He slid a finger from her knees to the inside of her thighs, savoring every moment, every discovery of the small planes of her. She bristled with heat and parted her legs to his touch.

Soon his hand reached for the hot center between her thighs, and he was thrilled to find her wet and ready for him.

He kissed the inside of her leg, right there near her damp juncture. He inhaled her sweet feminine scent and without another wasted moment, his tongue was exploring her intimately.

She jolted with a yelp of pleasure as he licked the sweet

folds filled with her heat, her taste, with her desire. Her longing of him.

Awash with his cravings, he was still stunned that she accepted him. That she had let him see through her cold persona, so much that she let him love her in such an intimate way.

His heart was full for her and he wanted to give her the world. He wanted to feel her come upon his tongue.

With his arms wrapped around her thighs, he teased that one little spot that made her moan harder, and she bucked under his mouth as he bit her gently. Her fingers dug into his scalp. She was so close.

He continued to pleasure her, alternating licks with sweet bites, his own body on fire to hear her breathless beneath him, guiding him along. He would not stop until he had her complete surrender.

When her hips seized with a powerful shake, she cried out his name as she came.

"Oh god." She held hard onto his shoulders and let out a small joyful laugh. "Oh, Mag. Wow. What was that?"

"That," he said, sitting back on his knees beside her, "was just the beginning."

His confidence soared and he was ready to take her now. Fully. To make her entirely his.

"Come," she said, her arms wide calling him. Her face was saying it all, her features both soft and alluring as she urged him with impatience.

She sat up on the couch, lowered his pants farther, and parted her legs to wrap them around him.

This was as it should be. Perfect bliss, the two of them together. He couldn't love her more.

He had the words on his lips when a scent of heather

reached his nostrils. A slight shift shimmered in the air above the couch.

The hair at the back of his neck stiffened and his body froze.

Nyssa stopped herself. "Something wrong?"

"Oh, Magnovald, *pitou*. I'm so proud of you." The familiar voice doused him like a frigid shower.

Half-dressed and poised above Nyssa on the couch, he stared with horror at the intruder. Fury mounted inside him and he clenched his teeth.

Muscles quivering, he slid his pants back up as fast as he could, shielding Nyssa from view. "What the fucking hell, Mom?"

# CHAPTER 26

*H*oly *motherly hell!* Nyssa went from the height of ecstasy to fear for her life in three seconds flat.

She dropped her top down and swiftly slid into her pants, snatching her panties from the floor, and tucking them under a cushion. She curled beside Mag on the couch, clinging to his arm with shock, her body pressed against his bare torso.

*"Maman,* what made you think it was okay to drop in on us like this?" His body was tense with irritation at his mother. He slid his arm at Nyssa's back and kissed the top of her head. "I'm so sorry, Nyss."

The witch's appearance had killed their passion like a bucket of ice water and left Nyssa dizzy with astonishment.

The woman had really appeared in her living room, just like that—in a poof of indigo fog. Nyssa shifted her legs from under her and struggled to reclaim her assertive persona.

"I was just talking to Emmeline at the *Serpent.* She filled me in. I think I figured out how to fix your problem, *mon pitou*." Charlotte Callan casually walked to Nyssa's wet bar, picked a low-ball glass, and poured herself a drink. She surveyed the living room with a shrewd eye. "This is a nice place you have, *chère*. Very elegant."

Nyssa tried to detect any sarcasm in the witch's voice but found none.

"What problem?" Mag grumbled. "I don't have any problems."

"Oh, but *mon fils*, you have many." Charlotte sat in the leather club chair across from them and rearranged her long velvet dress around her small body. "And your mother is here to help."

Nyssa, finding her wits, shot the witch a hard stare. "What gives you the right to materialized in my home like this," she scolded the woman. She was indignant of the intrusion yet fully aware the witch was that powerful to do so.

Charlotte shot Nyssa a side glance, then smirked at Mag with a raised brow. "Well, here's one of your problems. "

Before Nyssa could react, Mag tightened his embrace on her. "Nyssa's not a problem. In fact, she's everything to me."

Nyssa heart soared at his words. He had given so generously just a few minutes ago, thinking of her while she knew he was holding back his own needs. Her heart-felt attachment towards him intensified even more.

She blinked and in one sudden realization, admitted to herself that this was more than attachment—what she felt was love.

Pure, unadulterated and deepfelt love.

*Oh my god*, she did love him.

Her heart had opened for him the minute he'd bravely swept in Norwell's compound, indifferent for his own safety, just to bring her back.

Willing to give up everything, just for her.

And with her entire heart, she wished all of this, his mother, the club, and his enemy, would just disappear to leave them both in peace to explore their newfound feelings for each other.

Why did everything need to be so painful?

His mother whirled the amber liquid in one of the glasses Nyssa had brought back from a trip to Italy.

She recalled the awkward time. The drive along the Amalfi Coast with Baron von Hafner. He had almost proposed that day, but she'd made it clear she wasn't interested, the thought of Cat's wellbeing always nibbling at the back of her mind.

And here, with Mag, despite all the strange revelations, she knew Cat would always be safe. That she, Nyssa, would be protected.

She finally relaxed in his arms. There was nothing his mother could do to hurt her. She knew in her heart he wouldn't let it happen.

Charlotte looked at them both and waved a frustrated hand in their direction. "Well, if you say so."

"Mom, you have to let it go."

"I have, *pitou*. I know." Her irritated expression shifted into a pained look. "There's nothing I can do, you two are…."

"Yes, Mom. Together," Mag stated.

"Look, *chère*, I'm sorry about earlier." Charlotte's tone warmed as she leaned forward in her chair. "I was told you went to a mob gang to take on Prince Norwell by yourself because I turned you down."

"Well, not quite…" Nyssa hesitated, puzzled by the witch's changed demeanor.

Charlotte frowned as she fingered the pentacle at her neck. "You're gutsy. I see why he likes you."

"*Maman*, cut it out," Mag interrupted. "Can we please go back to the part where you decided that appearing in someone's house was an okay thing to do."

But Charlotte was ignoring her son, still focused on Nyssa.

"It was nothing personal." She smoothed the skirt of her black dress over her thighs and held Nyssa in a conflicted gaze. "You're human. I saw Justin bury a wife in the 18th century. And poor Valerian with Emmeline when they were teens. That didn't turn out well."

"You married a human," Nyssa rebutted carefully, not sure how far to press.

"My poor Antoine, yes. I loved him more than anyone could think possible." She tilted her head at them. "I wanted so badly to turn him immortal, but even if I had found a way, he wouldn't let me."

"Really?" Mag seemed surprised "I always thought Papa Antoine wanted to be like you."

"No, son. He was a religious man. And after seeing me cast spell after spell to try to keep him ageless, he told me to stop. My magic was drawing on darker energy—calling to the underworld—and he just wouldn't allow it."

"I never knew. So this means you might actually know how to make Nyssa immortal."

"Mag," Nyssa rasped, the mere thought shocking her. The one thing she had easily managed to ignore while Mag's lips were exploring her body was now returning to the forefront of her thoughts and deadening the pit of her stomach with anxiety.

"Wouldn't you want to be?" His face was eager and full of hope.

"I... I don't know." She slid her finger along his muscular forearm wrapped across her chest. "What about Cat?"

"Well." He lifted his shoulders. "Her, too. If she so wishes."

"Oh and should we turn her whole family and friends, too?" Charlotte retorted. "Magnovald, be reasonable. We can't do that."

"But Papa Antoine, you just said—"

"Stop." She held her palm up. "One learns a few lessons in three hundred years. Maybe if you had paid more attention, you would, too. We can't change the course of natural life. Whatever you decide to do about your relationship, she will stay human with a human life, and you will live forever as an immortal."

"Forever." Nyssa was still unable to wrap her mind around the concept. "Like until the end of time?"

"I don't know, dear." Charlotte shrugged. "Our cells regenerate constantly. We say forever but it could be thousands of years. Who knows?"

"That's it, then," Mag spat with force. "Mom, make me mortal."

"Mag. No!" Nyssa turned in his embrace, astounded with disbelief. He was willing to make himself mortal. For her!

"Why not." He shot her a devilish smile then plopped a light kiss on her temple. "I don't need a long life if you're not in it."

"Of all my sons, Magnovald, you're the one who most resembles my dear Antoine." Charlotte's eyes softened with affection. " But be serious, *pitou*. How can you protect her if you're mortal and lose your strength? And with this new enemy you have."

"Then do it after I take care of Prince Norwell." His jaw was firm with resolve at his decision.

"*Mon fils*, there will always be a Prince Norwell."

He took a deep breath and looked at Nyssa, his expression crestfallen. "So what do we do?"

"You care that much about me?" Nyssa asked him, aware of his mother's gaze on them. "To alter everything you are?"

"Of course he cares, Nyssa," Charlotte chimed, using her name for the very first time. "He loves you."

Hearing these words from his mother shook her to the core. He had never said he loved her.

But she had felt the deep emotion in him as he commanded her body earlier. She'd seen him broken at the prince's feet, willing to give everything away. Just for her. He hadn't said the words, but she had seen it all. His love for her. It had been there all this time.

"Would you mind if I was mortal, just like you?" His voice was hoarse with anticipation.

Uneasy with Charlotte watching them, she searched her heart, finding the love she held for him, and remembering how she had cast him away when she'd first found out about his true nature.

And with all her soul, she tried to express her true feelings for him.

"Don't change who you are, Mag," she said this with certainty. "Not for me."

"Oh." He broke their connection and, with a sudden drop in her stomach, she realized that she had said the wrong thing.

She laid a hand on his chest, ready to plead with him.

*Yes, honey, turn mortal or even better, make me like you.*

"Mag, I—"

"Well whatever you two decide," Charlotte abruptly stood from her chair, "now is not the time. We have to get rid of Prince Norwell and I know how."

"The bastard." Mag's demeanor shifted, his brow taking a decisive slant. "He wants the whole club. My waitstaff, too."

Nyssa's heart sank and her numbness reached her extremities. The moment to tell him how she actually felt had passed. And maybe it was for the best. His mom might be right. They shouldn't be together. If either one of them changed, there might be regrets. Regrets that would tear them apart.

"Well, that is why I'm here." Charlotte had dropped the subject of their relationship all together. "I know exactly how to get rid of Norwell."

"You do?" Mag took his arm off Nyssa shoulder.

"Well, son. I was going through your artifacts in your office—"

"*Maman.*"

"What?" She frowned.

"Privacy!"

"Nonsense." She waved her hand at him. "Anyway, I saw that you have the Goblet of Summon."

"And…"

"We call Merritt."

"His sister?" Nyssa asked, still crushed that Mag had pulled away from her but wanting to help.

"Yes," Charlotte confirmed. "Princess Merritt of the Daeva Realm. She outranks Norwell."

"Wouldn't it be better just to bring in Malcolm Dunsmuir?" Mag added. "Emme suggested it earlier. I'm

279

not fond of the guy, but he may be able to do something. He's Norwell's king.

"Not quite. I know he oversees the whole Daemon World, which technically encompasses the Daeva Realm, but they are more like friendly neighbors than a feudal colony." Charlotte stood to refill her drink. "So if Dunsmuir interferes without her knowledge, she may not take it kindly and start another uprising."

"So why do you think she would help us?"

"Oh, she will be furious. She's a fickle being but has grown in the last few years, both personally and within her position of royal." Charlotte turned from the wet bar. "She will hate that her little brother crossed over without her knowledge. She made a strict promise to the Black Oak Order that she would never return to the human world."

"So she'll bring her brother back," Nyssa interjected, her confident persona firmly back in place.

"That's my hope."

"Why the complicated summon? I still think we should first bring Malcolm in to talk to her," Mag griped. "Evan must know how to reach his sister. Harper is married to the guy."

"It will put Malcolm in a weird position with Merritt. Him knowing before she does, she won't like it." Charlotte took a delicate sip of her cognac. "I told you, she's fickle."

"So we summon her," Mag finally conceded.

"Yes. I say we wait until Norwell comes to claim your club with his daevas and right when he does, we do the ritual."

"Ritual?" Nyssa frowned at Charlotte, trying to keep up with all the supernatural information thrown around.

"Yes, *chère*. Go get dressed," Charlotte ordered above the rim of her glass.

"Oh hell no. She's not coming!" Mag bolted straight up from the couch.

Nyssa's heart cracked. Oh god, he truly thought she wanted nothing to do with him.

"Wait, no. I want to help." She unfolded herself from her seat and rested a hand upon his shoulder. "Mag, when I said I don't want you to change for me, it doesn't mean I want nothing to do with you. You have to know that."

He turned to cup her cheeks between his palms.

"I know, *mon amour*, I know." His voice was hoarse with emotion as he slid his finger along her chin. "I won't have you at harm's way. I just have to take care of this, and I will be back. We'll talk."

"But—"

"No." His gaze was full of love as he stopped her with a finger to her lips. "I almost lost you once."

"Magnovald, that's nonsense!" Charlotte interjected. "Nyssa is much stronger than she looks. She has proven it already. She comes with us."

Nyssa turned to the witch with disbelief, stunned at the words of support.

"Mom," Mag groaned.

"Look, son, if she's part of the family, she has to learn how to defend herself." She smiled warmly at Nyssa in the weirdest sudden turn of heart. "Don't you worry, *chère*, I'll teach you everything I know."

# CHAPTER 27

"You never said you were using Nyssa as bait," Mag grumbled between clenched teeth.

He was standing in front of his office desk, Nyssa right next to him, both looking at his mother who was drawing a salt circle on the ground while his brother Ren leaned casually by the door and Justin studied the spell Mom planned to use. Emme was slouched back in the club chair, slowly sharpening the blade of her short sword with a whetstone.

Nyssa tensed under his touch, but her spine was ramrod straight with determination.

They had called Vince and he'd agreed to keep watch over Cat with some of his people for the night—just in case they'd miscalculated Norwell's intentions and he decided to come for the kid.

Upon Mag's request, Vince had also sent Sandro and two other Moreno men to keep an eye on the compound. It was daytime so Mag couldn't send his own bodyguard vampires for risk they'd burn to a crisp in the late winter sun.

So far, all they knew was that the guests had left and the place was as sleepy as an abandoned tomb. Daevas, his mom had chimed, preferred the night since their world had no natural sun and relied on a sort of bioluminescence for energy.

"She's not really bait, *pitou*. I just need her human essence for the spell. Merritt is a *quarinah*, which is a special kind of daeva who prefers young human females for sustenance when in our world." She let out a heavy, frustrated sigh. "I can't use any of you. Unless we ask that spunky waitress of yours, what do you call her, Sandrine?"

"She's keeping an eye out on the floor." Mag splayed his palm wide against Nyssa's back. He had thought of shutting the club altogether but then Norwell was likely not to show if there were no patrons to impress.

"I'm fine, Mag," Nyssa countered, turning her pretty face to him with resolve. "I'll just be a conduit."

"I won't hurt her," Mom said. "I promise."

To prove her point, his mother took something out of her witch's satchel and got up to her feet to approach Nyssa with an open palm. "Here." A silver signet ring adorned with a pure clear blue crystal rested in Mom's hand.

"Oh. This is exquisite."

"Morag's Protection Ring," his mother said quietly. "You can always call on me wherever you are."

"Mom?" Justin looked up from the spell book with surprise.

"Listen, you two." She looked at Justin then at Ren with a firm gaze. "Magnovald is bringing a human into our family. It is now my duty to protect her at all costs. And I expect you both to do the same."

"Sure, *M'man*." Ren shrugged, his arms crossed at his

chest.

"Of course," Justin pinched his lips for a second and laid a heavy look on Mag. "Are you sure it's what you both want?"

Mag didn't reply and instead stared at Nyssa, his heart pounding, still unsure of her feelings. "Are you?"

The brave smile she gave him was the sweetest thing he ever witnessed. She carefully took the enchanted ring and slid it on her middle finger. "Yes."

"Wow." Emme smirked and tested the sharpness of her blade. "Morag's Ring! A big honor coming from Charlotte, here. She never did this for me when I was human."

"Well, Emmeline," Mom replied. "You and Valerian were too young to know what you were doing."

"Still, you didn't do anything to prevent my turning."

"I would have, had I known about it." Mom rolled her eyes impatiently at the blonde vampire. Mag knew his mother had always blamed Emme for Val's lifetime guilt. "You went behind my back."

The two of them never got along even when Emme was just a human kid behind the counter of her father's general store.

"Just because you wouldn't do it for us," Emme argued.

"Ancient history." Mom closed her satchel with a brisk pull. "I thought you were perfectly happy being who you are."

"Who told you that?" The vampire shot the witch a strained gaze, her brows drawn together.

"Justinien."

With slight amusement, Mag watched Emme turn a murderous look to his brother.

"Hey," Justin protested. "You told me yourself."

"You shouldn't believe everything I tell you." Emme smirked but her expression remained dark, leaving Mag wonder if Justin knew things about Emme that she wouldn't tell anyone else.

"Welcome to my family." Mag bent to Nyssa and brushed the curve of her neck with a kiss. His pants tightened with desire as he inhaled her fresh clean scent. When this was all over, he would finally be able to show her how he truly felt about her.

"Can we just move on?" Justin eventually added, resting a hard gaze on Emme who had returned to casually polish her sword. "We have a freakin' daeva prince and his horde of minions on our doorstep."

"I'm almost done with this." Mom placed her mystical paraphernalia—candles, mirrors, vials of herbs, and the goblet—at the center of her sacred circle.

"You have someone watching their compound, right?" Ren said. "How long do we have after they leave?"

"I don't know." Mag turned to his mother. "Can't they just materialize without us noticing?"

"It's a long way," his mom frowned. "I don't know about Norwell's power, but daevas can't just travel in dust form from that far. They'll have to drive, part of the way, at least. One of Moreno's men should catch sight of them."

"You really should have closed the club, Mag." Justin passed the spell book to their mother.

"No. From what I've noticed of him," Nyssa countered, "he'll want to be here when the place is full. He's very fond of himself. He'd want an audience."

"I guess you're right," Justin said.

"I don't think he'll want to hurt them," Mag noted. "He was pretty clear. He wants to run the nightlife in the city. He had human clients in his compound."

"He did." Nyssa shuddered with disgust. "I saw twenty or so."

"He'll want to impress my customers," Mag added.

"Yes. He'll want a showdown." She turned her alarmed expression at him. "He'll want a confrontation with you again. In front of all those people."

"You kicked his ass," Emme chuckled.

"Yep." A small, satisfied smile curled his lips at remembering Norwell's stunned expression as he disintegrated.

"With your birthright," his mother looked at him with pride. "My Callan legacy in you."

He silently shot a quick nod at his mother, letting her believe that she was the reason why he'd summoned her magic. But he had brought it back because of Nyssa. Only *she* had that kind of power to make him forget his resentment.

"He won't let that slide." Nyssa skated her hand at his waist and suddenly all he wanted was for this to be over so they could focus on what truly mattered. Each other.

"Then let's bring it on." Mag tingled with anticipation of a good fight. "We need to protect the human patrons at all costs, though."

"We will." His mother skimmed her palms on her dress and addressed Ren and Justin. "You boys, go set up wards around the place."

"It's already warded, Mom," Mag added. "Maisie did it before they left for Berwick Hollow."

"Val's wife did a good job, but I feel them loosened. You need to keep these things up, you know. Renaud, Justinien," she considered his brothers again. "You do remember how, I hope."

"We're not kids anymore, Mom," Justin said, his tone indulgent. "You have to stop bossing us around."

"Here." She passed them each a vial of what looked like tiny star anises mixed in with herbs. "Use these and go strengthen those defenses."

"Thanks, bros." Mag dipped his chin to his two brothers. "This club has nothing much to do with you."

"You know me," Justin said. "I need to see this through. Plus, that bastard abducted little Catalina. He can't get away with this."

Ren stared at Mag, his expression unreadable as usual. He then shrugged. "You're a pain. But you're family."

"Right." The corner of his lips curled into a half-smile. "Appreciate it, man."

"You want the wolves here?" Ren still held him in a dark gaze.

"Why?" It was an unexpected offer. "Not like you to involve them."

"This looks bad, man."

"Does it?" Mag chuckled. "Hell yeah, I suppose."

"Wolves?" Nyssa asked.

"Werewolves," he informed her. "Pack in Domaine-Lassalle. Ren's buddies."

"You're friends with werewolves?" Her eyebrows rose with astonishment.

Ren smirked. "Friend is a strong word. Let's say I'm close to the pack."

"Honorary member, I hear," Justin chimed in.

"Are they like… human that change into wolves with a full moon?" Nyssa was full of curiosity.

"Something like that." Ren's smile for Nyssa was warmhearted and Mag was relieved to detect some acceptance in his voice.

Both his brothers seemed okay with his relationship with a human. Now he just needed to figure out a way to make her immortal. But he'd cross that bridge when he'd get there.

"*Les enfants*, wards," mom shouted.

Ren rolled his eyes with amusement and silently followed Justin out of the office.

It was about ten in the evening. The place was still quiet but in two or three hours, the club would be packed. If Nyssa guessed right, that was when Norwell would show.

"Emme, you'd best wait at the entrance with Raphael," Mag instructed.

"Yeah, ok." She unfolded herself from the chair and strode to the door to disappear in a flash of blonde hair, dark suede, and confidence.

"That leaves us. You have everything you need, Mom?"

"Yes. But wait…" She was rummaging through his artifacts still on the chair. She removed a flat bronze necklace from the pile—the chain incrusted with tiny heather gems. "Aradia's Chain of Power. Wow, Magnovald. I didn't notice it earlier. Just what she needs."

"The ring will allow you to call on me," Mom added as she passed the jewelry to Nyssa. "But this necklace will enhance any physical strength you already have."

"Nyssa won't be fighting," Mag protested, his heart racing at the sudden possibility of Nyssa being caught in the crossfire.

"Oh, she looks like she can handle it." His mother impressed a serious look on Nyssa. "Can you not, *chère*?"

Nyssa stood straight, her body radiated strength and energy. "I can."

"Look, Nyss," he cleared his throat, trying to find the

right words, "I saw you fight off that daeva in the street and you have some skills, I know."

"Martial arts," she said.

He didn't need the reminder. "This is a prince of the Daeva Realm and even I couldn't take him without magic." He shuddered to remember the bastard's possessive hands on her body. "He *had* you."

But Nyssa's expression was full of righteous vengeance as she tied the necklace around her throat. "It will be okay, Mag. You've got to let me do this."

"She won't go near the prince, Magnovald," his mother said. "I promise."

"But Mom…" His heart pounded, his skull throbbing at the risk Nyssa was taking just by being here.

"Mag, if this, you and me, is going to be a thing, I need to be able to hold my own in your world." Nyssa put her hands on his shoulders and held him steady in her gaze, her words soothing. "I can fight. I have the sight of these poor abused children to sustain me."

Her tone was so strong that he realized how resilient she truly was. She had not only erected buildings in their city, but she had also built herself.

He stared at her with awe. She was both the ice queen he knew and the passionate woman he had held in his arms earlier. And in this time of need, the passion and strength melded in the formidably brave woman before him.

He gently sleeked her hair and tucked a silky strand behind her ear. "He can't hurt you."

"I won't let him." Her determination was unfaltering.

"Mom." He took a deep exhale. "You *will* watch after her."

"Actually, Mag," his mother said, "it's the other way

290

around. I need her to watch over me. Once I start this spell, I'll be vulnerable. I need her here in case any daeva comes in while I cast the summon."

"Fine. But put a ward on the door before you start," he extolled. "Only leave this room when Princess Merritt is here. Then you bring her to me."

"Do not put yourself at risk, Nyss," he added. "Stay in here."

She nodded with a small smile. "We got this."

Against his better judgement, he had no choice but let her help. She was right, if she were to stay in his world, he had to trust her strength. And trust that his mother would give her all the protection she could within her tremendous powers.

He squeezed Nyssa's shoulders once more to give himself the courage to accept that she was part of this.

"So we have Emme at the door, Justin and Ren on the periphery," he reviewed, "and me in my booth waiting for him."

"He'll want to take you in the middle of the club," Nyssa reiterated.

"The dance floor," he nodded in agreement. "Okay, so you both wait here for his arrival. How will you know?"

"Oh I will," Mom said. "That part is easy. I'll feel his essence."

"And you call upon his royal sister while we keep him occupied."

Nyssa seized both his cheeks in her palms, deep concern etched in her features. "Don't die, Mag."

"Don't you worry, *ma belle.*" He took her hands in his and as he lowered them to his chest, he brushed a kiss on her forehead. He then shot her a cocky smile. "I'm a Mount-Royal Immortal, remember?"

CHAPTER 28

"*S*o all I have to do is read this?" Sitting cross-legged in the middle of the complicated circle drawn with salt on the flagstone floor, Nyssa took her eyes off the spell book. She studied Mag's mother as the woman's rearranged an odd-looking ragdoll in front of three tall black candles.

"More or less." Charlotte's look on her was lit with a twinkle and Nyssa understood where Mag had gotten his playful streak.

"Why do you need the book? Mag told me you're the most powerful witch on the continent."

"Ah, sweet boy. I do have many abilities. But magic is a finite thing, like energy." Charlotte took an easy breath and placed the sacred goblet carefully in front of her. She emptied a vial of sweet-smelling herbs into the receptacle. "It cannot be created or destroyed. It is merely transferred. The spell helps me do that. Some spells, like this one, are so powerful that they are very fickle. Once cast, they vanish from memory, so they must be read."

Nyssa frowned, not sure where Charlotte was going

with that. "But why can't I do what you do, then. Read from a book and activate this energy?"

"Why can you write and a dog can't? Why can a bird fly but you will never be able to."

"We do have planes," Nyssa rebutted with a level-headed smile. The woman *was* intimidating, but Nyssa would have to learn how to deal with her.

"Indeed we do. Which is why you have the ring and the talisman," she clarified, no more the overbearing mother but the witch passing down her knowledge with patience. "You can't do magic by yourself alone, just like you cannot fly. But with the use of artifacts, you will be able to."

"Why aren't people using them all the time, then?"

"It took humanity a long while to build planes, didn't it?"

Nyssa nodded, pondering the analogy.

"Some humans do use them." She indicated to the club chair. "Look at Magnovald's artifacts. They go back centuries."

Nyssa stared at the jumble of objects, some so old, she couldn't pinpoint their origin. "Yes, quite the collection."

"True. I realize now how much he refused to use my magical legacy." A shadow crossed Charlotte's ageless features. "How much I hurt him."

"He used one spell." Nyssa shook her head in awe. "At the compound. Just one spell. There were ice crystals everywhere. And the prince just dematerialized."

Charlotte's expression brightened. "Yes…very clever."

"Why didn't you get in touch for so long?" Nyssa still hadn't wrapped her mind around the fact that a mother would ignore her son like that. And in the St-Amand's world, long had a whole new meaning.

The question shook Charlotte, and the woman took her time before answering. "I don't know. At first, I left because I was so stricken by grief because of Antoine, my husband. You see, they were all there, my boys, when their father died. Even Griffon, who was always gone on some expedition or another, attended his bedside. And I let Antoine die. With all my power, I couldn't persuade him to let me save him. I felt so much shame at letting it happen. I couldn't bear having my sons see me after this."

"But it was not your fault," Nyssa choked, witnessing a glimpse of the witch's tragedy.

"Oh, *chère*," sorrow touched Charlotte's tone, "can't you see how they should hate me? I'm one of the most powerful witches alive and I couldn't keep their father from death. I let him draw his last breath in front of his beloved sons. I failed when I was needed the most."

She paused and gave a tiny shrug, her features struck with grief. "They all ought to loathe me," she added. "But one by one, each of them came to see me in Lafourche. Or at least started to write me, like Renaud and Griffon. We all rekindled our lost connection. I hoped for so long to hear from Magnovald, but he never contacted me. It broke my heart."

"You could have called," Nyssa pointed out. "Does he even know how you feel?"

"I don't know. But the boys told me about his life. How he seemed happy. He was so close to Antoine, I didn't want to disturb his peace. And I guess in the end, pride kept me away. I failed and couldn't get past it." Her chin quivered with remorse. "Worst error of my life. Which is why, when I heard about you, I decided it was time to come and help."

"You knocked me unconscious." Nyssa tried to find it in her to forgive the intrusion.

"Sleep spell. Nothing more." Charlotte's shoulders fell and Nyssa suddenly saw a glimpse of a simple woman who had been carrying an immense burden for centuries. "But I'm sorry. I should have known he cared about you."

"Is that why you're helping me now?" Her heart thawed for the woman and she fingered the heather gems at her throat.

"Yes and no. You're a tough woman, Nyssa Vlahos." Charlotte gave her a warm, appreciative smile. "He chose well. But it will be hard for you two. One immortal, the other not."

Nyssa nodded slowly. "If you could go back in time, would you still be with a mortal?"

"You mean the boys' father, Antoine. Because to me, he was their only father."

"Yes. Would you still do it if you knew how hard it would be when he died?"

"For me, yes, I would do it again." Charlotte turned somber. "But Antoine, was it fair to him?"

"You feel guilt."

"I could never give him a child." The sorrow was visible in her dark eyes, so like Mag's. "One of his own blood."

"You think I could? Give Mag a baby?" Nyssa's hand seized upon Aradia's chain. The words had come out, just like that.

"If you two can't," Charlotte asked prudently, "are you still sure you want to be with him?"

Nyssa's lips thinned as she pondered the question with gravity.

"Yes," she finally said. "Absolutely. Plenty of couples

who cannot have children. It's just something you sort out together."

Charlotte nodded. "To be fair, I don't know why he can't have a child. His wretched birth father did. But I was told Magnovald tried many times. And couldn't."

"Oh." Nyssa was judiciously sorting through her feelings on the subject. She had always thought of having children but had been too busy building an empire to think on it very long. It was such a huge responsibility that, were she decide to bring one to this world, she would put all her efforts to doing it right. That Mag had tried to have offspring and never could, made her ache for him.

"Yes. He was always good with the little ones. You should have seen them all when they were children," Charlotte chuckled. "They were very much like they are now. Renaud disappearing in the woods for hours, Justinien at the school with the priests, and Magnovald leading the local kids to mischief in the streets."

"Really?"

"Kids just flocked to him. Quite the ringleader. They never did much bad, steal a loaf of bread from the baker, slide a frog in a rich lady's collar, that sort of thing. And he was constantly making powerful allies. Like the Moreno men helping us tonight. He's always been a very loyal person."

"He is," Nyssa agreed. He had never let her or Cat down.

"And he liked life around him." She looked around the office. "Probably why he built this place."

"He did build this." Her research had uncovered that the building's foundation dated from the late 17th century. She bit her lip with the wonder of it all, amazed that she had fallen for someone that was alive during that time.

297

"That is what I was told yes. I was gone by then. But Justinien kept me updated."

"And his father, his real one, never showed."

"That beast. Ambrus was his name." She snorted with scorn. "A real-life Count Dracula."

"Like for real?" With everything she had to swallow recently, she'd be unfazed if the infamous vampire actually turned out to be Mag's father.

"Who knows?" Charlotte shrugged. "The man was deadly handsome and came to my boarding room at night. Just before I embarked on the ship to New France with the other *Filles du Roy*."

Nyssa was entranced by her story and urged her to continue with a slight nod.

"I realized that I was pregnant aboard the ship taking us to the New World."

"But you still found a husband?"

"I waited for the ship to sail farther upriver to the next port, I was scared to be honest. A lot of the other girls found husbands in Quebec City. I still didn't know what to do. Being a witch, I could have ensnared anyone to take me, but I was still in shock to have been compelled and impregnated by a vampire. I was very young." Her gaze dropped to her spell components and she rearranged the doll's position on the floor. "When we finally landed in the Montreal port, I met Antoine. I fell in love and told him the truth."

"Wow."

"We expected one child, not six," she smiled at Nyssa.

"And he didn't mind that they were not his?"

"Love, my dear, it does move mountains."

"And how about Mag and his brothers being immortals. How did your husband react?"

"The Notresdame disciples showed up on the seventh day after their birth. The boys were fussy, and the priests insisted they needed their blood. Antoine was deeply religious. The disciples were part of a well-respected local order of monks and so he accepted the reality relatively easily. He loved his sons."

Nyssa parsed her multitudes of thoughts. "So Mag's father, this Ambrus, he doesn't know they exist."

"No. And I wish to keep it that way." Her voice hardened. "My son Griffon is out there, looking for him. Knowing how stubborn he is, it's only a matter of time."

Nyssa shuddered. It had been tough enough dealing with the mother, she had no desire to meet this Ambrus.

"Hard to take it all in?"

"Yes." She couldn't lie.

"Are you scared?" Charlotte frowned.

"Of Mag. Of you?

"Of any of this." The witch's eyes narrowed at her.

Nyssa huffed. "I'm not scared of you. But your powers, this prince. Yes, it scares me."

"Don't worry." Charlotte reached a jeweled hand to her and shifted her body in the circle. "We have a good plan. I could have asked my friend Lakota for this, but I feel it's best you get involved sooner than later."

"Sure." Nyssa said, her spine straightening with resolve. She had made her choice, there was no turning back.

"As soon as I feel his daeva essence, I will start."

"Okay." A few flutters churned in her stomach, but she steadied her grip on the spell book.

"You know, Mag is quite taken with that little sister of yours," Charlotte added. "What is her name again?"

"Catalina, she's very—"

*"Diable!"* Charlotte's eyes suddenly widened. Her entire body started to shake. "He's here! I can feel him."

Panic seized Nyssa's throat.

The witch mumbled under her breath, the woman's eyes now rolling back into her skull. *Oh god.*

"Do I start the spell?" Nyssa shrieked.

*"Dhio meih ban-dhia…"* The sacred goblet was now in Charlotte's hands. Her eyes were glassy and blank as a mist rose from the floor. "Read, girl. Now! Start reading. They are too close."

With trembling hands, Nyssa clung to the spell book and started reading the incantation to summon Princess Merritt.

A whiny but too familiar voice suddenly snarled in the room. "Not so fast."

A vicious, invisible blow kicked the book out of her hands.

The grimoire landed against the wall across from her and she looked in horror as a tall shape materialized right behind Charlotte.

*Prince Norwell.*

One of his minions appeared and towered over Nyssa.

"The Ice Witch." Norwell sneered as he pulled Mag's mother up by the back of her hair. "Oh, how fun!"

The daeva prince reached for Charlotte's throat with his massive hand.

"Run Nyssa," Charlotte managed to scream before choking on the prince's grip. "Get Mag!"

Norwell's underling attempted to grab her as she bolted to her feet in a familiar fighting stance. She briefly touched her chain and, with a surge of power, grabbed the daeva by the shoulders and kneed him in the groin. He screeched and his body flew across the room, leaving space for her to run towards the door.

"Oh look who's here, the big sis!"

*LaChance.* The sleezeball was at the doorway, blocking her exit. He had to have managed to sneak into the club amid all the other customers.

She touched the chain again but felt nothing. The artifact was already depleted of its energy. *Damn.*

She gave LaChance a hard squint. The scrawny rapper's limbs twitched with suppressed energy, his nasty knife jerking back and forth ready to take a slice of her flesh.

But she wouldn't have it. Not this time. Her pulse raced with wrath at her sister's molester.

She stilled as she slipped into her skillful defensive stance. Ignoring his self-satisfied sneer, she focused on the weapon, noticed the lax posture. He didn't know how to fight. Good.

A powerful sidekick was the first of her sequence. Years of dedicated training culminating in this single moment.

The knife flew out of his hand and she registered his stunned expression with a trickle of satisfaction.

But it was not enough for the bastard.

It took a mere few seconds, she struck where it hurt, knees, groin, kidneys, ending with a crack of his nose. She danced nimbly on her feet as he uselessly tried to take a swipe at her.

She bent forward as one of his punches sucked her breath, but her hatred fueled her, her discipline doing the rest. And the sturdy last roundhouse brought him down. He fell on all four and she slammed the outside edge of her hand at his neck.

He rolled on the floor and blinked at her hazily, his face a mess of blood and puffed-up flesh.

"Fuck you, asshole!" She spat in his face and finally caught her breath.

"Nyssa!" Charlotte's cry made her glance back.

The witch had somehow escaped Norwell's grasp and had backed into a corner. She was now surrounded by four daevas closing in as Prince Norwell supervised, a sanctimonious curl to his mouth.

"Go! Get them," Charlotte ordered before mumbling something under her breath.

The temperature in the room dropped to an instant freeze.

Every single object, from the walls to the office supplies and the glasses on the wet bar disappeared under a sheer coat of ice. Icicles dripped from the ceilings and crystalized from the ground, trapping LaChance's limbs under a thick layer of snow.

*Holy shit!* Nyssa watched in shock, her limbs still.

"*Anyenthex!*" The window crashed open at Charlotte's command and an icy blast stormed into the office, knocking two daevas down in its path.

Nyssa held onto the door handle to sustain the blizzard as she witnessed Prince Norwell's mocking laugh echo madly in the midst of Charlotte's ice storm.

*Dammit.* The plan had failed. Nyssa shot Charlotte one last look, shoved open the office door and, worried for the fighting witch she was leaving behind, fled breathlessly into the hall.

# CHAPTER 29

*C*oiled and ready for action, Mag was sipping his scotch with restless energy when he saw Nyssa bolt through the flap doors leading to his office.

Her hair was plastered on her cheeks, sweat beaded at her forehead and a veneer of white frost covered her clothing.

*Sacrament.* His glass fell on the table and he bolted from his seat to meet her.

"Mag. Come quick. "Her eyes feverish. "He's in there with your mom…"

"Wait, what?" His gut clenched as if he'd swallowed a stone. *Shit.*

"The prince." Nyssa's chest heaved up and down. "She's barely holding on."

"She's fighting him?" He seized her shoulders and noticed the nasty bruises on her forearm and the blood on her hands. "What happened to you?"

"I'm fine…but your mom, I don't know." She choked on the words. "She yelled at me to get you all."

Just above her shoulder, he caught sight of a lone daeva pushing open the swinging doors and enter the club.

He cupped Nyssa's cheeks. "Nyss, please. Go find my brothers. But be careful."

She nodded but his heart tumbled with angst as he watched her disappear into the busy crowd. But he had to help his mom. Despite being a powerful immortal witch, she could still be killed like any other human if her spells failed to protect her. The place was stocked with his vampire staff, and he had to trust that they'd look after Nyssa.

Mag strode towards the office and in seconds, faced the lone daeva scowling at him. In one brisk move, Mag grabbed the foe by the throat and dragged him back through the doors.

The monster croaked, his eyes bulging out of their sockets as he tried to take a swipe at Mag.

But Mag was done playing games. His entire focus was on destroying Norwell. He crushed the minion's windpipe and threw him back down the hallway. The daeva's body bounced on the far wall, just a foot from Mag's office.

"Norwell, leave my mother!" Mag marched down the hall. "Show your face."

But there was no sign of the prince. Another daeva came out of the office—his body compact in the khaki and brown parka— and charged at him, ramming into Mag's stomach.

*Shit*! That hurt. Mag folded at the blow, his breath briefly lost, while twisting sideways to grab the back of the daeva's collar.

His grip steady, he ran a quick left uppercut to his face, bashing the minion's nose. The foe grunted in pain as Mag followed with a few punches to his gut.

Fuckin' creature, invading his home like this. Mag hoisted him over his shoulder and threw him out to land him unconscious next to his buddy.

"Norwell, what the hell! It's me you want. Not my mother." Mag burst into his office. He nearly tripped over LaChance passed out and beaten bloody under a coat of ice blocking his path. A sheen of ice covered every surface of his office.

Then he saw his mother. *Sacrament.*

She lay unconscious in the middle of her circle, her summoning doll ripped open by her side, the salt markings broken.

Norwell was sitting behind his desk, rocking in his chair and shuffling snowflakes from Mag's paperwork.

"What have you done to my mother, you sick bastard?" Mag's fury knew no bounds, flushing his blood to his fists. His vision tunneled onto his one adversary. He would annihilate the fucker.

"*Vahrasth hyenthx!*" His palms were out, his mark burning. A ray of hope pierced his mind, his mom had to be alive if he could still call on her magic. "*Vahrasth!*"

But Norwell was faster. "*Du Akular!*"

Mag was propelled straight out of his office doorway and across the hallway. Agony struck his lower back as he slammed into the wall and fell to his knees.

"Fuck you!" he roared, jumping to his feet. His fangs were out, nails ready to slash that overly pretty face. He rushed back inside and dove over the desk and upon Norwell, catching the bastard's throat right where he had wounded him earlier.

Norwell yelped as he fell off the chair. He scrambled to his feet and pulled Mag up by the shoulders. "Not this time, worm."

His fingers dug into Mag's flesh and he landed a knee right at his solar plexus. The pain seared so hard that Mag's breath stopped.

An underling grabbed Mag from behind and tried to pull him off. But Mag wouldn't let go, fangs and nails digging into the prince's skin.

With unparalleled strength, Norwell punched him straight into the gut.

Mag almost let go from the wrenching shock, but as the prince struggled under Mag's grip and minions kicked his back viciously, he held on tight to try to topple Norwell's bulk.

"Enough of this. *Korilath!*" Norwell's body became searing hot.

*What in the sacred hell!* Mag let go with a curse and jerked backwards.

The daeva prince's entire body erupted with fire, white flames emerging from his very skin and topped at his head in a fiery blaze, his eyes burning red embers.

The minions had stopped kicking, their mouth slackened with equal shock.

Norwell advanced towards Mag and thundered, "I told you this is *my* club now. I want you out."

*Holy shit.* Why had no one told Mag of this? All their expectations of summoning the princess sister were gone and lay behind him, his mother out of the game and surrounded by his useless artifacts. There was no way in hell he could fight a daeva in flames.

He retreated slowly back and away from the blazing daemon.

His minions—Mag counted four of them—had recovered their wits and were circling him.

"Leave him to me," Norwell barked. "I want his admirers to see him defeated."

"Fucking hell, no," Mag boomed with angry denial, thinking of his staff, of his patrons.

As he slowly exited his private quarters, Mag's eyes oddly caught the bill he'd received earlier to fix the electrical system as Nyssa asked. Right beside it was the fountain pen his brother Val had gifted him on his three hundredth birthday. And toppled beside it on his desk, the small portrait of Papa Antoine at his forge drawn by a client.

The history, the sweat he had drained to build and maintain this place flashed through his mind. It fueled his rage further at the thought that someone would just take it all away.

Mag was now in the middle of the hallway, backing off while Norwell ambled toward him until they were both facing each other in front of the swinging doors.

*Sacrament.* His teeth were clenched with urgency. Where the hell were his brothers?

Magic might again be the only way. "*Strieahadhr—*" Mag started to intone the spell that had taken Norwell down in the compound.

"Ah. Fool me once." Norwell snapped his fingers and the incantation died on Mag's lips. The prince let out a derisive laugh, his body still smoldering with bluish white flame. "You think your magic can stop me. I am a prince of the underworld, you maggot."

With his skin an inferno, Norwell held on the deep bite at his neck, blood trickling down between his fingers.

The bastard *could* bleed. Hope rose inside Mag.

He considered the situation in a fraction of a second.

Norwell could be wounded. But this wasn't something he could do alone.

He needed his brothers. And Emme. Now.

One to subdue the fire. The other to rip his throat out.

They might succeed in dematerializing him as Mag had done before but he would be right back. And now that he had summoned the depth of hell into his body, it may be impossible.

Mag just required enough time to get his mom back. Stall him until his brothers came once Nyssa informed them.

"How did you get out of your palace, Norwell?" Mag sneered, blocking the monster's path to the busy club. "Did your big sister allow you out?"

"Leave my sister out of this," the prince scorned, his mouth taking an ugly downturn.

"Oh, did I touch a nerve?" Mag leaned back on his heels with a smirk. "Jealous she's inherited the title and you're only second best?"

"I am not second best." Norwell leveled with him, his chin high despite the hand at his wound. "I'm the first male in line. It should have been me."

"And that bugs you, doesn't it?" Mag continued to goad, shoulders loose and ready. "Being eclipsed by a female."

Echoes of clinking glasses and laughter emerged from the club behind him, the thumping of the beat pulsating through the walls. He could not let Norwell pass the swinging doors and show his burning body to everyone. Dammit. He should have closed the club. A bit late now. He'd have to figure out a way to end this discreetly, shield his customers from catching a glimpse of the daemon in flames.

"She's a dumb little thing," Norwell was grumbling, the envy obvious in his tone. "Doesn't know how to rule."

"And you do." Mag had no idea where he was going with this, but just wanted to keep the prince talking.

"Of course I do. And I'll start with this place." He narrowed burning eyes at Mag. "This club, this neighborhood. This city. I always thought I'd make a good mayor."

"No, motherfucker." Mag's blood boiled. "You won't. You'll be crawling under the rock you came from, under your sister's skirts."

"Enough." Norwell's face was flushed with anger. Small flames licked his cheeks, his pupils so dark they flicked with the evil of true hell.

"You'll never have my club," Mag spat, his face a mere foot from Norwell's. He vibrated with the urgency to obliterate him.

"Enough." A flash of fury sparked in Norwell's eyes and he doused the flames licking his body.

He took one step closer and with both hands, slammed Mag hard in the middle of his chest.

*Fuck!*

Mag's body sprang back in the air and crashed through the swinging doors.

He landed with a snap of his shoulder right in the middle of the dance floor.

Cries erupted everywhere. Dancers screamed as they parted from him. The music stopped abruptly.

Mag shuddered with lancing agony and he rolled to his side.

So much for discretion.

# CHAPTER 30

*N*yssa heard the screams of patrons erupt just as she reached Ren and Justin at the far end of the club. The music had stopped and they all turned toward the commotion.

As panicked dancers cleared the way, she saw Mag sprawled on his back on the floor. *Oh god.*

The crowd parted with hushed murmurs as Prince Norwell strode to the middle the dance floor to tower over Mag, now on all fours before the daeva royalty.

"Not so strong now, are you, St-Amand." The prince sneered.

Mag jumped to his feet. "Get off my property, you fucker."

"We need your mother," Nyssa whispered to Justin. "I don't know if she's alive."

"We got this," Justin quietly said, keeping his eyes on Mag and the prince with a grim twist of his mouth. "Help Mom in any way you can."

"How about Emme?"

"There's no time. Go check on Mom." He nodded at his brother Ren. "We'll help Mag."

Justin and Ren cut through the crowd while Prince Norwell and Mag circled each other surrounded by a row of baffled patrons.

"Your property? It's mine," the prince whined. "I got it fair and square."

Nyssa kept them in her line of sight as she made her way behind the bar.

The daeva prince's arms wide, he slowly pivoted as if wanting to be admired. "Behold, city dwellers. I am Prince Norwell, new owner of the *Serpent Maudit*." At his words, his entire body ignited with a low blue-white flames.

Holy mother of… Nyssa's jaw dropped as the club's customers gasped in shock.

*Mag*, she worried.

But Mag was posturing with a sneer. His stance steady, muscles tight under the black t-shirt, fangs out with that emaciated look on his features, both formidable and scary as hell.

"Should I kill you now," Prince Norwell mocked, "in front of all of them?"

Nyssa's heart pounded against her ribcage. They needed Charlotte. Get on with the plan. She prayed the witch was still alive.

She snaked her way through the crowd and to the corridor leading to the office. Her hands went straight for the talisman as she saw LaChance still down and blocking her way by the office door. He was crawling slowly, reaching for his blade on the icy floor, and hadn't noticed her yet.

Without thought, she delivered a bold kick to the head

312

that knocked him back unconscious. Bastard. This one was for the other kids he'd ensnared before her sister.

She did a quick scan of the room, empty of threat but covered in ice and snow everywhere. Charlotte lay on the floor, her head tucked under her arm, the witch's velvet skirts fanned across the sacred circle, its salt visible under a sheer coat of frost.

Nyssa slammed the door swiftly behind her and bolted it shut.

"Charlotte." She rushed to the witch's side and shook her shoulders. *Damn.* The woman was breathing but was unconscious. Nyssa patted Charlotte's face a few times, trying to revive her. But to no avail. She had to wake her, but how?

She scrambled to the small wet bar next to her. Everything was frozen solid. Finally, she found a full bottle of vodka, still in liquid state.

She grabbed it from the tray and dumped its content on Charlotte's head.

*"Mon dieu!"* The witch bolted straight up. She frowned. "Nyssa?"

"Sorry, you passed out."

Her hazy gaze refocused. *"Maudit Chien.* Norwell. He choked me."

"He's out there fighting Mag and his brothers."

"Are they…" Her eyes widened, alarm crossing her gaze.

"They're okay. For now." Nyssa pressed her lips with urgency. "There's no time. We need to call Merritt."

"Where's the book?" Charlotte's commanding presence returned.

"Here." Nyssa found the pages, creased but intact.

"Find the spell." She mumbled a quick incantation that

melted the ice immediately under her. She started to fix the salt lines of the broken circle.

Oh god, where was it? Nyssa flicked the pages of the spell book. *Here it is. Beckoning from the Other Planes.*

Charlotte rearranged the artifacts and scooped the herbs into the Summoning Goblet. "What will I do with this ripped doll?" she muttered, trying to put the fabric together again.

Nyssa reached for Mag's desk and passed her a roll of tape. "Here."

"Perfect." Charlotte shot her a thankful look before spinning tape all around the rag figure. "We're good. Let's do this."

Seated in the circle across from Charlotte, Nyssa stared at the words on the pages. She just had to read.

Charlotte seized her forearm. "Magic will flow through you," she said. "Just let it."

Flutters of apprehension in her stomach, Nyssa nodded, not willing to mess any of this up. She started to read.

"*Sus kahló sa aftón tin kósmo…*" As a tingle rushed through her limbs, Nyssa glanced down at her wrist and was overcome with shock.

Her throat tightened, almost preventing her from reading farther, at seeing faint symbols appear on her flesh. *The mark of the Ice Witch.*

Charlotte hadn't been kidding when she mentioned her being part of the family. She shook herself and endeavored to continue to read. The words sounded like ancient Greek, similar to her parents' language. As she said the words, it was as if her mother was alive again, assisting her in saving the man she loved.

She was three quarters into the spell when a scent of

ozone filled the air. As she neared the last line, a halo of gold shimmered on the floor, a vague shadow taking form and rising at its center.

Nyssa jumped as a loud knock battered the door.

A strained voice sounded out from the other side. "Charlotte, Nyssa, are you in there?"

*Emme.* The door handle rattled with force.

Charlotte shot Nyssa a hard warning to ignore the interruption, her grip hard solid on Nyssa's arms as she continued to mumble her own spell.

The witch's entire body glowed in a silvery hue, her features seemingly otherworldly as her familiar heathery scent overpowered the charged air.

"Charlotte, open the freakin' door. The guys need you real bad right now!" The knocks turned to kicks. "Nyssa. Are you in there?"

With a pressing stare, Charlotte directed Nyssa to look at the gilded fog.

Shock caught her by surprise and her mouth fell wide open at the apparition. Nothing could have prepared her for what, or who, stood above her.

Surrounded by a golden halo, the being looked like a true princess of fairytale. Her shiny dark hair glistened and flowed down along her bare pale shoulders. Her skin glimmered unnaturally under a white slip of a dress, the material covered in tiny crystals of many pastel hues. A fine bronze circlet encrusted with turquoise gems adorned her forehead. She was blinking with surprise as she took in the surroundings of Mag's office.

"*Merde*, you bloody stubborn witch!" The door suddenly crashed off its hinges and Emme bolted in the office.

*"Du Akular..."* The otherworldly creature leisurely pointed at Emme.

The blonde vampire screamed and tumbled to the floor unconscious.

"No!" Nyssa screamed.

"Oh dear." Charlotte gathered her skirt and gently stood to face the apparition while Nyssa ran to Emme's side.

"Who the hell are you, maggots? The princess leveled her stare, her chin high and her brows slightly raised with disdain.

"My apologies, Your Royal Highness." Charlotte bowed slightly. "I know this is a crude way to get you here. But it is a matter of urgency."

Nyssa searched for a pulse at Emme's throat and found none. Her heartbeat raced with worry. Did vampires even have a pulse?

"What did you do to her?" Nyssa blurted out at the royal apparition.

Princess Merritt slowly turned towards Nyssa. She gave her a look so stark that Nyssa gulped, chilled to the bones with dread.

She then turned back to Charlotte with a pleasant smile. "The Ice Witch of the Callan Clan."

"The one indeed, Princess. I call you to my city because your brother is here."

"Norwell is here?" Startled, she again looked around the office with a gentle frown at her brows. "What is this?"

"This is my son's abode, Princess. The *Serpent Maudit* nightclub." A hint of pride warmed Charlotte's tone.

"A human nightspot, lovely. I do like those." With a glint in her eye, she waved her hand to thaw the ice off a chair before taking a delicate seat, her hands folded in her lap. "How I've missed this world."

"Your brother, he wants this place for himself."

"Oh." The frown deepened on her forehead. She huffed with a tiny shrug. "Why should I care?"

"If it was a regular human bar, of course, it wouldn't matter," Charlotte noted. "But this one is connected to the Black Oak Order."

The contemptuous princess flinched. "I see," she said, grudgingly. "No, that wouldn't do."

"Exactly, Princess. You know what happens when our two worlds collide."

The princess pursed her lips, appearing to ponder Charlotte's words.

Nyssa felt a sudden shudder in Emme's chest under her palm. The blonde was still unconscious but drew in a shallow breath.

Emboldened that the female vampire seemed alive, Nyssa turned to the royal.

"Princess Merritt," Nyssa told her. "Your brother has brought these horrible daevas with him. He kidnapped my sister and countless other children."

The princess cast a shrewd eye to Nyssa. "And who is this?"

"My name is Nyssa Vlahos," she said coolly, bolstered to finally be acknowledged.

"Nyssa, how pretty." A predatory gleam crossed the daeva royal's eye and Nyssa repressed a hint of fear that Princess Merritt may not turn to be an ally.

"She's my son's girlfriend, Merritt." Charlotte's deferential address suddenly soured. Her curt tone contained a sharp warning. "Tread lightly."

"Oh, how sweet." The predatory look vanished

instantly, and the princess's features softened into a dreamy expression. "I lost my own boyfriend here in this world. We both liked it so."

"But you cannot be here, Merritt." Charlotte's voice remained stern.

"No, sadly. The Daemon King made it clear. He keeps the peace as long as we stay away." She sighed and her dress shimmered as her chest rose.

"Where's my brother, then." Her annoyance darkened her pretty traits. "He can be so bothersome. Clueless about diplomacy."

"In the club," Charlotte responded. "Fighting my sons. And you know what may happen to your precarious throne if any of them gets hurt."

"Lead the way, then." The princess stood and gathered her gossamer skirts within her alabaster hands. "Let's put an end to that."

Nyssa hesitated, her arm protectively around Emme, who was stirring on the floor.

"You, too, Nyssa Vlahos. Come." The princess cast her an authoritative look. "I like pretty little things like you around."

Nyssa frowned at the command. "But Emme."

"Oh, don't worry. She'll be fine." Her tone gave Nyssa no choice. Mag was out there fighting a daeva prince in flames and they needed the royal sister. "Let's get my tiresome little brother before he does anything serious."

# CHAPTER 31

"*A*re you ready to give up, maggot?" Norwell's chest was puffed with importance as he towered over Mag in the middle of the dance floor, the fire at his skin replaced with a golden hue.

"You know you won't be able to keep the club up for long." Standing tall, in a lose posture, Mag squinted at him. "Before you know it, my brother Val will bring the entire Black Oak Order upon you. They took your sister down once. They'll have *you* out in no time."

They'd been going at it for a couple of minutes and Norwell was obviously enjoying the verbal confrontation in front of everyone.

Where the hell were his brothers? And Nyssa? Mag's heart pounded as he assessed the situation.

The club's customers had scattered away from the dance floor, not wanting to be caught in the fight. But many remained at the edge, drawn by the pull of witnessing some implausible battle. Electronic devices were out, recording every words.

Norwell's daevas—Mag recognized six of them—were

319

scattered among the crowd watching their boss ready to take on the immortal.

*Finally*, Mag let out an internal sigh of relief as he caught sight of Justin and Ren in the shadows within the crowd. There was no sign of Emme.

Sandrine was at the back behind the bar with his bartender Jackson and had gathered a handful of humans with them. She had a loaded shotgun on the counter.

Evan and Louka were trying to convince the patrons to leave. But they wouldn't budge, unable to tear their eyes and cellphones off the impending fight.

"I don't care about some human realm warlocks." He wetted his lips as he preened before the crowd. "I have my own army."

"A few daevas?" Mag eyed one of them with a small curl of his lip and sneered at the prince. "That's who defends you? They better look out."

In one discrete move, Ren had padded behind one of Norwell's minion and slit its throat in a single cut of a small blade. The daeva silently slumped to the floor. Its grayish dusty blood splattered to the nearby people who shrieked with terror.

Justin had seized another by the throat and methodically crushed his windpipe as panic ran through the crowd like wildfire. This was no longer fascinating.

More screams erupted. People pushed on one another trying to get out, which, Mag realized, may have been Ren and Justin's plan all along.

"Hey, don't leave," Norwell shouted at them, his eyes darting left and right in a momentary panic. "We're just getting started."

But people were bolting for the front door, others rushing to the fire exit.

"Stop." Norwell's sudden booming command brought a chill to the whole room. He was no longer pleading, his tone shaking the flagstone flooring outside the dance area. "You will stay."

His arms rose to his side ominously and dark gray shadows twirled around him, obscuring his body for a moment.

A shock of terror fell over the entire club, freezing everyone in place. The shadows formed into, not the daevas Mag had expected, but a gaggle of living corpses. Emaciated, rotten flesh hung from protruding bones as they slowly rose and stretched their misshapen limbs from the ground.

*Oh fuck, ghouls.* How on earth had Norwell managed to raise ghouls?

"Justin," Mag roared, seeing his brother closest to the fire exit. "Get them all out. Now!"

Everyone moved and screamed at once. His staff tried to control the crowd as best they could. Jackson lifted a disabled veteran over the bar and Evan shielded two young women in his arms.

"Looks like they don't like your new management." Mag's tone was flippant but inside he was horrified.

The ghouls were fully raised and ready, forming a half-circle guard around Norwell and waiting for his command.

"Oh, by *Ell'zoth*." With surprising speed, Norwell dug into the departing crowd and came back with a tiny young woman, her eyes bulging wide with terror under a pair of horned-rimmed glasses.

Adrenaline raced through Mag's veins as rage pounded inside him. He narrowed the distance between them and fumed. "Let her go."

"I want you out, maggot." Norwell preened, holding his hostage by the top of her arm. "You and your brothers and all the vampires. Leave. I'll keep that human waitress."

Mag heard Sandrine pump the shotgun in response.

"Nobody moves." The prince pulled hard on the small girl, seizing her by the throat with one hand. "Or I kill her."

Panic finally caught up with Mag as he stared at his frightened patrons. Even the buffest of them was frozen in place.

*Sacrament.* He needed his mom alive and calling out to Merritt right now. And where were Nyssa and Emme? Mag searched the crowd for them and found nothing.

"Shut those doors," the prince ordered.

The club was dead quiet now. Many were hiding under tables or were huddled flat against the walls. Evan was still with the girls. Jackson was slowly lowering down the young veteran in his wheelchair behind the bar.

Mag saw Sandrine's gun move and shook his head to stop her. Bullets would not stop the prince and his ghouls. Especially as he was clinging to his hostage like a child with a prized toy.

Mag was just a few feet away from his foe. Close enough to snatch the girl safely away at the right moment.

With a measured exhale, he leaned back on his heels and slowly crossed his arms at his chest. "Do you always hide behind women, Norwell? Is that how you succeed in life?"

Mag glanced briefly at his brothers, his mouth in a grim twist. It looked like their plan had failed. Princess Merritt was not coming. Now it was all about getting everyone out alive.

"Don't come any closer, St-Amand." Norwell drew the girl into his chest. "I *will* kill her."

"What kind of host will you be if you start killing your patrons?" Mag a strode one foot closer. "Don't you want to run the nightlife here?"

He was keenly aware of the hostage. Sammi, she was called. He remembered now. She came sometimes with her group of girlfriends who loved to flirt with him. This one always stayed in the background, though. A little shy.

"It will be okay, Sammi," Mag said. "I won't let anything happen to you, okay?"

The girl just cried harder and clutched the strap of her crossbody purse tighter.

He quickly glanced sideways again at Ren and Justin. His right hand slid along his Ice Witch mark and he knew his brothers noticed the gesture. Neither of them had been fool enough to renege on their mother's magic and recognized Mag meant to start the attack with a coordinated spell. It had been centuries since they had done anything like it. But together, their immortal blood was linked through their mother's legacy and they would prevail., They had to.

He was so close now, he could smell Sammi's fear and the prince's otherworldly essence.

Together, the St-Amands would defeat the bastard.

"*Koir idash...*" He snapped his neck backward to direct the spell at the ceiling.

"*Koir idash!* " his brothers both repeated after him.

The humans screamed and rushed in one big mob to the exits.

The ceiling above the dance floor became covered with a multi-layered sheet of pure blue frost. Thunder rolled followed by the crackling of ice. The ceiling trembled and giant icicles descended in menacing spears towards the daevas and ghouls, who scattered, some impaled by the falling frozen spikes.

*"Colebex yth!"* Ren called out and a lightning bolt erupted from the ice to strike one of the ghoul dead. The others dived for cover and glanced at their leader for command.

"Oh, damn this!" the prince shoved Sammi out of the way and jumped straight at Mag.

*Oh shit.* The bulk of Norwell's body hit Mag like a mass of bricks and they both rolled to the ground.

His fangs and claws dug into the unearthly flesh while lightning ice sparks crackled all around them at Ren and Justin's commands.

Norwell managed to seize his wrist, the wide palm slammed against Mag's Ice Witch marks, and the brothers' link severed. Mag could no longer control its magical energy.

A heavy crack suddenly shook the entire club, sending bottles and light fixtures crashing to the flagstone floor. Sleet pounded every surface as an arctic wind blew hard across the club.

Norwell now had his hands around Mag's neck as he tried to pry him off. Mag dug his fangs deeper, not willing to give an inch. The daeva's blood tasted foul under his tongue, but dammit, he would drink him empty if he had to.

Norwell released him for a mere second then slammed his palms hard at each side of his skull.

Mag howled at the instant agony that swelled over him.

The pain was soon replaced by vision of pure horror as

if he'd been dropped into a pool of viscous crawling insects.

They were everywhere around and inside him, maggots worming their way across his eyelids, long centipedes inching feathery appendages under his clothes, small gnats burrowing in his nostrils. A buzz of flies hummed in a persistent ring of doom in his ears.

Gagging with disgust, he was fighting a raising panic when a giant velvety spider skidded across his chest. His eyes suddenly opened to the vision of a corpse sitting alone at a bench.

The bugs scattered away as he looked stunned at the gloomy sight. It was him he was looking at, himself as a living corpse. In the *Serpent*.

His club was a decrepit mausoleum, the dance floor coated with a thick and dry sheen of spiderwebs, the derelict bar crumbled under layers of dust. The fractured mirror was reflecting the poor soul crouched under the weight of centuries who sat at the faded booth. It was *himself*.

Undying and alone.

All alone. Just as he had always feared.

Despair descended down and along his throat. Why build this life when *he* only remained in the end?

They would all die. Just like Papa, just like Justin's wife and everyone else he knew. One after another. And here he would be, left behind to exist.

As the world died around him.

The hint of a fresh, elegant scent suddenly crossed his memories. He recalled a silky strand across his cheek. A tender touch on his skin.

As if Nyssa was calling him from the beyond.

His fists tensed with sudden protest. He was not alone. No!

He had *her*.

In the depth of the nightmare created by Norwell, he was hit with the realization that, for the first time since his father's death, he had hope.

Hope for a future.

He was not this immortal desiccated living corpse creaking over his drink in his long-forgotten bar. He had someone!

Someone he loved. A life worth fighting for.

A rush of euphoria swelled in his soul and returned him to the present.

His muscles tensed with a surge of energy, embolden by the frosty gusts blowing over his skin.

He slammed one heavy fist under the prince's chin and felt him relent. He released his throat, spat the blood out, and bit him once more. The prince flailed as Mag drained him further before letting go again. Straddling his foe's waist and ignoring the ice crystals pelting them down, he seized his head and banged it hard on the stone.

He had him, the bastard was close to being bled dry.

Mag had no time to savor his victory or ponder whether a daeva royalty could actually be drained when a bright flash of light blinded him.

"What is the meaning of this, Norwie?" The clear but commanding voice erupted above them.

Norwell froze under Mag's grip.

Mag lifted the prince again, ready to slam his head down. A blast of searing hot energy hit him in the center of his back. Pain radiated through his entire spine and he dropped the prince.

"You, fiend. Leave my brother alone."

Brother? Mag frowned with confusion.

"This is my son, Princess." The confident voice Mag knew so well echoed in the air.

*Mom?*

"*Daúscayrl*," his mother said, and the storm dissipated.

"You can let go of him, Mag." Nyssa lightly touched his shoulder. "Princess Merritt is here."

His heart soared. Nyssa had succeeded in summoning the royal. His own ice queen, the one he was so worried about protecting, had done it! He was flooded with a flurry of emotions as she urged him to his feet.

He finally got off Norwell and stood to slide an arm around her waist with incredible relief.

The prince was on his back, his blood everywhere on the floor. Bewildered, he stared at his royal sister. "Mer?"

Princess Merritt advanced in a shimmering pool of glittery white silk and a hush of reverence scattered across the crowd. No one could look at her and not be awed, even Ren and Justin looked impressed.

Everyone, except their mom. The lace of her velvet dress was torn, her dark hair in disarray, but she resonated with a power that seemed older than the world itself.

"He really shouldn't be on this plane, Princess," Mag's mother was saying, the censure audible in her tone. "You need to take him home."

"Norwie, my dumb little brother." The princess extended a pearly-gloved hand to the fallen prince who blinked through a puffed-up eye. "What were you thinking, coming here like this?"

"I tried, Mer. I really did." Lips pouting, Norwell gathered himself up and stared around at all the patrons. "I gave them what they really wanted. The drinks, the drugs. Forbidden sex with little humans."

"I had a chat with these two ladies here," the princess explained. "They tell me you want to take over this club. Expand in the city. Why?"

"Look at this place." Norwell circled in place to emphasize their surroundings. "It's packed. They keep coming. I asked around. They love him."

The princess sighed with a fond look over her brother, then her gaze narrowed onto Mag. "You almost killed him."

Mag stood tall and glowered back at her, his grip firm around Nyssa's waist. "He has no right to be here, Princess. He's been kidnapping and trafficking children. He was ready to harm my patrons."

And the bastard had dared capture the woman he loved. His blood still boiled with fury.

"I see." Merritt ambled a few steps across the dance floor, her forehead lined in thought, her long gauzy dress flowing gracefully behind her. She stopped and surveyed the club. "This is nice. Once it's cleaned up. It almost makes me want to take over."

"What?" Mag's heart seized as Nyssa let out a small yelp of surprise.

"That would be foolish, Merritt," Mag's mom warned. "Not only would you have Malcolm Dunsmuir and his daemon army after you, but I also only have to say the word and my sons' father would return from the underworld."

"Father?" She paused eying his mother.

"Ambrus the Exiled. Or as you know him, the Banished Death."

"The Banished Death." The princess brought a slow hand to her mouth, a disturbed shudder carrying all the way to her delicate brows. "Their father…"

"Mom?" Mag asked with disbelief.

Justin shook his head, equally puzzled while Ren shot his mother a blank look.

"You're right, Ice Witch. We need to leave," the princess relented. She took her brother's hand. "Come on Norwie, you've annoyed these people long enough."

"But Merritt," he whined, his tough persona faltering. "I was just beginning my empire—"

"Be quiet!" She had gone from understanding big sister to ruler in a half second flat.

Despite his height and size, Norwell cowered under her gaze, like a toddler caught doing something wrong.

"I do apologize for my brother's interference. I am now taking him home. Is there anything I can do...?" She casually waved her arm around. "To lessen the damage he caused."

"Actually, there is." Mag drew Nyssa closer to his chest. "What do you know about immortality?"

## CHAPTER 32

"Where's Emme?" Justin scanned the club with a frown.

"In the office." Nyssa nodded absentmindedly, still stunned by Mag's words. "She seemed okay."

Justin took off as Nyssa stared in turn at Mag and Princess Merritt. Norwell remained subdued beside his sister.

"Immortality." The female royal's brow rose curiously at Mag.

Charlotte chimed in. "That's not a bad idea."

"Wait, what's going on?" Ren side-eyed his brother.

Nyssa cast a look at the patrons and staff around the floor, who were all watching them with morbid curiosity.

"It's all good, folks," Mag shouted with a pleasant smile. "As you see my poor friend Norwell got injured in our little play fight today. But he's fine."

Charlotte was mumbling a spell to get rid of the ghouls' mishappen corpses and the broken ice chunks scattered everywhere. The club's patrons remained shocked, some taping the destruction left behind by event with their devices as she toiled to dissolve it all into nothingness with her magic.

She turned a shrewd eye at them and ended her enchantment with one powerful snap.

Everyone shook themselves as if out of a trance, puzzlement and doubt across their features. They found their seats and drinks, phones returned to their pockets, no doubts with the videos of the night erased along with any memories of the night beyond an exciting bar fight to discuss over the next few days—Mag's mom had likely seen to that.

Mag left Nyssa to approach the girl Norwell had clung to earlier and put his arm around her. "Raphael. Come here. Sandrine, you, too."

"I'm sorry you got caught in this fight with my old friend, Sammi," he said to the girl." My bouncer will take you home. Sandrine, too. Get some rest, okay?"

The girl nodded at him, confused and with her face still tear-stained behind the thick glasses.

As Raphael and Sandrine approached, Mag instructed, "Make sure she's okay, will you?"

"Sure thing, boss." Sandrine wrapped her arm around the girl in a sisterly hug. "Come with me, Sammi. Raphael, here, won't let anything happen to you, okay, *fille*? I'll stay the night with you if you want, have some girl talk. I've seen so many of these brawls, I'll tell you some stories."

The three of them walked away while Mag addressed the rest of the patrons, his arms splayed wide and welcoming. "Friends of the *Serpent*! Please enjoy the rest of the night with a free round! DJ Al-Whalid, take it!"

A shout of joy responded to his call and the thumping music resumed.

Customers huddled to discuss what they thought

they'd seen, calling out their drinks to Mag's busy wait-staff. The dance floor was soon packed again.

"Let's move to the office," Mag said over the beat as he motioned for Princess Merritt to lead the way. "Your Royal Highness, if you please?"

She beamed at him as they made their way towards the back. "This is so exciting. I wish we could stay. Maybe order one of those fancy cocktails with lots of bright colors."

Nyssa glanced at her royal brother with a shudder. He was sticking close to his sister, a look of bored annoyance distorting his pretty-boy features. She wanted those two gone from their world as soon as possible.

But Mag had other ideas. Her heart thumped at the request he had made.

The office was empty when they arrived, remnant of snow, ice, and broken glass everywhere.

"Where's Emme?" Nyssa said out loud.

"Justin texted," Ren reassured her. "He took her out. She was still in shock from her attack."

"Your little blonde friend that was here?" Merritt chimed. "I may have reacted a little too fast when I attacked her. I'm not used to being summoned like this."

"She'll be fine," Charlotte said, waving her arm to dissipate the snow and restore the window in one simple swoop. "She's a tough one."

Nyssa wanted to say otherwise, having seen Emme almost dead, and made note to check on her when the royal departed. But for now, all she could focus on was Mag's outlandish request.

Merritt brought the topic first. She took a careful seat in Mag's club chair while her brother remained behind her at attention.

"You want immortality?" she asked Mag. "But aren't you immortal?"

"For her. For Nyssa." Mag had his hand at Nyssa's back again. "Could you do it?"

"Mag…" Ren shot him an expressionless look. But the tone clearly showed that he was not on board with the idea.

"It's the best way." Mag was adamant.

"Is it?" Ren was looking at Nyssa now and she shuddered under the heavy gaze of the distant immortal. "Is this what you truly want, Nyssa?"

"She does," Mag insisted. "Of course, who wouldn't?"

"Mag, give her space." Ren said quietly, the corner of his eyes taking a kinder turn.

Nyssa was still speechless.

"We talked about this, didn't we?" Mag asked.

She frowned, her body completely still but her mind racing with contradicting thoughts. "Not exactly."

"It would solve everything."

"You mean us, together."

"Yes." His expression was so full of needs that it broke her heart.

"Can she do it?" Nyssa needed to grapple with all the facts before she could consider such a proposal.

"She probably could," Charlotte noted. "Wouldn't you say so, Princess?"

"Turn a human immortal?" The princess caught her chin in her delicate gloved fingers.

"You are a full-blooded royal from the underworld," Charlotte continued. "I noticed Mag has the *Tiare Eternelle* in his collection. Had we had that with Justin's late wife, we perhaps could have extended her life. But we need

Daemon blood to make someone fully immortal. Full blood from a royal line would do the trick."

"How about Malcolm Dunsmuir?" Ren asked.

"He's half-blood. His mother is a human witch." Charlotte shook her head. "Princess Merritt's blood would be needed."

"You asked me how you could pay for your brother overstepping my domain," Mag told the princess. "This is it."

"My blood?" Her tone turned icy. "Isn't that a tad excessive? Norwell wasn't that bad."

*Not that bad?* Nyssa shot the princess a side-eye. Her brother was so much worse than bad.

"Can we just go home now, sister?" His expression was churlish as he chimed in. As if he was done playing and ready to move onto something else.

"We just need a few drops, Princess." Charlotte clarified. "And your assistance in the spell."

"For her?" She shot Nyssa a puzzled look.

Nyssa silently bit her lips. They were making all these arrangements but she was overwhelmed with little time to mull over it all.

"It won't take long. An hour of your time."

"She's human," Mag explained. "I'm immortal. She needs a longer life span."

"Oh. I see." Merritt suddenly smiled. "For love, then."

Nyssa finally let out a breath and put her palm out to stop them. "Wait. This is my life you're all discussing."

"Why wouldn't you want to be immortal?" Charlotte squinted at her. "This mortal life is so... well, short."

"It's not for everyone, Mother. You know Val struggles with that. Hells, you do, too." Ren countered. "And what about Maisie? She almost went insane."

"But with Merritt's blood, Nyssa won't take any of those risks. She'll just have a longer life." Charlotte was now determined. "And I was there to help Maisie along, she is fine now."

"Nyssa." Mag was looking at her with such intensity that she was struck with the bond between them. "I want this for you. More than ever. But it's ultimately your decision."

"Immortal."

"Yes, *ma chère.*" Charlotte said. "And with similar physical strength that the Aradia's chain gave you. You could always keep the chain for the strength, but I cannot give you the lifespan without Merritt. You need to decide now, *ma fille.*"

"I'd be with you," she looked at Mag with a slow nod. "Forever."

"I certainly hope so." He shot her that half-smile that always made her melt. Then his gaze turned serious. "But you and I, together, it's on. Whether you're immortal or not."

"And Cat?"

"You will have to explain to her why you don't age."

And she'd have to accept that Cat would age and die in front of her eyes, Nyssa contemplated before adding, "And all my projects."

"You can build and reshape this entire city." His face was bright with the possibilities. "The whole country if you want. The world will be entirely yours."

Nyssa was still stunned. Shocked at the choice before her. On one hand, the mortal life she knew, her independence and all she had done as a human. The certainty that is this life, in this time. The certainty of death. On the other side was this whole world that Mag had opened up to her.

So much richer than anything she could have ever dreamed.

"No one will ever have power over you," Mag said gently.

He knew.

Knew her at her very core. He understood that despite all her successes, a part of her was still that child cowering in front of her stepmother, always wondering when the next blow or searing word would come. Even now, as an adult, after all that work, martial arts training, and therapy, she still avoided Doukas in fear of an encounter with the bitch.

Immortal meant she would never fear her stepmother or any human again. She'd move forward, safe in knowing that all the insecurities embedded in her from Lucinda would be left behind.

And she could protect Cat. Her spine lengthened in a determined stance at the thought.

Yes, she loved Mag and she knew he felt the same. They would be together regardless. But the immortality meant that she would be there always for her little sister. She would never die. She would be by Cat's side to assist and protect her for the entire span of her life.

Sure, she would grieve for her at the end, but knowing that she would always be there for Cat would appease the guilt always resting in the back of her mind for not doing more for her after she left Doukas.

She blinked once and quietly said, "I'll do it."

"You will?" Mag's face was ecstatic.

"Yes, I will." she said, her confidence returned. "Charlotte. Do what it takes. Make me immortal."

# CHAPTER 33

*S*acrament. Mag basked in the surge of feelings sailing through him.

For a moment there, after all she'd been through, he feared that she would return to her mortal life. To her life without him. That would have crushed him. But while he wanted nothing more, for the first time in his life, he genuinely wanted what was best for a woman he cared about.

Not what was best for him.

He had never questioned the motive of the women he spent nights with. Oh sure, they were willing. But they were lured by lust. His bite was what brought them to him.

But Nyssa, he wanted everything she chose to be her own. Independent of him.

"Are you sure?"

She smiled. "Yes, I'm sure... Didn't you just try to convince me? Isn't that what you want."

"Yes. More than ever. I love you." He held his breath. There, he'd said it out loud. "I don't know why but I know it's real. I've lived for three hundred years and never felt so deeply about anyone."

From the corner of his eye, he saw Ren leave the office without a word, casting one last deadly look at Norwell. The prince appeared bored while the princess beamed, looking upon them with captive attention. Mag's mom was searching through her satchel, her back to them.

"I love you, Nyssa Vlahos. I do," Mag insisted. "And because of that I don't want you to be pressured into making this choice." He gazed at her, hoping she would say those words back. Tell him she felt as strongly as he did.

Her skin flushed as she pressed her hand into hers. "When I said I will, I will. This is all my choice."

He nodded, his throat tight. He was so overrun by his emotions, he no longer knew what to add.

"Very well, *mes enfants*," his mother interrupted, "shall we get this done, then? The royals won't stay here forever."

"This is so beautiful. Such love." The princess was wringing her hands together with delight. "Dear Charlotte, thank you for bringing me here."

"Mag, take this." His mother gave him a set of binding cords.

He couldn't take his eyes off Nyssa who stood as she always did, strong and cool, her blonde hair oddly in place, as she watched Mom sweep the salt circle on his floor to create a new sacred space.

"It will be okay," he said. "I may have avoided her for centuries, but I respect every bit of her power. Mom knows what she is doing."

Nyssa turned to him and silently mouthed the words, *I love you*. Her eyes were bright and a little damp.

His heart hammered with joy and he swept her into his arms. "Oh god, Nyssa, you are the bravest woman I know. I love you so much."

"I love you too, Mag," she said against his chest, her arms around his waist.

A weightlessness opened up his heart and his soul soared with bliss at hearing the words finally expressed out loud from her lips.

And for the first time in centuries, he was the happiest man in the world. True happiness, not devilish amusement from assuaging his deepest cravings, but in experiencing the love and trust of another person. Two souls joined together. And in a few moments, for the possibility of an eternity.

And suddenly he could no longer wait.

"Come on, hurry," he barked at his mother over Nyssa's head.

"It would go faster if you could help, son," she grumbled. "Sorry for the wait, Merritt. It shouldn't be long."

The princess had made herself a drink and was reclining in one of Mag's club chairs. The prince still standing behind her was now taking a slug from Mag's best bottle of scotch.

He cast his sister a surly look. "Can we just go?"

"Oh, be quiet, Norwie. You've caused enough trouble."

Mom worked on setting her magic circle, laying candles at the edges, her athame and crystals at the center.

In his joy to have won over his blonde beauty, he had forgotten that his mother had a big part in making this happened. His anxiety receded. "What do you need, *Maman*?"

"Get me the Quaich of Perpetuity from your pile there. Where on earth did you find that?"

He fetched the flat silver vessel inscribed with Celtic runes, picking the object from the pile of fifty or so mismatched pieces from his collection. One of these days he would have to sort and catalogue them all.

"Nyssa, would you please look through my bag and find my wand? It's a plain gnarly old stick."

"A real wand?"

"Of course it's real, *chère*." She gave Nyssa a generous smile.

"Your Book of Shadow, *Maman*?" Mag passed the leather binding cords back to his mother, fond memories of childhood stirring inside him.

"Not this time, *mon pitou*. I will call on the raw source of my power." She took her wand from Nyssa and kneeled in front of her makeshift altar. "From my true home."

"Which is?" Nyssa asked.

"The Callanish Stones." She paused and impressed a dreamy look upon Nyssa.

"In Scotland," Nyssa said. "I've been there once."

"You have?" Mom was now positively beaming.

"Yes, there is a strange vibe to the place," Nyssa added. "Beautiful island."

"Where my essence still lingers." Mom nodded slowly, as she crushed herbs and dried flowers in the quaich.

Nyssa frowned, not quite understanding.

"Mom's existence is complicated." Mag was vaguely aware that his mother had lived many lives before this one.

"It is." His mother granted them a mischievous smile then touched the cords with her wand, causing mystical energies to shift.

But her smile became strained, almost apologetic. "I will need you to bite her."

"What?"

She nodded at the quaich. "The hemlock signifies her death, the holly seeds her rebirth. You will need to slow her heartbeat to a point where she is close to leaving us. "

"Am I not going to die?" Nyssa clasped her hands together, her brows drawn.

"Mom, no." He wrapped his arm protectively around Nyssa's shoulders. Damn, he'd been naïve to ignore that this could be dangerous to her life.

"Everything has a price, *mon fils*. Did you think I would just scatter some herbs, say a prayer, and there she'd be completely immortal?"

"Well, yeah, maybe?" He was such a fool.

"You should know better. Magic is all about balance. If we are to gift her with a long life, we need to give something back."

"Her mortal life?"

"In a way. She will have to be weak before being reborn."

"Weak, you didn't say dead, right?" Mag wouldn't chance it if he could lose her.

"Exactly. Nyssa, we need your original life to almost vanish, but what makes you, you, to stay within. So the spell can rebuild you stronger and make you invincible to illnesses and decay."

Nyssa swiveled in his embrace. "Do it, Mag."

"But—"

"I said I was in. I'm in all the way." There was absolute certainty in her tone.

He recalled something Emme had said earlier, that Nyssa knew how to get things done. And the female vampire was right, Nyssa got things done. No hesitations, just a very powerful drive.

"Okay." Mag finally gave in and imagined an eternal lifetime of being partnered to such force of will.

"I will be fine." She smiled, the fear gone from her gaze.

"I know." He skimmed the back of his fingers down her cheek. "I'll make sure of it."

"Take her in your arms. Now," his mother commanded.

Mag sat cross-legged at the center of Mom's circle, Nyssa in his arms across his lap. Her arms were tight around him.

"*Ceanthal.*" His office turned pitch dark, aside from for the glow of lit candles around the circle and radiance of the binding cords.

"Princess Merritt?"

"What would you have me do, Ice Witch?" the princess asked, her tone filled with respect.

"Kneel beside me."

Merritt did as asked.

"We will bind ourselves together and I will draw on your unearthly power." She wrapped the luminous cords around their joined hands.

"Ready, *mes enfants*?"

"We're ready." Nyssa clear and decisive words answered for them both.

Mag's mother seized Merritt's hand tighter. "Aradia, Aradia. I call thee. Aradia, *Rhònhla…*"

A shift disturbed the air. A peaty scent rose around them and Mag concentrated on his own hammering heart, ignoring his mom's droning. His love would soon be immortal. Just like him.

"Mag, now."

He didn't need more than this to start. His lips were on

the sweet cradle of Nyssa's neck, his tongue sampling her skin. When his fangs pierced her flesh, he felt her jolt in his arms before she settled against him with a moan as his saliva mixed with her blood.

Oh god. Her blood tasted as sweet as he'd ever imagined. Lightheaded from his own intoxication, he pulled stronger and faster.

Her heartbeat pounded against his and for an instant he feared he would never be able to stop feeding from her.

He had always ended before it was too late. Never wanting to drain anyone raw. But this was different. Pleasure and unsatiable hunger were building to a tempestuous tide inside him and he wanted all of her. Consume all of what she was, to her very core.

There was a bottomless need inside him that only *she* could fill. His entire body was on fire with terrible unquenchable thirst. He wanted to drink from her until he had reached the very depths of her soul.

A low possessive growl resonated at the back of his throat.

She had stopped moaning now and was nearly unconscious. Her heartbeat had slowed, and he suddenly became very aware of her limp hand on his forearm. Her grip on him was still there, faint but steady, with all the trust she had ever given him.

And he knew, in this precious moment, that no matter the thirst for her, he would never hurt her. Her love would always be there to restrain the worst instinct of the predator inside him.

His heartbeat slowed to match hers. And in that moment, they were one and only.

"I released my bite. Mom. I can't go further. It will kill her."

"*Sulat maldifidiich idira!*" Mom called out, circling her wand over the Celtic quaich.

A shimmering figure appeared before them. She towered above them all. The woman was dressed in long dark robes. Her red hair flowed passed her shoulders, her fingers adorned with many rings.

"Magnovald Callan St-Amand." The apparition looked at him and he felt transformed. "I am the Lady of the Callanish Stone. The First Witch of the First Coven and your magical ancestor. It appears I am here for you."

Mag swallowed carefully as he stared at her. He knew who she was. Mom used to tell them stories of her origin where the first coven had been decimated by a rogue warlock named Theuron. Where his mother had died that day with her coven sisters and had been reborn in the 17th century.

"Morag," Mom said.

"Lilith."

Mag frowned. This was new. He never knew his mom had a different name in her first life.

"And Merritt of the Daeva Realm."

"High Priestess." Merritt was strangely subdued in deference under Morag's gaze.

"You will go on to do great things, Princess," Morag said. "But you do need patience."

"What the hell is she talking about?" Norwell ranted.

"Ah, the little brother." Morag turned a fiery gaze at the prince who, frightened by the ethereal witch, retreated behind the club chair and took another swig of Mag's good scotch.

"My Lady," Mag said, keenly aware that Nyssa lay in his arms between life and death.

"Yes, my apologies, Son of Lilith and Ambrus."

She crossed the circle's boundary and kneeled beside him, her scent of heather caressing his senses. Very carefully, she traced Nyssa's pale cheek. "She is truly lovely." Her tone was infinitely gentle as she pushed Nyssa's hair from her forehead.

"Morag, I plead with you to bring her back." His voice was hoarse full of worries. What if she never woke?

"Sister," his mother urged.

"Of course, Magnovald. You do deserve happiness." Morag patted his cheek. "Fine young man you have here, Lilith."

"I go by Charlotte now, Morag. This is who I am. And I urge you to grant my son his wish," his mother spoke calmly. "Merritt has agreed to help. You can do the spell can you not?"

"Of course, sister." Morag placed herself in front of Merritt and Mag's mother. "Please add me to your binding."

As Merritt looked on utterly fascinated, Morag kept one wrist magically tied to the two women and lay a hand on Nyssa's forehead. The ancient high priestess closed her eyes. The small lines of her face disappeared.

As his arms tightened around the woman he loved, a glow rose around them at Morag and Charlotte's archaic words murmured in unison. The sacred circle seemed to shimmer in a silver hue. It was as if a gentle breeze had entered the room. It played with Nyssa's hair and Morag's robe fluttered up brushing his cheek. And for an instant, he felt as if he had been transported to another world, the Celtic isles perhaps, where Morag and his mother had originally been born.

Mag held his breath for what seemed like an eternity and sent a secret prayer to the Almighty to guard Nyssa's life. His heart full, he stared at her with unbreakable hope.

Morag let go and finally spoke. "Magnovald, I give you your soulmate. In the now and in eternity."

He peered down at his love's face, searching for the familiar scar above her lip. It was gone. The only physical thing in her that had changed at Morag's words.

Everything else had stayed the same, except for that small flaw. It was gone, the memory of her abuse erased. As if she had finally reached a peaceful place where her dramatic childhood experience had utterly vanished.

His pulse raced with trepidation as she opened her eyes.

And in a whisper, she called his name.

# CHAPTER 34

"I still can't believe you asked the Daeva princess to help grant me immortality."

Clad in a thick terry robe, she was coming out of the shower into his guest bedroom suite above the club to find him reclining on the couch. He'd washed up in his own quarters, his hair still damp at his neck.

Fresh drink in his hand, his gaze on her was both soft and lustful. She gulped at the intimacy in the air.

"You've healed already," she said. The deep wounds inflicted by Norwell were now faint scratches.

"So have you." He poured scotch into a lowball glass, added ice, and passed the drink to her.

She took it from his hand and sat beside him, her feet and knees together, her back straight. This felt so strange. Like being reborn. The hazy light of dawn rose outside. A clock ticked in the background. Time seemed suspended.

She grazed her fingers on her neck where he had bitten her earlier. "The scar is barely there."

"It should disappear in a few hours."

She frowned. "I will never get sick?"

"You shouldn't."

"Wow," she said quietly before taking a small sip of alcohol. "Another perk of immortality."

"Don't you feel different?"

She nodded, remembering the pounding of her heart as she'd slipped out of consciousness. That was the main thing she recalled from the ritual, her heart's constant hammer, slower and slower, in tune with his. Before a rush of electricity had jolted her and she'd awakened with Mag's concerned gaze searching her face.

"A little. Strong, for sure," she admitted. "I should feel drained from the night we just had, but I don't."

"More stamina." His half-smile raised a deep warmth within her.

"Yes, probably." She sat her glass down on the coffee table and flattened the belt ties of her robe on her lap. "Your mom said my immortality was more like hers than like Emme's. What does it mean?"

"Emme has some limitation. She cannot be in the sunlight without the special ring she wears and needs blood every day to survive." His gaze turned serious. "Mom is just like any human, she needs regular food and drink or she'll wither. She does love the sun."

With a need to do something with her hands to keep from fidgeting, she reached for her glass again and cupped the drink in both palms. Despite being strong, she felt mentally fragile, with everything new and complicated. "I cannot die, then?"

"Technically, you could, just like I could. We found out a few months ago that immortals could be taken down with the right drug cocktail."

"How?" There was so much she didn't know about them.

"My brother Val—he's looking forward to meeting you by the way—was overtaken by some lunatic scientist. He recovered with powerful magic but that shook us all. Apparently, some vampire hunter massacred a whole family of immortals some hundred years ago."

"Oh, that's awful." She turned somber. "Despite being immortal, you still need to be on alert for those who will destroy you?"

"Yes. Which is why we keep things quiet about our existence."

"The patrons were quite shocked tonight."

"Mom erased most of their memories of the royals. But that poor girl Norwell took hostage, Sammi, she was still pretty traumatized."

"You sent her out with your staff." She had noticed his kindness with the woman. It made her love him even more.

"Sandrine texted me earlier. The girl is fine. That's why I sent Raphael with them. A little vampire compelling helps now and again. Same in the club. Evan and Louka are used to cleaning up this kind of mess."

"Compelling?" She shifted in her seat. "Like the whole vampire trick?"

"Yes," he chuckled. "The very one."

"Oh god. Have you ever..." She stopped herself, not willing to consider the possibility, and took a swig of her drink.

"No, babe. I would never have done that to you."

"Why not?" She shot him a slow smile. "Didn't you say you fed on women. Isn't that how you have them agree to it?"

"Yes. And at first, I *was* extremely tempted to compel you to fall into my arms. I wanted you, Nyssa, from the

351

moment I met you." His gaze turned so sincere it thawed her from the inside. "It would have been so easy. But instead, I stalled you, hoping you'd keep coming."

"Mag…" She was awed by the confession, her heart tumbling in her ribcage. "I thought you hated me."

"Well, I didn't like that you wanted to take the club from me." His smile took a devilish turn. "But *you*, I couldn't get you out of my mind."

"I recall that day so well." She shook with lust at the memory of the unbearably handsome club owner, the casual leather jacket stretched against strapping shoulders, the enticing curl of his mocking smile. "You were so snarky. You sent me packing."

"And you were so frosty. Like an ice queen."

She laughed. "Really?"

"Oh yes." The lust in his tone was unmistakable. "Who knew there was so much passion inside you?"

"*You* knew." Her body feverish, she reached out for him.

"Yes. I knew and I wanted it all for myself." He clasped her hand in his and gave it a meaningful squeeze. "But I wouldn't compel you to be with me."

"Why not?"

"It just didn't feel right."

She breathed out, let go of his hand and stood up from the couch. "And all these girls you had?" Nervous about what he was about to say, she walked to the small desk to stare blandly at a collection of faded pictures from the times when the *Serpent* was a jazz club.

"They didn't matter, Nyssa." His voice was hoarse behind her. "Not like you do."

"You gave away your club for me," she said, not quite willing to look at him.

"I would have given my life for yours," he insisted, passion filling his tone. "And for Cat. "

She turned to look at him, so perfect and handsome, so striking. "You've lived for so long. All these pictures... I just can't imagine."

"You will, eventually."

She walked back to stand above him. "I will need your help with it," she rasped with sudden cravings, overly conscious of her nakedness under the thick white robe.

"And you will have it."

"I'll need directions." Her gaze boring heavily upon him, she untied the belt of her robe. "To guide me in this immortal life."

"Directions?" Amusement replaced his earlier somber tone, and he laid his drink on the table to reach out for the belt of her robe. He drew her towards him with a strong pull.

"Yes, handling."

"Handling?"

"Lots of handling." She wiggled to let the robe fall open, baring her chest. Completely naked, she straddled his lap, her knees at each side of him.

"Like this." His eyes feverish, he slid his hands upon her waist to secure her on his thighs and she felt his desire grow beneath her.

"Say you were to advise a brand-new immortal woman, what would you have her do now?"

"Now?" He swallowed, his expression suddenly filled with predatory lust.

"Yes," she purred. "Right now. What should she do?"

"Undo my belt, *poupée*." A primal growl erupted from deep inside him as his hand gripped her bare waist farther.

"Your belt?" She shot him a tantalizing smile. "That's it?"

"For now."

She bent to tug at his belt, and undid the buckle, very much aware of the hard bulge so close to her touch. She sat back and licked her bottom lip as she leveled with him, her pulse racing with desire. "Like that?"

"Now take my pants off." It was both a plea and a command, the urgency palpable in his tone.

She unzipped the jeans and took a moment to cup his crotch. With a gentle squeeze, she asked. "Just the pants?"

"Boxers, too," he croaked. "Take them off."

"As you wish."

She slid both hands at his bare hips and tugged the pants and shorts down. The waistband of his silk boxers caught on his erection and she very carefully, very slowly, pulled on them to free him totally.

Oh god. For the very first time, she got to admire him fully.

Longings shook her straight to her core. He was gorgeous. And all hers. She bit her bottom lip and stared at him, shared hunger reflecting in his eyes.

"You want it all off?" she managed to say despite the storm of needs overtaking her body.

"Do it." He could barely speak, his hands digging down into her hips.

She shifted to slide his pants and boxers down over his knees and took them off him, one leg at a time.

Naked at his feet, with his hands dug into her hair, she was a puddle of desires. But he had been so generous the first time they were together that she wanted to do every-thing to please him. Follow his lead.

She slowly stood up in front of him while he trailed his

touch down her shoulders and arms, his gaze taking her all in.

"You are just so beautiful, love. So perfect." His gaze settled at the juncture of her thighs and he trailed a slow finger along her navel. "A natural blonde."

With shivers scattering along her skin, she smiled and cocked a playful eyebrow at him. "And what would have your immortal girl do now?"

He reached out and pulled her onto his lap. "Come here, you. My ice empress."

She straddled him again and gasped at the intimate touch of her bare crotch against his erection. "I want you, Mag."

Their kiss felt like forever. She sensed its heat, its passion right to her very bones. His tongue exploring hers, his needs of her, were a deep pressure that seemed bottomless.

But they had time to fill the well. So much time. An eternity.

He broke their kiss with a growl and lifted her slightly above him. "Now! I need you right now."

His hand reached between her thighs and his fingers explored her slick folds. She panted as the intimate touch drew her near the edge. She was so wet, so ready for him. She had been for months.

"I won't wait this time," he urged.

"Don't." She melted in his embrace, wanting nothing more but let him take over every inch of her.

At her word, he lifted her a little higher and with her help slid her down and around him. She cried out as his thick, solid cock penetrated her, his urging and commandeering body deep and wide inside hers.

She sat with her back straight against his palms, taking

all of him, inside her. "I love you, Mag. There's nothing I wouldn't do for you."

And it was true. All this time she had thought he was wrong for her and now she knew without a doubt that he was who she had been waiting for all along.

His strength filled her, his hard erection taking control of her. She shifted a little around him and he groaned.

"*Je t'aime, mon amour.*" With one hand on her hip, the other reached between where their bodies were joined, his thumb finding her needy spot.

She moaned with intense pleasure as the pad of his finger flicked back and forth against her tender nerves. She held on tight to his shoulders as she rode him, knees digging into the couch, taking him deeper and deeper with each of her thrust.

"Nyssa," he growled. While his thumb still played with her, his free hand found one of her breasts. He cupped it and squeezed the flesh tenderly.

"Oh god," she cried out. "Mag."

He left her breast to seize her butt for leverage. His fingers were working faster and faster on her, mounting tides of hunger inside her, each wave stormier than the other.

"I want you to come, Nyssa," he ordered, his tone as urgent as his touch on her, tugging, flicking, pinching. "Right now. Come, babe. For me."

Lightheaded, she blinked. She could no longer hold it in. The powerful orgasm shattered her, wild and hard through her entire body and around his thick cock.

He grabbed her hips and rammed her into his crotch, his strong thrust making her ride the last waves of pleasure. Everything in her was raw and sensitive but she no longer had a mind of her own.

In a swift move, he flipped her onto the couch under him.

"God, Nyssa, you're mine." He thrust solid inside her, urging her to sigh with pleasure. "I love you. Just you."

Overtaken by all that he was, every movement more powerful than the next, she was completely at his mercy.

She let go of the last of her carefully erected barriers as he tensed in her arms and cried her name as he came.

He held himself there for a few second, his body exuding pure power, before he fell on top of her. Their sweaty bodies collided, their heart thumping against each other.

"Dang it, Mag," she rasped. "That was something."

"It's not over yet, babe." He brushed her lips with a kiss and her heart pulsed with eagerness—his fangs drawn out, his eyes the darkest of hue.

There he was, her immortal.

"Do it," she ordered. "I want *ALL* of you."

With a groan, he dug into her flesh.

She barely felt the sting of his bite. And as he drank her blood, a tide of passionate bliss rushed through her.

His erection grew inside her. And he slid himself slow and long, his body angled just right to tease her most sensitive zone. He took his time as hunger overtook both of them again. She sensed his hammering pulse as her blood entered his system to make her a part of him. His hand slid between them and he stroked her intimately with each of his unhurried thrusts inside her, with each of his long pull on her neck.

The effect was intoxicating.

And she no longer knew time. She was now immortal, suspended between intense delicious hunger and imminent release, with the man she loved in her arms.

She possessively cupped the strong muscles of his buttocks as she fell into his timeless entrapment.

He finally let go of her neck. The predator had retreated, replaced by the human side of him—because he was indeed human, his expression both vulnerable and fierce. And when they both came together, when the pleasure crushed through their melded bodies, the gaze between them was steadfast. Certain their bond would never break. They would remain forever entwined.

In true eternity.

# EPILOGUE

*Vlahos Tower, Montreal*
*Two months later*

"I can't believe the look on Lucinda's face at the divorce hearing when she learned she wasn't getting much now that Cat lives with me. "Nyssa was calling out from her kitchen. "Is it petty of me?"

"Okay, Mag. You have to ask her," Cat whispered to him from across the table.

"That bitch deserves everything coming to her," he responded back to Nyssa from the dining area of the penthouse.

Beyond the expansive windows, the late evening sun was setting on the streets below, radiating on the last few snow patches clinging to the darkest corners of the pavements, the few dormant trees below slowly returning to life. Spring was coming to Montreal.

"You have to," Cat insisted, and he cast her a fond smile.

The teen had changed from her school uniform into a pair of comfortable exercise pants and a t-shirt, her hair in two little buns at the sides of her head.

After her homework, they had settled for dinner.

Nyssa had dismissed the daily housekeeper as soon as she'd come back from her office and this was their time together before he headed down to the *Serpent*. Their time as a family.

He looked at the remnants of their dinner on the table. The little white wine left at the bottom of their sleek crystal glasses, the rest of the spanakopita casserole from Nyssa's mom's recipe, the Greek meal lying in a sleek stainless dish at the center of the table, and the now empty square white plates that he would soon take back to the kitchen.

Everything so modern and glossy. So efficient.

How had he, the immortal who spent his time in the dark recesses of his club watching the sins of this world as time ticked on, found himself living the busy bustle of a partnership in raising a teenager.

Because he was kind of a dad now.

LaChance hadn't been mentioned since Cat's abduction. And Mag knew for a fact that his friend Amelia Akande had built a case against him. He was now rotting in jail with others like him who had run the children traffic for Norwell. The kids had been turned over to child protection services, with heavy counseling paid by the Catalina Vlahos Foundation. Señora Moreno had somehow managed to claim the compound and its former clientele had received chilling visits from Vince and his squad.

"Come on, Mag." Cat wouldn't let it go and she was right. It *was* time.

Mag shot Cat a complicit smile, thrilled at her beaming expression. "You think I should do it now?"

A few flutters kicked in his stomach as he fingered the small velvet box in his pocket. But his heart was certain.

"Yes," Cat stated. "It's been months."

"Just two months, kiddo."

"What's been two months?" Nyssa walked in with a warm pie plate.

She still had her business attire on, a pencil skirt that cuddled every part of her sleek curves and a light blue silk shell that drew out the glow of her soft gray eyes. She had discarded her jacket and her bare arms were strong, just as she was.

The immortality suited her perfectly.

She beamed at him and his heart pounded in his chest like it did every time he set his eyes upon her, every time his touch settled upon her skin.

And every moment when he crawled under their bed sheet at dawn, still amazed at his happiness, at his incredible luck to have found her. They would make love in the early morning, her body warm from sleep, his seeking her freshness after a night at the *Serpent*.

"Come on." Cat elbowed him in the rib.

"Maybe wait for Saturday?"

"No!" Cat protested. "I want to be there when you do."

He was just teasing the kid. Nyssa always came to the club on Saturdays while Cat either stayed over at her friend Livy or caught a movie with Mr. Julien.

While he was blissfully happy in their domesticity and had made his home in her penthouse, she also wanted to be part of his nightclub life. She'd wear the skimpiest dress and the highest heels, eclipsing any of his dancers with her classic sexy aura, her blonde hair curlier than usual, her makeup a little more dramatic. His blood would boil with intense lust, pushing him to lose himself in her supple body and drink from her, deep into the night in his apartments above the *Serpent*.

"What are you two talking about?" Nyssa placed the pie dish at the center of the table and took off the oven mitts. She sat and poured herself more wine. "Go ahead, Cat. You serve. It's strawberry rhubarb, your favorite. Mrs. Daviot said the market was open today and she made it just for you."

"Not now, Nyssa." Cat's serious expression strummed his heart. The kid was as invested as he was. "Mag has something to tell you."

"Really?" She turned to him. "Has Charlotte returned from Louisiana? She said she was thinking about coming back now that spring is here."

His mother had left as soon as Merritt and her nasty brother had been dispatched, calling her mission to help him a success. He'd promised to call, not sure where that left them, but he was aware that Nyssa was in constant communication with her as she had decided to study and catalogue each of his artifacts as her new project.

"No. This has nothing to do with Mom." Before he realized it, he was kneeling at Nyssa's feet.

"Oh my god, Mag." Her hands flew to her mouth. "What are you doing?"

"Nyssa, *mon amour*." He opened the jewelry box where a sleek diamond rested, the design made by a local modern artist, commissioned the month before by Cat and himself. "Would you do me the honor of being my wife?"

"Your wife?" Her eyes were bright, her cheeks flushed as she gazed at him in shock.

He waited, his heart crashing in his chest. They were both immortals, living together with no end in sight. He knew how his touch made her feel, how she trusted him with her sister. He knew how she loved him, body, and soul.

But this, this proposal, made it right. Made it official to the whole world.

"Magnovald." Her tone was filled with emotions. "I don't know what to say. I—"

"Just say yes!" Cat blurted.

"Yes." Her palms pressed together. "Of course. Yes!"

She dropped to her knees in front of him and wrapped her arms around his neck. "Oh god, Mag, I love you so much. "

His heart soared. She was his. All of her, now entirely his.

"Put it on," Cat gushed. "Put the ring on."

Nyssa pulled back and took the ring from its velvet cradle. "Oh wow, this is gorgeous."

"At first I wanted to look for something antique, but then I remembered your taste." Mag was near overcome with emotions. "You prefer this, right?"

"Honey, I love it." She gazed at him with nothing but adoration in her eyes. "I would have loved anything you chose."

She slid the ring on her finger and it fit perfectly. The sleek design was set with the biggest diamond he could find.

"Were you in on this, Cat?" Still kneeling on the floor in front of him, Nyssa rested her cheek on his shoulder.

"You bet I was. We chose the design together."

"Your sister's even tougher than you are when it comes to getting what she wants," he chuckled. "She drove the guy mad."

He gathered Nyssa in his arms and lifted her from the floor. Drawing her in his embrace, his chin at the top of her head, he inhaled her familiar daytime perfume and he let the warm feeling of her body pressed against him fill his soul.

The sunset cast early evening shadows in the wide-open living space of the penthouse, its rays playing with the silver drapes, dancing on the living room furniture where they usually settled on Fridays for pizza-movie night with Cat.

This special time, when the day was over and night just started, was theirs.

The time they came as a family. Soon to be blessed by the world as husband and wife, with Cat as the youth he had always wanted to guide through life.

When he had wanted a child of his own, it hadn't been about legacy. He realized it now—he had actually wanted a family.

He breathed in his happiness, his gaze taking in the spectacular reds and oranges of the sunset announcing good days to come.

He loved the woman in his arms more than anything.

And she was his now.

DEAR READER

The idea for this book came to me when I was visiting my mother outside Montreal and watched a local documentary on young girls being groomed into sex trafficking by predators pretending to be their boyfriend, the girls being broken down with repetitive sexual assaults and drugs, before being shipped to Toronto and the US. Some escaped and recovered, some disappeared for good, and their family never heard back from them. Many of these teens did have families who loved them, but they became easy preys during that difficult transition into adulthood.

As a teacher working daily with young teens, this report broke my heart and, while I work daily to support their social-emotional needs here in Seattle, I also thought they needed a staunch savior in the shape of a bad-boy vampire willing to risk anything to save them.

And that is how I created this story, which is also steeped into the history of my people in Québec. While I distorted a few facts for story's sake, the Daughters of the King and the Society of the Sons of Liberty are a real parts of French Canadian history.

Thank you for taking this journey with me into Magno-vald's search for happiness and, as always…

…trust your heart,

Marie-Claude xoxo

*P.S. WANT to know if there is anything going on between vampire Emmeline Dubois and Mag's more serious immortal brother, Justin St-Amand? Find out in A VAMPIRE'S SOUL,* **Book 3 in the Vampires of the Black Oak series.**

A FREE STORY FOR YOU...

Enjoyed A Vampire's Sin? Not ready to stop reading yet? A copy of *A VAMPIRE'S HEART*, the story of Mag's brother Val and Maisie's first meeting, is yours to download as a thank you for joining my Secret Circle.

Get your download code at:
marieclaudebourque.com/a-vampires-heart

## A VAMPIRE'S HEART

### *A Witch-Vampire Meet Cute Paranormal Romance Prequel*

To prove her worth as a leader to her coven, awkward witch Maisie Thibodeau must battle a horrible monster in front of the whole supernatural community. But the White Holly sorceresses are not the only ones watching.

Immortal Valerian St-Amand can't tear his eyes from the small but powerful witch as she battles a dangerous troll set on her small mystic town.

While he had vowed not to interfere in witches' business, his unexpected fear for her life makes it impossible for him to keep his distance.

Read on for a taste of *A Vampire's Heart…*

"Hey, it's her!" Mag elbowed him as the pub's door opened, letting some fresh air in.

"Who?" Val frowned as he continued to scan the room, casting a brief nod at the waitress bringing them their drinks.

"The girl from the shop," Mag explained with eagerness.

Val reluctantly looked to see what made his brother so enthusiastic. The young witch from the craft store stood there, a small figure in an anime logoed t-shirt, plain jeans, and faded sneakers. Her poker-straight black hair fanned against her cheek and down to her chest.

A little geeky, but yes, there was something about her. He felt a kinship in her awkwardness. She, too, didn't seem to want to be there.

She perused the crowd, waved at a few people, before settling her eyes on him.

His breath remained caught in his throat as her gaze of the deepest jade connected with his own. The contact disturbed something in him that had been dormant for centuries.

*Seigneur*!

The strange force stirring within him had gone straight to his core. His heartbeat pounded madly as a flush of warmth spread down to his groin.

Oh damn. Val instinctively searched for Sasha, who was vigorously lapping water from his bowl at his feet. He couldn't remember ever feeling anything so intense before. He shook himself as he sunk his fingers into the fur of his loyal companion. This could mean trouble.

"I wonder if I should hit on her," Mag was saying.

Val moved his head bleakly as she broke their connection to survey the bar with her head held high before waving with animation at a group of women at the back.

"Sure, why not." He let out a slow exhale, his pulse now steadier, and leaned further back in his chair. He forced himself to look away from her and continue to study the patrons. But he couldn't shake the feeling that this young witch was something else.

And with his entire being, he strongly prayed that Mag would leave this one girl alone.

*You probably wonder about some of the characters you met here... such as Diesel Stanford, Malcolm Dunsmuir and Harper Grant—as well as what happens to Val's five brothers and Emmeline Dubois.*

*Here is the list of books current and to-be-released in the Black Oak world:*

### ~ Vampires of the Black Oak ~

**A Vampire's Heart (Val and Maisie's first meet cute)**: In this prequel to A Vampire's Spell, awkward witch Maisie Thibodeau must prove her worth as leader to her coven by battling a horrible monster in front of the whole supernatural community.

**A Vampire's Spell (Val and Maisie):** Guilt-ridden legacy vampire Valerian St-Amand teams with powerful witch Maisie Thibodeau to protect his city from a crazed scientist seeking immortality.

**A Vampire's Sin (Mag and Nyssa):** Immortal Montreal vampire Mag St-Amand teams up with ambitious real estate tycoon Nyssa Vlahos to rescue her kid sister from a child-trafficking ring run by a pack of daemons.

**A Vampire's Soul (Emme and Justin):** When female vampire Emmeline Dubois teams up with faithful immortal friend Justin St-Amand to escape a vicious hunter set to kill her, the centuries-old friendship turns into so much more than she'd anticipated.

**A Vampire's Fate (Ren and Rosalie):** When female wolf-shifter Rosalie Gauthier returns to her town to take on the leadership of her pack after her father's illness, her birthright is challenged by a tyrannic rival and marriage to powerful vampire Ren St-Amand is her only option to save her family's legacy.

**A Vampire's Star (Cass and Tilly)** Can an immortal truly father a child? That's what rock star Cass St-Amand finds out when Tilly Davenport, a strong-headed music producer banshee, shows up backstage at his latest concert claiming to be carrying his child.

**A Vampire's Blood (Griff and Isabelle)** Can you fall in love with your lifelong enemy? Griff St-Amand has his hands full when he finds himself having to rescue French supernatural hunter Isabelle LeGall despite her hatred for his family.

### ~ Warlocks of the Black Oak ~

**A Warlock's Kiss (Diesel and Kera):** Stoic warlock leader Diesel Stanford must convince his panther-shifter ex-girlfriend Kerala Clarke to return the only magical artifact that can cure his sister from a terrible hex.

**A Sorcerer's Night (Sin and Celeste):** Protective panther-shifter sorcerer Sinclair Clarke battles a powerful demon who holds hostage his fiancee, legacy witch Celeste Stanford.

**An Alchemist's Desire (Thorn and Raven):** Recluse alchemist Thornwood Huntington must help talented violinist Raven Giancola unlock the magic of her enchanted violin despite his vow to keep all things magic away from non-sorcerers.

**An Archmage's Destiny (Knight and Bryce):**
With her reputation on the line, steadfast attorney Bryce Jackson must convince daredevil warlock Knightley Morgan to return to the folds of his powerful New England family or apply the devastating consequences herself.

**A Spellbinder's Denial (Duke and Sloane):**
Riddled with guilt after his unleashed powers wrecked lives decades ago, billionaire warlock Duke Morgan still refuses to unlock his powers to make amends, but when savvy banshee Sloane Davenport crosses his path again, even his fortune won't be enough to protect her.

**A Necromancer's Love (Mal and Harper):**
When vampires descend on his city, Seattle necromancer Malcolm Dunsmuir can no longer hide from the darkness of his demon side, especially when the enticing life-loving human Harper Grant tries her very best to bring him to the light.

**A Warlock's Storm (Rey and Saira):** Stranded on a boat in a haunted New England harbor, rugged warlock Rey Stanford and sassy female panther-shifter Saira Varma battle sea-monsters and revenants as they try to survive the night.

# FRENCH-ENGLISH GLOSSARY

**Serpent Maudit** – *Cursed Serpent*

**tiens, tiens** – *well, well*

**sacrament** - *sacrament, as in the Christian rite. (common French Canadian curse)*

**fille** - *girl*

**Sanctuaire des Truands** - *Sanctuary of the Miscreants*

**pour l'amour de Dieu** – *for the love of God*

**maman** - *mom*

**mon pitou** – *my puppy ( a common French Canadian term of affection from a mother to a son)*

**mon fils** – *my son*

**mon enfant** – *my child*

**Fils de la Liberté** – *In this story, refers to the Montreal-based French Canadian society who supported the Sons of Liberty American patriots against the British government in the beginning of the 1800s*

**Sortilège** - *spell*

**Guerre des Motards** – *Biker War, in this story, refers to the Québec Biker War which was a turf war that began in 1994 and continued until late 2002 in Montreal.*

**Vous êtes de Montréal?** - *Are you from Montreal?*

**J'viens de Gaspé** - *I come from Gaspé*

**Un vrai beau pays** - *a really nice area*

**Sorcière des Glaces** – *Ice Witch*

**oui** - *yes*

**merde** – *shit (common French curse)*

**mon amour** – *my love*

**m'man** – *mom (shorten version)*

**chère** - *dear*

**les enfants** - *kids*

**Filles du Roy** – *Daughters of the King, in this story, refers to the young French women who immigrated to New France between 1663 and 1673 as part of a program sponsored by King Louis XIV.*

**diable** - *devil*

**mon dieu** – *my god*

**ma belle** - *beautiful*

**poupée** - *doll*

**Tiare Eternelle** – *Eternity Tiara*

**Je t'aime** – *I love you*

# CAST OF MAIN CHARACTERS

**Vampires:**

**Magnovald (Mag) St-Amand**: Mount-Royal Immortal and owner of the *Serpent Maudit* night club in Montreal. Brother to Val, Justin, Ren, Cass and Griff.

**Professor Justinien (Justin) St-Amand:** Mount-Royal Immortal and professor of Astronomy at McDougall College in Montreal. Brother to Val, Mag, Ren, Cass and Griff

**Renaud (Ren) St-Amand:** Mount-Royal Immortal and honorary member of the Domaine-Lassalle Wolf Pack.

**Valerian (Val) St-Amand:** Mount-Royal Immortal and founder of the *Sanctuaire des Truands* shelter in Montreal. Brother to Mag, Justin, Ren, Cass and Griff.

**Cassiodore (Cass) St-Amand:** Mount-Royal Immortal and brother to Val, Mag, Justin, Ren and Griff.

**Griffon (Griff) St-Amand:** Mount-Royal Immortal and brother to Val, Mag, Justin, Ren and Cass.

**Emmeline (Emme) Dubois:** Montreal immortal vampire

and former fiancée of Val St-Amand. Friend to the St-Amand brothers and Maisie Thibodeau.

**Evan Grant:** cursed Montreal vampire, sister to the Daemon Queen Harper Grant, and bodyguard to Mag St-Amand. Turned by Emmeline Dubois and saved from blood addiction by Val St-Amand and the *Sanctuaire des Truands* shelter.

**Raphael Chung:** Cursed Montreal vampire and bouncer at the Serpent Maudit club. Turned by Emmeline Dubois and saved from blood addiction by Val St-Amand and the *Sanctuaire des Truands* shelter.

### Witches:

**Charlotte Callan (aka The Ice Witch):** Ancient witch of the Callanish tradition and mother of the Mount-Royal Immortals.

**Morag Callan (aka The First Witch):** Ancient coven sister of Charlotte Callan and High Priestess of the Callanish Coven, consort of Alchemyst Iain Callan of the Celtic Isles.

**Maisie Thibodeau:** Witch of the White Holly Coven in Berwick Hollow. Wife to Valerian St-Amand and best friend to Emmeline Dubois

**Madame Lakota Ioshta:** Eclectic Witch of the Mohawks of Kahnawá:ke clan and close friend to Charlotte Callan.

### Warlock:

**Diesel Stanford:** Warlock and leader of the Order of the Black Oak. Resides in Seaport with his wife panther-shifter Kerala Clarke and their young son Sai Stanford.

### Disciples of Nostredame:

**Father Grégoire:** Oldest disciple of Nostredame, living at the *Sanctuaire des Truands* in Montreal and assigned to Val St-Amand

**Ariane:** Young female disciple of Nostredame, living at the *Sanctuaire des Truands* and assigned to Justin St-Amand.

## Humans:

**Nyssa Vlahos:** CEO of Vlahos Enterprise and love interest to Mag St-Amand. half-sister to Catalina Vlahos.

**Catalina (Cat) Vlahos:** 13 years-old half-sister to Nyssa Vlahos.

**Vincenzo (Vince) deLuca:** veteran and former Montreal biker, now man-at-arms for the Moreno mob and loyal friend to Mag St-Amand.

**Sandrine Boudreau:** Waitress at *Serpent Maudit* night-club and loyal friend to Mag St-Amand.

**Lucinda Vlahos:** Stepmother to Nyssa Vlahos and mother of Catalina Vlahos

**Señora Moreno** – Elderly Italian widow and Montreal's mob boss

**Oliver LaChance** – Montreal rapper and sex trafficker, claims to be Catalina's boyfriend

**Mr. Julien** – Chauffeur to Nyssa Vlahos and good friend to Catalina Vlahos

**Captain Akande**: Female police officer and Captain of the Sureté du Québec provincial police. Mag St-Amand's loyal friend.

## Daemons:

**Prince Norwell:** Royal of the Daeva Realm, little brother of Princess Merritt and late Daeva King Morgius

**Princess Merritt:** Royal of the Daeva Realm, older sister to Prince Norwell and younger sister to the late King Morgious. Briefly came to the human word and was defeated by Black Oak Warlock Knightley Morgan before returning to the Daemon world to rule her realm.

**King Malcolm (Mal) Dunsmuir:** Warlock of the Black Oak, Necromancer and King of the Daemon and Daeva Realm. Consort to Harper Grant.

**Queen Harper Grant:** Queen of the Daemon and Daeva Realm, consort to Mal Dunsmuir and sister to cursed vampire Evan Grant.

# ACKNOWLEDGEMENTS

I want to thank all the readers who have waited so patiently for me to finish this story that was interrupted so many times during the 2020 pandemic. Your constant support means a lot of me.

Deep-felt thanks to editor and career coach Angela James for her helpful comments on the opening of this book and for her motivation in getting it completed.

I am also very grateful to talented romance author, friend and amazing editor Jenn Bray-Webber who helped turn this book into my vision. Thank you also to Em Petrova and Deb Burchfield for their help with copy editing and Frauke Spanuth for a great set of covers.

Marie-Claude Bourque is a Montreal-born Seattle-based author of gothic paranormal romance and the winner of the American Title V award with her first novel ANCIENT WHISPERS.

Her writing features modern-day fantasy skillfully weaved into infinitely romantic stories between smart strong women and complex passionate heroes. Happily Ever After always absolutely guaranteed! Find more at www.marieclaudebourque.com

To be first to hear about her latest book, win free copies and more, subscribe to Marie-Claude's Secret Circle at www.marieclaudebourque.com/secret-circle

Or connect directly with her at www.facebook.com/mcbourque